A Mansion on the Moon

A Mansion on the Moon

A Guam Love Story

C. Sablan Gault

Library of Congress Control Number:		2015919065
ISBN:	Hardcover	978-1-5144-2704-0
	Softcover	978-1-5144-2705-7
	eBook	978-1-5144-2706-4

Print information available on the last page.

Rev. date: 08/29/2016

To order additional copies of this book, contact:
Xlibris
1-888-795-4274
www.Xlibris.com
Orders@Xlibris.com
707099

To my husband David and best friend Faye Camacho Kaible,
for believing in me.

PART ONE

Chapter 1

Amanda couldn't sleep. She tossed about, restless and wide-eyed for hours. The heat in the small room she shared with her sisters was stifling; the air stagnant. The sun that afternoon, in the beginning of July, had roasted the land and sea, and now every rock and living thing was giving off heat into the night. Even her sister Ana, sleeping beside her, seemed warmer than normal. She stirred when Amanda felt her forehead, but Ana was fine; she didn't have a fever. Amanda threw aside the blanket covering them, but it didn't help. She stared up at the rafters and underside of the thatched roof above her head, resigned to another sleepless night. Then in the distance, above the barking of a dog and the surf breaking against the reef, she heard the low rumbling of thunder. It came from far out at sea to the north and heralded welcome respite from the heat. Rain would soon drive cool wind toward shore. Amanda listened as the wind and rain approached.

The rustling of the fronds of the coconut trees along the shore and the bushes outside her window announced their arrival. The wind arrived first; the squall followed close behind. A cold damp gust washed into the room and drove out the heat. Amanda closed her eyes with relief. Whipped by the wind, hard rain followed loudly and heavily, splattering against the thatched roof for several minutes. It then stopped abruptly, the cloud containing it wrung dry. Rainwater spilled from the roof for many minutes before slowing to a trickle. To the hypnotic plinking of rainwater dripping into puddles on the ground, Amanda fell asleep.

More than the heat, the heartache of losing Tim Laney, the man she loved, was what kept Amanda awake. Tim was a navy seaman. He sailed away that morning. It was not his choice to leave. He loved Amanda as well, and didn't want to leave her, but his assignment in Guam was at an end. Amanda slept with Tim two nights prior, knowing it was a sin to do so. It was her parting gift, her body the only thing she had worth giving. She expected to be tormented with guilt and shame afterward, but it was love, not lust, that motivated her. She was certain of Tim's love and wanted to be one with him, if not by the laws of God and man, then by their own accord.

Now that Tim was gone, Amanda was haunted by the single night she spent in his arms. She called it to mind again and again, remembering his face, his smile, his kisses, the warmth of his skin against hers. A million stars twinkled in the blue-black sky that night, and silvery moonlight drenched the beach. The ocean was calm. Gentle swells broke against the reef and washed little ripples onto shore. Tim gazed upon her nakedness with reverence. He draped a blanket around her shoulders, as if to shield her from the world and keep her only to himself. The beautiful words from the Bible about a man leaving his father and mother and clinging to his wife echoed in Amanda's mind. So did the warning about not tearing apart what God had joined together.

Tim was six months shy of nineteen when they met. He was far from home, far from his parents and two younger sisters, far from their small farm north of San Diego, California. He didn't want to end up a pain-racked farmer like his father and had lied to get into the navy. He was on his own, a carefree boy out to see the world. Amanda made him feel confident, more sure of himself, a man in command of his own fate. She made him see the world differently, simply because her world was unlike his. He didn't know how deeply he could love someone until he met her.

"Are you all right, my love? Did I hurt you?" Tim whispered after making love to her. He had tried to be gentle. He stroked her hair and kissed her. "I love you, Amanda," he said, gazing steadily into her eyes and hoping she could see in his that he meant it.

"No," Amanda replied and smiled. She had felt some pain, but it was not intolerable, nor did it diminish the sensation of being joined as one. As Tim lay breathless and helpless in her arms, Amanda realized how vulnerable he was at that moment. She recognized the strength of her own body and the power it had over his. She marveled at the balance and wondered whether God had intended it to be so.

Amanda caressed Tim's face. The contrast of her brown hand against his ivory cheek saddened her. Tim kissed her fingers and repeated his desire to marry her, no matter who objected. The impossibility of it caused Amanda more pain than had his body. God had allowed them to fall in love, but the world stood in defiance against them. Neither Amanda's parents nor the United States Navy would sanction a marriage between them. Tim was an American, a member of the new ruling class. He was white. Amanda was not, although some Castilian blood coursed through her veins. Tim belonged to the navy and was subject to its regulations and to the laws of his home state, both of which prohibited interracial marriage. If it was possible, Amanda would have run away with Tim, but where could they go?

They wanted desperately to believe they could defy convention, but in those days, there was little hope of it.

The year was 1899. The Spanish-American War had ended the year before. The United States was reveling in triumph over the liberation of Spain's rich colonies in the Caribbean and the Philippines in the Pacific, and puzzling over its acquisition of the nearby lesser known Mariana Islands. Few knew or cared about the resource-poor Marianas, not even the Spanish empire itself, which had controlled the tiny archipelago since the seventeenth century. The Marianas were not relegated to obscurity; they were already there.

While en route to Manila with reinforcements in June 1898, the navy fleet received orders at sea to stop and capture Guam, the largest and most inhabited of the Marianas. The Americans were expecting to find battle-ready Spaniards and half-naked aboriginals. Instead they found apathetic, mixed-race colonial administrators and the indigenous Chamorros civilized by nearly three centuries of Spanish Catholic influence and domination.

There was nothing to remember about the capture of Guam, except that the Spanish governor didn't know his country was at war with the U.S. There was no vengeful attack over the sinking of the USS *Maine*, no heroic charge up San Juan Hill or lopsided Battle of Manila Bay. There was only a cannon shot mistaken as an arrival salute. The Spanish governor was stunned by the American order to surrender the island and be taken prisoner along with the officials of his administration. That done, the navy sailed on to the Philippines, leaving no one in charge. The absence of authority led to political instability and rivalry. Into the vacuum raced the social elite who jockeyed with low-level ex-government officials. All thought themselves natural ruling successors. The squabbling eventually prompted the navy to station a small contingent on the island until a duly appointed governor arrived to restore order, inaugurate American governance, and exercise authority over Guam, the Chamorros, and a few others of various nationalities. Seaman Tim Laney was in that contingent on temporary assignment.

Although they were as racially prejudiced as the ousted Spanish, the Americans were less concerned about social rank and status. The American navy men were charming and bold, and equally enthusiastic about submitting to their carnal urges and sowing their seeds. In short order, especially as the number of Americans increased, their daring smiles and audacious flattery enamored many a rebellious Chamorro maiden. Not all love affairs lasted, and some didn't end happily. Tim and Amanda's story was one of many. They met in March 1899, four months prior to Tim's scheduled rotation.

Tim had been in the navy for nearly three years and was ready for advancement to petty officer third class, the next pay grade, and assignment to a new duty station. His ship was anchored in the Piti[1] Harbor, an arm of the larger Apra Harbor. Tim and his shipmates kept mainly to the port villages of Piti, some four miles from Agaña, or to Sumay, on the southern shore of Apra Harbor. Most of the amenities they wanted or needed were nearby, and rarely did anyone need to go into Agaña, the island's capital.

The captain remained on board ship and sent his executive officer, a lieutenant, into Agaña with instructions to observe and send back regular reports on the situation. The lieutenant billeted himself in the crumbling *casa de gobiernador*, or governor's "palace," in the heart of town. The palace was originally built in the seventeenth century and was a dilapidated hulk when the Americans took over. In the years that followed, the navy went to great expense to repair, renovate, and modernize the building, eventually wiring it with electricity and installing indoor plumbing and telephone lines. It was renamed Government House, but most people continued to call it the Governor's Palace.

The lieutenant was a scientist first and a politician last. His interests were in exploring and studying the island's flora, fauna, and geology. He sometimes called for assistance in these endeavors, and on one such occasion, Tim and his friend Scott Jones were assigned. They rode into Agaña with the captain's courier then followed him across a wide plaza to the run-down Spanish headquarters. They heard heated voices and saw several men arguing loudly with the lieutenant, who looked exasperated. The men, each claiming to be the rightful representative of the people, were clamoring for official recognition and pressing the navy on all sorts of community issues and needs. The lieutenant didn't have the authority, the means, or the inclination to meet any of their demands. He wanted only to explore the island, identify and catalog plants species, collect samples, and write of his findings for various scientific journals and magazines. He resented having to put up with the infighting while the man duly assigned with the responsibility hid away on his ship. The lieutenant spotted Tim, Scott, and the courier and summarily dismissed the local leaders.

"Thanks for the rescue, boys," he said. "I couldn't take much more of that crap. Assholes think we're here to serve them." His day ruined, his mood fouled, the lieutenant canceled his planned excursion and released Tim and Scott to return to the ship. "Hell, it looks like rain, anyway," he muttered as he headed into the compound and the courier headed off to tend to the horses.

---

1 Pronounced "Pee-tee."

Before returning to Piti, Tim and Scott decided to get a bite to eat and have a few drinks at El Gato, which was more a rowdy saloon than a respectable eatery, on the town's main street. It boasted a piano, and someone was always banging out lusty tunes that enticed early drinkers into raucous song. It was also where the prettiest barflies could be found. Tim and Scott had heard about the place and were eager to see for themselves. As they walked down the street, a sudden downpour forced them into Castro's Retail Store, where Amanda worked and where their story began.

Amanda was at her station behind the sundries counter when the two men burst through the store's swinging doors. The rain was falling heavily outside. Laughing and hooting boisterously and adding to the din of the rain, the sailors pushed and shoved each other good-naturedly. They were glad to be relieved of their assignment and freed for the day. They stamped their feet and whipped their "Dixie cup" caps against their jumpers to slough the rainwater from their uniforms. Their shoes and bell-bottom trousers were wet and splattered with mud. Tan[2] Chai, the widow who owned the store, looked irately at them and then at the muddy, wet floor.

"Ricutdo!" she called out. Her grandson, a scrawny little eight-year old, appeared from the back room. Tan Chai jutted her chin toward the wet floor. Without a word, the boy turned around, disappeared into the back room, and reappeared a moment later with a mop. Tan Chai had an uncanny way of saying one's name in a particularly stern way that was at once both a summons and a command. She didn't need to voice the command, merely one's name. As Ricardo mopped up the wet spots, Tan Chai grumbled to herself and followed the sailors who started wandering about in her store. She hissed at her salesgirls to stop gawking. That command was issued with a stony glare and a scowled, "Ssst!" that Amanda and the three other salesgirls quickly obeyed.

The sailors had no intention of buying anything; they were simply curious about the store and its wares. They marveled at the variety of Japanese and Chinese products in bottles, boxes, tins, and packages with undecipherable labels and at the unfamiliar fruits and vegetables. Large jars of loose hard candy, twists of tobacco, and pickled things—boiled hen eggs, pig's feet, and strange fruits—lined the counters. Castro's Retail Store was alien to their browsing experience. It had a peculiar smell—not an unpleasant one but a strange, musky scent combined with the odor of tobacco, dried fish, and seaweed. Tim ambled toward Amanda's counter

---

[2] Tan (feminine) and Tun (masculine) are derivatives of the Spanish Tia (aunt) and Tio (uncle). In Chamorro society, all elders, whether blood relatives or not, are addressed with Tan or Tun, as a sign of respect.

for a closer look at the contents of the pickle jars. Her back was to him and she turned around as he approached. Tim froze, transfixed by her beauty.

"Come on, Laney, the rain stopped," Scott urged. But Tim stood cemented in place. Scott shrugged his shoulders. "Suit yourself," he said, "meet me over there when you're ready."

Tim ignored his companion and stared unabashedly at Amanda. As he drew toward her, Tan Chai again summoned her grandson. Ricardo appeared immediately. He saw the sailor making his way toward Amanda's counter and hurried over to stand beside her—a witness to any untoward exchange that might occur or diminutive chaperone and bodyguard, if needed. Amanda welcomed the boy's presence, wary of the rain-soaked sailor approaching her.

Tim knew that the local girls were sheltered, reserved, and bashful around strangers, especially around American sailors, so he approached carefully. He knew that the people of the island, the Chamorros, shared the same history of Spanish conquest as the native peoples of the southern United States and Central and South America, but the Spanish language did not supplant the language of the Chamorros. Tim understood Spanish as it was spoken back home, and he recognized Spanish words as they were spoken in Chamorro, but he could not understand Chamorro at all; it was a completely different language, as were the people who spoke it.

"Hello," he said to Amanda in English. "My name's Tim. What is yours?" He tried to be polite and friendly.

The sailor at her counter was nice looking. He had pretty blue eyes and reddish brown hair. He was taller than her father and more muscular. His manner was respectful and his eyes sparkled. Still, Amanda was unaccustomed to such brazenness, but she blushed and shyly said her name. Her attraction to him was as immediate as his seemed to be to her. He told her she was the prettiest girl he had ever seen and she wanted to believe him.

Indeed, Maria Amanda de Leon was a beauty, an attractive girl by anyone's standard. She wore only a smile; she didn't need any other enhancement. Her dark brown eyes were large and mesmerizing, rimmed by thick, long lashes. Her nose was almost childlike, small, with a rounded tip, and not widely splayed. Her lips were full and inviting. Her hair was long and dark. She wore it in a bun at the back of her head while at work but set it free when she finished her shift. Her skin was smooth and golden brown, like coffee with milk. She was short, barely reaching five feet. Her lower half was hidden behind the counter so Tim couldn't appreciate her figure. All he could see of the salesgirl was her top half—a plain cotton blouse draped over a pair of generous breasts, assuring him that the rest of her would be equally enchanting. Tim was instantly aroused; it had been more than a year since he slept with a woman.

Chapter 2

Amanda was the only one in her family who knew enough English and was schooled enough to land the job at Castro's. Although her English skills were marginal, she could speak and understand enough to manage, but could not yet read English. With the American navy taking over the island, Tan Chai anticipated an increase in the number of English-speaking browsers and customers, and hired accordingly. A shrewd businesswoman, she knew that with daily practice, pretty young novice speakers like Amanda would eventually master the language and attract customers as well. Tim was no English professor, but his gentle corrections and patient explanation of words and phrases, over the course of their acquaintance, improved Amanda's proficiency. She was sixteen years old, the eldest of six children. She was bright, beautiful, and dependable, her proud father's darling.

Her father, Sylvino de Leon, was a fisherman and part-time carpenter. He was hired occasionally on labor crews working for the Spanish and later the Americans on various construction and renovation jobs. By 1900, as the navy presence increased and settled in more permanently, more work was available and day laborers were in demand. Amanda's mother, Pilar, was a deeply religious woman who was devoted to the Blessed Mother. She named her daughters Maria, either as a first or middle name, in honor of the Virgin Mary. The name wasn't generally mentioned, except when their parents were cross. Pilar was small in stature, spry, and stronger than she looked. As with other Chamorro households, Sylvino appeared in the public view to be the head of his household, but everyone knew that it was the woman of the house who truly ruled. The Spanish had imposed their patriarchal and patrilineal social order on the Chamorros, but many aspects of the inherent matriarchal/matrilineal order remained. Like other Chamorro wives, Pilar ruled her household. She kept a small garden and sometimes made some money doing alterations by hand.

Pilar bore ten children in all, but only six survived. Rafael, who was born before Amanda, died of a fever when he was two years old. After Amanda, Pilar lost two more babies; both were stillborn males. Ana Maria, who was twelve, followed next. Her survival was welcomed but not as greatly celebrated as Juan's arrival a year later. Juan was eleven years old and was a miniature version of their father, both in looks and character. Pilar suffered a miscarriage between Esther Maria, who was eight, and Maria Elena, four. The girls were sandwiched between Juan and three-year-old Jaime, and lost in their parents' unabashed appreciation over Juan's survival and baby Jaime's birth. Had they all survived, Pilar and Sylvino would have had six sons. Pilar was certain that the child she miscarried was a boy also, as it seemed she had difficulty bearing male babies. The boys were Pilar's pride and joy, but Amanda commanded a special place in her heart. As eldest daughter, Amanda was destined someday to rule her own home and family, and to carry on the culture, traditions, and language of the Chamorro people.

Amanda and her siblings attended school only in the morning. Until the Americans instituted their own system of education, the old one, established under Spanish rule, remained in place. Staffed by Chamorro teachers, the system developed a character and curriculum of its own, more Chamorro than Spanish, and influenced heavily by Catholic teaching. More formal religious learning took place once a week at *escuelan pale*[3], literally "priest's school." After their school day, Amanda herded the children home, fixed their noon meal, started them on their chores then went to work at the store. She worked five days a week, either from one o'clock until six or from five o'clock until the store closed at ten, depending on the schedule Tan Chai worked out for her salesgirls. On Saturdays Amanda worked the entire day, from nine in the morning until closing. Like other commercial establishments, the store was closed on Sunday. Amanda had landed the job in February, a month after her sixteenth birthday. She was among three other salesgirls and was the youngest, hence her shorter work hours.

"May I call you 'Mandy'?" Tim asked after their initial meeting. Amanda had never heard her name shortened that way and liked it very much. "Mandy" sounded so American, unlike the harsh way Chamorros pronounced names, whether Spanish, English, or some other origin. Like Tan Chai's "Ricutdo," for "Ricardo," "Amanda" was pronounced "Amunda," which made her feel like an old washerwoman. "Mandy" was so much prettier and made her feel worthy of Tim's attention. Her pronunciation of his name tickled him immensely. She called him "Teem." He never tried to correct her. Although childlike, her pronunciation soon became part of his changing view of himself as a man growing in maturity. He also liked hearing her say it.

---

[3] Pronounced "pah-lee," *pale'* is the Chamorro pronunciation of the Spanish *padre.*

Tim's initial intentions were not noble. He felt challenged by the shyness of the local women but had had no luck in bedding any in Piti or Sumay, not even among the bar girls. Although he wanted to win over the pretty girl at Castro's Store merely to satisfy his lust, something about her appealed to other parts of his body as well. Something about her struck him differently, but he had little opportunity to discover what or why. Amanda was difficult prey. Stationed aboard ship in Piti, he was distanced from her. He couldn't see her every day and had no official reason to travel into Agaña. Within days of their initial meeting, Tim began volunteering for any assignment into town, even if he could only steal away for a few minutes to see Amanda. Within a month, Tim spent his every off-duty day in Agaña. Scott sometimes accompanied him, but Tim more often went alone. He hitched rides with the captain's courier or with passersby, and sometimes, if he couldn't hire a horse, he walked the four miles to see her. Without ever touching or kissing her, he was falling in love.

Tim would station himself at Amanda's counter or mill about the store, trying to look like a genuine customer whenever Tan Chai glared at him. It frustrated him to have to mask his efforts to woo Amanda. Courting her in the only way he knew how became his aim, but he couldn't sit in her parlor and hold her hand, or bring flowers to flatter her mother and cower under her father's scrutiny. He couldn't try to steal kisses behind her parents' back, or simply take her for a walk. He could only linger at her counter, trying to charm her between customers. Perhaps it was the difficulty of such courting that made him more determined and her more desirable. Nonetheless, Amanda welcomed his attention and never ordered him away. She, too, was falling in love.

Over the course of several visits, Tim told Amanda about his home in California and all the other wonderful places he had visited. He entertained her with stories of his adventures in cities that she could only dream about. There was little chance, at the start of the twentieth century that a girl from a tiny Pacific island could travel the world; it was as unlikely as voyaging to the moon. Amanda was mesmerized, not only by his stories, but also by the animation of his face as he spoke. Tim would prop his elbows on her counter, rest his chin on his fists, and smile into her eyes whenever she spoke. In her eyes, he saw the future he wanted for himself, the one he had always dreamed of. It was one full of exotic adventure on the high seas, far from cornfields and chicken manure. Their conversations could only occur in brief spurts, interrupted often by customers Amanda had to attend to, or by Tan Chai's watchful proximity.

On the days of his visits, Tim consumed as much of Amanda's work time and attention as he could, and it didn't escape Tan Chai's notice. She pulled

Amanda aside and scolded her for paying too much attention to her sailor and not enough to the customers who were really there to spend money. Her command of English was worse than Amanda's, but she was eloquent in Chamorro, their native tongue. Typical of the privilege, authority, and influence of women her age, she cautioned Amanda about consorting with sailors and warned her of the dangers.

"Be careful, my daughter," Tan Chai started, "these sailors are not here to shop for wives. They are looking for what they can get free. If you make it available, they will take advantage." She motioned toward Amanda's skirt. Amanda understood her message immediately and thought her impolite for suggesting something so crass.

Amanda had already been betrothed at birth to Elias de Gracia, the nephew of her high-ranking godmother, the indomitable Tan Julianna Calderon y de Gracia, who was the indisputable matriarch of her clan. As a young girl, Pilar worked for Tan Julianna as a housemaid and admired her as much as feared her. Tan Julianna's grandparents came from Salamanca, Spain, at the end of the eighteenth century and grew rich exploiting the huge tracts of land awarded to her grandfather by the Spanish king. Tan Julianna and her younger brothers inherited the *lanchos*, the Chamorro pronunciation of the Spanish *ranchos*, which produced copra and cattle. Anselmo de Gracia, Elias's father, was among the men who thought they should have been appointed interim governor. When Amanda was born, Tan Julianna rewarded Pilar by becoming Amanda's baptismal godmother and betrothing the children to each other. The arrangement was to have bound and benefited the three families: the de Leons to a higher social rank, the de Gracias to a wealth of heirs, and Tan Julianna to greater prestige. Amanda was simply a pawn in her game.

Amanda disliked Elias. He grew into a handsome young man who turned the heads of many girls jealous of Amanda's good fortune, but he was arrogant and narcissistic. Elias would ride one of his family's beautiful imported horses through town, from their orchards and farm in the north to the cattle ranch in the south, basking in the attention and admiration of all the women along the way. He thought the de Leons were too far below his family's rank and was not quiet about his disdain for the betrothal. He felt his parents were goaded into it by his aunt, Tan Julianna, but he dared not protest it. He wanted Amanda only as a mistress, not a wife entitled to his inheritance. If Amanda's parents had known about Tim, they too would have preferred she be kept as a mistress rather than the wife of a Protestant foreigner. They were not above the contradictions of Spanish cultural influence and practice, in which wives of high-ranking men were expected to produce numerous children and remain silent abc husbands' dalliances with one or more well-rewarded mistresses.

Like many of the ranking women of her generation, Tan Chai was aware that her husband had one long-term mistress and had fathered at least five children with her. Such offspring were known as "outside children." Although the mistress knew better than to show her face in Castro's Store, her children were frequent customers. Tan Chai knew who they were and they knew who she was. Tan Chai tried to dislike her husband's outside children, but could not. They were always humble, well-mannered, and exceedingly respectful toward her. Tan Chai couldn't help but accept them simply as innocent children. She herself bore eleven children, six boys and five girls. Her husband was long in his grave and all her children were grown and married when American rule began, but she was never alone or lonely. Ricardo was only one among the dozens of both legitimate and outside grandchildren and great grandchildren always underfoot or nearby.

Tan Chai cared about her salesgirls as if they were her own daughters. She was their employer, with the authority to manage their conduct on the job, but she also had a motherly obligation to watch over them and ensure their behavior as proper young ladies. Amanda was the youngest and most innocent and vulnerable of the salesgirls.

As Tim's appearance in Castro's Store became more regular, especially as he almost never bought anything, Amanda feared Tan Chai would say something about it to her parents. They relied on her small income for payments requiring cash, especially as U.S. dollars became the exclusive new medium of exchange. Amanda couldn't risk losing the job, so she tried to be more discreet about entertaining Tim, sometimes ignoring him, scolding him, or pleading with him to leave the store.

"Can't we sit somewhere and talk—just you and me?" Tim pressed. "Mandy, I can only see you on my days off. I want to spend every minute I can with you."

Amanda could not oblige him. She had to keep their budding relationship secret. It would have been reckless and scandalous for a proper young lady to be discovered unchaperoned in the company of any man unrelated to her, especially if that man was one of those drunken, uncouth, foul-mouthed American sailors whose only aim was to have sex. Amanda knew that Tim Laney was not one of those, at least not when he was with her. Within a month of their meeting, she wanted to be alone with him as much as he wanted to be with her. She began to skip her half-hour dinner breaks whenever he came to town, which was only once or twice a week. Tim would buy a boxed meal from the canteen at the old Spanish government compound. The meal boxes were prepared for the men working to repair and rebuild the compound and who lived too far away to go home to eat. Anyone could buy the meals for a nickel. Tim and Amanda would share the meal in a stairwell in the alley next to the store. Amanda had suggested it as their private meeting place. Tim laughed when she tried to describe where it was. There were no "steps to the wall by the alley."

"You laugh to me?" she snapped indignantly. "Never mind, we stay here."

The irritation in Amanda's voice and the hurt in her face put a quick end to Tim's amusement. He didn't mean to offend her, especially about speaking English.

"I'm sorry, Mandy," he whispered. He was standing at her counter, within earshot of Tan Chai. "I'll meet you anytime, anyplace. I'll find those steps to the wall," he said softly.

"Hmph!" she sniffed and turned away. "Ricutdo!" she commanded, "Tell this man, 'Go away.'"

Ricardo marched bravely toward Tim, scowling like his grandmother. To avert dismissal, Tim drew a penny from his pocket and held it out to Ricardo.

"I'll give you a penny if you let me stay." Tim then drew out another penny. "Two, if you don't tell your grandma."

Ricardo had no idea what Tim was saying, but he was easily bribed. Ricardo grinned, grabbed the two pennies from Tim's hand, and scurried away to the candy counter.

Amanda's "steps to the wall" was a flight of stairs recessed into the store's exterior wall in the narrow alley between the store and the adjacent barbershop. The stairs led to Tan Chai's home on the floor above the store. The door at the top had been nailed shut and unused since Tan Chai's husband's death years earlier. The staircase was in a narrow alcove hidden from the street. It offered the concealment and privacy that both Amanda and Tim wanted. They mounted the stairs quietly and sat on a step about halfway up. In daylight, they could not be seen from the street; at night, they could not be seen at all.

From their first secret meeting in the staircase, Tim wanted to kiss Amanda but worried that she would balk and reject his advances if he was too abrupt. She was of a society far more straitlaced and conservative than his. He waited patiently, breaking down her reserve with small talk in their initial encounters. Later, as she grew more trusting, he advanced slowly and gently, simply toying with her fingers and hands as they talked. At their fourth session, Tim brought her hands to his lips and kissed them as she spoke. On their fifth session, in late April, he decided to make his move. He played with her fingers and kissed her hand as usual then kissed his way from her hand and along her arm to her neck. Tim's kisses sent chills and breathtaking sensations throughout Amanda's body. When he reached her face and pressed his lips to hers, she received him eagerly. She and Tim sat halfway up the staircase in the dark, forgetting about dinner entirely.

"We show our love like this," she said. She pressed her nose to the side of his face and inhaled deeply. She noisily breathed in the scent of the skin on his cheek then inhaled her way down his neck to his throat and the opening of his shirt. Her action startled Tim, but the sensation drove him wild.

"You smell good, Teem," she whispered. "I breathe you in. Now you try."

Tim eagerly obliged, pressing his face to the side of her neck. He wasn't sure what he was supposed to sniff for, but the feeling it gave him was rousing. Amanda's skin was smooth and smelled sweet and clean.

"When you breathe in someone they become part of you," she explained. Tim preferred kissing, but decided "smelling" was enjoyable too.

After Amanda returned to work, Tim waited at El Gato for Castro's Store to close. He hid in the shadows in the alley for Amanda to exit then secretly followed her home. He wanted to know where she lived. Her house was not far from the store and was like a few others in the neighborhood: wood plank walls with a thatched roof. Dim lantern light shone through the two front windows, and the sound of children's voices and laughter poured from inside. He listened for Amanda's voice until he heard her sweet laugh. She was saying something in her native tongue, which Tim didn't understand, but by the tone of her voice, he assumed she was herding her siblings off to bed. A few minutes later, the light in one of the windows went out and the house was quiet except for the low murmur of adult voices, including Amanda's. Somehow, knowing where she lived and a bit more about her life brought her closer to him. Satisfied, Tim walked back to the government compound, hoping to catch a ride back to Piti.

Chapter 3

Looking forward to more kisses, on his next day off, Tim caught a lift to Agaña with a carriage driver who wasn't going all the way into town. Tim thanked him on the outskirts and walked the rest of the way to Castro's Store. Amanda was not at her counter. He spotted Ricardo and asked if Amanda had come to work that day. The boy looked at Tim but made no answer.

"Amanda?" Tim pressed, realizing Ricardo didn't understand English.

Ricardo made his way to the main doors, opened one side, and pointed to a goldsmith's shop across the street. Tim hurried over and found Amanda admiring the gold chains, dainty necklaces, heavy "bamboo" bracelets and bangles, and the variety of rings and earrings in the showcase. Tim pretended not to know her, so as not to embarrass her in front of other customers, and she pretended not to know him. He stood a little way away from her, watching to see what she was admiring.

"Tan 'Sabet, *akuanto esti*[4]?" Amanda asked timidly, pointing down at a pair of gold earrings. Tan Isabel, the saleslady, was an elegant woman whose silver hair was in stark contrast with her milk-chocolate complexion. Her gleaming hair was piled on top of her head and held in place by a large Spanish-style comb. She was dressed in a richly embroidered Spanish satin gown and looked to Tim like a character from a stage play. Tan Isabel answered, "*Sientu sinquentai-sinko pesos*[5], *haga-hu*[6]."

Tim understood both Amanda's question and the saleslady's response: a hundred and fifty-five pesos, but he didn't know what kind of pesos, whether Mexican, Filipino, or one of the dreaded and nearly worthless South American dollars, which he hoped was the case.

After a thoughtful moment, Amanda thanked Tan Isabel and left the shop without acknowledging Tim's presence. He lingered behind, allowing

4 "How much is this?"

5 The Chamorro pronunciation for the Spanish "one hundred and fifty-five dollars."

6 "My daughter."

some time to pass before following her back to Castro's. He studied the pieces in the showcase, especially the earrings that had attracted Amanda's interest. Unlike the heavy, garishly ornate Spanish style jewelry on display, Amanda's earrings were a pair of plain, pea-sized gold spheres on studs. To Tim's mind, they matched Amanda's unadorned beauty and simplicity.

"May I help you, sir?" asked the elegant saleslady. Her English was perfect. She had no accent. If Tim hadn't seen her and only heard her voice, he would have thought she was an American. He wondered how she had acquired such fluency. He couldn't have known that her father was an American whaler who jumped ship to marry her mother seventy years earlier. Or that her four brothers sailed away as deckhands on British, German, and American merchant vessels. Tan Isabel received sporadic letters from them but never saw her brothers again before she died.

"Yes, ma'am," Tim said. "I'm interested in these earrings."

"My husband made these," the saleslady said proudly. "It's quite difficult to produce small, perfect spheres of equal size and weight. These are made of eighteen-karat gold, which is more malleable and more costly than the standard fourteen karats for jewelry."

"What are you asking for them?"

Tan Isabel raised an eyebrow, certain that Tim could not afford the cost. "Fifteen American dollars, sir," she said.

Tim swallowed hard. Fifteen dollars was far less than a hundred and fifty-five foreign dollars but much greater than he could afford. It was more than half his monthly pay.

"We do allow payment in installments. Would you like to purchase them that way?" Tan Isabel was eager to make the sale to the American, the first one to enter her shop, not knowing whether he was a common sailor or a better-paid officer.

"Yes, thank you. I'd like to buy them for my girl. I can put three dollars down right now," he said as he pulled the bills from his billfold. The three dollars were his spending money for the rest of the week and the next.

"I'm sure your sweetheart will be very happy. I'll draw up a receipt," she said, but didn't seem pleased. Tim looked at her questioningly, wondering whether she regretted having to give up her husband's special handiwork and worried that she would decide not to sell them.

Tan Isabel sighed heavily as she took the earrings from the showcase. "That young lady who left a moment ago will be so disappointed. She comes into the shop at least once a month to admire them. Today was the first time she asked about the price, but I know she can't afford them," she explained.

"I'm sure she'll get over it," Tim said without smiling.

Tim wasn't sure how he was going to pay the twelve-dollar balance on the earrings. Twelve dollars a month was what he lived on after sending his mother half his pay. He wouldn't have considered sending her any less. At the agreed-upon payment of two dollars a month, the earrings wouldn't be paid off for six months. Tim had only two months left on the island. To redeem them in time, he would have to pay six dollars a month and live frugally on the remaining six. He thought about canceling the purchase, but that would have been like giving up on Amanda. He would have to suffer a little, but Amanda was worth the sacrifice. She would have something of value, a reminder of her value to him.

While Tim was excited about his parting gift for Amanda, she was pensive at their next encounter. She had invested too much time in her relationship with Tim and was now too deeply attached to give him up. As impossible as it was, she had to end their secret meetings, and as painful as it was to think about, she knew someone else would win his heart and not have to ever give it up. Maybe someone already had; maybe there had always been someone else.

"Teem," she said, looking him in the eye, "you have girlfriend in your place?" Tim tried not to laugh; he knew what she meant but dared not correct her—not on a question of such obvious importance to her.

"Not anymore," he answered.

"Why no more?" she pressed.

"Well, I'm here and she's in San Diego. I'm not with her."

"You want to be with her, no?"

Tim didn't say anything and was quiet for a moment. Amanda waited for an answer, but none came. Then she asked, "She have blue eyes like you? Her hair is yellow?

"Blonde. Her hair is blonde," Tim corrected. "Yes, her eyes are blue."

"She's pretty?" Amanda's heart was sinking fast.

"I don't want to talk about her," he said, growing a little irritated. Yes, she had blue eyes, like robin's eggs. And yes, she had blonde hair, the color of sweet corn. But he didn't want to be reminded.

"Why, Teem? You still like her?"

"Stop it, Mandy!" He had pined for Sarah Chapin for months after he joined the navy. Sarah was his girl throughout high school. He thought he loved her and would eventually return to San Diego and marry her, even though he took every advantage to satisfy his urges with willing women in Honolulu's bars. Amanda's questions made him realize that he hadn't thought about her since he arrived in Guam, long before he met Amanda. Sarah had become a faded memory that was no longer painful to recall.

Amanda was now all he could think about, and he wondered whether she would be as easy to forget.

"What's her name?" Amanda demanded.

"Why do you want to know? It's not important," Tim said, his irritation growing.

"It's important to me."

"Why should it matter, Mandy?"

"Because I want to know who's in your heart when it's not me."

Exasperated, Tim finally said, "Sarah. Her name is Sarah."

"When you go back, you will look for Sarah? You love her?" There was sadness in Amanda's voice. She knew that Tim was hers only while he was in Guam.

"I don't know, Mandy," he said. "Don't ask me questions I can't answer." Tim couldn't give her a truthful answer. He was fond of Sarah; she commanded a place in his heart. She was still there, a part of his past, and probably his future as well. Sarah and her parents expected them to get married. His parents expected it also. It was not what he wanted, but he feared he would acquiesce. The prospect was disheartening. He didn't feel about Sarah the same way he felt about Amanda. Sarah was a warm and wispy memory. Amanda was a burning reality that he wanted more than anything.

The exchange in the stairwell ended on a sad and uncomfortable note that day. Tim and Amanda left much unsaid. Amanda was jealous of Sarah, someone she didn't know, someone who had been in Tim's affection long before her, someone he was likely to return to and marry. Tim didn't want to be a farmer. There was nothing wrong with farming but it wasn't what he wanted. He wanted to sail the seas and see the world. Tim wanted to be his own man, to make his own decisions and carve his own way in life. He wanted to marry who he chose. He wanted Amanda, but he was afraid of the scorn and rejection he would face for marrying outside his race. He couldn't bring her back to the States. He didn't have the courage to defy the law or the expectations of the people back home, the norms of society, or the navy's prohibition against marriage to native women.

In May, Tim received word that he was to depart Guam on the first of July. He thought he was supposed to leave later in the month. He dreaded having to break the news to Amanda. He never told her how long he had been on Guam or how much time he had left. He assumed she knew that he would have to leave eventually, but only he knew that his assignment was never meant to last more than six months. Tim didn't think leaving would be difficult. The thought now made him anxious. He didn't want to leave, didn't want to leave Amanda. Tim feared that news of an actual date, and the discomforting conversation about Sarah, would cause Amanda to end their relationship. As he toyed with her hands on their usual step in the stairwell, Tim quietly said, "I'm leaving in July, Amanda."

Amanda's heart dropped. Tim was serious; he didn't call her by his pet name. The time had come; the end was near. Amanda had tried to steel herself against the inevitable, but the heartache was inescapable. Her chest began to quiver, and her eyes filled with tears. Before they could spill, she stood up and said, "You go now, Teem. Good-bye!" She tried to hurry down the stairs, but Tim grabbed her arm and held her fast.

"Wait, Mandy, please don't send me away."

"I go back to work now. You go home!" She struggled against his grip and made it to the bottom of the stairs. Her tears were now streaming down her face. Tim rushed after her, and the two stood in the shadows in the alleyway. He tried to embrace her, but she pushed him away.

"Go away, Teem," she said angrily, wiping away tears with the back of her hand. She dashed back into the store, leaving him alone in the alley. It was the right way to end a love affair: cease contact, remove oneself, commence separation, and start nursing a broken heart. Tim stood stooped-shouldered in the silvery moonlight. He made his way back to Piti on foot, too dejected to thumb a ride, the bright full moon his only companion.

The following week, when Tim entered the store, Amanda escaped into the back room and refused to come out. Tim hung his head and left. He crossed the street to the goldsmith's, to make another payment on Amanda's earrings. He paid as much as he could spare. He denied himself any beer or soda pop and ate only in the ship's galley in order to pay off the earrings faster. He had only two payments left, but wouldn't be able to make the last one before his ship sailed.

For the next two weeks, Tim didn't go to Agaña or make any attempt to see Amanda. During that time, Amanda waited for Tim to come into the store as usual. Despite the way she had brushed him away, she hoped he would not give up. They had only a few weeks left before Tim's departure. Of those weeks, they had only two or three days, and of those few days, even fewer moments. She yearned to see him again. She watched and waited, her heart soaring each time a sailor came through the doors, but Tim was never one of them. Even Tan Chai noticed his absence.

"What happened to the sailor?" she asked snidely. "I hope you didn't give him what he wanted."

Amanda held her head proudly but said nothing. *No, Tim hasn't gotten what you're suggesting,* she answered in her head, incensed that Tan Chai would think such a thing. Unlike the drunken local scoundrels who wandered in from El Gato and taunted Amanda with the crude and nasty things they wanted to do to her, Tim was never disrespectful or indecent. He was a gentleman, and she loved him for it. *Ai Tan Chai, if he wanted me, I'd let him.* The desire was growing in her mind.

To Amanda's joy, Tim came into the store the following day. Amanda tried but couldn't hide her happiness. The look on Tim's face was not as joyful. Despite the widest welcoming smile he had ever seen on Amanda's face, Tim was somber.

"I must speak with you," he said. "Can we talk in the alley?"

Tan Chai glared at them, but Amanda ignored her unspoken warning. "I'll be right back, Tan Chai," she said as she came around the counter, took Tim's hand, and led him outside. In broad daylight, in the alleyway where anyone could see them, Amanda threw her arms around Tim's neck and kissed him deeply. She didn't care whether anyone saw them.

"Amanda, I'm leaving in three days. That's all the time I have left," he said with a sadness that stabbed into Amanda's heart. "I love you, Amanda. I don't want to leave you. I want to be with you. Not just for a few minutes, but for always."

At that moment, Amanda made up her mind. If they could not be together forever as man and wife, they could be as one for at least one night. "I will come to you tonight, but not here," she said. "I love you, Teem, and I will be with you." She gave him precise instructions as to when and where to meet. "You go there and wait for me."

Chapter 4

Amanda hurried home at six o'clock, anxious about what she had committed to, but exhilarated by the prospect of intimacy with Tim, desperate and dangerous as it would be. She rushed through her chores and supper and waited for nightfall and for her family to retire for the night. She worried about Tim and wondered where he would go, what he would do, to pass the time. She hoped he wouldn't be tempted to wait out the hours at El Gato and show up drunk at where they were to meet.

Tim had only a few pennies in his pocket, enough for a ride back to Piti but not enough for even one beer. He spent an hour or so listening to the piano player at El Gato then lounged at the enlisted men's temporary barracks in the government compound. He dozed off and woke with a start at ten thirty. He stole a couple of blankets from the barracks and headed to the beach. Since the last carriage run to Piti, Sumay, and Agat left at ten o'clock, he would be stuck in Agaña until morning, but it didn't matter. He would take the first carriage at six, or walk back if necessary. He would catch hell for missing muster and being absent without leave, and was bound to go up for captain's mast, but he was willing to pay the price to spend the night with Amanda.

At long last, after Amanda's mother concluded the family's nightly rosary, her father extinguished the lanterns and signaled that time had come for bed. Amanda did not change into her nightclothes but covered herself with her blanket in case her mother looked in on them. Until she turned thirteen and was already a menstruating young woman, Amanda shared the largest bed in the house with her sisters Ana, Esther, and Elena. They squabbled nightly over who was taking up the most space and who was not sharing the blanket. They shared the bedroom with their brothers Juan and Jaime, who slept in their own shared bed. When the situation became untenable and no longer appropriate, Sylvino de Leon built another bed and divided the room. The smaller section became the boys' room; the larger section and the new bed were for the girls. Ana and Amanda shared the new bed, closest to the window. Esther and Elena had the old bed, closer to the bedroom door.

Amanda extinguished the lamp between the two beds and pretended to sleep. She lay wide awake, waiting restlessly in the dark and listening to her father's old clock on the wall. Time passed so slowly. The minutes seemed interminable; the hours lasted an eternity. When all she could hear was the slow, rhythmic breathing of her parents and siblings sleeping in their rooms, Amanda arose from her bed and laced her shoes back on her feet. She tiptoed out the door and into the cool night. Her heart pounding with nervous anticipation, she dashed across several streets and alleyways to get to the beach, which was only a few hundred yards from her house. In daylight, the walk would have taken only a few minutes, but trying to navigate quietly through people's yards and over a footbridge in the dark took longer. Amanda had never been outside her house that late at night, and neither had most of her neighbors. Every house and street she passed was dark and quiet. She worried that Tim would lose his way in the dark and not find her. Only El Gato and Billy's Tavern, at the other end of the block and four streets behind her, were alive with lights and the distant, muffled sounds of music and liquored laughter. She prayed again that Tim was not also getting liquored up. She would not go through with her plan if he was drunk.

With only the moon to light the way, Amanda hurried to the spot on the beach she had described to Tim. It was behind several large rocks near the water, well away from where the *galaide*[7] (ga-LIE-dee) and light proa[8] of fishermen were pulled up onto the sand above the high tide mark. She thought she would have to wait for Tim, but he was already waiting for her. He had spread out one of the blankets on the sand and had taken off his shirt, undershirt, shoes, and socks. Amanda ran her hands across his chest, feeling his bare skin and filling her lungs with the scent of his body. Tim lifted her blouse and camisole and eased them over her head. He ran his hands over her velvety skin and cupped her breasts while he kissed her neck and the top of her shoulder. He held up the second blanket behind her as she finished undressing. She clasped the blanket around herself and shivered while he disrobed. Tim gently pulled her down onto the blanket on the sand and began kissing her, touching her body slowly, awaiting her arousal before taking her.

After lovemaking, Tim rolled over beside Amanda. Panting, he whispered, "I love you, Amanda." They giggled and cuddled and kissed again and again then lay quietly, watching dark wispy clouds glide slowly across the face of the moon. A few minutes later, Tim was breathing slowly

---

[7] Dugout paddling canoes.

[8] Oceangoing outrigger canoes.

and deeply. He was asleep, his arms still wrapped around her. *My poor Tim,* she thought, *how tired you must be.* She nestled her head against his shoulder and ran a finger along his jaw. In his sleep, Tim reached for her hand and kissed it. "I love you too," Amanda said. Tim smiled.

Amanda awoke in a panic when she heard the cathedral bell start ringing at four thirty. It was still dark, but early churchgoers, including her mother, would soon be heading to the cathedral for Mass at five. The stars were beginning to fade and the black sky would soon give way to the colors of dawn. She had to slip back home before sunrise, before her family woke up to start their day, her father to feed the chickens and her mother to start the breakfast fire after she returned from Mass; she never missed a morning. Amanda wanted to spend eternity in Tim's arms, but the time had come for them to part. She nudged Tim's shoulder and jarred him awake. He opened his eyes and smiled. He wanted to make love again and reached for her, but Amanda pulled away.

"No more time, Teem," she said, "I must go home."

"I'll walk you home," Tim said as they reached for their clothes and started dressing.

"No, you can't," she said, "People will see us."

"Are you ashamed of me, Mandy?" The hurt in his eyes broke her heart.

"I never be ashamed of you, but we will get in real bad trouble; you and me."

"So this is it? Mandy, this can't be it. We can't end like this."

"It must, but in here," she said, placing his hand on her chest, "it will never end. In my heart, you are my husband, Teem."

The darkness was fading and the sky was beginning to glow purple, royal blue, and pink. Time was running out. Amanda's heart started pounding in fear. She reached up and kissed Tim one last time. "I love you, Teem, I always will love you," she said and hurried away. Tim tried to choke down the lump in his throat as he watched her go.

As he made his way back to Piti, Tim thought about reenlisting. He had less than a year left to decide whether to stay in the navy or get out. Reenlisting for another four years would allow him to build up a nest egg for return passage to Guam, pay for a proper wedding, and maybe even purchase a small house for his bride. But as a sailor, he had no say in where he would be sent. There was no guarantee of a reassignment to Guam, and waiting another four years to return to Amanda was too long. He contemplated signing onto a merchant ship after leaving the navy and working his way back with money to spare. That would take time also, but as a civilian, he wouldn't be bound by the navy's marriage ban and could still send money home to his parents. By the time he reached Piti, his mind was made up. He would work his way back as a civilian.

As he expected, Tim was in trouble for not showing up for muster and was called up for captain's mast. He expected to be docked some pay, denied liberty, and probably penalized a few weeks of extra duty. What he received was more devastating than he could bear. Instead of punishment, Tim was given the news that his father and youngest sister were dead, killed in a fire that burned down the family farmhouse. His father managed to get his mother and sister to safety. He then returned to the burning house and died along with his daughter who was only ten years old. His mother and sister, Tim was told, were relying on the charity of neighbors for food and shelter. The bodies of his father and sister were at the county morgue, awaiting disposition. Tim didn't know how he was going to afford paying for their funerals; his last paychecks would not be enough. He also needed to build a new house, but how and with what?

Tim departed Guam as ordered, but not to return to the fleet in Manila. As an only son, he was obliged to care for his family as its new head. His discharge papers had already been drawn up and signed. A day later, he was on board a ship bound for Honolulu and California. Tim stood at the stern watching as the island of Guam grew smaller and smaller. He fought back his tears, his heart heavy with grief over the deaths of his father and baby sister. He also mourned the loss of all his dreams, his independence, and any future with Amanda.

He gave Scott the last payment on Amanda's earrings and asked him to deliver them with a letter. Scott could not fulfill Tim's request until nearly a month later.

CHAPTER 5

Amanda cried into her pillow for several nights after Tim left, smothering her sobs from her sisters' hearing. Although she saw him only for a few minutes once or twice a week, she missed him every minute of every day that followed his departure. For nearly a month, she couldn't sleep, either because of the pain in her heart or because she fought to relive every moment she spent with Tim, especially their night on the beach. Everyone noticed her unhappiness, but she refused to explain its cause. Amanda tried desperately to hide her sorrow, especially from her family, but they knew she was in pain. They sometimes heard her late at night calling out forlornly in her sleep, but they didn't know who or what a "teem" was. In the morning Amanda would be cheerful and pretend to be her usual self, but her father and mother could see that the sparkle in her eyes was gone. Even Tan Chai recognized Amanda's melancholy and was sympathetic, although she never offered any soothing words. She knew what it was to love deeply and to mourn its loss.

About three weeks after Tim sailed away, Scott came into Castro's Retail Store. He walked straight to Amanda's counter and greeted her uncomfortably.

"Tim asked me to give these to you. I've only now had the chance," he said, and handed her a small satin pouch and an envelope. Amanda stared at the items then up at Scott.

"I'm leaving in the morning and I figured I'd better get these to you," he said.

Si Yu'us ma'ase[9], she muttered the Chamorro equivalent of "thank you" without realizing it, her attention focused only on Tim's letter.

She was both elated and discouraged. She recognized her name on the front of the envelope and was certain it contained Tim's words of love and promise. Amanda could read her name but nothing else. She knew several people, like Tan 'Sabet, who could read English, but dared not ask their help. Doing so would have exposed her relationship with an American sailor and with his private message to her. She didn't want to share Tim's

---

[9] Pronounced "see joo oos ma ah see," literally, "God is merciful."

words—whether good or bad—with anyone, not even Scott. Whatever Tim wrote, whatever he had to say to her, would remain a mystery until she could read English. She folded the letter and stuffed it in her pocket along with the satin pouch. She was eager to examine its contents but waited for a private moment.

"He really liked you, you know," Scott said. "Well, good-bye, Amanda."

"Good-bye, Scott." Amanda watched him nervously back out of the store with a crooked smile on his face and his cap in his hands. He seemed reluctant to leave, as if he had more to say but chose not to voice it.

Scott didn't have the heart to tell her the tragic news about the fire, the deaths of Tim's father and sister, and the plight of his mother and surviving sister. A farm boy also, Scott couldn't bring himself to tell her what a massive burden was now resting on Tim's shoulders, a burden so heavy it would anchor him to the family farm for good. Tim was not likely to return to her, no matter how much he wanted. Scott assumed Tim's letter would explain everything, although it seemed cruel not to give Amanda some warning of the letter's sad contents. But it was not his place to divulge it prematurely.

At her dinner break, Amanda hurried out to the alley and climbed to the step that she and Tim shared on his days off. She took the satin pouch from her pocket and carefully opened it. The gold earrings spilled out and sparkled in her hand. They were the ones she had always admired in the goldsmith's shop, the expensive ones. She started to cry. The earrings she loved were now hers, a gift from her beloved Tim. That made them even more valuable and more deeply cherished. Amanda carefully removed her old Spanish-style dangling cross earrings, a gift from her godmother at her christening, and replaced them with Tim's. She would later give her old ones to Elena and tell anyone who asked that she had saved and bought the new earrings herself. No one needed to know that they were from Tim.

Amanda removed Tim's letter from her pocket and kissed the places she knew Tim had touched. She broke the wax seal and opened the envelope. Inside was a single page of writing. She unfolded the page and studied Tim's handwriting. His hand had rested on the page; his eyes gazed on every word as he wrote. She followed his words across the page, recognizing individual letters and some small words, but not understanding what they meant all together. At home that night, while Ana was washing the supper dishes, Amanda hid Tim's letter in the back of a drawer under her camisoles and petticoats. She was sharing the bed with Ana but not any secrets.

About a week later, Amanda woke with a queasy stomach. She roused Ana and tried to ignore her stomach as she headed to awaken her sisters and brothers for breakfast. She got as far as the girls' bed and could not hold down her heaving stomach. She dashed to the pee pot in the corner of the bedroom and threw up bitter yellow bile. The smell emanating from the pot caused her to gag even harder. The sounds frightened Ana.

"What's wrong, Amanda? Did you eat something bad?" Ana asked, worried that whatever made Amanda sick would sicken them as well. Food poisoning was a real concern.

"I'll go get Mama," Esther said as she jumped from bed to race for the door.

"No!"

"Why?" Esther pleaded, afraid for her sister and anxious for their mother's help.

"Because Mama will make me stay home from work," Amanda said. "I'm all right. I just have a bad stomach." Although she was puzzled by the nausea, Amanda worried only about missing work. If she missed a day's work, her family would lose a day's wages, especially the American money mandated to eventually replace Mexican and Filipino pesos. Tan Chai paid her employees a combination of currencies, the American money being less plentiful but more valuable. Amanda gave no thought to her nausea until it happened again when she got to her counter. The odors in the store made her queasy again. The following morning, the nausea returned, as did the queasy stomach at work. Amanda was certain that she ate nothing to cause such lasting upset and began to suspect the only other possible reason for having morning sickness. Sworn to secrecy, Amanda's worried siblings could only listen to her discomfort, which lasted over several mornings.

Amanda missed her menstrual cycle and waited with a mixture of both hope and fear for the next telling symptom. Even before the morning sickness subsided, her breasts began to swell and became tender and painful. When the time for her next cycle came and went with no bleeding, Amanda was certain she was pregnant. Tim's child was growing inside her. The thought filled her with joy and sadness. A pregnancy was supposed to be a joyous development, a welcome event, but hers was not the product of marriage. She had no proud husband eager to share the happy news with relatives and friends. She had only the memory of a tender lover and a single night spent in his arms. Bringing new life into the world was supposed to be in fulfillment of God's command to be fruitful and multiply, but the father of her child would not be present to receive and cradle their gift from God. Tim was miles away on some other shore, not knowing that he had left her with child. Amanda would give birth alone. By her calculation, Tim's baby would be born sometime in late March, probably on the anniversary of their first meeting. That thought warmed her heart.

As the weeks crept by, the thoughts of what lay ahead filled Amanda with both fear and anticipation. She feared the pain of childbirth and wasn't sure she could endure it. She became a woman at age twelve. Jaime was born that same year. Amanda knew the pain of menstrual cramps firsthand and had witnessed the apex of such pain when her mother gave birth to Jaime. More frightening than the pain of delivery was the anguish of discovery. She was now three months pregnant, and her parents were bound to find out. She didn't know how they would react or what they would do. She knew only that they would be angry and disappointed in her. But the thought of holding Tim's baby in her arms and trying to imagine what he or she looked like was thrilling. Thinking of names soon filled her thoughts and warmed her heart. She was ashamed at having betrayed her parents' trust, but not of having loved Tim or of having his child. She was determined to face her parents' wrath bravely.

Before heading to work, as she entered her fourth month, Amanda headed to the beach and stopped at the place where she had slept with Tim. It was a lovely spot, private and cozy, even in daylight. The sun was shining warmly, and pure white clouds towered into the heavens. As they did that night, gentle waves washed against the reef. She sat on a rock, slipped off her shoes, and dipped her feet into the warm shallow water, remembering how Tim had been so gentle and tender. She gazed at the horizon, out to where the dark blue ocean meets the cloud-studded sky, and wondered how far Tim was beyond that line. A part of him, more precious than the earrings she was wearing, was growing inside her. A new human being, the product of their bodies, was making its presence known. The baby's movements, which began as slight flutters, were now stronger thumps and jabs. Amanda rested a hand on her belly and smiled sadly.

"Your father knows nothing of your coming," she whispered, "he can't be here for either of us."

The changes in her body were easy to disguise in the first six months. When her waist started to expand, she moved the buttons on the waistband of her skirts and stretched out the plackets by hand. She wore only her largest and loosest blouses or hid behind loosely tied smocks and aprons. The festivities and activities of the Christmas season drew attention away from her condition, especially as her seventeenth birthday loomed, the island faced the start of a new century and settled under American naval rule. By her seventh month, Amanda could no longer hide or disguise her swollen belly, and she waited fearfully for the moment of discovery. It was now inevitable. The moment arrived while she was washing dishes after supper.

Pilar had been observing Amanda over the months, noting how her downcast spirit gradually lifted into something happier. The sparkle had returned to Amanda's eyes, and she was putting on some weight. There was even a tempered cheerfulness in her daughter. Pilar initially attributed it to the holiday season and her coming birthday, but something in Amanda's changing demeanor and appearance became troubling. Shortly after the Feast of the Three Kings, Pilar noted that Amanda's weight gain was centered at her belly. Hoping her suspicion was wrong, Pilar confronted Amanda. She pressed her hand against Amanda's firm belly and shrank back in horror, her face growing pale, her anger rising rapidly.

"When did this happen?" she demanded. Not waiting for an answer, Pilar began shouting at Amanda and slapping at her face and head with both hands. Amanda held up her arms to block the blows, but her mother was much stronger. Pilar grabbed hanks of Amanda's hair and yanked with all her might. Their cries and screams brought Sylvino rushing into the kitchen.

"Your daughter is pregnant!" Pilar spat out the words as if Amanda had desecrated some holy object. Sylvino pushed his wife aside and faced Amanda.

"Amanda, is this true?" the hurt in her father's voice and in his eyes broke Amanda's heart. She bowed her head, shame-faced. Sylvino blanched when Amanda told him that her lover, the father of her child, was an American sailor. For an hour, he and Pilar questioned her. When? Where? "Why, Amanda, why did you allow this?"

"Because I love him, Papa, and he loves me," Amanda sobbed.

Pilar crossed herself and looked heavenward, imploring, "Ai, Santa Maria!"

"Who is he? What is his name? What do you mean 'he's gone'?" Sylvino demanded. He intended to hunt the man down and beat him. Amanda could see it in her father's eyes. As they watched from their bedroom doorway, her sisters and brothers trembled in fear and tried hard to suppress their sobs so as not to add fuel to their father's anger.

"I will not tell you, Papa, not until he comes back," she said with as much respectful defiance as she could marshal. "If I tell you his name now, you will hate him. He loves me and he is coming back. Trust me, Papa, he will."

"How, my daughter?" her father said as tears filled his eyes. "How can we trust you when you have already betrayed us?"

Sylvino de Leon walked away from his daughter and out the door. He was certain that his daughter had been seduced, duped, and abandoned in the worst possible way. Neither he nor Pilar believed that Amanda's lover would ever return. Pilar sat in a kitchen chair sobbing into a dish towel. Amanda approached her and tried to put a hand on her shoulder, but her mother shrank from her touch.

"He will come back, Mama, you'll see," Amanda whispered, desperately trying to make herself believe it also. For the first time since Tim left, doubt entered her mind. *What if he couldn't come back? What if something happens to him?* The thought sparked other terrible questions in her mind. Amanda retired to her room and cried into her pillow. Her parents now knew that she was pregnant, but she now also had doubts about Tim's return—not because he didn't want to, but because he couldn't, because returning was not in his power.

Ana sat by her sister and listened to her sobs. She didn't know whether to share their parents' disappointment and anger or to feel sad for Amanda. Part of her wanted to shrink from her in revulsion—Amanda had done that secret act that belonged only to married people. Another part wanted to know how someone as strong and virtuous as her sister could be led into corruption, but she dared not ask for fear of sharing Amanda's sin. Ana could only listen to her sister's misery, unsure how to feel.

Chapter 6

The prospects for Amanda's future were bleak. Once her condition became known about town, she would be the object of many months, maybe even years, of snickered gossip. Although Elias de Gracia, her betrothed, would no longer be obligated to marry her, he was likely to be her loudest accuser, condemning her as the despoiled and pregnant cast-off of one of those vulgar American sailors. Amanda would be whispered about, laughed at, and scorned as a foolish and shameless woman. Only she would know that none of it was true, that Tim truly loved her, that he would return eventually and prove everyone wrong. Even if she spent the rest of her days in her parents' home, with no husband or home of her own, Amanda believed she could withstand the mockery until Tim returned.

Amanda did not quit her job at Castro's Store until the beginning of February. Quitting wasn't what she wanted, but her parents insisted on it. For an unmarried young woman heavy with child to parade herself shamelessly in public was unacceptable. The need to disguise her belly was no longer possible or necessary. She knew when she entered the store that the salesgirls and the customers would either stare at her in shock or smirk at the confirmation of their suspicion. Word of her condition would spread rapidly.

Amanda held her head up proudly as she approached Tan Chai. She expected the old woman to cackle with satisfaction. Instead, the look on her face was one of recognition and sympathy. Tan Chai felt no triumph at having been proved correct about the compulsions of transient servicemen and was saddened by Amanda's loss of innocence. She felt sorry for the foolish girl who had disregarded her warnings and was now beginning to pay the lasting price.

"And now you are pregnant," Tan Chai said once they were in the privacy of her upstairs apartment. Amanda nodded and started to cry. "It's too late for tears, child," Tan Chai said, believing there would be many more tears to follow in the girl's life.

"He is coming back, Tan Chai," Amanda countered. "I know he will."

Tan Chai heaved a heavy sigh and thought, *Why, Lord, do you deny young girls the wisdom they need and give it instead to old women who don't?* She didn't believe the sailor who regularly flirted with Amanda would return. Having had his way with her, he was gone for good. "What are you going to do now? What do your parents want you to do?"

"I must go to Tan Julianna after I leave here. Whatever comes of this, I will take care of my child, with or without my parents' help," Amanda insisted.

"If they won't, I will help you," Tan Chai said.

Amanda's parents had also demanded she confess her disgrace to Tan Julianna and Elias directly. She dreaded having to face them and giving them more reason to look down on her and her family. She organized her thoughts and rehearsed what she needed to say during the carriage ride to Tan Julianna's hacienda in the hills above town. A *muchacha*, a housemaid, met her at the beautifully carved front door and led her to a gazebo near a small fountain on the grounds.

"Tan Julianna instructed me to tell you that she will not see you," the maid said, "but you are to wait here for Don Elias. You are to tell him what you need to say. Then you are to leave here."

The terse dismissal humiliated Amanda. She blushed with shame and seated herself in the gazebo. She and Elias saw each other frequently as small children, placed together by their parents to play as the way to get to know each other. They got along as children, although Elias frequently punched or pinched her and made her cry. As they got older and their interests broadened, they drifted apart: Amanda, to work and help her family, Elias, to enjoy the fruits of his parent's wealth. As such, they had little need or occasion to interact. Amanda waited in the gazebo for nearly half an hour before Elias emerged from the house. She stood up as he approached.

"Buenas dias, Amanda," he greeted. Amanda nodded and curtsied quickly.

"You have something to tell me?" he asked snidely.

"You need not marry me, Elias. Our engagement is nullified."

"And to whom do I owe my deliverance?"

Amanda wanted to spit in his face. It was obvious that he already knew what she had to report. "You may thank the great United States Navy," she said proudly.

She didn't wait for his reaction, or for the return of the carriage back to town. She hurried away from the gazebo and started to walk down the road, her heart soaring with joy. Her only regret was that any benefits her family might have derived from her marriage to Elias were now gone. She reached home and went into exile until after her baby was born—or until

Tim returned and restored her honor. She was the only one who believed it would happen.

Sylvino became cold and aloof toward her. He rarely spoke more than two or three words to her and would not acknowledge her presence. If she entered the parlor, he left it, ashamed even to be near her. Amanda was his *kirida*, his pet, but she betrayed his trust, and it broke his heart.

Amanda was heartbroken also, not only because she disappointed her father, but because she brought shame down upon all in her family. People would vilify her for her scandalous affair with one of those obnoxious American sailors. They would criticize her father as an inept provider of wisdom and discipline, and fault her mother as an incompetent tutor of proper womanhood. And the other children? Well, if the eldest was so easily seduced, the younger ones were probably also unruly. Her family certainly didn't deserve the disparagement; the sin was hers alone. While they would be the recipients of community derision, Tan Julianna and the de Gracias would be the recipients of its sympathy. Amanda was sure that Elias would ride the waves of public indignation as the unfortunate victim of her treachery, but to her surprise, he remained quiet.

As her pregnancy progressed into its final weeks, Amanda grew more uncomfortable and fearful. Ana moved to quilts on the floor so that Amanda could have the bed to herself. Pilar also felt sympathy for Amanda's discomfort and fears. She arranged with Tan Elisa, the *pattera*, the midwife who delivered all her children, to attend to the birth of Amanda's child.

Amanda's labor began early one morning before sunrise. Ana was allowed to stay home from school to help Amanda and their mother. They took turns looking in on Amanda and taking care of Elena and Jamie, who were curious but frightened about what was happening. Sylvino left as usual to go fishing, and to stay out of the way. His anger and disappointment in Amanda had subsided, and upon his return that afternoon he sat with her intermittently, believing his presence would somehow be of some comfort and assurance to her. Amanda's labor continued throughout the day, progressing and intensifying steadily into the evening. By sunset, she was sweaty and pale. When Amanda's bag of waters broke, Ana was sent to fetch Tan Elisa.

Tan Elisa emerged with a worried look after making her examination. Amanda was far from ready to give birth but was already weakened and fatigued. Pilar prepared supper, but only Tan Elisa and the children ate. Tan Elisa encouraged Ana, Pilar, and Sylvino to nourish themselves for the long night ahead, but none had an appetite. Pilar sat at the kitchen table and buried her head in her hands each time Amanda cried out in pain. Sylvino couldn't bear to hear his daughter's agony and left the house to walk along the beach until the ordeal was over. Ana stayed faithfully by her sister's side, holding her hand and mopping her forehead.

"I'm sorry, Mama, I'm so sorry," Amanda said through a veil of sweat and tears when she sensed her mother's presence. "I will tell Papa who the father is as soon as my baby is born."

"I know," Pilar said, stroking Amanda's brow and knowing that no amount of love for a man can lessen the pain of childbirth. Sylvino was at her side or nearby for the birth of all her children. She hated him with each contraction, cried with him when their baby emerged, and loved him even deeper when he smiled proudly into his newborn's face. Pilar couldn't imagine how lonely Amanda must have felt to be without the father of her baby, to be the focus of her frustration and pain, to see him become a father at the moment of birth and witness his pride, and to love him even more.

"Please don't give my baby away," Amanda said weakly.

"Your baby will stay here, with us, where it belongs," her mother said.

On the morning of April 2, 1900, after a long and difficult labor, Amanda gave birth to an eight-pound baby girl. Ana and Pilar were at her side as Tan Elisa tied and clipped the infant's umbilical cord. She wiped the baby clean, wrapped her in a blanket, and placed her beside her mother. Amanda could barely lift her head to look at her child. Her vision was blurred and her head spun, but she managed to see her baby's face.

As Tan Elisa awaited delivery of the afterbirth, Pilar carried the baby into the parlor for Sylvino and the children to see.

"She wants to name her Sylvia, after you," Pilar said as she handed the child to her husband. "I am adding Maria. Here is Sylvia Maria de Leon, our first grandchild."

Wiping her hands with a large towel, Tan Elisa joined them in the parlor. "She's a big baby, bigger than most, and a fine one," she said, "healthy and strong."

Ana stayed behind with Amanda while the rest of the family fawned over baby Sylvia. She tried to get Amanda to tell her the name of the baby's father, but Amanda smiled and, through half-closed eyes, said, "Papa first. I have to tell Papa first. I promised."

"Did he really love you, Amanda?" Ana kept probing. Amanda tried to nod, but managed only to lift her chin slightly. A minute later, her eyes shot wide open in sudden fear. She turned toward Ana and tried to speak. Ana watched in horror as Amanda's face grew ghostly white and blood began to seep through the thin blanket covering her sister's body. The stain rapidly grew larger and larger. In a voice barely audible, Amanda whispered, "Ana, get Mama."

Ana dashed out in a panic. "Mama, Tan Elisa, come quick! Something's wrong. Amanda's bleeding."

Pilar, Tan Elisa, and Ana rushed back to Amanda's bedside. Tan Elisa ripped off the blanket and pulled blood-soaked cotton wadding and towels from between Amanda's legs. Blood was gushing from her womb. The wadding and the thin mattress beneath her also were soaked with blood. Tan Elisa tried desperately to get to the source of the bleeding but could not stanch it. Amanda was quickly bleeding to death.

Pilar bent her face to Amanda's and ordered her not to die. She rubbed her nose against her daughter's temple and cheek and begged her to keep breathing, but Amanda slowly slipped away. Tan Elisa placed her metal listening horn against Amanda's chest and listened to her heart beat its last. She then looked at Pilar and shook her head. Pilar squeezed her eyes shut and rested her forehead against Amanda's, but did not utter a sound. Beside her, Ana was trembling in shock and horror. She began the kind of choked whimpering that would burst into loud, mournful wailing if both Pilar and Tan Elisa hadn't shushed her immediately.

"Not yet, Ana, do not cry yet," Pilar said softly but sternly. "We must let your sister go in peace."

Ana stifled the sobs struggling to break free from her chest. She stared at her sister's body in disbelief. She knelt beside Amanda and stroked her face. It had been warm just minutes earlier and Amanda was there, speaking to her. Now it was cold, lifeless, and Amanda was gone.

"Where are you, Amanda? Where did you go?" Ana whispered into Amanda's ear, unable to accept or understand why her sister's body lay before her, but Amanda was not in it.

Sylvino, still carrying the baby, watched from the doorway and ordered the younger children to stay away. The de Leon family remained quiet and still for more than an hour, to allow Amanda's spirit to pass into the next life without mournful cries to distract and detain her. In whispers, Pilar and Tan Elisa began stripping off Amanda's bloody night dress and washing the blood from her body. Choking back his grief, Sylvino handed the baby to Ana and gathered up the blood-soaked dress, rags, and bedding. He took them outside along with the afterbirth, which was already wrapped and ready to be burned. With tears streaming down his face, Sylvino added kindling and kerosene to the pile and set it ablaze.

When baby Sylvia began to whimper, Tan Elisa took from her midwife's bag a glass bottle and rubber nipple. Into the bottle she poured a bit of sugar and some boiled water from a kettle on the wood fire stove. She handed the bottle to Ana and said, "See if she'll take this. Don't force her. Just rub the nipple gently on her lips."

Meanwhile, Pilar and Tan Elisa wrapped Amanda's body in clean sheets and laid it directly on the rope webbing of the bed. Only then did Pilar wrap her arms around Amanda's body and start weeping. She allowed herself some tears and a few minutes' grief then summoned the rest of her family and began a rosary. Tan Elisa stayed for the rosary then departed for home. Ana continued to tremble in shock. She remained silent during the rosary and stared blankly at nothing.

Over the next nine days, as Amanda's body and casket were prepared, the family recited the rosary for the dead twice a day, at noon and at eight o'clock. Neighbors and relatives from far and near joined them at one or the other rosaries and for Amanda's funeral Mass and burial. Tan Chai, several of her daughters and grandchildren, and Amanda's coworkers attended almost every rosary. Tan Chai, the salesgirls, and Ricardo were especially grieved, shedding tears with the de Leons.

"I promised Amanda that I would help her take care of her baby," Tan Chai told Sylvino and Pilar. "If there is anything you need for the child, you let me know. If there is anything you need at all, I will provide it."

Sylvino pressed Tan Chai for as much information on Amanda's activities on the job, trying desperately to learn more about the man who had impregnated her. She told him about the American sailor who came to the store often, but she didn't know his name or very much about him. Even Ricardo could tell him only that the sailor was a nice man who gave him pennies for candy.

Tan Julianna attended some of the nightly rosaries but left for home immediately afterward. She never stayed to talk with Pilar and Sylvino or any of their neighbors. Tan Julianna, Anselmo, his wife, and Elias attended Amanda's requiem Mass and burial. The de Leons never saw them again afterward.

Chapter 7

Sylvino de Leon was still young enough to father more children but old enough to cry unchecked at losing one. He had now lost four. Losing his firstborn son Rafael and the two sons who followed Amanda was painful, but losing Amanda was excruciating. Amanda was his beautiful, firstborn daughter, the jewel of his making. He had wasted so many days and weeks being angry with her instead of talking, teasing, and laughing with her and her siblings. Now she was gone. He would never see her again and it saddened him more than he could understand. The spark that had once brightened Sylvino's being was snuffed out. He wore his sadness like a heavy cloak that stooped his shoulders. He was only thirty-seven but seemed to age another ten years after Amanda's death.

After the funeral, Pilar and her daughters packed away Amanda's only treasure—the gold earrings Tim had given her. She was wearing them when she died. Amanda had told them proudly how she had saved her money and did extra chores for Tan Chai to purchase them. It wasn't the truth, but it ended any question as to how she came to have them. Pilar planned to give the earrings to Sylvia. As they picked through Amanda's belongings, deciding what to keep and what to burn, Ana found Tim's letter hidden beneath Amanda's undergarments.

"Mama, look," Ana said, holding up the letter, the gold anchor and stars in the dark blue emblem of a navy ship glittered in the upper-left corner. Pilar and the girls took turns examining the envelope and the single page tucked inside. Ana and Esther could not read English yet; Pilar never learned. Like Amanda, they only recognized Amanda's name written on the front of the envelope. "Give it to Papa," Pilar instructed.

Sylvino stared at the letter for a long time. He could speak, read, and write Spanish, but knew nothing of American English. He recognized Amanda's name and individual letters in the text, but could not read it. He was certain that the letter was from Amanda's lover. The writing was in a masculine hand. Sylvino wanted to hate the man who had written to his daughter, taken her innocence, and caused her death, but he had no face, no name; no target for his anger. The only connection he had with that unknown man was a beautiful baby girl named in his honor. Sylvino folded the letter and placed it in the leather satchel, a gift from Anselmo de Gracia when Amanda was betrothed. Sylvino had no use for the satchel except as a safe place to keep important documents. Someday, he thought, he would ask someone to read and translate the letter. Then he would know who to hate.

There was little joy in the de Leon house after Amanda's death; the family grieved over the circumstances. Amanda had left them with a scandal and a mystery: Who was Sylvia's father? What was his name? Where did he come from? Who were his family, his people? Did he truly love their daughter, or was he a scoundrel who took advantage of an innocent young girl? They had no answers, no clue. They knew only that he was an American sailor, and only God knew what sort of person he was.

Sylvino was ashamed to show his face, especially to the de Gracias. The children were pestered and teased at school. Pilar was embarrassed and ashamed too, but could not give in to the grief and apathy weighing down on her. She was exhausted, yet there were meals to prepare, a house to clean, laundry to do, clothing to mend, vegetables to harvest, prayers to be said, and most important, five children and a newborn to care for. Without Amanda to nurse her, baby Sylvia had to be fed from a bottle. Since all of her babies were breastfed, Pilar had no idea how to bottle-feed. Tan Elisa showed Pilar and Ana how to dilute canned, evaporated milk with boiled water and how to properly wash and assemble the glass bottles and rubber nipples. Tan Chai provided as many nipples, bottles, cotton diapers, baby clothing, and canned milk as the de Leons needed, never asking or expecting payment. Preparing bottles and washing diapers soon became a seemingly unending chore. Without Ana, Esther, and Elena to help, Pilar would have collapsed from exhaustion. She didn't realize how reliant she had become on Ana or the burden she was placing on her, a burden that would profoundly affect Ana's future.

Baby Sylvia was the bright spot in their lives; she brought back meaning and purpose beyond the ordinary and every day. At first, she was simply Amanda's sleepy newborn who needed to be fed and cared for, tasks that fell mainly upon Ana. But as Sylvia's personality emerged, she became their beloved new baby sister. In Sylvia, Esther and Elena had a living doll to care for and play with, and Juan and Jaime didn't mind being outnumbered two to one. They were the big brothers, duty-bound to look after and protect their sisters.

Sylvia brought back joy and laughter into their home. Her first crooked little smile washed away some of the hurt, even for Sylvino. Her giggles and happy baby laughter and her cooing and babbling were effective antidotes for grief. By naming her baby after her father, Amanda ensured that baby

Sylvia would be endeared to him as surely as she had been. Sylvino could not reject his namesake, especially as she grew, even though her father was some unknown stranger. When Sylvia started teething and fussed with fever, her grandfather was the only one who could calm and soothe her. When she struggled to her feet and took her first steps, she would toddle only toward Sylvino. Like her mother, Sylvia was Papa's girl.

The entire neighborhood knew of Sylvia's birth. There was no hiding such news in so small and so tightly knit a community. Nearly all of the de Leons' neighbors condemned Amanda's sexual romp with a sailor and her illegitimate pregnancy, but lamented her death in childbirth. Many viewed it as God's punishment, but a few others saw it simply as a tragedy. To Pilar's relief, most sympathized with the de Leon family's heartaches and were understandably curious about the baby—what did this half-Chamorro, half-American baby look like; was she more of one than the other? Pilar refused to expose Sylvia to anyone's view until after she was baptized, which occurred two months after her birth, delayed because the family first had to bury Amanda. Tan Elisa and Tan Chai were the only outsiders Pilar allowed. Not only for her generosity but mainly for her closeness to Amanda, Pilar asked Tan Chai to be Sylvia's godmother. Tan Chai tearfully agreed. "I will most likely be dead and gone when she gets old enough to get married, but I would be most honored," she said.

When Sylvia was six months old, Ana and Esther pierced her earlobes with a sewing needle and thick thread. The process was a grueling one, especially for Sylvia, who struggled and screamed mightily. A few days later, after her earlobes healed and the thread loops were removed, Ana inserted Amanda's treasured gold earrings into Sylvia's earlobes. Without knowing it, Sylvia wore the earrings her father bought for her mother.

No one could mistake that Sylvia was a half-breed, the child of a white person. Her skin was light tan and flawless. Her hair was dark auburn; the redness stood out especially in sunlight. Her nose had a raised bridge and was not bulbous at the tip. She had Amanda's eyes, though not as dark. Sylvia's were a rich brick-brown. As she grew older, Sylvia looked more and more like her mother, but her American father also emerged. The family didn't know his name or what he looked like, but there were unmistakable traits of him in his daughter. Her nose was the clearest evidence. And so were her smooth, creamy complexion, her lighter eye color, and her height. Sylvia eventually towered over Pilar, the girls, and Jaime. She grew to be as tall as Juan and two inches shorter than Sylvino, who stood five feet six inches.

Like her mother, Sylvia had a special bond with her grandfather. Ana, Esther, and Elena were much closer to their mother and were interested and eager students of womanly skills and chores—cooking, keeping house, sewing, and taking care of family. Sylvia learned those lessons also, but she was curious about many more areas. Her interests were broader. She liked tinkering and working with her hands. She was a whiz at solving spatial puzzles and was no stranger to hammers, saws, and nails. She became an excellent carpenter's assistant before her twelfth birthday. Her birthday could be celebrated that year because it fell after Lent and Easter, unlike the year before and other years—the misfortune of being born in April. She enjoyed going fishing with her grandfather, Juan, and Jaime, learning how to cast *talaya*, or throw nets, help set out fish weirs, and repair fishnets and equipment. She learned, along with Juan and Jaime, how to be proper family providers, often to Sylvino's amusement.

Despite the circumstances of her birth, Sylvia was deeply loved and cherished. Amanda's siblings treated her more like a sister than a niece. Ana was the exception; she had witnessed Sylvia's birth, took charge of much of her care, and felt more motherly than sisterly toward her. Sylvia grew into a sweet and loving but shy young woman. The taint of illegitimacy followed her everywhere; she could not escape it. Everyone in the neighborhood knew that she was a child born out of wedlock. When she was five years old, Sylvia began asking about her parents, particularly her father. Her grandparents could tell her much about her mother and why she was absent from their lives, but nothing about her father. Not even his real name. They made up a name—Henry—and avoided all her other questions as long as they could, often telling her that he died in the war.

"What war, Papa?"

"The one that brought the Americans here."

"Oh."

Or that he ran away to sea.

"Why, Papa?"

"Because he wanted to catch whales."

"What for?"

"To get their fat and render it for oil to sell."

"Oh. But you said he died in the war."

"He did. That was after."

"After what?"

"After he went to sea."

"Oh."

Probing for answers was her favorite pastime, especially during long and scary typhoons and lesser storms. It was easy to distract her when she was little, but after she turned seven, the age the Church recognizes as the age of reason, and she received First Holy Communion, they knew they had to tell her the truth, which was that they knew nothing about her father or his relationship with her mother. They knew only that Amanda loved him, that she would not divulge his name until his promised return, and that she died before she could tell them. They knew nothing about her parents' relationship. They didn't know whether her father knew that Amanda had become pregnant, whether he left without knowing or fled to avoid responsibility. It was easy to think the worst of him; an honest, decent man—a genuine lover—would have come in search of Amanda, but no sailor ever came to their home, pleading to see her. They knew only that he left behind a letter, which they could not read and kept hidden away. Sylvino forbade his wife and daughters from saying anything to Sylvia about the letter. He wanted to be the first to know its contents but would not share it with anyone who could read English. Pilar didn't agree with his decision to withhold the letter, but she dared not question her husband.

"I will give it to her when the time is right," Sylvino assured his wife.

For want of a story less painful than the bits she knew, Sylvia romanticized the missing pieces. She had been told since childhood that her mother was a beautiful girl with long dark hair and big brown eyes. Sylvia's own reflection in the mirror was not that of a dark-haired beauty. Although she was only ten years old, Sylvia didn't think she was beautiful and decided she looked more like her father, who probably wasn't a bad-looking sailor. He was at least nice-looking enough to attract her mother. He, of course, could not help but fall in love with her mother. They did the unthinkable "it," and Sylvia was the result. They wanted to marry, but jealous officers, envious of her father's good fortune, sent him away, never to return.

Sylvia knew that her imaginary story was not the truth. If her father had truly loved her mother, she would have known everything about him and she would have secretly shared his identity at least with Ana. But Ana denied any knowledge. The family would have known something about him as well, if nothing else, at least that Amanda had a secret lover. Why would her mother have yielded to a stranger? She told her family that she loved him. She couldn't have loved a stranger. If he loved her, why didn't he ever write her a letter? How could he have left her with nothing to remember him by? Did he know that she became pregnant? The answers seemed obvious: since he wasn't present in her life, he must have deceived her mother, taken advantage of her, and left her. *Oh, well,* Sylvia decided sadly, *maybe someday I'll know the truth.*

Chapter 8

Officially established in August 1899, the navy government of Guam quickly assumed exclusive control of public education. In 1900, the year Sylvia was born, Guam's first navy governor ordered education to be compulsory for children aged eight to fourteen years. He also ordered the introduction of the English language to be used and taught in all schools, as soon as some English-speaking teachers could be imported and new ones trained. The governor also banned religious teaching in the public schools. Ana, Juan, and Esther made the transition from the Spanish-Chamorro-Church-based school system to the American system with some difficulty, as did their contemporaries. From the start, Elena, Jaime, and Sylvia's schooling began in the American system.

Sylvia started religious instruction in escuelan pale' earlier, at age six, to prepare for First Holy Communion, along with a small number of other six-year-olds. They learned under the watchful eyes of their parish priest, who didn't tolerate teasing or tomfoolery. He had limited time to instill important lessons about their faith and the sacredness of the sacrament they were preparing to receive. Life in the public school, which she entered at age eight, was difficult. There were many more children and fewer adults to oversee their behavior, especially on the playground. Sylvia's schoolmates knew that she was an illegitimate orphan and teased her mercilessly about it. Her classmates, in particular, harassed her about being an American half-breed who spoke broken English. The other children mocked her as an *Amerikanan pao asu*, an "American who smells of wood smoke." It was the ridicule heaped on anyone who tried to pass himself or herself off as a sophisticated American, or someone who was ashamed of his ethnicity. Or, in Sylvia's case, someone who wasn't what she was supposed to be.

Despite the taunts, Sylvia made excellent grades in arithmetic but struggled with English. Until she entered school, Sylvia spoke Chamorro, her first and only language. Her English grammar skills were especially poor. Since the Chamorro language does not distinguish genders, Sylvia (and many others) had difficulty with the English language's pronouns: *he*, *she*, *him*, and *her*. Prepositions were challenging also; the Chamorro language has no prepositions as such and has its own way of handling prepositional phrases.

After failing another English grammar test when she was ten, Sylvia found a quiet spot behind one of the school buildings to sit alone and cry. She was afraid to go home. Ana and her grandmother would tell her sternly to study harder, but Jaime's harassment would be relentless. He was thirteen.

Jaime, Ana, Elena, and Sylvia were the only ones still at home. Ana was twenty-two and unmarried. She was so traumatized by Amanda's death that she swore never to marry, never to have children. Having witnessed Amanda's death in childbirth, Ana was genuinely afraid of having children. She knew that getting married was usually the first step in the process. Juan was a year younger than Ana but had no such fears. He was twenty-one, already married, and the father of two. He and his family lived only a few houses away. Esther, who was eighteen, got married earlier that year but had no children yet. Elena was going on sixteen and was working at Castro's Retail Store. Jaime was the closest to Sylvia in age and was her most ardent tormentor throughout their childhood, despite Ana's admonitions.

Most of the time, Jaime's teasing was good-natured and funny but true. At others, it was cutting and mean, and he didn't seem to know the difference, or when to stop, even after bringing Sylvia to tears. His jibes about being half Chamorro and half stupid hurt her deeply. Her American half—the part that should have excelled at English—was as alien, as absent, and as useless to her as her American father, and she resented him for it. What good was it for her to be half American yet not have any of the benefits it was supposed to impart? Failing an English test was bound to bring out Jaime's sharpest cuts. Sylvia lingered behind the school. She was afraid to face Jaime's ridicule. Then, from around a corner, came her classmate, Natividad "Natty" Mendiola.

Natty wasn't merely the smartest girl in class, she was the smartest girl in the whole school. Even the school superintendent, a stern-faced navy officer who didn't seem to like his job, would come to their class to look at Natty's seat work and test scores. He couldn't believe that a native—especially a girl—could equal a white man in intelligence. He was sure Natty was cheating somehow. He eventually drew up a test of his own, with a variety of questions and problems in different subjects—some in even more advanced subject areas—and administered it to Natty himself, with several teachers present to ensure she didn't cheat. Under the watchful eyes of the navy's superintendent of public education, the school principal, and six teachers sitting in a circle around her, Natty nervously took the test. She scored ninety-seven out of a hundred. Only then were the superintendent and his colleagues assured that Natty didn't cheat. She was truly a gifted child, but that was never acknowledged, nor was Natty ever groomed or encouraged beyond the navy's established curriculum for native children. Not long after Natty passed the test, a rumor circulated that the same test was administered to the twelve-year-olds in the school the navy operated separately for its children. None passed the test.

Embarrassed that Natty caught her crying, Sylvia quickly turned to hide her tear-streaked face and walk away. It was one thing to flunk a test; it was another to be caught crying over it by the smartest girl in school, the classmate who not only spoke Chamorro and Spanish but Japanese and English as well. Natty's parents and grandparents spoke Spanish fluently and spoke both Chamorro and Spanish at home regularly. Natty's Auntie Chang, her father's sister, was married to a Japanese. He was a teacher who spoke both Japanese and Chamorro to his wife and children and to Natty; they all acquired Japanese the same way. Natty couldn't explain how she came to understand and speak English. She was no more or less exposed to it than her contemporaries, but simply hearing it seemed to be enough for her perceptive mind.

"Wait," Natty said. "What's the matter, Sylvia?"

Sylvia ignored Natty's question and didn't answer. She didn't think anyone in the world cared about her troubles and was a little suspicious of Natty's interest. Was she also going to make fun of her? Sylvia didn't want to have to explain her embarrassing predicament, but something in Natty's tone of voice stirred her desperate need for a friend, someone with a sympathetic ear. Pressed to answer, Sylvia slowly opened up to Natty.

"I know what you mean," Natty said. "You're half American and don't understand why English is so hard and I'm all Chamorro and don't understand why English is so easy. We have the same problem, only backwards." The bit of humor made Sylvia laugh and feel comfortable. The two soon became inseparable friends.

As their friendship grew, Sylvia discovered that Natty also was a lonely child. The children in their school, both their age and older, were intimidated by her intelligence; the younger ones thought she was strange and avoided her. Their teachers were in awe of her brilliance. Only her cousins and Sylvia loved her in spite of her brains. Natty tutored Sylvia in English, and in time, Sylvia's command of the language and grammar improved significantly. She became truly half American, both in appearance and speaking ability.

Much to her grandfather's worry, Sylvia's ability to read English outpaced everyone else's in the family. He realized he would soon have to give her the letter from her father. After waiting more than a decade to hear what the man had to say, Sylvino feared Sylvia's reaction more than his own. He didn't want her to be hurt and thought about destroying the letter so that she would never know, never possibly be hurt by anything her absent father might say. Torn between his concern for Sylvia and his own curiosity, Sylvino let any decision slide. Sylvia was growing up and would be mature enough to handle whatever the letter contained. In the meantime, he watched proudly as Sylvia grew into a beautiful young woman.

When Sylvia and Natty reached secondary school, Natty fell in love with Atanacio "Tass" Nauta, a boy a year ahead of them. Tass had a crush on Sylvia, who by then was the prettiest girl in school. The situation could have ended a truly wonderful friendship between the smartest girl and the prettiest girl, but Natty could see that Sylvia had no interest in Tass.

"It hurts so much to be in love all by yourself," Natty said one day as they watched Tass playing baseball after school. She was talking about herself, and Sylvia knew it.

"Yes, I'm sure he cries himself to sleep every night," Sylvia said, and they both laughed.

With Natty's help, Sylvia successfully completed the mandatory curriculum for girls, which involved lessons in mathematics and household budgeting, English language, and health and hygiene, as well as training in housekeeping, cooking, and sewing, mainly as job skills and avenues for employment. When she and Natty turned fourteen, Natty urged her not to give up on school, to press on for as long and as far as they could take their education, even though they were no longer required to do so.

Tass Nauta eventually turned his attention elsewhere and Natty decided she was never truly in love with him. In time, she met Alejandro "Andy" Castillo, the boy she would eventually marry. He would take her to the United States and encourage her to go with him to college. Natty Mendiola Castillo eventually earned a doctorate in medicine, her husband a doctorate in law.

Chapter 9

Sylvino de Leon died of heart failure the summer after Sylvia turned fourteen. He had just turned fifty-one. His death was sudden; no one was prepared for it, and no one was more devastated than Sylvia. Sylvino was preparing to go fishing that morning when he suddenly grabbed at his chest and crumpled to the floor. Pilar screamed. Jaime jumped to his father's side and, with Elena and Sylvia's help, carried Sylvino to his bed. His face was gray, his breathing raspy and erratic. Seconds later, he let out a long, drawn-out breath and died. They waited in fear for him to inhale, but his chest did not rise. They watched in horror as the color slowly drained from his face.

While Jamie ran out to inform his brother and sister, Pilar sat at her husband's side, stroking his face and whispering into his ear. Sylvia could not hear what she was saying. She sat on the opposite side of her grandfather's bed, holding his hand and rubbing it against the tears streaming down her cheeks. She knew better than to give voice to her grief and sorrow so that his soul could leave in peace. After Juan and Esther arrived with their spouses and children, and said their good-byes, Pilar started the rosary, the first of many to be said over the following days.

After the rosary, Pilar, Ana, Juan, and his wife went to the undertakers, to arrange for a casket. While Esther and Elena prepared the parlor for their father's rosary and wake, Sylvia stole into her grandparents' closet. She had to hurry because her grandmother would be returning soon and the rest of the family, their relatives, friends, and neighbors would be gathering at the house for the midday rosary. Sylvia retrieved her grandfather's old leather satchel from high on a shelf in the closet. The opportunity to discover its contents was at hand. She had wondered about the satchel's contents throughout her childhood but had been forbidden to touch it. The prohibition made it something of a mystery too tempting to leave alone. Her grandfather had caught her several times trying to get to it and she got spanked, but that never stopped her from trying. She knew that it held the secrets to her birth, her mother's death, and maybe even something about her father. With the bedroom to herself, she could finally open the satchel for some answers. Her grandfather's body still lay in his bed.

"Papa," she whispered gently, "it's time for me to know."

The satchel's two exterior buckles were rusted and sticking to the leather straps they clasped. The cracked and stiffly curled straps were difficult to undo. The hinges at the sides were rusty also. The satchel hadn't been opened in a long time and seemed unwilling to give up its secrets. Sylvia struggled to pry it open. The hinges creaked and finally gave way. The musty smell of dry leather and antiquity wafted into her face. Inside was a sheaf of papers. Some sheets were folded, others were not. The largest unfolded piece was a parchment document, beautifully illustrated with a bride and groom kneeling before a richly robed priest standing in front of an altar. All the printed words were in Spanish. Written by hand in beautiful calligraphy were her grandparents' names: Sylvino de Leon y Santiago and Pilar Mesa y Balthazar. The document was her grandparents' marriage certificate. It listed the name of the church, Nuestra Señora de Los Angeles, and was dated 25 de Mayo 1883. At the bottom was the flowery signature of the priest who had officiated.

Sylvia stared at the date and calculated her grandparents' ages when they married. Her grandfather was twenty. Her grandmother was eighteen. Sylvia wondered what their lives were like during the "Spanish times," which began in 1668 and ended in 1898, when the Americans arrived. Sylvino and Pilar often spoke about the "old days," but Sylvia couldn't relate to their stories. She knew life only under American naval rule.

Sylvia carefully replaced the marriage certificate and withdrew several smaller documents which looked official and were yellowed with age. They didn't have pretty illustrations. Their only decorations were frayed bits of red satin ribbon affixed to the paper with sealing wax. The hard red wax had deepened in color and bore the impression of the Spanish government seal. The documents were worded entirely in Spanish. Sylvia could read only the names and dates and realized they were the birth records of her grandparents and her aunts and uncles, including her mother.

Similar to the marriage certificate in style, illustration, and fine quality paper but smaller were seven baptismal certificates, including Raphael's, six First Holy Communion certificates, and six Confirmation certificates. The certificates for her own religious milestones were not as fancy and were printed in English. Sylvia picked those of her mother and studied them carefully. Holding them in her hands was the closest she felt to Amanda.

There were two more documents in the pile. They were on plain white paper, written in English, and bore the unadorned stamp of the U.S. Navy government. One was Amanda's death certificate, and the other Sylvia's birth certificate. The date listed on both was April 2, 1900. Sylvia pored over both documents, reading every slightly blurred, typewritten line twice. According to the certificate, Amanda's cause of death was "uncontrollable postpartum exsanguination due to rupture of the uterine artery." Sylvia didn't understand the words but knew from Ana and her grandmother that her mother had bled to death. Ana's description was particularly frightening. The document recorded Amanda's age at "seventeen years, three months at time of death." A description of her height ("58 in."), weight ("97 lb.") and hair color ("dk. brn.") was included. Under "Remarks" was written, "The decedent expired at place of residence in the presence of both parents and a government-certified midwife in attendance. Death occurred at approximately 0732 hours." The words were a cold, unfeeling way to learn how and when her mother died.

Sylvia then turned to her birth certificate. She had never seen it before. She weighed eight pounds, two ounces at birth and measured twenty-one inches long. She entered the world at "approximately 0708," twenty-four minutes before her mother left it. The name "Maria Amanda Mesa de Leon" was listed as "mother," but the line for "father" listed only the word, "Unknown." Sylvia's heart sank; she hoped she would at last learn her father's name. She stared at the word for several minutes, hoping it would somehow shed some light.

As she opened the satchel to replace the documents, Sylvia spotted a hidden slot that was revealed when she widened the satchel's opening. She reached into the slot and felt a folded envelope tucked deep down inside. She pulled it out. Scrawled on the front of the envelope was the name "Amanda," written in well-practiced penmanship, beautifully executed. A chill swept through Sylvia's body; she knew instinctively that the letter was from her father. Inside was a single sheet of paper. Trembling, Sylvia open the page and read:

1 July 1899

My Darling,

My heart aches to write this. The weeks with you have been the happiest of my life. I wish to God that I could stay with you forever, but I am needed at home and must leave.

My heart is yours, Amanda, as are these earrings. I know how much you liked them. Wear them as if they were the wedding rings I wish for us. I love you, Amanda. I will always love you. Pray as I will that I can return to you soon.

Forever yours,
T.

Tears filled Sylvia's eyes, and her heart soared with a joy she could barely contain.

"He loved her, Papa! My father loved your daughter," she cried and caressed her grandfather's lifeless face. "I was made with love, Papa. I'm not a stupid mistake."

Sylvia stared at her father's initial. His name began with a *T.* But what did it mean? What did it stand for? Was it for his first name? Thomas? Teddy? Timothy? His last name? Which? Only he and her mother knew. Sylvia ran her fingers across the page, feeling where her parents' hands might have touched. She read the letter again and again until she suddenly realized that her mother would not have known how to read English. Sylvia knew that her grandparents also couldn't read English. The joy she was feeling melted into sadness. Had they not known of his love? Had they been denied this knowledge, this important information? Had something happened to her father? What could have prevented his return, even after fourteen years? Sylvia couldn't speculate further. She heard rustling behind her and turned to see Ana and her grandmother at the bedroom door. She didn't know how long they had been standing there, watching and listening.

"You were never a mistake, my daughter. God doesn't make mistakes," Pilar said, edging forward. Esther and Elena followed her into the bedroom.

"Let me read it, Sylvia. Please," Ana implored. "Papa kept it secret. He never let anyone see it."

"He was afraid it would hurt you," Pilar added. "Read it, Ana, I want to hear it."

Pilar didn't understand English very well, but the tone in Ana's voice and the look on her face as she read the letter out loud conveyed as much meaning and feeling as the foreign words intended. When Ana finished, tears were streaming from her eyes. She remembered how she had tried to get Amanda to reveal her lover's name and how Amanda smiled but refused. Ana recalled the sudden terrified look on her sister's face as death took her away, and the feeling of horror and helplessness returned with stinging sharpness.

Death and grief were upon them again. Juan poked his head into the bedroom. "Mama," he whispered, "the men are here with the casket."

Sylvia, Ana, and Esther helped Pilar prepare Sylvino's body and watched sadly as the undertaker's men carried and arranged him in his coffin. Elena was too grieved to help, but she placed her father's rosary and crucifix in his folded hands. The men then carried the casket into the parlor, placing it before the little shrine that Esther and Elena had set up. It was where people were already gathering to recite the rosary. Sylvino's wake would last for three days before he was carried to church and then to the cemetery.

Life in the de Leon household changed significantly after Sylvino's death. Their number had dwindled from eight to five. Only Sylvino, Juan, and Esther were no longer resident, but the house seemed emptier. Sylvino had commanded such a presence that his absence left a large void in their home. Sylvia missed her grandfather dearly and mourned him for more than a year. She felt a loneliness that seemed no one could fill. Pilar urged her to channel her grief into prayer instead of depression, but she didn't take her own advice. Pilar didn't pray as often as she used to, was less patient, and suffered bouts of depression, each lasting longer than the previous one. Ana too grew more reclusive. The atmosphere at home became unpredictable and was sometimes stifling and uncomfortable. Jaime couldn't wait to get out on his own. He often fled to Juan's house when Pilar's behavior became erratic and worrisome. Elena, the youngest of the de Leon daughters, was the most patient and unaffected by the tension and strain that seemed to grow as the days passed.

It had become a tradition somewhat for the de Leon girls to work at Castro's Retail Store. After Amanda's death, Tan Chai assured Sylvino and Pilar that she would employ their other daughters, if they wanted. Ana was the only one who never worked, never got married, and rarely left the house, not even to go to church. Esther worked at Castro's until she got married. Elena started working there when she turned fifteen, long before her father's death. After he passed, working at the store was where she could escape the strangeness growing at home.

Chapter 10

In January 1916, shortly after Elena turned twenty, three German sailors came into Castro's Retail Store to buy supplies. They were from the warship that had been marooned in Guam since 1914, when they steamed into Apra Harbor in violation of U.S. neutrality. The Germans had sought to replenish their coal supply, but the U.S. Navy refused to accommodate them.

Despite its isolation in the western Pacific, American-held Guam was not isolated from the war raging in Europe. Much to the U.S. Navy's discomfort, German ships regularly plied the oceans around Guam. Germany had purchased the remaining Mariana Islands to the north, the Palau Islands to the south, and the Eastern and Western Caroline Islands from Spain after the Spanish-American War. In 1914, when Japan entered the war against Germany, Japanese ships began to prowl the same waters for its enemy. The possibility for hostilities to affect Guam was not unreasonable. Without fuel, and their enemy waiting to pounce outside the harbor, the German ship couldn't leave Guam, despite the navy's order to do so. A stalemate ensued for the next two years. Without the means, the funds, or the authority to imprison the Germans, the Americans allowed them to roam the island at will, fending for themselves.

The German sailors were down to their last coins when they entered Castro's Store. Mrs. Aurelia "Tan Layla" Santiago, Tan Chai's sixty-year-old daughter, took over to run the store after her mother's death four years earlier. Tan Layla felt sorry for the sailors—they were unwelcome foreigners who were cut off from their country and unable to leave Guam. The navy bank wouldn't lend them any money, and their German marks were worth almost nothing. Tan Layla was among several local merchants who accepted marks at a better rate, more as a humanitarian gesture than a business decision. Although they didn't have enough money, the sailors sought to buy five-pound sacks of coffee and sugar, some tobacco, and cigarette papers, which they brought to Elena's counter. Tan Layla signaled her to accept whatever they could pay. One of the sailors, who was much younger than his bearded companions, smiled at Elena, but she didn't acknowledge him.

She had seen him come into the store once or twice before, usually with others of his countrymen.

"Buenas dias, señorita," he offered awkwardly, smiling at Elena as one of the petty officers handed him the sack of sugar. Elena nodded slightly but said nothing. Another man who seemed to be senior to the others handed Elena the money. She looked at the strange coins then at Tan Layla, who nodded approval. "Go ahead and take it, 'Lena. It's all they have," she instructed in Chamorro.

"*Danke schoen,*" the senior man said and bowed curtly to Tan Layla.

"What did he say?" Elena whispered to Tan Layla in alarm.

"I think he said 'thank you.'"

To Elena's surprise, the young German came back to the store by himself later that day. He again said "Buenas dias" to her. He said it as if it cost him every bit of courage and confidence he could muster. Something about his bright, shy smile appealed to her and she smiled back. Elena was a pretty but quiet girl with a reserved personality. She was content to adhere to her parents' instructions and advice concerning men. Although she was too young at the time to understand what happened to Amanda, Elena grew up hearing the story again and again, and, along with her sisters and Sylvia, had the lesson pounded into their heads. Ana took the lesson too literally and refused to get married. Esther married the man her parents chose for her. After Sylvino died, Pilar was in no hurry to give up Elena and the income she provided. Elena was in no hurry either.

"*Mein name ist* Hans," the sailor said shyly, pausing after each word, hoping she would recognize his meaning. Hans Deiter was from Hamburg and was twenty years old. He was new in the navy and on his first assignment. His German words were close enough to English for Elena to interpret and understand. "And you?"

Hoping to discourage him, she blurted out her entire name. The smile on the German's face didn't change.

"Maria Elena Concepcion Mesa de Leon," he repeated without hesitating or stumbling. Elena was taken aback; she didn't expect him to remember all her names correctly and in order. Impressed, she smiled against her will and said, "Just Elena. Mine is Elena." She was intrigued by what seemed to be a word game."

Despite the language barrier, or perhaps because of it, Hans and Elena spent several afternoons trading words, gesturing and groping for those each could comprehend, laughing and learning without realizing it. Hans, of course, spoke German but knew a little English and some words in Spanish. Elena spoke Chamorro and had a fair command of Spanish and English. What was a language barrier turned into a communications bridge to friendship and then to deepening affection. Within weeks of their meeting, Hans and Elena were connecting effectively, not only with their shared words but also with their eyes, their smiles, and the touch of their hands.

In his company, Elena blossomed. Although she was never an untidy or unkempt person, she started taking greater care in her appearance, as if finally discovering her femininity. She saw herself in Hans's eyes and realized that she was beautiful. She wasn't just the youngest sister of the legendary Amanda or the virginal Ana. She wasn't the married and matronly Esther or Sylvia, everyone's sweetheart. She was Elena, the object of Hans's attention and affection, and she basked in his admiration. She smiled more easily, laughed a little louder, spoke up more often, and glowed with happiness.

Hans was unlike the American navy men, who had no trouble flirting with any of the salesgirls or customers, teasing them to elicit a giggle or a laugh. They even flirted with old married women, including Tan Layla. Everyone knew such flirtations were mostly in jest and took them to be part of American boldness and friendliness. Hans was white-skinned also, but his manner and behavior, especially toward Elena, was different. He wasn't shy and retiring, but neither was he outgoing and loud. Hans was always polite and gentlemanly. He was more regimented and levelheaded. Elena wasn't sure whether it was due to his ethnicity and culture or just his upbringing. However it came to be, Elena admired him for it. He was from a different culture, but it was similar in many ways to hers.

Unlike Amanda's relationship with her sailor, Elena didn't want to hide her relationship with Hans. It was not immoral in any way, and she saw no need to keep his identity a secret. They never engaged in any shameful or sinful behavior and had nothing to be ashamed of. She conversed openly with him in the store and was sometimes seen sharing a meal with him in restaurants. Many people saw them strolling together in the plaza, in full view of whoever cared to observe. Her public display made everyone think Pilar knew of their companionship. Even Hans assumed Elena's mother sanctioned his attentions.

Like Elena's family, Hans's family was devoutly Roman Catholic. He attended parochial schools in Hamburg and was reared under a strict code of proper behavior. Despite their distance from home and the difficulty of their circumstances, Hans and many of his shipmates attended Mass every Sunday in the nearby villages of Sumay or Piti. Traveling to Agaña, to attend Mass at the cathedral, was more difficult, but Hans made the effort. He would seek out Elena and her family and always sat in the pew behind them, politely asking for the space if necessary. Smiling, Elena would know he was behind her and she would always reach her hand back and wriggle a greeting with her fingers.

Although it still wasn't proper for young people to arrange their own matches, either in his culture or hers, times were changing and young people like Elena and Hans were feeling it. At twenty, both felt old enough to make their own choices and decisions. Elena wanted to introduce Hans to her mother and the rest of her family, but waited until he asked to be presented. When he was certain about his feelings for Elena, Hans decided to surprise her and present himself for her mother's approval. He wanted to continue his courtship properly, with an eye toward marriage.

After Mass on Easter Sunday, Hans followed discreetly behind Elena, her mother, brother, and younger sister (he assumed Sylvia was a sister) and waited until they entered their home before mounting the steps and knocking at their door. Elena answered and her face lit up to see him. She had been afraid Hans wouldn't want to meet her family. Elena excitedly took his hand and brought him before her mother, but Pilar's reaction was not what Hans and Elena anticipated. Pilar blanched when she saw the slender fair-haired man. Hans bowed deeply but before he could say a word, Pilar screamed at him to get out. Fearing she would lose another daughter to an untrustworthy sailor—one who wasn't even American, Pilar angrily threatened to have him arrested. Shocked, Elena cried and pleaded with her mother to stop screaming, to hear them out, but Pilar was beyond reason. Elena threw herself in front of Hans, trying to shield him from her mother as he tried to back his way out the door. The commotion drew the attention of a passing marine policeman, a big, burly man who was greatly feared in the neighborhood.

"What the hell is going on here?" the policeman demanded angrily. Not waiting for an answer or an explanation, the policeman mounted the steps, grabbed Hans by the collar, and threw him out into the street.

"I'll teach you to bother these ladies," he growled as he pushed Hans to the ground. Elena wailed in anguish, trying to hold on to Hans while the heavyset policeman tossed him about with ease, and knocking Elena to the ground as well. Hans tried desperately in broken English to explain himself, but the policeman refused to listen. He was among the American military men who resented the presence of the Germans on the island and were quick to find fault with them.

Pilar's angry shrieks, Elena's frantic cries, and the policeman's shouted obscenities drew shocked neighbors to their doors and windows. They watched in horror, not knowing who was at fault or what caused such outrage. Panting heavily from her exertion, Pilar watched from her doorstep as the policeman dragged Hans off to jail for disturbing the peace. She was satisfied that she had rid herself and Elena of the foreigner. Reeling from the terrible emotional upset and angered by what her mother and the policeman had done to Hans, Elena glared at her mother, pushed past her roughly, and stormed into the bedroom she shared with Ana and Sylvia. Without a word, she tucked her coin purse into her pocket, emptied a pillowcase, and stuffed it with her clothes.

"What are you doing?" Pilar demanded. Elena didn't answer. She pushed past her mother and hurried out the door. "Where are you going? Elena! Come back here!"

When Elena did not return home by nightfall, Pilar sent Jaime to fetch her, but he couldn't find her. He searched well into the night without success. Elena, meanwhile, sought refuge at Castro's. She had the keys and was supposed to open the store Monday morning. Since Tan Chai's apartment was left vacant since her death, Elena hid there until morning. She let herself out at sunrise and waited outside the jail for Hans's release. She knew the policeman's charge was a trumped-up way to assault one of the Germans. Hans hadn't broken any law.

Hans was battered and bruised when he was released. The marines at the jailhouse badgered and harassed him all night, punching and slapping him for their amusement. Elena shrank in horror and started to cry when she saw his face. His lip was split and bloodied, his eye blackened, and his clothing was torn.

"I am sorry, Elena. I meant no harm. I will leave you now," he said sadly. His intentions for showing up unannounced on her doorstep were honorable and heartfelt. He never meant to embarrass Elena or ignite such incomprehensible fury in her mother. He didn't think his effort would result in so painful and unwarranted a thrashing. His heart soared to find her awaiting his release, but he was resigned to exit her life and spare her any more hurt.

"Hans, I'm going with you. I ran away. I'm not going back," she said tearfully.

"Then I will run away too," he said and tried to smile despite his cut lip.

The decision to run away together, to face whatever was to be their fate, was borne out of a sense of betrayal. It seemed that all the years of behaving properly, of being obedient and dutiful, of being good children and good adults, were meaningless and empty. They wanted only to remain honest, proper, and good, to be kindly and to receive kindness. Instead, they were forced to become fugitives, to flee like criminals simply because they loved each other. They had been open and honest about their relationship. They did nothing sinful or wrong. They had never even kissed.

Elena led Hans back to Castro's. The store wouldn't be opening for another two hours, so they had time to prepare for their getaway. While Hans washed himself upstairs, Elena collected some new clothing for him. She was owed a week's pay and tried to take only what would have amounted to its equivalent. She added the new clothes to hers in the pillowcase. They left the store before eight and made their way to the carriage station. With twenty cents from her coin purse, double the regular cost for passage, Elena paid for seats on a carriage to Piti.

"If anyone asks, you never saw us," Elena said sternly to the carriage driver.

"What happened to him? Are you two in trouble?" the driver demanded as he stared at Hans's bruised and swollen face.

"He's my friend. The policeman got him," Elena answered.

The driver was not surprised. Everyone in town knew of the policeman's brutality, except the people who could stop him. Or if they knew, they did nothing. "What did he do to get beat up?"

"Nothing. He's from the German ship. He just came to visit me," Elena said. "I want to help him get back to his ship."

"Then hurry up and get in," the driver said.

"That policeman gets off soon and will be heading back to Sumay also. He's going to be mad as heck to find this carriage gone before he gets here. He'll just have to take the next one," the driver added with a wicked smirk.

Along the way, Elena wanted to talk about their next move, but Hans was too sore and exhausted to think clearly. He leaned against Elena and fell asleep. She cradled him in her arms and gently stroked his bruised face. They reached Piti at midmorning. Elena used the last of her money to buy some sweet flour *titiyas*[10], grilled strips of dried beef, and some cheese. Neither of them had eaten since the day before and were famished. As they sat on the dock and ate their meal, Hans spotted a Yapese family, a fisherman, his wife, and twin sons who looked about twelve years old, loading supplies onto their large, oceangoing outrigger canoe. Since Yap, the tiny island between Guam and Palau, was under German rule, Hans hoped someone in the family understood German. He approached them and asked. Both boys answered affirmatively. Hans spoke to the boys but looked at their parents. He apologized for his battered appearance, explained that he had gotten into a fight in a bar, and asked if he and Elena could sail with them. The man and his wife looked back and forth between Hans and their sons as

[10] "Tee-tee-jas," the Chamorro pronunciation of "tortillas." Titiyas, made either of corn or white flour, are much larger and thicker than the Mexican original.

their exchange took place. One of the boys then spoke to their father, who looked at Hans, smiled, and gestured to him to come aboard.

"Come, Elena. They will take us with them," Hans called out. He took the bulging pillowcase from her and helped her climb into the canoe. He put his arm around her and smiled. "We will be fine," he whispered to her in German.

Hans and Elena remained in Yap for six months, doing what they could to earn their keep. Elena sold the gold cross earrings that Amanda had given her for food and lodging and still had enough to pay for passage to Babeldaob, the largest of the Palau Islands. They sailed to Palau in November 1916 in hopes of settling in the village of Koror. There they learned that Hans had been declared a deserter, and a warrant for his arrest was still in effect. To hide his identity, Hans began using his middle name, Peter, and Elena's surname. They lived in hiding for several months, living off Palauan sympathy and generosity. When Elena became pregnant, they got married as Peter and Maria Leon. They were married by a Spanish Capuchin in January 1917 and waited until after the birth of their son before fleeing again.

Before he could be discovered and arrested, Hans fled with Elena and their baby to Australia, to a small German community near Darwin. Hans hoped he could return to Germany someday, to introduce his wife and son to his parents and siblings. He longed to go home to Hamburg and grew more deeply saddened as the years passed and the journey remained impossible. Elena could see the sadness in his countenance when he was homesick, as well as the glow in his being whenever he was speaking in his native tongue to one of his countrymen about their homeland. Elena, too, got homesick, especially for her mother and brothers and sisters. Hans tried to convince her into returning to Guam and facing whatever their punishment was to be, but she refused. If he could never see his family and his homeland again, she would suffer the same fate.

Hans Deiter's shipmates searched for him and eventually gave up, unsure whether he had deserted or was the victim of some nefarious deed. They heard a rumor that the police had detained a young German sailor on Sunday but released him the next morning. No one had heard or seen him since. Shortly after ending their search, the Germans learned that the U.S. had entered the war. They were no longer unwelcome guests of the navy; now they were enemies. The navy governor ordered the German captain to surrender his men and his ship and be taken prisoner. The captain surrendered all but a handful of his men, but refused to surrender his ship. Instead, he ordered it scuttled in the harbor. The captain and the men who scuttled it with explosives went down with the ship. The rest of the sailors were confined in hastily built shacks for several months before being shipped to prison camps in the U.S. later in 1917.

Chapter 11

The Spanish influenza arrived on Guam in 1918, not long after the German prisoners left. Dozens of people were getting sick and many were dying. As the scourge spread, the undertakers and coffin makers were overwhelmed by the numbers of the dead. At the height of the epidemic, it was no longer possible to provide individual caskets and funeral services; the dead were piling up too quickly. The priests in every village were conducting funeral Masses daily, often with three or more coffins before the sanctuary. Pilar de Leon was among the first to contract the flu and die from it. She was fifty years old. Ana and Juan were convinced that her death had as much to do with Elena's defiance and disappearance as with the influenza. Pilar had waited for months for Elena to come home, fully expecting her youngest daughter to beg for forgiveness, but as the months passed with no sign of Elena, Pilar's spirits sank and her health deteriorated. She had neither the will nor the strength to fight the flu. Juan's youngest daughter, who was only a year old, died also. She was placed beside her grandmother in the same casket. Jaime and Sylvia also came down with the flu but survived. Esther and her husband were spared.

When Sylvia recovered, Natty persuaded her to try for jobs in the navy government's secretarial pool. The flu epidemic had left many jobs wanting, even in the government.

The secretarial pool and other administrative offices of the navy government filled the first floor of the Governor's Palace. The second floor housed the governor and his family. The palace and the adjacent Dulce Nombre de Maria Cathedral were the largest and most impressive buildings in Agaña. The palace was the centerpiece of the navy government compound, which was surrounded by a pillared concrete wall that enclosed several smaller buildings. Since taking over, the navy continually upgraded and modernized the old Spanish infrastructure and added new buildings as needed. Stables became garages, oil lamps were replaced by electricity, and indoor plumbing and sewer lines were added. The town of Agaña was modernized in the process as well.

Landing a government job was a real coup for those able to qualify and be selected. Working in the compound was prestigious, and government pay was higher than the average.

"Come on, Sibby, it'll be fun and the pay is great," Natty urged. "Fifty cents an hour! Can you imagine that?"

Sylvia was reluctant. She had had no training in any of the skills needed, especially in secretarial work. Natty had no actual hands-on training either, but she bought and borrowed several books on the subject and was confident she could do the work.

"Don't worry, I'll teach you what I know and we'll learn together," Natty said, refusing to accept Sylvia's excuses. Sylvia agreed to try but hoped she wouldn't qualify or be selected. Working in the compound meant close and daily exposure to more sailors than her mother Amanda or Elena had ever been. As they grew up, Sylvia and her mother's sisters were cautioned regularly against falling for the empty promises of philandering sailors. The message became so ingrained that Sylvia actually thought all sailors were wicked and were to be avoided and feared. The prospect of being so near them on a daily basis worried her, but Natty convinced her that she had nothing to fear.

"Don't be silly, Sibby," Natty chided. "They're not ogres. They're just boys who grew up. They're no different from the boys we grew up with. If they flirt with you, just ignore them or tell them you're not interested."

Natty qualified as a clerk-typist and was selected immediately. She later trained as a stenographer. Sylvia also was selected but initially could only qualify as a file clerk. With their supervisor's permission, she and Natty spent an hour in the office after work every day so that Natty could teach Sylvia how to type, where to position her fingers on the keys, and how to rely on her brain, not her eyes, to keep her fingers positioned correctly. She also trained her on how to execute the various format standards the navy government required. Sylvia excelled at typing. She was even better at mastering the mechanics of the pool's Underwood and Royal typewriters—changing ribbons, setting margins, leveling papers and envelopes, and calculating centers and column widths. Within months, Sylvia was promoted to clerk-typist and was one of the pool's fastest and most accurate typists. She could even troubleshoot typewriter malfunctions and repair minor breakdowns.

To her relief, most of the sailors Sylvia met were diligent about their duties and didn't seem like philanderers. She concluded that men didn't have to be sailors to be rogues. Despite what her grandmother had preached, married men were more likely to be bothersome. Her grandmother had said that she and her mother's sisters should keep themselves pure and untainted until they were married to men who truly loved them. Such a man, she had told them, would give up anything for the woman he loved, even his life if needed. Sylvia no longer believed it. All the evidence available to her spoke otherwise.

Sylvia was among several young female workers who had to fend off the unwanted attention, crude remarks, and blatant advances of some of the married men at the office. She knew of coworkers whose husbands got drunk and beat them. Some didn't even need to be drunk, just angry. She worked with women whose husbands treated their dogs and livestock more lovingly than their wives. She would pass people's homes and hear husbands and wives screaming angrily at each other as their children sat frightened and crying on their front step. Given such evidence, Sylvia believed that no man could love so fully, so unselfishly. Marriage, Sylvia decided, was not for her. Then she met Tino.

Constantino "Tino" Flores Camacho was well-known among the girls in the secretarial pool as a good catch. He was a well-paid bachelor without a steady girlfriend. He was college-educated, articulate, and able to support a family comfortably. He had average looks—not handsome but not ugly either. He had a pleasant, friendly face with sparkling dark brown eyes and a bright, engaging smile. His skin was a rich brown and was evenly shaded from head to toe. His hair was wavy and almost black. He was taller than average; he stood five feet nine and was muscular. He had all the attributes of a fine husband, including being heir to a fine house and large property in Sumay.

Tino's parents, Maria Flores and Alberto Camacho, had owned and operated a small bakery in Sumay, the village nestled on the southern shore of Apra Harbor. They made breads and pastries in traditional beehive stone ovens. Initially, they made and sold bread to their neighbors, those who didn't make their own. Later, as the American presence on the island increased, their largest regular bread customer was the mess hall at the U.S. Marine Barracks, which was located on a ridge overlooking the village and the harbor. In time, the Camachos became successful enough to build one of the largest and nicest homes in Sumay, and to afford to send Tino to college. The Camachos employed a childless, middle-aged couple, Bitta and Carlos Taiañao. Bitta kept house and cooked the family meals, and Carlos delivered bread orders in a small, horse-drawn carriage. He also took care of the horse and maintained the ovens and firewood supply. Bitta and Carlos lived in a small cottage near the Camachos' compound, which enclosed their home, the bakery, a stable and storehouse, and a vegetable garden.

Tino was born in 1896, two years before the war and the start of navy rule. He was the only one of his parents' seven children to survive to adulthood. He was also the youngest. His parents grew up under Spanish rule and their parents, the Flores and Camacho families, were among the local elite. Tino's parents were married in the waning days of Spanish rule, when social status could not shield against the poverty, disease, and the governmental inertia and neglect that had become commonplace. The newly wedded Camachos had expected to live their lives as their parents and grandparents had, but it was not to be. Their world would be rocked by tragic loss and significant change.

Maria's first two pregnancies ended in miscarriages. Her next two babies were stillborn. Her fifth and sixth children, a boy and a girl, were born healthy. The boy, Antonio, lived until his fifteenth year but drowned when he ventured too close to the reef and was caught in strong currents. His body was never recovered. Maria didn't think her grief would ever end. Then life dealt one more blow. Her only daughter, Josefina, then only three years old, and baby Tino contracted influenza during one of several epidemics that swept through the population over the centuries since the arrival of the Spanish. The influenza outbreak in 1897 killed dozens. Tino was among the children who survived. The arrival of the American navy the following year marked the start of tremendous social, cultural, political, and economic change.

Although Tino was his parents' only child, he was not spoiled. His mother was protective but not oppressive. As soon as he was able, he was put to work helping his parents in the bakery or making deliveries with Carlos. By age twelve, Tino could make several kinds of bread and pastries and could handle the horse and carriage on his own. Carlos passed away when Tino was fifteen. He then took over as the delivery driver every morning before heading to school. He attended the newly established American schools and learned English, farming, and animal husbandry. He was an excellent student and earned good grades, especially in mathematics. In anticipation of furthering his education, Alberto and Maria began saving a portion of their bakery profits to send Tino to college. After graduating from school, Tino applied to and was accepted by the prestigious University of Santo Tomas in the Philippines. He left Guam in 1913, at age seventeen, to study civil engineering and public administration.

Except for the language barrier, which didn't last long because he acquired enough Tagalog to get by, Tino blended comfortably into the Filipino countryside. He also attracted several female admirers. He welcomed their attentions, but none of them could dissuade him from his studies. He was a serious student who appreciated his parents' sacrifice.

Halfway through his studies, which included preparatory areas that the navy's education curriculum did not include, Tino received word that his father had passed away. He wanted to quit school and return to Guam to bury his father, take care of his mother, and run the bakery, but his mother insisted he stay, finish school, and not waste the opportunity his father worked hard to provide. Tino was twenty-one when he returned with an engineering degree in late 1917.

Since Tino's degree wasn't earned at an American institution, the navy government gave it little credibility, but quickly hired him as a technical clerk in its Public Works Department. The pay for a young man was exceptional. He was assigned to the civil engineering division, to shuffle and file blueprints and project specification documents. The Public Works offices were scattered in warehouses and government yards around the island while the engineering division was headquartered in the Governor's Palace in Agaña. Within a year on the job, Tino impressed his navy bosses with his engineering knowledge and competence. The only discouraging aspect of his job was that navy engineers, like the navy governor, rarely stayed on Guam for more than two years. Constantly getting to know new people, learning to work with them, and hoping to finish ongoing projects without delaying changes, brought about by bad weather, failed supply arrival, or simply egotistical reasons, made for an erratic work environment.

Tino knew almost everyone in all the divisions housed in the Governor's Palace. The largest, the secretarial pool, was located down the hall from the engineering division. About a dozen young women worked there as typists and clerks. Some were trained in shorthand and were among the highest paid. One day, as he passed through the pool, with all the clickety-clickety sounds of typists at work, he noticed a new girl, a pretty one. She was about eighteen years old and had the prettiest eyes Tino had ever seen. She had nicely molded features and was light-skinned. Her hair was a dark auburn; its red highlights glinted in the sunlight. She was taller than the other girls. Her name was Sylvia de Leon. Tino mistook her for the daughter of a mixed marriage. There were several among American civilians and local women by then. Although most states had laws prohibiting interracial marriage, the law on Guam was what the navy governor decreed; some upheld the prohibition, others ignored it.

Until he laid eyes on Sylvia, Tino had no interest in a serious relationship. He had several female friends, but none who he considered a love interest. Marriage, like death, was a vague future event. Sylvia made him think beyond casual friendship. The more he saw of her, the more attracted he became, but each time he tried to approach her, she turned away and peered down into the innards of her typewriter or pretended to be busy.

He wasn't sure if she was shy or found him unattractive and was trying to discourage him. He was, after all, four years older than she was. Most men his age were already settled and married with children. Unwilling to give up, he placed a flower on Sylvia's desk and introduced himself.

"I know who you are," Sylvia said coolly and walked away, leaving him standing alone and confused. He didn't think he would win her over instantly, but he didn't expect her to cut him off so abruptly. Not one to give up, he tried again and again to make friends, at least. Sylvia's coworkers noticed Tino's growing interest and teased her about it. At the same time they egged her to accept his attention before someone else stole him away. Even Natty encouraged her, but Sylvia continued to avoid him.

"I'd like to get to know you, if you'll let me," Tino said.

"I'm sure you will without my help," she said and walked away from him again. Sylvia was sure that Tino would hear the office gossip about her background, and once he knew, he was likely to walk away and leave her alone. But Tino didn't walk away. He persisted. Challenged by her aloofness, Tino was determined to win her over. He would pick a flower—whatever was in bloom from a neighbor's yard—on his way to the palace and leave it on her desk every morning.

Tino was indeed bothered to learn that Sylvia was the bastard daughter of an unknown, long-gone navy sailor and a teenaged mother who died in childbirth. He did hear the gossip about her from her coworkers, not from Sylvia herself. That was understandable; who would want to admit such parentage? Sylvia's pedigree was dubious; what other mysteries might be lurking in her background? Unbeknownst to Sylvia, Natty approached him and vouched for Sylvia's good character and worthiness of his affection. But Tino didn't need an endorsement. He was deeply smitten and wanted only to be with Sylvia. He had never felt that way about anyone else. Tino was falling in love.

Chapter 12

Sylvia was hesitant about entertaining his advances at first, fearful that he would eventually use her illegitimacy and the scandals in her family as weapons to insult and hurt her if they ever argued. But Tino was sweet and kind and always respectful. Something about his persistence, his earnestness, and his inner strength appealed to her vulnerability, the same way Natty did. She liked him well enough to give him a chance and occasionally accommodated his attentions over the course of several months. She didn't sense any questionable facets in his character and began to grow fond of him. Her fondness soon deepened.

As they shared lunch on a park bench in the shade of a flame tree in the plaza one afternoon, Sylvia decided the time had come to reveal her past to Tino and to pray that he would continue to pursue her. If he ever chose to hurt her with the details, the onus would be on him; she would not be guilty of withholding shameful particulars. Sylvia had never shared her story with anyone else but Natty. She was confident by then that their friendship was strong enough to withstand the scandal and that her friend would not judge her poorly or look down on her and treat her as a lesser being. She hoped Tino would react the same way, but since doubt remains akin to hope, she was afraid.

Tino sensed her anxiety as she started to speak; he could almost hear her heart pounding. He took her trembling hands in his. "You don't need to tell me anything, Sibby," he said. "I love you, not your history. I don't care how you came into this world. I'm just glad you're here."

Sylvia insisted, telling him first about her grandfather and how he was the only father she ever knew. "Everyone says he doted on my mother and on me, too. She named me after him. I still miss him very much."

She found it easier to start her story with her grandfather then progress to the unhappier parts—about her mother's dying in childbirth, the lasting effect it had on Ana, the only spinster in the neighborhood, and about Elena.

The scandal involving Elena and her German sailor was well-known. It was the subject of widespread and long-lived rumormongering after the public brawl in the street and their disappearance. Sylvia was certain Tino had heard about it and, like many others, wondered what really happened. Since no one knew what happened to Elena and her paramour, all sorts of stories arose. Many knew the marine policeman to be mean and spiteful and too ready to mete out his judgment whenever, however, and to whomever gave him the slightest cause. No one complained about him because even his superiors feared him. The man truly belonged in jail. Some blamed Pilar for not allowing the lovers to make their case before calling on the police to drag the German boy away to jail. Many thought she deserved the punishment. Others faulted Elena, saying she was a despicable person for carrying on an illicit affair with a foreigner and dishonoring her family. In the end, people concluded that either they hid on the German ship and died when it exploded or they fled deep into the jungle and were still living there like savages.

Sylvia related the story as she witnessed and remembered it. She studied Tino's face and eyes as she spoke and watched for signs of disapproval or disenchantment, but there were none. Tino's smile never changed.

"Sibby, I heard about it, but I wasn't home yet when that happened. I was still away at school," Tino said. "I don't care what happened. If they were as happy as we are, then I hope they will remain so whether in heaven or in hell, or wherever they are."

Sylvia also related how she found her father's letter in her grandfather's satchel. "I still have the letter. All I know about him is that he was a sailor and his name began with a *T.* He said he loved my mother and would try to come back to her, but he never did."

Sylvia's background didn't change how Tino felt about her. On a weekend visit to his mother in Sumay, Tino announced his decision to propose to Sylvia and to ask his mother's blessing. Maria was fifty-eight years old. She and Bitta were alone and living together in the big house. After Alberto's death, Maria sold the bakery, the stable and storehouse, and the carriage. She didn't have the heart or the strength to carry on the business alone, and she didn't expect Tino to give up the profession he had studied and worked so hard for, no matter how limited he was allowed to practice it. Maria listened soberly as Tino poured out his heart to her. Her face darkened as Tino related the details of Sylvia's origins. She watched her son's face, saw the depth of his sincerity and the love he had for Sylvia, and her heart softened. Maria knew what it was to be the object of gossip and derision. As she lost her children, one by one, friends, neighbors, and even relatives whispered that it was punishment from God. In her grief, Maria also suffered scorn. How now could she perpetuate the same kind of anguish for an innocent child who bore no guilt for the manner of her entry into the world? How could she fault her son who was willing to ignore hurtful whispers to love this girl and take her as his wife?

"When you marry her you will be giving me a daughter," Maria said, and smiled.

With his mother's blessing and encouragement, Tino courted Sylvia for several more weeks before he proposed. With Tino, Sylvia didn't feel like an orphaned love child. He treated her as someone special, and she felt special. When he proposed, Sylvia did not hesitate.

"Whose permission should I seek?" he asked. Sylvia wished her grandfather was still alive to grant permission and give her away, but he was long dead. Juan was her uncle and more like a big brother, but she didn't think of him as a father figure. She thought even less of Jaime.

"Maybe Pale' Joe?" Sylvia offered. She and Tino were aware of the irony. The parish priest of the church in her district in Agaña, Pale' Joseph O'Brien, was a redheaded Irishman from New York. To fulfill an expected marriage tradition, Tino would have to ask a pious American cleric for the hand of the illegitimate daughter of an American sailor.

Pale' Joe was among several American Capuchin priests who came to Guam after the turn of the century. Suspicious of the great influence the Spanish Augustinian Recollects had over the people, the navy deported them, leaving the only Chamorro priest to serve the entire island. He eventually received help from Spanish Capuchins serving in the German-held colonies around Guam. American Capuchins eventually arrived to replace the Spanish priests. Many of the American priests learned to speak Chamorro and spent the rest of their lives serving in the Marianas. Pale' Joe was among the first to preach and sing in Chamorro and who became much-loved and respected. He also loved Chamorro food and grew to be quite rotund. With his white hair and goatee, his brown cassock and chubby sandaled feet, he was always smiling and seemed happy all the time.

Pale' Joe assumed Tino and Sylvia had come to arrange for the requisite marriage preparation and was pleasantly surprised when the couple explained their purpose. Pale' said it was a bit unorthodox but understandable under the circumstances. Thus, Tino formally asked Pale' Joe for his blessing and permission to marry Sylvia.

"And will you promise to love, protect, and support my daughter?" Pale' asked, relishing playing the role of Sylvia's father. From that day on, whenever Tino met Pale' Joe on the street, Pale' would ask, "Are you taking care of Sylvia?" He would similarly ask Sylvia if Tino was taking good care of her. In time, it became a well-worn but much-loved anecdote among them.

As Tino and Sylvia began their marriage preparations, even before the first of three bands of matrimony was announced from the pulpit, Tino's mother passed away. Bitta died earlier that year, leaving Maria alone in the big house. Tino tried to convince her to move in with him in the tiny apartment he rented in Agaña, but she refused. She was a resident of Sumay, born and bred, she insisted, and there she would stay.

"Now I know why you're so stubborn," Sylvia teased as she and Tino rode the bus back to Agaña.

Sylvia and Tino spent their Saturdays with Maria in Sumay. They increased their visits to the whole weekend as Maria's health declined. On one of their visits, after starting their marriage preparation, Maria took Sylvia aside and led her into her bedroom. She barred Tino from joining them and said she needed to speak with Sylvia alone. From her closet, Maria tried to pull out a beautifully carved wooden chest. Sylvia had to help her because the chest was made of ifil wood (*Intsia bijuga*) and was heavy.

"It's my trousseau," she said with a wide smile and a twinkle in her eyes. "I've used and worn out everything over the years, but there are a few pieces that are special to me."

With Sylvia's help, Maria lifted the heavy lid and brought out three parcels wrapped in lengths of butcher paper. Beneath the paper, each parcel was wrapped in coarse muslin. Inside the first parcel, the largest, was Maria's wedding ensemble. The second contained a long lace veil, the third a baby's christening gown and bonnet. All the items were slightly yellowed with age but in excellent condition. They were all handmade; the lace hand-tatted and more beautiful than anything Sylvia ever saw in any shop downtown.

"I was seventeen when Tino's father asked for my hand and eighteen when we got married. Alberto's mother had this made in Spain especially for me. Isn't it beautiful?" Maria said as she handed Sylvia the wedding garments. "We were married in 1878, in the most beautiful ceremony I have ever seen. No one's wedding before or since was as beautiful as mine."

The dress, which was in separate pieces, was made of white silk taffeta, trimmed with handmade lace, floral silk brocade ribbon, and thousands of tiny crystals. The bodice was a tight-fitting jacket with what seemed like a hundred small, satin-covered buttons, from the neck to the abdomen, but the buttons were only an illusion. Only every tenth button actually closed the bodice. Its long trumpet sleeves ended in lace-edged cuffs that would have draped demurely over the bride's hands. The skirt was not the huge bell shape in vogue near the end of the nineteenth century, but it was quite full, with a tiered, linen underskirt and a muslin petticoat. The outfit also came with a whale-bone corset, a camisole, and a simple, short-sleeved cotton underdress. Maria explained that the underdress protected the outer pieces from the wearer's perspiration and was washable, whereas the outer pieces were not.

"In those days," Maria continued, "the bride didn't eat until after she changed, or else she wore a ridiculous bib to protect her gown."

The entire ensemble was beautiful, but impossibly old-fashioned and was obviously made at a time when showing any skin was not appropriate.

"It would honor me if you would consider it for your wedding," Maria said. She noted the look of concern on Sylvia's face and quickly added, "Of course, you will want to have it altered. It is so out of fashion."

Sylvia was relieved. She would have worn Maria's wedding garments as they were, if she had asked, but they were too small and too short, and no one wore that many pieces of clothing all at once anymore. As Maria spoke, Sylvia started thinking about how to reconstruct the pieces, which unnecessary ones to eliminate, and how to get from too short and too small to just right. The fabrics were gorgeous and were worth a small fortune. She wasn't sure how she wanted the outfit reconstructed, but she was glad to have the freedom to change it. As Sylvia pondered the possibilities, Maria lifted the lace veil from its wrappings and placed it in Sylvia's lap. The veil was folded several times and weighed almost two pounds because of its great length. Sylvia lifted a corner of the top layer and studied the tatting. It was indeed beautiful.

Tears glistened in Maria's eyes as she spread out the christening gown and ran her gnarled hand gently over its length. Like the veil, it was unusually long, almost five feet from neckline to hem. The bodice, neckline, and puffed sleeves were made of satin-lined tulle and ringed with tiny white handmade satin roses. Satin ribbon streamers at the shoulders accentuated the gown's length. The lower half of the skirt was made of heavy lace. The bonnet was made of the same lace and matched the tiny roses on the bodice.

"Mother Camacho had this made in Manila, in anticipation of my first baby's baptism," Maria said sadly. "I lost four babies, one after another. Then Antonio came along. Then my little Josefina. Then Tino. All three were christened in this gown. Now I give these to you, the chest also. I hope you will accept them with the same love and respect and happiness I felt when they were given to me."

"I will cherish them as long as I live," Sylvia said. She was excited and eager to return to Agaña, to show the items to Natty and to confer with her on the most advisable and flattering way to have the wedding ensemble altered to fit.

Natty knew just the seamstress to approach. Tan Loli' was the best; she could turn a flour sack into a ball gown, Natty said. They were disappointed though when they showed Maria's wedding clothing to Tan Loli'. The seamstress scowled as she examined the pieces.

"Daughter," Tan Loli' said with a sad look on her face, "it would be a sin to cut up something so beautiful. I am afraid to touch it. Santa Ana[11] would be so unhappy with me."

"Please, Tan Loli', help me with this," Sylvia pleaded. "I promised my future mother-in-law that I would wear it. If it fit me, I would wear it as it is, but it doesn't. What can we do?"

The three women spent several evenings studying the pieces and discussing various options. In the end, with ideas Natty offered, Tan Loli' opened the sides of the bodice-jacket under the sleeves; fitted the front, back, and shoulders to Sylvia's torso, and filled in the gaps with smocked heavy satin, which she smocked by hand and ornamented with some of the crystal beads carefully taken from the skirt. Nestled between the smocked panels at the back, Tan Loli' inserted a new type of closure called a zipper. She lowered and scalloped the neckline in the front and lined it with the extra buttons. Since the sleeves of the bodice were long enough and large enough to fit Sylvia's arms, they needed no alteration. The laced edges reached her wrists. Tan Loli' then attached the reconstructed bodice to the skirt, which needed only to be altered for length. A band of smocked satin provided the added length and married the new design together.

Maria did not live to see her son's wedding, but her daughter-in-law proudly wore Maria's redesigned and reconstructed wedding gown and veil. Sylvia kept the christening gown carefully tucked away in the ifil wood chest for the day when she and Tino would have need of it. She wanted to continue Maria's tradition and have all her children christened in Tino's gown.

Several months before the wedding, Tino purchased a heavy Spanish gold chain and rose-shaped pendant with matching earrings and bracelet. He also bought a silk-lined Japanese lacquer jewelry box. The jewelry and box were his wedding gifts for his bride. At three hundred dollars, the jewelry set and lacquer box were the most expensive items he had ever purchased and had paid for it in installments. Sylvia paled when she saw the jewelry. She had never owned anything so costly.

"I have nothing to give to you," she said to Tino, tears welling in her eyes.

"There is no need," Tino said, "I have you."

Sylvia wore the jewelry on her wedding day.

---

[11] The mother of the Blessed Virgin Mary and patron saint of seamstresses.

Chapter 13

Constantino Flores Camacho and Sylvia Maria de Leon were married on February 23, 1920, shortly before his twenty-fourth birthday and Sylvia's twentieth. Sylvia moved into Tino's small apartment in the San Ignacio district near the cathedral. She and Tino walked to work at the Governor's Palace every morning. Sylvia, who grew up sharing a bed with one or more of her mother's sisters, was not uncomfortable about sharing Tino's bed, although it was an altogether different experience. Tino, who never had to share his bed, had to get used to Sylvia's presence in it, although he liked having her body so close. Ten months after their wedding, on December 20, 1920, their daughter, Vivian Amanda de Leon Camacho, was born. Tino would have preferred a melodious, old-fashion Spanish name, like Mariquita or Asuncion, but Sylvia wanted to honor her mother's memory and to give her baby a first name that was more modern, more American.

"The American flag has flown over us since I was born," she said. "Maybe someday, when Vivian grows up, she'll become an American citizen, a real American."

"Sure, and maybe men will walk on the moon," Tino said sarcastically.

Tino didn't share Sylvia's optimism. Calls for the grant of citizenship had been made regularly since the start of American rule, but all were ignored or rejected. Tino was content to remain a native resident of Guam, a citizen of nowhere else. Sylvia was among the many young people who wanted to fully embrace Americanism. At the time, the movement was gaining popularity. Youngsters in the schools launched a crusade to distinguish themselves in a more American flavor. They called themselves "Guamanians," to distinguish themselves as the Chamorros of Guam under American rule, as opposed to the Chamorros of the rest of the Marianas under Japanese rule. In their native tongue, however, everyone was still Chamorro. Initially, only the Chamorros of Guam were "Guamanian" and only white Americans were American. Vivian would grow up with all three identities: a Chamorro Guamanian American.

Vivian was a beautiful baby, dark haired but pale skinned. Tino held her in his arms and wondered what her missing American grandfather would think of her. It irked him that his baby, another generation removed from that unknown stranger, had inherited some of his physical characteristics, forgetting that his own mother, who was part Spanish, was also very light skinned. Vivian was only hours old, and it was too soon to determine whose traits she inherited. Nevertheless, Tino thought about all the wonders and milestones that American would miss and took pleasure in knowing those joys would be his.

Although fatherhood suited him well, Tino thought he would enjoy welcoming more babies until just days after Vivian was born. Tino had lived alone for most of his life. As an only child, he never had to share his parent's affections or his living arrangements, even when he was away at college. After getting married, living with Sylvia in his small apartment was sometimes stifling and uncomfortable, even though he loved her deeply and liked sharing his bed. Sylvia's presence was sometimes challenging. The addition of an infant tested his patience and tolerance, especially as he discovered how often a newborn demanded to be fed and changed.

Sylvia bounced back to good health right away but gave up her job. She now had a husband and a newborn, and taking care of them was her new full-time job. Ana wanted to move in with them, to help care for Vivian, but Tino tried to dissuade Sylvia from allowing it.

"But Ana has no one, Tino," Sylvia said, "and I could use the help."

"She was the one who chose not to get married, Sibby," Tino insisted. "She should be driving her husband crazy and drowning in children and grandchildren by now."

"I know, my darling, but that isn't the case," Sylvia said. "I know that watching my mother die deeply affected her."

"Well, if it's what you want, I'll try to be patient. I just hope it won't be forever," he said. Sylvia recognized the discomfort and reticence in her husband's voice and in his face. She was touched that he would consider allowing it, if it was what she wanted. Sylvia wasn't keen on Ana's constant presence either. She wanted to care for Vivian herself, but she felt sorry for Ana, who was thirty-two years old and all alone in the de Leon house. Without the heart to say no, Sylvia sidestepped the issue until Ana realized she was not going to get the answer she wanted. Ana would never have asked Tino directly; it was his house and she respected his right to manage it.

Sylvia asked Natty to be Vivian's baptismal godmother, her *matlina*. Natty was engaged but not yet married to Alejandro Castillo, who had dreams of going to college in the U.S. and was working and saving up to fulfill his dreams. Marrying Natty was his first priority. Tino asked his friend and coworker, Francisco "Kiko" Taisipic to be Vivian's godfather, her *patlino*. Thus, the foursome's friendship was made stronger, as *commadre* and *compadre*, or joint parents. Natty was going to have a christening gown made for Vivian, but Sylvia told her there would be no need. She explained how Tino's grandmother had had a gown made in the Philippines, how Tino and his two older siblings had been christened in it, and how she wanted Vivian to wear it also.

"For an American, you're such a romantic," Natty said. It was well-known that Americans, particularly the navy men, were not sentimental about anything that had to do with the history or culture of their charges; the mission was always the priority. If anything stood in their way, like the ancient Chamorro stone building supports called *latte*, it was bulldozed away without consideration of its historical value.

"I'm only half, remember?" Sylvia said. She retrieved the gown from Maria's ifil wood chest and presented it for Natty to see. Natty spent several minutes examining every inch of it and marveling at the workmanship and the gown's beauty.

Vivian was baptized by the bishop himself on a Sunday after Mass at the cathedral. After the ceremony, Tino and Sylvia hosted a large celebration under several *palapalas*[12] beside the de Leon house in the Santa Cruz district. Esther, Juan, Jaime, and their spouses and children gathered at the old house the Friday before and worked through the weekend to prepare the house and grounds for the festivities on Sunday afternoon. Ana was the only one still living in Agaña. Esther and her family lived in Sumay. Juan landed a job at the transpacific cable station and moved his family to Sumay also. Jaime and his wife lived in Agat.

Vivian's baptismal celebration was large and well attended, with two *palapalas* for the food buffet and another for the desserts alone. Natty and Alejandro outdid themselves in providing the great quantity and variety of sweets and confections. Four other *palapalas* filled the front and side yards to shield guests from the sun. The bishop blessed the new family of three, offered grace, and "opened" the tables to the hungry crowd. Ana was beside herself with joy, welcoming the bishop, the navy officers Tino worked for, their wives, and all the other invited neighbors and guests to her home. Tino's coworkers, their families, and the girls from the secretarial pool and their families attended also. Juan and a couple of his friends provided live music, playing guitars, a violin, and a trumpet all afternoon. It was the busiest, loudest, most crowded, and liveliest the house had ever been. The party was even larger than Tino and Sylvia's wedding reception. For Vivian's first birthday, Tino and Sylvia arranged another celebration, dipping into

---

[12] A *palapala*—a temporary shelter usually of rough wooden uprights with a roof of woven palm fronds or canvas and decorated with fruits in season, fresh flowers, and decorative shapes woven from palm fronds.

their savings to make the affair special, hosting thirty-five children and their parents. Eighteen of the children and teenagers were Sylvia's first cousins.

A day after the birthday party, Sylvia and Natty pierced Vivian's ears in the same way theirs had been: someone held them down and pushed a threaded sewing needle into their earlobes. From the time she was six months old, Sylvia wore her mother's small gold earrings. She didn't know until she was fourteen years old that they were a gift from her father to her mother. Tino bought her a pair of ruby earrings so that Vivian could receive her old ones. Just as Sylvia grew up wearing Amanda's small gold earrings, Vivian would do the same, but she would know where they came from and why she inherited them. She would also inherit Sylvia's wedding jewelry someday.

"Did you know these are eighteen-karat gold?" Natty asked, examining Sylvia's old earrings while Sylvia prepared the alcohol, cotton, needle, and threat they would need.

"No, I never really paid attention," Sylvia answered. "I rarely took them off."

"Well, they are, and that means they weren't cheap. Your mother couldn't have made much working at Castro's old store. How could she have afforded these?"

"She didn't. I wore them for years before I found out that my father bought them for her. Are they really expensive?"

"Oh yes, indeed. They're more expensive than fourteen-karat jewelry. How do you know they're from your father?"

"It was in his letter," Sylvia said. "He told her he wished they were wedding rings."

"He must have really loved her," Natty mused. "Sailors didn't make much back then. They don't make that much even now. Either he was rich or he sacrificed a lot to buy these earrings."

"I don't think he was rich. If he was, he could have bought his way back to her," Sylvia responded. "I like to think he made the sacrifice. Maybe he knew that he couldn't come back to her."

"Or maybe he stole them," Natty added, and laughed.

"Maybe he did," Sylvia said with a feigned chuckle. "Stole the earrings, stole my mother's heart, stole my mother from me, then stole away, never to be seen or heard from again."

The thoughts lingered in Sylvia's head. She wanted to wish her mysterious father ill, but knew deep in her heart that *T.* loved her mother. *If you're dead, and that's why you couldn't come back for us, then may God forgive you and grant you peace, Father T., whoever you are,* she said in her mind. The feeling of having been cheated returned in a flash. She didn't know either of her parents, didn't even know what they looked like. She couldn't say she loved them, nor could she say she hated them; she just didn't know who they were as real persons. It was the sadness she bore all her life, and all she could do was pretend it didn't bother her.

"Shhhh, my sweet baby," she said, trying to soothe her traumatized baby. "You will know your mama and papa." She rocked Vivian in her arms until she fell asleep, still sniffing raggedly.

Chapter 14

In 1923, Sylvia learned of a house for sale at the base of San Ramon Hill, not far from the navy government compound. She was among several individuals interested in it. The navy government was interested in purchasing it also and adding it to their inventory of dependent living quarters. Sylvia convinced Natty to go with her to see it.

The house was built and owned by Providencio "Tun Vid" Mandapat, a successful Filipino tailor who was much sought after for his beautiful *barong Tagalog* formal wear for men and his breathtaking "Maria Clara" gowns and mestizas for women. He was the one who made Natty's wedding gown for her wedding two years earlier. Tun Vid was a longtime resident of Agaña and an active member of the Dulce Nombre de Maria parish. His friends and neighbors were sad to see him leave. He was moving his family and business back to the Philippines to care for his aging parents. Several young women, who were already engaged to be married, ordered and purchased in advance Tun Vid's tailor-made, one-of-a-kind gowns for their wedding.

Tun Vid built the house at the turn of the century with fine narra, ifil, and mahogany, which he imported from the Philippines. It was among several tile-roofed, whitewashed *mamposteria*[13] buildings in town. It fronted the street that led directly to the government compound's rear gate. The house had two levels: the main living area on the upper floor and a workshop, storage area, and utility space at ground level.

A flight of concrete stairs along the front led up from the street to a veranda and the main entrance, which featured two sets of double doors. The outer doors were of heavy ifil wood and were usually left open. They were shut and bolted securely for typhoons, otherwise there was rarely any need to close them at night. The second set were wire-screened, which allowed breezes in and kept insects out. The doors opened onto a comfortable parlor with a bank of screened windows overlooking the veranda. Two large bedrooms flanked the parlor on the right. Another large bedroom and the

---

[13] A traditional method of wall construction featuring coral rubble sandwiched between interior and exterior layers of plaster. Such walls may measure two to three feet thick.

bathroom were on the left. Beyond the parlor, through an archway, was the dining room. Adjacent to it was the kitchen, with an electric stove and an ice box. A door in the kitchen opened onto an exterior flight of wooden stairs that led down to Tun Vid's shop and the open-air laundry and utility area. Tun Vid did his work, conducted his business, and stored his fabrics, notions, and supplies on the first floor. The workshop, which included a small fitting room and storage room, took up most of the ground level space. The backyard was small and narrow; much of it sloped uphill.

Although the backyard was disappointing—there was no space for a vegetable garden—Sylvia liked everything about the house. Natty thought the asking price was too high, but they could negotiate a lower price because of the sloped backyard. The navy also thought the price too high and made an insultingly low offer, which Tun Vid refused. Sylvia remained the last buyer still interested. Beaming with excitement and eager to see it again, Sylvia persuaded Tino to take time off to go and look at the house. After a quick tour, Tino was skeptical. He liked the house also but didn't like the looks of the slope in the backyard.

"Hmmm," Tino said, rubbing his chin pensively. "I'll bet the backyard turns into a muddy swamp during the rainy season. That's not good, Sibby. Anyway, I think the house is too big for us."

"It's too big now, but we'll grow into it," Sylvia countered. She assumed she would bear more children and was only a little concerned that month after month had passed without another pregnancy. "And as for the slope, you can fix it. That's what you went to college for, isn't it?"

Tino couldn't resist his wife's gentle sarcasm and the twinkle in her eyes. It warmed his heart to see the happiness in her face. If buying this house would make her even happier, he would buy it, damn the slope. They sought out Tun Vid and managed to get the price lowered by enough to cover the cost of digging a dry well and shoring up the slope with a low retaining wall. They closed the deal on the house and lived frugally for several months, buying new furniture as they could afford it, a few pieces at a time. The first thing Sylvia did to make the house her own was to plant a hedge of alternating red and white bougainvillea bushes in the front. Vivian was a toddler at the time and happily played in the dirt as Sylvia worked.

"You know those things have wicked thorns and will have to be pruned regularly or we won't be able to get into the house," Tino said as he watched Sylvia wrestle with a pick. "Would you like me to do that for you?"

Sylvia looked up at him and scowled. "And here I thought I married a gentleman," she said, and tipped the pick in his direction.

"You did, my queen, but I was busy watching over the princess of this castle," he teased.

"You can do the pruning, too, when the time comes," Sylvia said with a smirk.

Sylvia's bougainvillea hedge helped keep dust from the street from wafting up the stairs and into the parlor. When in full bloom, the bougainvillea became a dazzling wall of red and white papery flowers. Sylvia saw them that way only once.

In 1924, after Sylvia turned twenty-four, she began to complain of mild fatigue almost daily. Caring for her child and her home seemed to grow more and more physically exhausting, although it never had been before. While her inexplicable fatigue worried her, her failure to conceive troubled her deeply. Something was wrong, but she was afraid to see a doctor or to tell Tino. At first, Tino didn't notice anything different about his wife, but he also wondered why she wasn't getting pregnant. He was doing his part regularly, but still no pregnancy.

When Sylvia began to lose weight and look pale, Tino began to worry. Natty noticed the changes also and urged Sylvia to seek help. Sylvia refused her advice, certain that whatever ailed her was minor and would eventually pass. She told no one about the pain in her abdomen. By the middle of 1925, however, the symptoms, especially the pain, worsened, and Sylvia could no longer hide or deny her health problems. They were plain to see. She lost more weight and lost her appetite, even for her most favorite foods. Her hair was no longer healthy and shiny. Her skin was dry and sallow. She would sometimes get so weak and lethargic that she couldn't get out of bed.

At Tino's insistence, Sylvia finally sought medical help and underwent several tests at the navy's Maria Schroeder Women's Hospital. When the results returned a few weeks later, the diagnosis was devastating: Sylvia had advanced cancer. Her doctor encouraged the couple to settle her affairs and to enjoy the time she had left.

After they returned from the hospital that day, Sylvia immediately took to her bed, more angry than frightened. There was so much yet she wanted to do with her life. She wanted more time with her husband, more children to bear for him. She wanted to see Vivian grow up, become a young woman, and eventually get married. She wanted someday to become a grandmother and to grow old with Tino. Sylvia was too emotionally and physically drained to cry. Vivian, who was not yet five years old, lay with her to nap. Tino went downstairs to the laundry area. He dropped to his knees and prayed, begging God to spare his wife and grant them a little more time. But the cancer had already spread beyond any hope. God had decided their fate as a family, and Tino cried harder than he ever had before.

Sylvia spent the next month in the hospital. Tino and Natty visited her every day. Natty looked after Vivian so that Tino could stay longer at

Sylvia's bedside. The doctors and nurses did what they could to ease her suffering. When there was nothing more they could do, her doctor, a tall navy lieutenant with a stern face but a gentle voice, asked Sylvia if she preferred to remain in the hospital or go home.

"Mrs. Camacho, if you stay here, we will do whatever we can to make you more comfortable," the doctor said, adding that he didn't think she would have to suffer much longer, that the end was near. "We can give you some powerful medications to alleviate the pain, but they must be administered here in the hospital."

"Thank you, doctor, but I want to be with my husband and baby. I want to go home," Sylvia said, her voice barely audible.

Although the hospital was less than half a mile from the Camacho home, Sylvia's doctor ordered an ambulance and two corpsmen to be provided to transport Vivian back home and upstairs to her bed. Over the ensuing weeks, as the disease took its course, Sylvia suffered bouts of intense pain. She also repeated to Tino again and again how he was to raise their daughter, what to teach her, what to tell her, and how to prepare her for adulthood.

"My mother was reaching for the moon in her belief that my father would return to her someday," she said, disappointment bubbling under her words. "She died believing it, but I know it never happened.

"Promise me, Tino, promise me you'll teach our daughter to be wiser. Promise you will do this for me," she whispered, tears streaming from her eyes.

Tino waited on Sylvia hand and foot, trying to feed her, although she either ate very little or refused to eat. He carried her to the bathroom and cleaned her body when her bladder or bowels failed. Humiliated by her incapacitation, she would cry and apologize to him for having to attend to such an offensive task. Tino would kiss her and assure her that nothing she did could offend him. He bathed her, dressed her, and combed what remained of her beautiful hair, caring for her as best he could. Until she could no longer speak, Sylvia thanked her husband for loving her. Tino in turn would kiss her forehead and thank her for allowing him into her life. Afterward, exhausted and heartsick, he would retreat downstairs to weep.

Sylvia grew weaker and thinner until there was hardly anything left of her. Tino could no longer carry her as any movement caused her intense pain. Even sponge bathing was painful, but she insisted on being cleaned. Natty often came to help Tino with the bathing, but he insisted on doing everything himself. Pale' Joe also came daily to visit her. On his last visit, when it was clear that she was at death's door, he heard her confession, granted absolution, and administered last rites. When he completed the ritual, he kissed her forehead and said his good-byes. There were tears in his eyes.

On October 22, 1925, shortly after midnight, Sylvia Maria de Leon Camacho died in her husband's arms. Her death was inevitable, but Tino grieved more deeply for her than he had for his parents. He embraced her lifeless body, caressed her gaunt cheeks, and kissed her bony fingers and hands for hours, whispering words meant only for her, quietly refusing to let go. Vivian was asleep beside her mother but awoke before dawn to her father's sobbing. Not understanding anything except that her mama wouldn't wake up and her papa was crying, Vivian began crying also. That night and every night thereafter, Vivian would wake in terror and cry uncontrollably.

Numbed, Tino was barely conscious of his actions and decisions as he attended to the process of burying his wife. Although he was a self-reliant man, not eager to ask for help, Tino relied on Natty, Kiko, and his neighbors and coworkers to help him so that he could make arrangements. They came to his aid immediately, mourning as he did and sharing his grief. Natty was especially grieved. She was supposed to be on the next ship out, to join her husband Alejandro in California, but put off the trip to bury her dearest friend. She kept breaking down in tears as she watched over Vivian, did some household chores, and prepared meals for everyone who came to grieve and pray the nine-day rosary for the dead. Natty and another of Sylvia's former coworkers took charge of setting up a small shrine in the parlor, with flowers, candles, and a crucifix, where the rosary would be said and where Sylvia's coffin would lie during the wake.

The first thing Tino had to do was to report Sylvia's death to the authorities and to accompany the coroner's assistant to Sylvia's bedside to certify her death. Tino also called on Pale' Joseph, to inform him of Sylvia's passing and to ask that he conduct Sylvia's funeral Mass in his parish in the Santa Cruz district, as well as the burial rites at the cemetery. Tino and Sylvia were parishioners of the Dulce Nombre de Maria Cathedral, but since Pale' Joe had been reassigned from the cathedral to the Santa Cruz parish, just a half mile away, Tino wanted Sylvia to be prayed over by the parish priest who was like a father to them both. Tino also had to arrange with the cemetery director for a plot, as well as with the coffin maker and the stone carver. These were the tasks he dreaded most.

Tino's navy bosses gave him as much time as he needed to mourn. Even the navy governor himself told him that the navy stood ready to support him in any way needed. The officers knew how much Tino loved his wife—she and his daughter were all he talked about. Tino was a loyal, longtime navy government employee who deserved and received special accommodation.

For months after Sylvia's death, Tino was a sad, unhappy man. Five-year-old Vivian was inconsolable too. She cried for her mother almost every night for weeks. Heartbroken, Tino couldn't bear to hear her in such sorrow. Vivian needed her mother and clung stubbornly to her father, refusing to let go of his arm or leg when he tried to leave for work. Pushing her away so that he could leave broke Tino's heart. Vivian could sleep peacefully only in the crook of his arm on her mother's side of the bed. Tino later moved her little bed into his room. Vivian didn't have her own bedroom until she was six years old.

Chapter 15

Tino couldn't remember what his life had been like before Sylvia entered it. He had lived alone for much of his life but never knew loneliness until Sylvia was no longer with him. The pain of her absence was almost unbearable. If not for Vivian, Tino would have ended his own life. He couldn't bear the loneliness and the unfulfilled dreams lurking in every corner of his house. He and Sylvia had been together as man and wife for less than six years, and only two as owners of the house at the base of San Ramon Hill. Tino thought it was too big, but Sylvia loved it. She wanted to fill it with children and surround it with plants and flowers. Her bougainvillea bushes were in full bloom again, but she was not there to revel in them. Her presence filled the house with love and laughter, with life and light. Without her, it was dark and hollow and empty. Tino and Vivian were now its only occupants. Their echoed voices amplified their loneliness.

Tino wouldn't have considered selling the house, but he and Vivian didn't need all the space. He decided the best thing to do was to put it up for rent, as he had done with his mother's house and property in Sumay. The proximity of the house to the government compound made it a convenient and an especially desirable choice for navy renters. He threw himself into doing much of the renovation work himself, hoping it would occupy his time and fill his thoughts with something other than the pain of missing Sylvia. Tino renovated the upper floor, decreasing the size of the two adjacent bedrooms to make space for another bathroom. His house was among the first on Guam to have three full bathrooms. He modernized the old bathroom and installed new electric appliances in the kitchen.

Tino converted the ground floor workshop into a cozy two-bedroom apartment for Vivian and himself. He extended the concrete floor, enlarged the storage area, and put in a small bathroom and kitchen, using the old stove and ice box from upstairs and doing much of the plumbing himself. He purchased a table, four chairs, and a narrow bed and small wardrobe for each bedroom. The ifil wood chest that Tino's mother gave to Sylvia and which she bequeathed to Vivian went into Vivian's room. It was the best piece of furniture in the entire house.

The laundry area, which had taken up a quarter of the ground-level space, was reduced to one small area. The new laundry remained without walls and housed an electric wringer-washer, an electric water heater, and a homemade wooden wash trough. Since the stairs from the kitchen above ended in his new apartment below, Tino enclosed them completely. To get to the laundry, tenants would have to pass through his kitchen-dining area and out a side door. To minimize the intrusion, Tino offered his tenants laundry service for a small addition to the rent. He and Vivian otherwise didn't venture upstairs unless invited. The ground-floor apartment had two entrances: a door at the side of the house that opened into the kitchen and the other in the laundry. Neither door was ever locked; there was never a need.

Vivian knew only this lower level apartment as her home and never thought of it as small and cramped, or humble. Many of her neighbors and playmates lived in thatched-roofed houses, which were not beautiful to look at but wonderful to live in, especially when it rained. The sound of the rain on a thatch roof at night was like a lullaby. Vivian couldn't hear the rain on her roof, but what she didn't have, she didn't miss.

As Vivian grew out of infancy, the resemblance to her unknown American grandfather gradually diminished, except for the nose. She had Sylvia's nose: a nice bridge with nostrils narrower than wide, flat noses. Her complexion was lighter than her contemporaries, but all the days of playing in the sunshine tanned her skin. Even after her playground years, Vivian retained some color, at least wherever her skin was exposed. Vivian inherited the red highlights of her mother's dark auburn hair and the waves and soft curls of her father's. She also inherited her father's eyes, dark, sparkling, and seemingly fathomless. She was not beautiful like her mother or grandmother, but like her father, she had a pleasant, friendly face. She was pretty in her own way, especially when she smiled.

After Sylvia's death, Tino paid Tan Eugenia Santos, who lived close to the plaza, to care for Vivian while he was at work. Tan Eugenia had four children; three sons and a daughter, Dorothea, who was a year older than Vivian. Dorothea was the closest thing to a sister Vivian had. Although she spent more years with Tan Eugenia than she did with her mother, Vivian never thought of her as a mother figure. She spent more time in Dorothea's company and care than in Tan Eugenia's. In 1931, before Vivian turned eleven, she announced to her father that she was old enough to stay at home and take care of herself. She assured him that if she needed help, his office was nearby and so were the tenants upstairs. By then the apartment was usually occupied by navy families. After announcing that she no longer needed to go to Tan Eugenia's house after school, Vivian effectively became the lady of the house. Since he had taught her how to bake and cook and keep house at an early age, Tino was certain that she could indeed look after herself.

Tino was not strict but was protective. He knew Vivian would be the only child he would ever have and was his only lasting connection to Sylvia. He would readily give his permission for her school outings and activities, but was not keen to let her go without him to see a movie, which she dearly loved, or to traipse around town without reason, not that she was ever interested in such. As she got older, Vivian began to look more and more like Sylvia, but exhibited many of Tino's characteristics and personality traits. Like Tino, she took her studies seriously and was a bright student. Tino often had to encourage her to attend the birthday parties of her schoolmates. She was either not interested in going or outright refused to go to some.

Vivian was unlike most other young girls in the community. While other girls her age were either flirtatious or shy, Vivian was neither. She was more studious and serious, like her father. Having lost her mother at such an early age and having only her father as her most constant companion, Vivian grew to be like him in many ways. She lived a quiet, sheltered life with her father and was greatly influenced by his sense of duty and commitment—that work was an inescapable part of life and that the only leisure worth pursuing was that which produced some benefit. Even though she was exposed to other girls at school, Vivian never developed an interest in activities she thought were frivolous. She never learned how to flirt with boys, or how to dance, or wear makeup. Reading a book was easier and, in her mind, more beneficial than experimenting with make up or trying out new hairstyles. She was not a tomboy and was not shy, but neither was she outgoing. She was not without humor and could be mischievous and playful.

Vivian grew up hearing the stories about how her mother was born out of wedlock and died before her time, how her grandmother fell in love with a navy sailor and died giving birth to her mother, and how her grandaunt ran away with a German sailor (Vivian always thought that story was romantic). She had heard the stories from her father, who swore that the same would never happen to his daughter. Sylvia made him promise. The stories, often told on long, scary nights during typhoons, brought father and daughter close. They could confide in each other and share their thoughts and opinions easily. There were some issues, however, that couldn't be shared. Before Vivian turned twelve, Tino came to her school, hat in hand, nervously asking to speak with Mrs. Perez, Vivian's teacher. Vivian couldn't imagine why there was a need. She was a good student; she didn't misbehave and hadn't been in trouble any time that week. Tino shooed her home so that he could speak privately.

"Mrs. Perez, I've come to ask a big favor of you," Tino started.

Mrs. Perez raised an eyebrow, suspecting (correctly) what that favor was. She assured him she would see to it and he didn't need to worry. When he came home, he said nothing to Vivian about his conference and seemed pleased with himself at supper. At school the next day, Mrs. Perez sent only the boys out for recess. To the annoyance of the girls who already knew, Mrs. Perez explained the mysteries of menstruation. Some of the girls had started as early as nine years and were already "experts." There were also some among the eleven- and twelve-year-olds, including Vivian, for whom the presentation was unnecessary.

When Vivian was eleven, three navy nurses were renting the upstairs apartment. Noting that Vivian was nearing the age (and that her father was not qualified or equipped to prepare her), one of the nurses detained her when she came upstairs to collect the bedding for the wash, an extra service Tino offered for a small but optional addition to the rent. Vivian did the laundry and was allowed to keep the fee. The nurse's name was Jeanne Turner. She was the nicest and friendliest of the tenants, and Vivian liked her very much. Until Nurse Turner left Guam, Vivian saw her every Sunday at Mass, usually in her white uniform and nurse's cap. Over several afternoons, and with motherly patience, Nurse Turner explained the function of menstruation and the process for attending to its arrival every month. She explained sexual reproduction, pregnancy, and delivery. Vivian had listened wide-eyed and frightened, but Nurse Turner assured her that all was normal and natural and that it was better for her to know the whole story rather than only what to do when the bleeding starts "down there." True to form, Mrs. Perez's explanation was limited to "what to do."

Believing Mrs. Perez had handled the delicate matter, Tino was greatly relieved. He had worried about how to prepare his daughter for something so privately feminine, and for which he was ignorant; Sylvia never shared that part of her life with him. He had frightful visions of trying to attend to a panicked and bleeding preteen daughter. Vivian giggled all the way home from school that day; only then did she realize what a worrisome task rearing her was for her father.

When menstruation began for her, at age thirteen, Vivian was prepared. Unbeknownst to her father, Vivian had purchased in advance everything she would need to attend to "what to do." Nurse Turner was long gone by then and Vivian wished she could have told her how much she appreciated the lessons and how well she had done on her own. She was sure Nurse Turner would have been proud of her. Vivian never announced to her father that she had become a full-fledged woman, and he never inquired. He knew the signs: uncharacteristic irritability, a pimple or two on her otherwise clear face, a grimace of abdominal pain now and then but no complaint, frequent and prolonged visits to the bathroom, and more than the usual number of cotton panties on the clothesline.

On the subject of sex, Tino tried to be frank but was terribly uncomfortable. He had asked Mrs. Perez to handle that issue also, but she refused. That, she told him, was his duty and obligation since he did not have a wife who would have borne the responsibility. He suspected that Mrs. Perez was as prudish and uncomfortable about talking about sex as he was. Tino knew that he couldn't avoid it or foist the responsibility onto someone else. Sylvia made him promise to prepare their daughter as best he could just as her grandmother had done for her and her aunts after Amanda's death. In preparing for her own death and while she could still speak, Sylvia asked Tino not to let their daughter reach her teen years without knowing.

"If my mother had known better, if she had known how to read a man's intentions, she would still be alive today," Sylvia labored to say. She had long given up the veracity of the love *T.* professed to have for her mother.

"That's true, Sibby, but if she had known, you wouldn't be here and I would have been an unhappy man," Tino said, knowing that he truly would be when Sylvia passed on.

Tino vacillated another two years, until Vivian was fifteen, before uneasily fulfilling his promise to Sylvia to prepare their daughter for adulthood. He avoided describing the sex act, not knowing that Vivian already knew about it; Nurse Turner's narrative, which included the terrifying disclosure that sexual intercourse would hurt at first, was graphic and complete.

"Vivian," he started uncomfortably, "men are ruled by the thing in their pants. For us, the urge is very strong. God made us that way so that babies would always be born into the world."

Vivian tried hard not to laugh, not at her father's simplistic, almost comical description, but at his heartrending discomfort. He couldn't even bring himself to name "the thing in their pants." She never knew her father to be anything less than strong and confident in his convictions, his beliefs, and in himself. Watching and listening to him struggle was painfully funny—if something so serious can be funny that way.

"But God also made a law—His law," her father continued. "His law states that men and women must be married before they make babies." Vivian raised a skeptical eyebrow; there were mothers in the neighborhood who weren't married or never were married. They were often the objects of condescending gossip and snide whispers. Vivian's thoughts instantly turned to her grandmother and wondered whether she too was whispered about, certain that she must have been. Shaken from the distraction, she cleared her mind to pay attention to her father.

Once beyond what he thought was a tasteful and acceptable description of sex, Tino's demeanor changed. He was now on more certain and comfortable ground, and he spoke with confidence and conviction on the point he wanted to drive home. It was a warning, a father's attempt to protect his daughter against the abuse, the heartache, and the physical, emotional, and even spiritual damage the members of his gender could inflict on the members of hers. He especially cautioned against engaging in relationships, even friendly ones, with transient servicemen who might do to her what one of them had done to her grandmother.

"Think of it this way, Vivvy," he said. "Pursuing a love affair with a serviceman is foolhardy. It's like reaching for the moon; you cannot have it. These servicemen are different from us. Their ways are different, their beliefs are different. They come from different places, and none of those places are like ours. Many of them look down on us. They think we are beneath them and that we were placed on this earth for their service and pleasure.

"If a sailor or a marine pays attention to you, I'm sure it will be because there is some attraction. But what is behind that attraction? What does he want from you? Does he want to marry you and make you his life's partner? Does he want to take care of you even though he knows that he is here only for a limited time and must return to a place that most likely will not accept you? These men cannot stay and make Guam their home, not while they remain in the service. They will leave when their time comes. They must; they have orders. When your serviceman leaves, will he take you with him? *Can* he take you with him?

"Vivvy, there are men in this world, not only among the Americans, but even among our own people, who will use you only for their own pleasure. There are dangerous men who will force themselves upon you and take from you the most precious gift you can give to a husband. They are the ones I fear most. They can be charming and attentive. They see women as a challenge to their abilities. They will do whatever it takes to persuade you to let them have your body," Tino paused. There was a faraway look in his eyes. Vivian guessed that he was thinking of Amanda, the naive young girl who gave up her virginity to a sailor who left her, probably unknowingly, with a baby—with Sylvia, the love of his life. Conflicted by the paradox, Tino was pensive for several moments before he spoke again.

"Vivvy, a serviceman who truly loves you will find a way to come back to you. He must conquer all the obstacles that lay in his path. There are many.

For him, it would also be like reaching for the moon. I tell you all this now so that you won't try. No one can have the moon."

"Don't worry, Papa, I won't reach for the moon," she said. "It's not among my goals, and I'm in no hurry to get married, especially to some sailor who thinks he can get the better of me." She laughed and hugged her father, glad that the uncomfortable lesson was over.

Vivian was sixteen and slated to graduate from high school a year early. She was among the top students in her class and was selected to undergo the navy government's teacher training program, something that appealed to her very much. Tino thought about sending her to college in the United States. He could afford the trip and some of the initial expenses, and she was bright enough to earn scholarships once she was there and proved her worth. When he broached the subject, Vivian said she would prefer to attend his alma mater, the University of Santo Tomas in the Philippines, because it was closer to home. Tino countered that since they were under American rule it made more sense to acquire an American college education. If she wanted, she could do much better and could go much further than with the limited training and teaching certificate the navy government offered. Although it chilled his heart to think of the great distance and long absence that would exist between them if she left Guam, he had to make the opportunity available. Vivian had a mind worthy of broadened horizons and further advancement, and he had to offer her the choice.

"Papa, I want to teach here. I don't need to go anywhere else. Besides, I would never leave you," she said, putting an end to the discussion. Tino was both disappointed and relieved. He had been torn between letting her go and keeping her at home.

Vivian accepted the navy government's teacher training offer and completed the program successfully. She was recruited to teach at Leary School, the grade school for local children, not far from the plaza. The children of navy personnel attended a segregated school within the government compound. Their teachers were imported from the States, as were their books and supplies.

Not long after landing her teaching position, Vivian agreed to become one of Dorothea Santos's twelve bridesmaids. Vivian was looking forward to wearing a fancy gown and carrying a bouquet of flowers, believing it would be the closest she would ever come to walking down the aisle. She and Dorothea remained close friends throughout grade school and high school. The two were a lot alike. Having a distracted mother and three older brothers, Dorothea also was not given to developing feminine skills and guiles, but she did fall in love and was getting married at eighteen. As she stood among the bridal party, Vivian wondered if she would ever meet and fall in love with any man. She hadn't yet.

"Don't worry, Bib," Dorothea told her. "When you meet him, you'll know. He'll make your heart skip and take your breath away."

"Does Danny do that to you?"

Dorothea smiled widely. "Oh yes!" she said. Vivian remained skeptical. None of the boys she knew had that kind of effect on her, not even the ones other girls thought were handsome.

Dorothea and her husband, Daniel Mateo, moved to Piti, and Vivian didn't see them as often as she wished. She was flattered when Dorothea gave birth to a baby girl and named her Vivian. She was deeply moved when Dorothea asked her to be the baby's godmother. As is custom, the godmother provides the baby's christening gown and accessories and the desserts for the celebration following the baptismal ceremony. Vivian ordered a gown from a seamstress in Agaña who was well-known for making beautiful but expensive ones. She also ordered cakes, pies, and other sweets from the family who bought Tino's parents' bakery in Sumay. She and Tino spent the weekend in Piti helping Dorothea's and Danny's families prepare for more than a hundred guests. Baby Vivian Mateo was the first grandchild for both families. Their pride and joy had to be reflected in the size and splendidness of their celebration.

PART TWO

Chapter 16

"*Guam*! Where the hell is that?" Preston Avery roared indignantly. He was a man accustomed to knowing all the important things that needed to be known, at least in his universe. A place he never heard of was completely outside his realm. Worse, his son Philip was being sent there. Twenty-three-year-old Philip Thomas Avery, a navy lieutenant, junior grade, was at home on leave before shipping out to his new duty station. After dinner, as the family retired to Preston's den for coffee and dessert, he announced to his parents and sister where he would be going.

"It's a little island in the western Pacific, Father," Philip answered. "We took it in the Spanish-American War." Philip was sitting in a leather wingback chair facing his father, who sat behind a large cherry wood desk. Philip's mother and sister Jennifer lounged on a settee having tea instead of coffee. "I did some research on it but couldn't find much information. There's not much available, save some outdated navy reports," he added.

Philip loved the navy and wanted to make a career of it, but the scuttlebutt was that an assignment to Guam was bad news for the career-minded. He did not welcome his orders to Guam and wondered how such bad luck had befallen him. With so little information available about the island, it might well have been a port of banishment—a dumping ground for navy misfits and troublemakers. Philip was neither a misfit—he excelled at everything he attempted and was well-liked by his professors and classmates—nor was he a troublemaker. While Philip was not happy about his orders, his father was incensed that his well-deserving son did not receive a better—nay, a choice—assignment, one more prestigious or at least closer to home.

Preston Avery was a successful businessman who thrice served as a New York state senator. He amassed his fortune in real estate and shrewd investing. He did not grow up in poverty, as had some of his wealthy contemporaries, but he did not grow up in wealth either. He inherited his father's small retail business in Albany and managed successfully to bring it through the Great Depression. Then he branched out cautiously into the real estate market, borrowing the money to make his first purchase. His first success was followed by many others. In time, he rose to prominence financially, politically, and socially.

His wife, Lydia, Philip's mother, was the daughter of a wealthy and well-respected New England family. Lydia Porter Avery was a socialite famed for her beauty and poise in her youth and for her organizational brilliance in her community and charity work in her later years. Before he passed away, Lydia's father set up generous trust funds for his daughters and grandchildren. Lydia, her three children, her sister Mavis, and her two daughters were Grandfather Porter's only surviving family. Philip's older brother, William, used some of his inheritance to put himself through medical school. Their parents paid for all three to attend private schools and college, but any postgraduate pursuits would be at their own expense. Philip was an excellent rugby player throughout high school and won scholarships to the college of his choice. He left his inheritance in the fund and drew from it as he needed. He spent generously on the girls he dated and on freewheeling nights with friends at the bars and restaurants around his school. Jennifer could not touch her share until she turned twenty-one.

The Avery offspring were accustomed to rank and privilege, but they were also compelled to strive for excellence. They were neither spoiled nor indulged. William, a medical doctor, worked in a community hospital in the poorest part of town, to get a taste of the real world before going into private practice in Boston. At age six, Philip boldly announced his intention to become an engineer. He earned architectural and civil engineering degrees from New York City's Columbia University sixteen years later. To his father's disappointment, Philip accepted a direct commission in the navy right out of college. Jennifer, the youngest Avery, was seventeen, finishing high school, and already slated to attend her mother's alma mater. All three had inherited their good looks from their mother and their drive and intelligence from their father, although not in equal proportions.

"Is it true the women there wear no clothes?" Jennifer asked. She had visions of dark-skinned natives, like the ones in *National Geographic*, bedecked with colorful feathers, bleached animal bones, and beads that did little to qualify as clothing. "Naked natives! That would be so exciting," she gushed. At that, Lydia swooned, nearly toppling the teacup and saucer in her hand.

"No," Philip said with a laugh, "it's not that primitive. I understand there's electricity as well as indoor plumbing and telephones, although those might be limited to the navy station. The people dress as we do. I've seen a few photos; they're dark-skinned but don't look like Negroes."

Philip's father was still fuming. "With Hitler causing havoc in Europe and the Japanese attacking China, and rattling their sabers at us, the navy department wants to deliver my son to some godforsaken little speck on Hirohito's doorstep? I won't stand for it," Preston said. For all his blustering,

Preston believed the United States would eventually go to war, either willingly or unwillingly. With his son in the navy, the prospect of war and Philip's inevitable involvement in it gave him cause for concern. Lydia feared for Philip also, but as long as Preston didn't appear worried, she could control her fears.

Philip avoided telling his father that the Japanese maintained a sizeable military base on Guam's sister island, Saipan, less than a hundred and fifty miles to the north. By League of Nations mandate after World War I, Saipan, the rest of the Mariana Islands, as well as several other island groups in Micronesia, formerly German possessions, were given up to Japan, which established thriving colonies. The Philippines and Guam were the only American footholds in the western Pacific. And Guam was hemmed in on three sides by the Japanese.

Philip didn't necessarily want his father to intervene on his behalf, to call upon his many powerful political connections. But he knew better than to thwart his father once his mind was set. Neither did he want his career jeopardized. He would have preferred fighting alongside the Allies in Europe than banishment to oblivion in the Pacific. If his father could do something either way, Philip wouldn't object.

Philip rose from his chair, excused himself, and went upstairs to shower and dress for an evening out. Jennifer followed behind him, hoping she could spend more time with him before he went overseas. She would soon be graduating from high school and heading off to college in Massachusetts. She didn't know how long it would be before she saw her brother again.

Jennifer was nagged by a strange foreboding about her brother's assignment and had tried to sound enthusiastic about it. She shared her father's concerns about Philip's choice of a military career in the face of geopolitical instability, but there was something more than the possibility of war that fed her dread; she couldn't name it or attribute it to anything specific. She waited until Philip had come out of his bath and was dressed before she knocked on his door.

"Are you going out tonight?" she asked as she watched him tying a Windsor knot. He obviously was, and Jennifer's hopes were dashed.

"Yes, little sister, I have a date," Philip said as he pulled on his suit jacket.

"How can you already have a date? You've only been home one day," she asked but wasn't surprised. Philip's Little Black Book listed at least a dozen girls who would jump at the chance to go out with him. He was, and probably would always be, a ladies' man, but not an ungentlemanly one. He truly loved women, but on his terms and at his convenience. The women he dated knew that he was not one to be tied down and that they had his attention only temporarily. He was honest about playing the field and never gave any female the impression that he was theirs alone. If they couldn't accept his conditions, he would wish them well and move on. He was a firm believer in the great numbers of fish in the sea.

"Who are you seeing?" Jennifer pressed.

"Libby Morton."

"Oh," she said and scrunched her nose. Of all Philip's girlfriends, Libby was the one Jennifer disliked most. Libby was beautiful but haughty. Jennifer's distaste for the woman came about two years earlier when Philip invited Jennifer to go Christmas shopping with them. Libby dared not protest Jennifer's presence but quietly tried to dissuade her from joining them. Jennifer tried to beg off at the last minute, as Libby had suggested, but Philip wouldn't let her. He had promised to help Jennifer pay for her gift for their mother and he wanted to see it beforehand. Throughout that afternoon, Libby made several snide comments to Jennifer, carefully couching her put-downs in words and phrases that a man wouldn't catch. "That color is a bit too bright for you, dear," Libby said about Jennifer's lipstick. "I think a more subdued pink would enhance your lovely face." Jennifer wasn't wearing lipstick.

Philip was oblivious to the cutting remarks that Libby, the older woman, was inflicting on the fifteen-year-old Jennifer. It was obvious to Jennifer that Libby resented having to share her brief time with Philip. While Libby fawned and cooed all over Philip, she gave Jennifer dagger looks. Jennifer retaliated by clinging to Philip's arm and monopolizing the conversation, deliberately annoying Libby. She was glad her brother rotated his girlfriends; Libby would not get another call from him until spring.

"You know she's a phony, don't you?" Jennifer said.

"I know, but she's easy," he said with a sly smile as he tweaked her nose.

"You are such a cad!"

"I love you too, Jenny," he called as he raced down the stairs and out the door.

Jennifer knew she would not be seeing him again for a long time when he went overseas and felt compelled to stay near him. She couldn't shake the strange foreboding she felt. She couldn't and wouldn't have voiced it to Philip for fear of jinxing him. Philip sensed his sister's anxiety but didn't ask her about it. He came home early that night and spent the rest of his leave either at home or out on the town with Jennifer. He even brought Jennifer with him on the long drive to Boston to visit William and his family.

Upon Philip's departure, a few days later, his parents soberly bade him farewell at the train station. In a rare show of affection, Preston gave him a bear hug. Lydia kissed both his cheeks and his forehead, as she did when her children were little. Jennifer hugged Philip tightly but said nothing. She feared acknowledging her misgivings would somehow bring them to reality.

Unlike the trip from the navy's officer training center in Rhode Island to Albany, which was filled with anticipation and excitement, the coast-to-coast train trip from New York to California was exhausting and boring. Philip had been eager to see his parents and brother and sister again, and to get his fill of home. With all that done, he now waited for the train to reach its destination. He had a few drinks at the bar in the club car, read every newspaper and magazine in the lounge, and slept late. He didn't smoke, so the smoking car didn't interest him, although he would have liked to play a hand or two of poker. He didn't know that the trip to Guam by ship would be even worse; it was grueling.

Chapter 17

Philip's ship, the USS *Henderson*, took several days to get to Honolulu, Hawaii, a few more to Wake Island (which looked to be no more than a large sandbar), and an eternity to get to Guam. Philip didn't think the trip would ever end. He was seasick the first few days out and threw up almost everything he ate. He was miserable for several days. Every unpleasant smell made his stomach heave. Sailing a large navy transport that reeked of oil and coal and sweaty sailors was not at all like yacht sailing on Long Island Sound. Philip was essentially a landlubber. He spent a good part of each day at the rails, watching flying fish skittering across the waves and schools of dolphins racing in the ship's wake. Once he even saw a large sea turtle rise almost to the surface then disappear into the deep. The only other distraction came when the ship crossed the international date line and time jumped one day ahead. There was a small celebration on board—not as elaborate as crossing the line at the equator (Guam lies at thirteen degrees north of it), but a commemoration nonetheless, and first-timers like Philip were initiated into a particular fraternity of sailors.

The *Henderson* pulled into Apra Harbor in mid-August 1939. Philip stood on the deck, scanning the island. It was a true tropical paradise, a mound of emerald green rising out of a royal blue sea. As the ship drew closer, he could see small buildings hugging the shore at two places around the harbor, one of the largest and deepest in the western Pacific. Behind the villages rose hills that were thickly carpeted in vegetation in various shades of green—from dark, almost black, to emerald and pale yellow-green. With a stiff cool breeze whipping at him in the launch to shore, Philip didn't feel the heat and humidity until he stood on the pier in Piti, one of the villages he spied from the ship. He was dressed in his travel uniform and standing in the warm sunshine. A seaman with a vehicle was there to drive him the four miles to Agaña, the island's capital.

The drive was picturesque and interesting. Because a ship had arrived in port, the roadsides were dotted with makeshift stalls from which brown-skinned people were hawking strange fruits, vegetables, foodstuff, and souvenirs—ashtrays, bowls, and other knickknacks made from coconuts and seashells—and purses, cigarette cases, decorative mats, and bric-a-brac made with tiny snail shells.

On Philip's left, behind the peddlers, was the ocean. It was crystal clear and turquoise in the shallow reef flats and deep blue beyond the fringing reef, which lay several yards away from the shore. Much of the reef was hidden underwater and marked only by pure white ribbons of sea foam. The parts that were visible jutted just above the surface as rocky outcroppings. There were a few fishermen in the water; some were standing in the shallows with their throw nets at the ready. Two or three others were standing waist deep at the edge of the reef. On Philip's right, the jungle blanketed a series of hills stacked one upon another. About halfway between Piti and Agaña, they passed the village of Asan, a cluster of thatch-roofed A-frame houses at the base of the hills. There were fewer and fewer houses as they passed the village, but among the trees and thick vegetation here and there, Philip spotted little houses and some ramshackle huts. As they drew closer to town, the number of both thatch-roofed and tile-roofed houses grew more numerous.

In Agaña, the houses were packed tightly together in irregularly shaped blocks which were separated by narrow lanes of crushed coral. The widest, Hernan Cortez Avenue, was the main street of the town. The crowded blocks soon gave way to a wide open space lined with royal palms. Situated in the center of the open space was a large gazebo.

"That's the Plaza de España," the driver announced before turning right onto a wide boulevard lined with more royal palms. The boulevard ended in front of a long, two-story building. "And this is your stop, sir," he added. "This is Government House. It's the headquarters of the navy government. The locals still call it the Governor's Palace, a throwback to the old Spanish days, I guess. The governor and his family live on the floor above. The bottom is where you'll be working."

Philip climbed out of the vehicle while the sailor unloaded his garment bag, suitcase, and valise and delivered them to the reception foyer. The men then saluted each other and the sailor drove off.

Philip stood outside the palace, studying his surroundings. A large church, the Dulce Nombre de Maria Cathedral, was adjacent to the plaza on his left. The marine barracks and several smaller buildings were on his right. Behind him, past the narrow streets and crowded houses, lay the beach and the channel dredged by the navy in the shallow bay for the coal barges that fueled the electric power plant. Its towering black smokestack was the tallest, most recognizable structure in town. The navy government compound stretched out in front of him from the church on his left to beyond the barracks on his right. The Tutujan Ridge and San Ramon Hill rose up behind it. A few people were strolling in the plaza and lounging on park benches. Others, who appeared to be native government employees, were entering and leaving the first-floor offices of the Governor's Palace and moving purposefully about in the compound. No one seemed to be in any hurry. Indeed, Guam was a sleepy little place basking under a hot sun. Within minutes, Philip was sweating even more profusely than earlier at the docks. He hurried into the Governor's Palace, which was only a little cooler.

After reporting to the governor and delivering his orders, Philip was introduced to the rest of the navy contingent assigned to the Governor's Palace, as well as to the Chamorro employees who worked there. The latter were short by his standards (he stood over six feet) and were brown-skinned with polite manners, pleasant demeanors, wide smiles, and white teeth. They reminded him of zoo monkeys. In the engineering division, Philip would be working with two other navy civil engineers, Lieutenant Commander William Pitt and Lieutenant Harvey Kaplan, and three Chamorros, Tino Camacho, Francisco Taisipic, and eighteen-year-old Jesus Rojas, the office messenger. Within weeks of working together, the men became friends.

Philip spent his first week in the bachelor officers' quarters, the BOQ, but didn't like having to share space with others, even at one occupant to each small room. The bed too was disappointing but not surprisingly. It was narrow and uncomfortable, like a dorm-room bed, with a squeaky spring frame and a thin mattress. It was too short to accommodate his height. Even worse, the ensign who occupied the next room snored so loudly that Philip found it impossible to sleep. He hadn't heard from his father since leaving California and wondered whether or not his effort to redeem him from this career-damaging assignment bore fruit. If so, Philip wanted to be ready to ship out at a moment's notice, but living out of his suitcase and valise was as disruptive as living in the barracks next to a chronic snorer. The heat and humidity truly bothered him, especially at night. If he opened the window screen to let in the cooler night air, he was plagued by mosquitoes. He put up a mosquito net around his bed, but it blocked air movement and was as stifling as leaving the window screen closed.

The heat, humidity, mosquitoes, and short length of his bed, combined with the loud snoring of his neighbor, robbed him of sound sleep. Exhausted after only his second week on the island, Philip thought about writing to his father and begging him to do something—anything—to get him off Guam. In thinking about it, he realized he was letting minor irritations dictate drastic measures. He chuckled at what his father's reaction would have been to such a letter and gave up the idea. He casually asked the snorer how long he had been on Guam and learned that he had arrived only a month before. At that, Philip became determined to find quarters in town. He hoped he could find a small apartment or even a house, some place near the beach, which was only a few hundred yards in front of the plaza. Until then, he had to find a solution to his misery. He bought an electric fan at the navy store and slept with it running all night. The whirling blades, humming motor, and oscillations cooled his body, muffled the snoring, and lulled him to sleep.

Except for the heat and humidity, Philip found no other reason to resent being assigned to the island—the people seemed nice enough, but he still worried that the assignment would negatively affect his advancement up the ranks. He enjoyed the work and got along well with the men he worked with, both his superior officers and his Chamorro subordinates. Lieutenant Commander Pitt and Lieutenant Kaplan were upstanding men who didn't seem concerned about any danger to their careers. The discomforts aside, Philip decided the island wasn't a bad place. If he had to stay for his entire two-year assignment, he would make the best of it. Two years in the tropics didn't seem like banishment. Perhaps the people who thought of Guam as a backwater dumping ground had never been to it, Philip decided. He was eager to explore the island, to go sightseeing, and enjoy the beaches—even do some deep-sea fishing. He also wanted to check out the nightlife and what the island had to offer in the way of available women. The local women he saw on the drive into town were not appealing at all. Of course, the only ones he saw were girls under ten years of age and gray-haired old ladies puffing on hand-rolled stogies.

A couple of weeks after signing on board, while shooting the breeze with other navy men, Philip learned that Ensign Parker Reed was looking for someone to share the cost of quarters he was renting outside the compound. Reed was from North Carolina. He was an accountant who worked in the comptroller's office. He arrived on Guam six months ahead of Philip. Reed didn't like the BOQ either and was fortunate to find a room for rent in a house near the compound. Parker's face lit up when Philip inquired about the space. He said he would be more than happy to introduce him to his landlord, Tino Camacho, who worked in the civil engineering division—the same Tino Camacho who worked with Philip.

Parker was greatly relieved when Philip expressed interest in living outside the government compound. Tino was glad too; he felt badly for the young ensign, the lowest paid of the officer ranks. Parker was a good tenant. He was neat, clean, quiet, and always on time with the rent. He took his meals in the compound or in town, and sometimes with Tino and Vivian. He also spent many evenings at the officers' club, but never came home inebriated or with a "guest" of dubious repute. He was friendly and good-natured, and Tino and Vivian liked him very much.

In the fourteen years since Tino began renting his upper-floor apartment, most of his tenants had been navy families, married couples, or small groups of nurses or junior officers who shared the rent. The rental income, along with their salaries, provided Tino and his daughter with a comfortable living. When Parker moved in, a lieutenant and his wife and two nurses were sharing the upstairs. The couple occupied the large bedroom, the nurses the smaller ones. Since the nurses were leaving the island soon, they agreed to double up into one bedroom so that Parker could take the third. They then split the rent three ways, with Parker paying one-third. The nurses moved out in April 1939. The married couple followed in June. Parker was then faced with the choice of moving out or paying the fifty dollars a month by himself. Tino would have preferred to rent to his usual clientele, but when the other tenants moved on, Parker chose to shoulder the rent alone. For Parker's sake, Tino hoped other renters would come along to share the burden.

That night, Tino told Vivian that Parker would be bringing home the new man in the engineering division. Tino had been working with Philip since he arrived on Guam, and he seemed like a nice fellow.

"He found out today that Parker was our tenant and is interested in sharing the apartment," Tino said. "Parker will be bringing him here tomorrow after work. I'm going to the lancho, so you'll have to handle it, all right?" Vivian nodded. She would show the house and conduct the transaction if the prospective tenant decided to take the space. She had done it before.

As he did almost every day, either in the morning before sunrise or in the afternoon after work, Tino went to his lancho to check on his garden, feed his chickens, and collect their eggs. If needed, he weeded and watered his garden, and harvested any vegetables or fruits that were ready for picking. Long before the end of Spanish rule and well after the start of American rule, Chamorros, who owned, rented, or were permitted by property owners to use a plot of land, kept a lancho, a place to get away from the rules and regimentation of living in town, to return to nature, to grow food to supplement their larders, or to make extra income. Depending on the owner's means, a lancho could be large and elaborate—an actual farm with a house, fields, and livestock—or humble, with a garden, some pens or coops, and a coarse structure in which to store farming supplies and tools. Tino's lancho was located in Tutujan, a farming area east of Agaña and further inland behind the brow of San Ramon Hill.

Chapter 18

Since her father was going to the lancho and wouldn't get home until sundown, Vivian left school early and rushed home to straighten up the apartment before Parker arrived with the new lieutenant. Parker was not a messy tenant, but since he confined himself mainly to his bedroom, the rest of the house would need dusting and the vacant rooms made ready. Vivian shared her father's concern for Parker. He was a nice person and the only American she knew to any degree. She hoped the lieutenant would agree to the rental and relieve Parker of some of the burden. Vivian and Tino knew that the fifty dollars a month he paid for July and August wasn't easy for the ensign. If the new man agreed to share the house beginning on the first of September, Parker would only have to pay twenty-five. If the men could find another renter, Parker's share would shrink even more.

As Parker and Philip left the government compound, Parker described the house, how spacious it was, and how there was room for additional tenants. He hoped they would find another bachelor or another couple to share the apartment, but Philip nixed that idea right away. He looked forward to the privacy of his own quarters, and a large apartment with only one incumbent resident was as good as he could expect. Cost for him was not an issue. If and when Ensign Reed moved on, Philip was happy to pay to live alone. As they crossed the street, Parker pointed out the house with a row of red and white bougainvillea bushes in front. The bougainvillea was in full bloom and ablaze with color.

"Well, there it is, Lieutenant Avery. There's where I live," Parker said proudly, almost as if the house belonged to him. "You'll like Tino's daughter, Vivian. She's a sweet kid."

"How old is she?" Philip asked. He was curious also about Parker's obvious familiarity with his landlords. Philip had only known Tino for a few days and found him to be likable, and while Parker knew him longer, his relationship with Tino and his daughter seemed friendlier than a mere landlord-tenant association.

"I don't know. Eighteen or nineteen, I think. She's a teacher."

Too young, Philip thought.

Vivian dusted the floors and furniture, opened the windows, and made the beds in the vacant rooms. She completed the tasks before the navy men came up the front steps and entered the house. She emerged from the large bedroom as Parker announced their presence.

"Hi, Miss Vivian," Parker said. "I'd like you to meet Lieutenant Philip Avery. He's the new guy in your dad's office. He may be moving in with us."

Standing beside Parker was a tall, extraordinarily handsome man with his bill cap pinched under his left arm. Vivian's heart skipped a beat. She had never met anyone so tall and so good-looking. Lieutenant Avery stood six feet, three inches and was athletically built. The black-and-gold shoulder boards of his crisp, white uniform accentuated his square shoulders. He had light, honey-brown hair and piercing gray-blue eyes. His nose and lips were finely sculpted, and his complexion was evenly suntanned but still light. He was older than she was, she guessed maybe by four or five years. Vivian wondered why her father didn't tell her that the new man in his office was so tall and handsome. He had told her that the engineering division was receiving another officer, a junior lieutenant, and he even mentioned that the new man had arrived and had started working, but he never told her his name or said anything else about him. Lieutenant Avery was reserved and was as poised and as self-assured as one would expect of a navy officer, but his manner and demeanor seemed inborn, not simply the result of officer training. He also seemed a bit snobbish.

Ensign Reed was the only naval officer Vivian knew. He could be equally as formal and impressive, but Vivian and her father knew that Parker could relax and be as down-to-earth as ordinary people and that he had a fun-loving side. Lieutenant Avery didn't seem like someone who would howl with unbridled laughter at a funny joke as Parker would and always did. *Maybe that's why Papa said so little about him,* she decided.

Lieutenant Avery nodded politely and held out his hand.

"How do you do, Miss Camacho?" he said with a slight smile. He spoke with unnerving formality, the same detached way the bishop did as he greeted parishioners after Mass on Sundays—not cold and unfriendly, but not warm and welcoming either. Just distant. Vivian was intimidated. Nevertheless, she put on her brightest smile and reached out to take the lieutenant's offered hand.

"I'm glad to meet you, Mr. Avery. Please call me Vivian," she said cheerfully.

Vivian's smile took his breath away. The girl was not a great beauty, but her dark eyes and her warm smile were the most beautiful he had ever seen. As they clasped hands, something strangely warm and intimate crossed between them. Neither expected such a reaction, and neither wanted to let go. They did not acknowledge it outwardly, but both were perplexed. Vivian was the first to pull her hand away. She did so slowly.

Without inspecting the house or the vacant bedrooms, Philip immediately agreed to the rental. He was eager to vacate the BOQ and was curious about the girl with the intriguing smile. As they ironed out the details, they wondered about their reaction to each other. Vivian decided hers was because Lieutenant Avery looked like a movie star and behaved like Prince Charming, and she was simply awestruck. Philip was bewildered. Vivian's smile and sparkling dark eyes disarmed him. It was an entirely new sensation. He was usually the disarming one.

Philip had always been drawn to tall, sophisticated blue-eyed blondes, and they to him. Vivian was the polar opposite; she was dark-haired and dark-eyed and stood only about five feet three or four, shorter than the women he dated back home. Her hair was pulled back and tied loosely at the nape of her neck. She had a nice nose and a tan complexion and was young—eighteen or nineteen as Parker had guessed, but she was dressed too starkly for her age. Her unpretentious appearance seemed to mask a more mysterious and complex nature. He thought about the Civil War stories he had read regarding Southern plantation owners who took slave girls as lovers. He could appreciate the attraction; Vivian was exotic, like a rare orchid to be coveted but never truly possessed. Philip had never met a female who struck him so profoundly.

That night, he and Parker ate supper at the mess then went up to the officers' club, which was on San Ramon Hill, overlooking the town. Philip was eager to be distracted by something other than Vivian's smile. He hoped a couple of drinks and some music and dancing would provide it. Predictably, the club was a humdrum military joint, one restricted to officers, but a boring watering hole nonetheless. It was dim and gloomy and decorated with frayed old tinsel garlands. It reeked of ashtrays and stale cigarette smoke. Philip was curious about what sort of people, especially women, frequented the club but was unimpressed. The few women present were either with their husbands or were not great beauties. Nevertheless, he and Parker had no trouble finding dance partners. Later, as they lingered over a couple of beers, Philip's mind wandered back to Vivian. He couldn't stop thinking about her.

"So did Lieutenant Avery take the room?" Tino asked as he handed Vivian two dozen eggs and some vegetables from the lancho.

"Yes, Papa, he did," she answered. "You didn't tell me he was so tall."

"Why? Does it bother you?"

"No," she said with a slight smile. "He's handsome too."

"If you say so," Tino said, masking his reaction to her statement. Vivian had never before offered such an observation about any man or boy. Her smile, though tempered, told him that his daughter was intrigued. "He went to a good school, but he still has to prove himself."

Shortly after renting the apartment, Philip took leave to get settled. The large bedroom was his. Parker remained in his bedroom closer to the front door. He also kept the smaller of the two bathrooms, leaving the larger one with the bathtub to Philip. They used the third bedroom as storage. Unbeknownst to their landlords, the men had negotiated beforehand over how to split the monthly rent. Since he took the large bedroom and insisted they turn down any inquiries or offers to share the house, Philip paid two-thirds of the cost.

Philip liked the big bedroom. It had a large window facing the government compound, and a nice breeze always seemed to come through it despite the screen. A small closet and a mirrored wardrobe with a bank of small drawers stood in one corner. The bed, as with all others since he left home, was too short for his frame, but it was a standard double bed, one that was wider than a single. Still, his feet stuck out beyond the mattress, so he slept on it diagonally. The bedding came with blankets, which weren't necessary. Because of the heat, he couldn't stand to be swathed in a blanket or even a sheet and had come to rely on his trusty electric fan to keep him cool at night. He had abandoned pajamas while in the officers' quarters and slept only in his skivvies. On sweltering nights, he slept in the nude after a tepid shower.

Philip ignored his hunger until he finished unpacking and arranging his belongings. Not surprisingly, the refrigerator and the cupboards in the kitchen were empty. As he rummaged through the kitchen, hoping to find something edible, he heard someone moving about downstairs. Not yet knowing the schedules of everyone in the household, he wasn't sure who had entered. Concerned, he opened the kitchen door to the downstairs apartment and called out a hello. Vivian moved into view and looked up the staircase at him and smiled.

"Oh, hello, Mr. Avery, I didn't know you were upstairs," she said brightly.

Philip could have grabbed a bite at the canteen in the compound or at a restaurant in town, but he was delighted with the opportunity to get to know the girl who beguiled him.

"May I come down there?" he asked. Not waiting for an answer, he clattered quickly down the stairs and stood in her kitchen, which was much smaller than the one upstairs.

"I haven't had lunch, and there's nothing upstairs. Might I trouble you for a couple of slices of bread and some peanut butter and jelly if you have any?" He didn't like peanut butter, but it was the only thing he could think of that didn't need much preparation.

"It's no trouble, Mr. Avery. Would you care to join me in some leftovers?" she said, trying not to look directly at him. The color of his eyes was too strange and startling.

"I certainly would. Thank you," he said with a wide smile. The invitation to sit with her was more than he expected.

The girl was again dressed in another ordinary cotton dress. It had a Peter Pan collar and was buttoned down the front, with a pair of buttons nipping the waist. It was the kind of plain, starched-and-ironed work dress that cleaning ladies wore. She wore no makeup or adornments except for a pair of small gold earrings. She was like a blank canvas. Philip wondered what she would look like in something more attractive, more colorful, and stylish—like a cherry-red tailored wool suit with a smart chapeau to match and white kidskin gloves. And pearls. Philip liked the picture in his mind; the girl would have been stunning.

Vivian opened and looked inside the new electric refrigerator. Tino had purchased it a couple of months earlier. Vivian had complained regularly about the old ice box, which was inefficient, messy, and old-fashioned. She wanted a modern one like the one upstairs, which had a freezer compartment with trays to make ice cubes and a light that came on when the door was opened. Tino didn't plan to replace the old one until he saw how the ice delivery man stared at Vivian. He happened to be at home at the time and didn't like the look on the man's face. Vivian clapped happily and kissed her father when the new refrigerator was delivered, glad that she no longer had to put up with the ice man's lewd looks.

She studied the leftovers in the refrigerator and decided against serving them. Lieutenant Avery was still new to the island and unacquainted with local cooking. She had heard that Americans didn't like fish unless it came in a can or was served without its head, tail, and entrails. Her cold leftover, pan-fried mackerel with all but its scales intact might have scared him off.

"I'm sorry, Mr. Avery, the leftovers won't do. How 'bout ham and cheese sandwiches?"

Philip nodded and smiled, trying to think of something to say to engage her in small talk, but he was at a loss. He knew how to charm the pants off giddy coeds but had no idea how to dazzle an exotic orchid. He watched how Vivian waltzed back and forth between the refrigerator and the counter, between the sink and the cupboard. She moved fluidly, gracefully, and was clearly at home in the kitchen. Philip wondered if she had the cooking skills to match. His college buddies said girls who knew how to cook were the kind to marry. He surprised himself at the thought; why would he wonder such a thing? He had grown up with Mrs. Mueller, his family's full-time cook. At college, he ate whenever and wherever it was convenient, never giving much thought to who prepared his food. He never knew or cared if his dates knew how to cook. It was not the feminine skill that interested him. He was never looking to get married either. But watching and wondering about Vivian was strangely entertaining.

Vivian made three ham-and-cheese sandwiches and a pitcher of lemonade. She kept one sandwich for herself and put two on a plate for him. The very tall Lieutenant Avery didn't look like a man who would be satisfied with only one thin sandwich. As she handed him the plate, their eyes locked. Philip was transfixed; he had never looked into eyes so dark and mysterious yet so warm and welcoming. Vivian broke the gaze and looked away; the lieutenant's eyes were too strange and otherworldly.

"You go ahead, Mr. Avery, I have to get supper going," she said. Philip sat himself at the small dining table in Vivian's kitchen. She stood by the sink and ate her sandwich quickly. She wanted to sit with him, but being alone with him in the house would have already ignited gossip in the neighborhood. Philip sensed her discomfort and decided discretion was in order.

While she busied herself with supper preparations, at a respectable distance away from him, Vivian stole furtive glances at Philip. She marveled at how attractive he was, even without his handsome uniform. He was still remarkable, even in his unremarkable civilian clothes—tan pants and a cotton plaid shirt. Everything about him seemed perfect. His eyes, with their unusual color, were the same size, not one slightly smaller or squinty. His eyebrows were slightly arched and even on both sides. His ears were not too big or too small or too pink; they were not flat against his head or sticking out too far. The collar of his shirt fitted nicely around his neck, which was not too skinny or too thick. His shoulders, even as he ate his sandwich, were still square. His hands were beautiful but masculine. He had long, tapered fingers with short, clean fingernails.

When Philip finished the sandwiches, he thanked her politely and headed back upstairs. Unlike his hurried descent, he stood straight-backed as he climbed the stairs, aware of her watchful eyes. Vivian studied him from behind. His back was wide at the shoulders and narrow at the waist. His backside looked nice also.

God sure was feeling good when he made that man, she said to herself and giggled out loud as she washed the lieutenant's plate. Vivian wondered why God created only a few people like Mr. Avery, so beautiful and perfect, yet made everyone else plain and imperfect and some even ugly. She hated how one of her ears seemed higher than the other and how her hair was thicker on the left than on the right, and why did one shoe always fit better than the other? She accepted that she was not a beautiful girl, never believing that she was a beauty in her own right. Her standard for beauty was among the half-American girls she went to school with, the girls of Chamorro mothers and American fathers. They were light-skinned and had beautiful faces; some had pale brown or hazel eyes and reddish, almost blonde hair. Their fathers owned many of the most successful businesses on the island, and their families were the upper crust of island society. *Lieutenant Avery must be from the upper crust of his hometown,* she concluded.

Philip had felt Vivian's eyes on him as he ate. He never liked being watched or stared at, although it happened all the time. It made him feel that something about him was amiss. It never occurred to him that he was being admired. Vivian's scrutiny was different; it didn't make him feel self-conscious and uncomfortable. Instead, it pleased him and made him feel good—like a proud little boy who had done well and delighted his mother or his teacher. The orchid he was curious about seemed equally curious about him.

Philip thought it would have been fun to explore their mutual curiosity. Something about the girl fascinated him; he wasn't sure whether it was because she was so different from his usual taste in females or because she was young and wore her innocence and inexperience without shame or guile. Yet there was an air of maturity and seriousness about her. She wasn't flirtatious or giddy. She didn't flirt with him, as many other girls did, or try to impress him. She just did, and did so genuinely. She also was entirely off-limits to him. Vivian was not someone he could trifle with at his leisure and leave behind when his curiosity was satisfied. She lived close at hand, downstairs with her father, his landlord, a man he worked with every day. As difficult as it would be for him, Philip would have to appreciate her from a safe distance.

Chapter 19

The navy tenants and the Chamorro property owners usually kept to themselves—the officers upstairs and father and daughter downstairs, although Parker never turned down an invitation to have supper with them. He would sometimes linger downstairs with Vivian, talking about a book or magazine article he was reading. Philip lived in the same house for three months but rarely crossed paths with Vivian, although he and Tino saw each other at work every day. The door in the upstairs kitchen, the only direct connection between the apartments, was always closed but not locked. Vivian needed the access to collect the bedding for the wash. She usually waited until after the tenants left in the morning. If her father was going to the lancho in the morning, he left before sunrise so that he would get back in time for work. Parker and the lieutenant left together before eight o'clock, exiting down the front stairs and walking across the street to the Governor's Palace. Parker then split off to his office in another part of the compound. Vivian was the last to leave.

When they were not on duty, the officers, especially Philip, spent little time at the house. They socialized with their navy friends and attended formal and official government functions and dinner parties as required. They sometimes landed dates with nurses from the hospital or the dispensary in Sumay and went on picnics or took in a movie. They went to dances at the officers' club or simply lingered there and stayed out late, long after Vivian and Tino retired for the night. They also joined other servicemen and women to explore the island, go to a beach, waterski, golf, or play baseball.

Philip was the outdoorsman and was physically active. He never passed up an opportunity to play ball, go hiking or swimming or, much to his delight, go deep-sea fishing. On such outings, he and his companions would pool their money to buy drinks and supplies, as well as to pay for the boat owner's fuel. They would be gone for two or three days, fishing all day, camping out at night on a secluded beach at Urunao, Hila'an, or Tomhom on the island's northwestern coast, fire-roasting their catch, and sleeping under the stars then motoring back to the coal barge channel in Agaña. Until his first visit to Tino's lancho, Philip was rarely at the house. Parker went fishing with him only once in a while, preferring his books instead.

Parker was a bookworm. In addition to borrowing a book or two from the library every week, he ordered the latest paperbacks by mail every other month. He also subscribed to several magazines. He read his books and magazines at lunch or after his workday and in the evenings at home or at the officers' club. He could often be found on a park bench reading in the shade of the trees in the compound or the plaza. Vivian loved to read too, but not as avidly as Parker. She would wait until after he had finished reading before asking to borrow a book or magazine. Parker never turned her down and always let her keep the magazines to use in her classroom.

Like their tenants, Tino and Vivian similarly pursued their own agenda. On weekends, when they didn't have a wedding, christening, or fiesta to attend, they would take the bus to Sumay and spend the day making repairs or doing yard work at Tino's mother's house, which was also rented out, usually to marine officers. The imposing U.S. Marine Barracks, which was much larger than the barracks in Agaña, was located on a rise above the village and was the marines' headquarters on Guam.

At least once a month, they would go to the cemetery in Anigua, on the outskirts of Agaña, to clean Sylvia's headstone and decorate her grave with fresh flowers. Tino had planted two small gardenia bushes on either side of Sylvia's headstone. They grew large and scraggly over the years and needed to be trimmed back periodically. The cemetery visit was a must on November first, All Saints' Day, to prepare for All Souls' Day the following day, when hundreds would gather for Mass at the cemetery. Tino and Vivian helped Sylvia's uncle and aunts tidy the graves of their parents, Tan Pilar and Tun Sylvino. By the time Vivian was ten, Ana was gone too, and Elena was still missing. Juan, Esther, Jaime, and their respective families split their time among four different village cemeteries where their spouses' families were buried. Jamie and his family always brought fresh flowers to place on all four graves, as well as on the graves of his wife's family in Agat. After the All Souls' Day Mass, almost everyone lingered in the cemetery to enjoy the scent of flowers filling the air and the glow of hundreds of candles flickering in the gloom as the sun set behind the hills. The flowers and candlelight made the cemetery a beautiful place, not a place to fear.

More often than not, Tino and his daughter spent their free days at the lancho, planting or harvesting vegetables and fruits, dispatching a chicken or two, and collecting the eggs to bring back home for breakfast and supper. Initially, they prepared food only for themselves, and in the old Spanish style: they ate heartily at breakfast and lunch, had a *merienda* of tea and sweets late in the afternoon, and had a light supper of some soup.

Philip and Parker usually took their meals at the officers' mess, the officers' club, or at a restaurant downtown. Both men were accustomed to eating cafeteria style and neither of them cooked so the stove upstairs was never used. Their refrigerator usually contained some bottles of beer or Coca-Cola, a loaf of store-bought bread, and a jar of jam. There also might be a jar of peanut butter and a tin of cookies or potato chips alongside a set of dishes gathering dust in their cupboard. Parker was never averse to Tino's invitation to dine with them, but Philip was rarely at home on such occasions.

Although meals were not part of the rental agreement, Tino and Vivian often came home from neighborhood celebrations—birthday and baptismal parties, weddings, and fiestas—with more food than they could possibly eat. To avoid embarrassment, Chamorros usually prepare more food for a celebration than is necessary. It is also customary for family members and friends to offer hosts something for the table. Fishermen might send fresh seafood; hunters, a side of venison, pigeons, or land or coconut crabs. Others might send special desserts or produce and fruits from their gardens and lanchos. At the end of celebrations, guests are expected and encouraged to take food home to enjoy later. On such occasions, Tino often insisted the officers join them to eat. Sharing the bounty of food paved the way for landlords and tenants to come together more often. Tino treated all his previous tenants with the same generosity and invitation; most politely turned him down, choosing not to mix with the locals. Parker, and eventually Philip, didn't seem to be bothered by mixing, especially since neither cooked. Tino would also invite them when they had to work late or during the rainy season when the skies opened up with nonstop torrential rains for days at a time. Slowly, under the navy men's influence, mealtime at the Camacho house transformed into the American "three squares a day."

As the men developed a taste for home-cooked Chamorro food, their eating out became less frequent. If they ate supper at home, it was understood that the only item on the menu was whatever Vivian or Tino prepared. They eventually helped with the groceries, buying staples for the kitchen as needed, or as Vivian requested. It tickled her to watch them eat. Parker ate with gusto and always seemed hungry. Philip was finicky but became less so as his tastes changed.

The men sent their uniforms and regular laundry to the cleaners at the compound or in town, but since neither had limitless wardrobes, they sometimes ran out of clean laundry. Parker had no trouble washing his clothes; his loads were usually small and easy—undershirts, underwear, handkerchiefs, socks, towels, and washcloths. His uniforms, heavier clothing, dress shirts, and anything that needed ironing always went to the laundry and dry cleaners. Philip sent out all of his laundry; he had no idea how to wash clothes. If he ran out of clean socks and underwear, he simply bought new ones. Vivian offered to teach him how to sort his laundry and how to use the washing machine. He welcomed the lessons as legitimate opportunities to be with her and get to know her better. In time, he sent only certain items to the cleaners and sometimes washed his whites himself. But he always seemed to "forget" how to operate the machine. Vivian had to repeat the lessons again and again until it became obvious that he was only pretending. His boyish efforts to be near her tickled her. She didn't mind his forgetfulness, although she never did his laundry for him.

She only washed the men's sheets once a week, following what her father said was her mother's rule: maintain at least three sets of sheets and towels—one set in use, a fresh set in the closet, and one set in the wash, and rotate accordingly. It didn't always work out properly, especially during the rainy season. She washed her unmentionables at night or after the men left for work and hung them to dry in her bedroom, preserving her privacy as best she could.

On Saturdays, if he felt up to it, Tino would bake some cinnamon rolls and at least four loaves of bread. As his "family" expanded, he increased the number of loaves. If the men were at home, the fragrance of baking bread lured them downstairs to wait for the first loaves to emerge from the oven. The third and fourth loaves would be gone a day or two later. Philip decided he liked peanut butter after all but only in a sandwich with sliced sweet bananas and honey. The aroma of fresh brewed coffee in the mornings also brought the men downstairs. Before long, they all ate breakfast together, the navy men in their undershirts to keep from staining their uniform tunics. Parker liked his coffee with cream and sugar, as did Tino and Vivian; Philip took his black. After breakfast, they would linger at the table and talk, the way families do, until it was time to leave and face their respective workdays. Always the last to leave, Vivian would clean up and do the dishes first.

By the middle of 1940, landlords and tenants had become an odd little family: a Chamorro father and daughter and two American naval officers, a Southerner and a Northerner. To Vivian, Parker seemed almost like a big brother and Philip was his best friend, the one on whom she had a crush. Life in the house at the base of San Ramon Hill was odd but cozy and insulated from the world outside. As they grew to know one another, they were unaware that they were also setting aside their respective prejudices. While those racial and cultural prejudices raged outside, inside their home, they were simply four people who liked one another's company. Eventually, the upstairs kitchen door stayed open all the time.

Chapter 20

Vivian enjoyed watching the officers. Comparing their behavior and personalities was entertaining. Parker, she knew, was the typical American from an average working family, a charming Southern gentleman who loved his books and breezed through the courses and training to become a naval officer. He was twenty-two years old and had the unusual and rather fascinating combination of black hair and blue eyes. His great-grandmother was full-blooded Cherokee, which probably explained his indifference to mixing with the locals. He was stocky but not fat and was light on his feet. Philip was like a thoroughbred—the product of quality stock—lean and healthy, beautiful of body and sharp of mind. Parker, the Southerner, was open and friendly. Philip, the Yankee, was staid and aloof, except in rare moments, she soon discovered, when he revealed a less guarded side of himself.

She loved to watch Philip without his knowledge, to study him the same way one studies beautiful things, like formal gardens, fairytale castles, and Gothic cathedrals, things she could only admire in magazine photos. Philip was like a beautiful mansion that she especially admired. It was photographed on the Connecticut coast and featured in *Life* magazine because it was out of place—a Southern-style plantation mansion on a rocky New England coast. It was an imposing building with a columned façade and a second-floor balcony that ran the length of the front. The mansion was painted white and its roof was covered in black slate tiles. It stood gleaming in the sunshine on a rise with its back to the sea. There were sailboats on the water in the background. A wide carpet of manicured lawn, a spectacular bed of roses, and other colorful flowers, and a low wrought iron fence separated the viewer from the mansion. Vivian liked the photo so much that she clipped the page and tacked it to a wall in her bedroom. Philip was like that mansion—a New Yorker with Hollywood looks, attractive to behold, entertaining to study, separate from her reality, and utterly unattainable.

Vivian watched how Philip walked, how he talked, how he carried himself, how he crossed his long legs—always like a man—with his ankle on his knee. His feet were bigger than Parker's. She wondered what size shoes he wore; they were huge. He had to be too tall for the bed upstairs. She wondered how he managed. He was not given to loud laughter—at least she never heard him laugh—and she wondered whether his laugh was as charming as his smile. She loved to watch him from afar, at official government events in the plaza, or the opening of the annual island fair, and during other public occasions. She didn't have to attend many such events but never passed up the opportunity, just to watch Philip. He would be on the grandstand among the other navy officers with his visor cap pulled low over his brow, looking stone-faced, authoritative, and breathtakingly handsome. Those occasions, however, emphasized the great gulf between them—not merely the physical distance of the moment, but the insurmountable racial, social, educational, and even religious distance and differences. Philip, the handsome navy lieutenant who slept upstairs and ate breakfast with her every morning, was among the ruling elite, the handful of Americans who, with the navy governor, were in charge of over twenty thousand native wards. Vivian was just one of the natives, one among the crowd of wards.

From his position on a reviewing stand, Philip could always spot Vivian in the crowd. As the governor, some important visiting guest or elected official droned on about Guam's importance to the navy and to the nation, Philip would keep his eyes on Vivian, watching her every move until she left the plaza. The only time she stayed for an entire event was during school competitions when students from all the schools on the island gathered in the plaza to compete in marching drills, oratorical and performance contests, calisthenics, games, and races. Philip's presence was required only for the opening ceremonies, but he could linger afterward, to watch for a while if he so chose. He got a kick out of watching Vivian cheer on the students from her school. She would dart about, jumping up and down, and running alongside the racers. Her enthusiasm—laughing, whistling loudly, and shouting encouragement—lifted his spirits for the rest of the day.

Vivian noted how Philip seemed to keep people at a distance. She didn't often observe him interacting with other people, but in those that she did, his reserved manner and behavior never deviated. She couldn't decide whether he truly was a snob or wary of people, especially of her, not that he was unfriendly or cold toward her. Maybe he detected her nosiness about him and didn't care for it, she concluded. It was like him to shield himself from her curiosity.

Parker noticed how Vivian studied people, especially Philip and himself, since they were the people closest at hand. He also noted how she paid particular attention to Philip.

"Rich folks are like that," he said, answering a question she didn't ask. He was downstairs waiting to drain the washing machine and wring out his wash. Philip had walked out the side door to go hiking to the waterfall he had heard about in Talofofo in the southern part of the island. Vivian's gaze lingered on the door as Philip closed it behind him. Parker's remark jolted her, and she shot him a quizzical look.

"His family back east has money. Rich people in that part of the country tend to be snooty. He's not a bad guy, it's just his way," Parker added.

Until that moment, Vivian knew only that Philip was from New York. She knew nothing about his family or his circumstances. Parker's comments explained a lot about what she had observed. She had long wondered why the people in movies were always dressed to the nines—men in suits and hats and women in beautiful dresses, hats, and gloves. All the movies seemed to take place in big, bustling cities like New York or San Francisco. Philip's demeanor and formality were like that of the men in the movies. She now knew why paying rent and buying new underwear didn't bother him. He truly was like her fairytale mansion—and probably actually grew up in one like it.

Vivian's heart skipped whenever Philip looked at her or spoke to her directly. His handsome face and his eyes always took her breath away—only for a second, but always. She recalled Dorothea's words about the right man taking her breath away and making her heart skip. Philip had that effect on her, but he couldn't have been the right man. He was a white, wealthy, ranking American. She was a humble, brown Chamorro girl. He was a prince; she was a peasant. Philip's clear gray-blue eyes were like an Arctic crevasse. Although she had never seen a crevasse, she imagined that looking steadily into his eyes would be like falling endlessly into deep ice, never to emerge. Vivian wondered what it was like to see the world through such incredible eyes.

Philip noted how Vivian would not face him directly, how she either looked down or away from him if and when they spoke. Although he went out of his way to avoid her, afraid of the feelings she stirred in him, it bothered him that she wouldn't look him in the eye. He couldn't understand why. Vivian didn't seem to have anything to hide nor was she untruthful. She wasn't bashful or meek. In fact, she was almost too candid. At some appropriate moment, he would ask her to explain. It also bothered him that she addressed him as "Mr. Avery." They had become familiar enough for her to call him by his first name, at least at home. He liked the sound of her voice and wanted to hear her say his name, as if he meant something to her—not with a title, as if the only thing between them was a business arrangement. She was a kind and caring soul with a fiery spirit, and the combination was exhilarating. Despite the restriction he had placed on himself to keep her at arm's length, Philip was drawn to her. He wanted her friendship. He wanted to know all about her—what she thought, how she felt. She was such a different kind of female. When she was with him or near him, he felt different too. She was the first and only girl to make him feel that way.

In the months that followed Philip's entry into her home, Vivian discovered that Lieutenant Avery was not the snob she first thought. He was reserved but always courteous and polite. He addressed her father as "Mr. Camacho," even at work, although the other officers did not. When his associates asked him why he was so formal with the hired help, Philip explained that he and his siblings were required by their parents to address the domestic staff formally, as a measure of respect. The officers were bemused, although they were not unfamiliar with the practice. Tino told Vivian about the discussion, which had taken place within his hearing. In defending his manners, Philip regarded her father as someone worthy of respect. That didn't often happen among American navy men.

Philip's good looks and wonderful eyes captivated Vivian. His formal education and military rank intimidated her but won her admiration. Philip was no ordinary young man; he was an engineer with professional credentials. He was not an average, everyday sailor; he was an officer. His lofty family background and upbringing made her feel inadequate and inferior. She was just a simple island girl, no one special at all. But his deference to her father earned her affection. Liking him soon turned into falling in love with him, although she knew nothing could come of it. Tino was growing fond of Philip as well. He and Parker were feeling more like foster sons than paying tenants.

Tino often sat on a bench in his outside kitchen, a lean-to adjoining the laundry, to enjoy the evening air. He would indulge in a scotch and water and a cigarette before going to bed. Philip would sometimes join him. Tino would offer some of his treasured scotch, and Philip always welcomed it. The scotch was mediocre, a brand that Tino could afford and which he drank sparingly. Philip asked about the outside kitchen and Tino explained that, like lanchos, most families had one. It was a place to clean and fry fish, peel breadfruit, husk and grate coconuts, hang banana bunches to ripen, or undertake any unpleasant tasks.

Tino's outside kitchen featured a raised fire pit, about five feet long, with cords of dried firewood stacked neatly underneath. A wire above the fire pit stretched from one post to another on either side. A couple of soot-covered pots and pans hung from hooks on a rafter behind it. Philip asked about the wire, and Tino explained that it was for drying strips of meat or fish over a low smoky fire. There was a sink and faucet fed by a pipe that had been T-jointed to the water main. Water from the sink drained into a pipe that ran along the ground and into the larger drain pipe in the laundry. Tino did all the connections himself and called it "jungle plumbing." He turned an old door into a work table and built a couple of benches with lengths of two-by-twelve lumber.

Whenever Philip joined Tino outside, they would talk about the projects they were working on, the project managers and construction folks they were dealing with, and even about the differences between them. They shared each other's history. Philip described his family and home and growing up in New York. Tino talked about growing up in Guam, first as a ward of Spain then of the United States, and about losing his brothers and sisters and being the only one of his parents' children to survive. He told about going to school in the Philippines, which interested Philip immensely. They spent many nights talking about going to college to study the same profession and how their courses differed or were exactly the same.

Tino talked a lot about Sylvia, about who she was, and about losing her. Philip could tell that Tino loved his wife and still grieved for her despite the passage of many years. He marveled at how strong and lasting it was, and he wondered whether it was that kind of love or simply convention and habit that kept his parents together. Until that moment, he never thought about their relationship. Philip didn't think he was capable of lasting love. His history with women was clear evidence of it. He believed love affairs were fleeting fancies that eventually fizzled out. When the sparks faded for him, he walked away without regret. His heart had never been broken—bruised, but never broken.

In the telling of Sylvia's mother's story, Tino's resentment toward her American father was evident, not because he was an American or a navy man, but because he was a coward. It was the only conclusion Tino could draw. Sylvia's father never wrote a second letter to Amanda to explain why he couldn't or wouldn't return. The man at least owed Amanda that, and Sylvia, at least his name.

"How could a man profess to love someone, take her virginity, and leave her with only a vague hope for his return? I know we'll never know the whole story, but he didn't seem to care what happened to the girl he claimed to love," Tino grumbled. He allowed himself a second scotch and was feeling its effect.

"Sylvia's mother was only sixteen; she was a good girl until he came along," Tino continued, not expecting answers. "Lieutenant, I've struggled with this for a long time. If not for that man, Sylvia would not have been born, and I would never have met her. Should I be grateful to him? I can't.

I loved my wife, and I would have died in her place if it were possible. If an early death was her legacy from him, then Lord forgive me, I hope he suffered the same fate."

"Maybe he did," Philip said quietly.

Tino grieved for the children Sylvia wanted but could not have. After learning how to live with baby Vivian, he wanted to have more too. Vivian was the only fruit of his marriage. He didn't say it out loud, but he thought to himself that if Vivian ever had a child out of wedlock, he would not reject her or her child, but he would hunt down the father with a vengeance.

Philip was equally pensive. The abandonment of illegitimate children was not uncommon in the States. He suddenly realized that he might have been guilty himself. He had taken girlfriends to bed, but since he had never been named in a paternity suit or threatened with blackmail, he never gave his affairs further thought. To lift Tino's spirits, as well as distract his own, Philip asked about Vivian's childhood. He sincerely meant to move the conversation to a happier subject. Jarred from his thoughts, Tino took Philip's question as an alarming curiosity and growing interest in Vivian.

"Next time, sir, it's getting late," Tino said as he stood up, signaling the end to their conversation.

Chapter 21

In light of the growing tensions with Japan, the navy increased a number of improvements to its various facilities and sought to build up its defense posture overall, hence the addition of a third civil engineer, but Congress stalled on the bulk of the funding request and, in the end, voted against fortifying Guam. Yet with all the projects the navy government had planned, Philip was in his element and enjoying his assignment. He had even forgotten about his father's effort to get him reassigned, although he knew his father wasn't one to give up. Philip worked well with Commander Pitt and Lieutenant Kaplan. They were men of caliber, as were many of the other officers and enlisted men Philip met. He wouldn't have characterized any of them as misfits and troublemakers, and from what he had heard, none of their predecessors' careers suffered from a Guam assignment. Guam too was not the hellhole he had been led to think. All of it, Philip decided, was bunk.

He especially enjoyed bantering in the office with Tino; Kiko Taisipic, who he later learned was Vivian's godfather; and young Chu' Rojas, the messenger. The Chamorros addressed the officers formally by their ranks and used nicknames among themselves, which puzzled Philip when he first heard them. Kiko's real name was Francisco; Chu's was Jesus. Although Tino was already short for Constantino, the boys called him "Toh." Philip knew that it was common among the Spanish and the native peoples they conquered and Christianized to name their sons Jesus, and that it was pronounced "Hey-soos," but it still rattled him to see the name in print. Although he was of no particular religious denomination, he thought it sacrilegious and most improper to take the Lord's name. He was glad to have the alternative and used it almost exclusively. As they pored over some schematics one day, Philip asked out loud, certain that someone would respond.

"How do you get *Kiko* out of Francisco and *Chu'* out of Hey-soos," he asked, deliberately exaggerating the sound of Jesus's name.

"The same way you get Jack out of John and Dick out of Richard," Kiko said. "Makes no sense to us either."

And they laughed the hearty laugh of men who can share risqué jokes and talk freely about work, sports, and women. Philip recalled meeting them initially and how he had thought them so polite, overly friendly, and too eager to please. Over the course of a few months, he learned to read them much better, to know when they were jokingly serious or seriously joking, when they were seething with anger or frustration internally but outwardly remaining unflustered and composed. He observed their curious reaction to racial discrimination, chafing quietly while conceding the futility of dissent; the prejudices were too powerful, too ingrained to ever change. Philip also learned that they were as sharp and as clever as his navy colleagues. It shamed him to recall his badly influenced and mistaken first impression.

Prior to his assignment in the Pacific, Philip's encounters with people of color were infrequent. Such people, mostly Negroes and Latinos, were scarce in the rarified atmosphere of his conservative upper-class enclave of the 1930s, even rarer in his social circle. He never thought about them one way or another, although he was not immune to the attitudes, beliefs, and perceptions of them prevalent at the time. The brown-skinned Pacific islanders he met en route to Guam—Hawaiians, Filipinos, the various Carolinians (they are not all the same ethnically), and the Chamorros themselves—were entirely new to his experience. Until he met Tino, Vivian, Kiko, and Chu', Philip had no reason to disbelieve any of the unflattering stories he had heard about Pacific islanders—that they were lazy, dirty, dishonest, barely civilized, and not very intelligent. The navy government, in general, maintained that the Chamorros were in desperate need of education, training, health care, and social improvement. Philip, like his navy colleagues, thought of nonwhites as lesser beings, inferior to themselves. Within three months of his arrival, however, and without his realizing it, Philip's feelings and beliefs changed. So did his attitudes toward women.

Although speaking Chamorro in the government offices was prohibited, the Chamorros often forgot or simply slipped into their native tongue without realizing it, sometimes even inadvertently speaking to the officers, stopping in midsentence, to apologize in English. As a result of the frequent tongue slips, the officers picked up several Chamorro words and phrases, especially swear words and the ones in dirty jokes. When Philip asked how to say "I love you," the men, especially Tino, stiffened. Philip changed the subject immediately. Machismo is the same in any language. Unbeknownst to the officers, the Chamorros had nicknames for them too. William Pitt, the senior man, was *Bustus*, meaning "rough" or "unrefined," because he wasn't the most graceful or nimble of people. Harvey Kaplan, who was

Jewish, was *Arun,* their pronunciation of Aaron. They often taunted Philip about his height, both to his face and behind his back. His nickname was *Haligi*[14].

"What does it mean?" Philip asked Tino in the outside kitchen one evening. He hoped it didn't mean something too unflattering.

"It means a pillar or a post. You know, like a telephone pole."

Philip didn't think himself tall enough or thin enough to be likened to a telephone pole. Although he was tall even among his fellow officers and the enlisted men, he was not the only one. He also weighed a healthy one hundred and eighty-five pounds. Reed weighed almost as much but was four inches shorter. He decided the nickname related only to his height. It could still have been something meant to be flattering, perhaps like "upstanding."

Philip also liked listening to the boys at work talking about their lanchos. He understood how people might keep vegetable gardens, but lanchos, as Tino, Kiko, and Chu' spoke of them, seemed to be much more than places away from town to keep a garden.

"You fellows make lanchos sound like summer camps," Philip observed.

"What's a summer camp?" Kiko asked.

Philip's explanation left Tino, Kiko, and Chu' looking puzzled. They could not relate to anything Philip described. There were no cabins or counselors or storytelling around campfires or paddling canoes on a lake. They saw no connection.

"Would you like to see what a lancho is?" Tino said. "I invite you to come to mine any time."

Tino owned his lancho. He had purchased two acres of land in Tutujan about five years earlier, but not all of it was level. The back part of his property sloped down to a small stream, which marked the boundary. Tino's lancho was simple; it consisted of a small open-air shack with an adjoining chicken coop and a garden, where he grew long beans or wing beans—depending on the season—Chinese cabbage, eggplants, sweet potatoes, tomatoes, cucumbers, hot peppers, bell peppers, and sometimes corn and melons. He also had some stands of cooking and sweet bananas, some papayas, a tangerine and a lemon tree, a large old breadfruit tree, and two mature mango trees. The trees bordered his property. When he produced more than they could consume, he gave away the excess to coworkers and neighbors. Likewise, he and Vivian were often the recipients of their neighbors' overabundance. Tino described his lancho and what he planted there.

---

14 Pronounced "Ha-LEE-gee."

The following Saturday, while Parker opted to stay home and start a new book, Philip followed Tino and Vivian through the yard behind the house and on a well-worn path up San Ramon Hill. Philip was impressed with Vivian's ability to keep up. She had no trouble making the steep, uphill climb and was not breathless at the top. It was only then that he realized how she had probably made the climb since childhood and it was nothing new (as it was for him) or difficult for her. Philip admired the way Vivian marched along, never asking for them to slow down or for a rest stop. He never guessed that such a fragile-looking orchid could be so resilient. Vivian was stronger and more physically fit than she looked.

From the top of the hill, the three followed a path inland through more thick jungle. The path broke off in various directions along the way, and Tino explained that they led to the lanchos of other people. They continued until they came to a small clearing on a plateau overlooking a ravine. A freshwater stream ran at the bottom. Tino's shack was the only structure in the clearing. He had built it himself and covered it with corrugated metal roofing sheets. The shack was flanked by the furrows of his garden.

"See, there are my beanpoles and my long beans," Tino said proudly, pointing to a tall spindly A-frame made with dozens of tree branches trimmed into thin, straight poles propped against each other and bound with string. Thick vines and long skinny beans, some as long as eighteen inches, were growing on the frame.

While he gave Philip a tour of the garden, pointing out what was growing and how it was eaten, Vivian picked some long beans and bell peppers. She collected eggs and fed the chickens. She then retrieved an empty tin can to draw water for them from an old oil drum, which stood under a makeshift downspout at a corner of the shack. Tino had used roofing sheets to fashion a gutter to catch the rain and funnel it into the drum, as well as to enclose parts of the adjoining chicken coop. Philip felt chastened by Tino's handiwork. Although all his materials were discards and cast-offs, Tino had put his engineering knowledge and skills to practical use and had built a serviceable outside kitchen at home and a functional hut at the lancho. Philip, with his fancy stateside engineering degree, had never built anything with his own hands.

"Papa," Vivian called out. "The drum's almost empty."

"I know. Get water from the stream. I'll need it for the plants," he said.

They spoke to each other in Chamorro; they always did but apologized and switched to English in mixed company. Philip liked listening to them speak, even though he didn't understand what they were saying. He could tell by their expression and behavior that they weren't necessarily talking about him. He wondered why his countrymen didn't also infer meaning from expression. They seemed always to assume that they were the topic of every Chamorro conversation and took offense to it being spoken on the job, hence the ban. The Americans even warned that speaking a native language in mixed company was impolite, yet they thought nothing of speaking English exclusively to people who may or may not speak or understand English very well or at all.

The clanging Vivian made as she carried two empty four-sided five-gallon kerosene cans from the shack prompted Philip to rush to her aid. Thick wooden dowels, cut to the exact width and nailed into two sides of the square tops of the opened cans, served as handles. The makeshift water cans also bespoke of Tino's engineering. Philip reached to take the cans from Vivian, but she waved him off.

"That's all right, Mr. Avery, I can manage," she said. "But will you help me carry them back up?"

Philip didn't anticipate the hike down to the stream to be difficult. It was below a slope of only about fifteen or twenty feet, but he was surprised at how steep and slippery it was. Although he and Vivian had no trouble making the descent, Philip wondered how she would manage carrying a heavy water-filled can back up. She gave no indication that the task would be difficult.

The jungle at the bottom of the ravine was glorious. A canopy of green vines, huge leaves, and tree branches arched high above their heads. Dappled sunlight peeked through the canopy and sparkled on the slowly running stream. A cool breeze whispered soothingly through a swaying stand of tall bamboo nearby. Philip stepped across the stream and studied their surroundings. Around them grew several varieties of vegetation that were unknown to him. The scene was what he imagined paradise would look like.

Vivian dropped the kerosene cans on the bank and surveyed the water, looking for a certain deep spot in the stream. Philip watched her. Against the backdrop of the slope, with dappled sunlight in her hair, she was as beautiful as the plants and trees and the lazy stream at her feet. She was as much a part of the tropical imagery as he was alien to it.

The stream was small and shallow, but the water was fresh and cool. Philip wanted to take off his shoes and socks, roll up his pant legs, and wade in, even though the water would only have reached the top of his ankles. As if she had read his mind, Vivian said, "Take off your shoes, Mr. Avery. We have to wade in and you don't want to get them wet."

Philip happily obliged. Vivian kicked off her own shoes and socks, lifted her skirt only high enough to expose her knees, and waded in. He rolled up his pant legs and followed her into the water. She wadded up her skirt and pinched it between her thighs then dipped her hands in the water and playfully splashed him. She wanted to hear him laugh out loud, to know for sure whether he knew how. She giggled as he flinched. When he reached his hands into the water, Vivian assumed he was going to splash back at her. She cowered, expecting the attack, but Philip instead wiped the wetness onto his face and neck. She sighed, her shoulders slumped, and she headed back to the bank, disappointed that he didn't take the hint, although she half expected it. Lieutenant Avery was too stiff and proper to loosen up, relax, and have a little fun.

Philip didn't miss her cue. He wanted very much to play with her, to push her off her feet and tickle her, to roll around in the water until they were both soaking wet. He wanted to feel her body against his and to laugh with her. He liked the sound of her laughter. He also wanted to lay flat on his back and feel the cool water trickling around his heated body. But he worried that Tino would get the wrong idea if they returned soaking wet. He wanted to earn Tino's trust almost as much as he liked Vivian's attention.

Philip watched curiously as Vivian reached between her legs, grabbed the hem at the back of her skirt, pulled it up in front, and pinched it into her waistband. The result reminded him of a genie's pantaloons but shorter and more snugly fitting. The cinched-up skirt exposed Vivian's thighs well above her knees. The effect was arousing, even though Philip knew she didn't mean it to be. Vivian retrieved the empty kerosene cans and waded a few yards further upstream.

"Over here, Mr. Avery. The water's deeper here."

As he followed her into deeper water, he said, "May I ask you a question?"

Vivian stopped and turned to face him with a puzzled look.

"Why won't you call me Philip?"

She smiled that special smile. "It wouldn't be right, Mr. Avery. My father cannot address you by your first name, and neither should I."

Indeed, it would have been inappropriate for Tino, an underling, to assume such informality with a superior officer, no matter how friendly and familiar they had become. Tino was among the most senior native employees in the Governor's Palace, but he was still subordinate to Philip, the newest and youngest officer in the engineering division. Philip would not have taken offense to Tino's familiarity, but Pitt and Kaplan would not have tolerated it. And they outranked Philip.

"Well," he pressed, "you can if you'd like, at least when we're alone." Philip hoped there would be more opportunities to be alone with Vivian. He wanted her to feel free enough to call him by his first name and for him to try to charm her for a kiss, although it wouldn't have been appropriate for either of them.

To Philip's relief, Vivian made him fill the cans only three-quarters full. The can he carried was as heavy as Vivian's, but she had no trouble with the load.

"Don't put your shoes on yet," she said. "We'll have to make more trips."

Philip flinched. He had never gone barefoot outdoors except at the beach and only on clean sand. The thought of walking in dirt and possibly contracting hookworms or some other strange tropical infection and disease truly alarmed him. He cringed, not only because the pebbles along the bank hurt the bottoms of his tender feet, but also because he didn't like the feel of mud squishing between his toes. As they ascended the slope, Vivian showed him how to feel around with his toes for places to dig into the soft earth and which deeply embedded stones to step on to gain better footholds. Philip kept thinking about how thoroughly he would have to scrub his toes and toenails during his bath that night.

At the top of the slope, Vivian fell behind him and hid her amusement as she watched him waddle up the path to the shack. He was more uncomfortable about being barefoot than about carrying water. It tickled her to know that a handsome navy lieutenant would so gallantly stoop to carrying water for her. *Oh, how I wish you really could be my shining prince with dirty feet,* she thought to herself and giggled quietly.

Vivian and Philip made three more trips to the stream. Vivian brought an old towel with her on the last trip so that they could wash and dry off their feet before putting their shoes back on. They filled Tino's water drum almost to the top. Vivian kept one can aside for drinking and cooking. Mosquito larvae were wriggling in the oil drum.

"It should start raining soon, and then we won't have to worry about drawing water," Tino said, looking up at the sky. "Guam has only two seasons, Lieutenant, wet and dry. Sometimes it's dry in the wet season, and sometimes it's wet in the dry season. You take what you get."

Chapter 22

Tino built a fire in a raised pit, which was like the one in the outside kitchen but smaller. He filled a large soot-coated pot with water and put it on the fire to boil. He then took a fat hen from the coop. Philip watched in revolted astonishment as Tino twisted and yanked the hen's head, killing it quickly. Philip saw Vivian outside the shack, picking through a pile of ripe brown coconuts. He didn't want to see what was next for the dead chicken, so he wandered over to offer Vivian a hand. No need, she said.

She picked up a coconut, shook it, listened for the liquid sloshing inside then walked over to a thick sharpened stake embedded in the ground. Philip watched in amazement as she jammed the coconut onto the spike and, with three or four thrusts, quickly peeled off the husk. He didn't notice the machete on the ground beside her until she picked it up. She held the peeled coconut in her left hand and struck it firmly in the middle with the machete in her right. She tossed the coconut slightly, turning it and hitting it twice more until it cracked cleanly around the middle. Before all the juice could drain from the crack, she turned the coconut upright to save what remained. She stuck the tip of the machete into the crevice and pried off the top half. The bottom half held the remaining juice. She handed Philip the machete and the empty half of the coconut. Then she took a sip of the liquid in the other half.

"Try it. It's sweet," she said as she took back the machete and handed him the coconut.

He had never seen a coconut peeled and cracked open, nor had he ever tasted coconut juice. It was slightly sweet and mild tasting. He liked it.

"Someday, you're going to have to teach me how to do that," Philip said.

"I don't think there are coconut trees in New York, Mr. Avery," Vivian said, amused by his interest in coconuts.

"No, but there are in Florida. My parents have a bungalow in Sarasota."

Now that doesn't surprise me, Vivian thought to herself. If his parents own a bungalow in Florida then he probably did grow up in a mansion in New York. It was another indication of Philip's lofty social status and of the disparity between them.

From his vantage in the shack, Tino watched Philip following Vivian around the grounds. He knew Philip was developing an interest in his daughter; he could see it in his eyes, even if Philip didn't realize it himself. Seeing no change in Vivian's behavior toward Philip, Tino felt secure that she was not similarly smitten. He did not know that his daughter was struggling to hide her feelings from both men.

From atop a shelf in the shack, Vivian tried to reach for an odd little stool with a lethal-looking iron bar protruding from one end. The bar ended in a flat, two-inch circle edged with small, sharp triangular points, like a saw blade. Even on tiptoe, Vivian couldn't reach the stool. Philip retrieved it for her.

"Thank you, Mr. Avery," she said and flashed him that smile again. She didn't know that her smiles deepened his fondness for her, and he didn't know that her certain smile emerged only for him.

Vivian set the stool on the ground and positioned an old pie plate beneath the saw-blade circle. She sat on the stool and placed one of the coconut halves over the saw-blade head. Holding the coconut firmly in both hands, she scraped the flesh out in fine bits and fragments. Philip was again amazed by Vivian's strength, skill, and speed. Both halves of the coconut were clean and empty in minutes, and the grated white coconut meat looked like a little mound of coarse snow.

Vivian wasn't trying to impress Philip with her coconut-grating skill; she wasn't even aware that he was watching her. She was lost in thought about New York mansions and Florida bungalows and how Philip was from a world so different and so far removed from her own. His wonderful eyes had already seen such wonders while hers probably never would. She didn't think she would ever see a real mansion, let alone live in one in her lifetime, nor would she ever see New York or Florida. For her, those places were as far away as the moon.

This is my reality, Vivian thought to herself as she added some water to the grated coconut, kneaded it, and squeezed out the milk. *And there's nothing wrong with it,* she told herself contentedly as she scattered the used coconut pulp in the coop for the chickens. Visiting a New York mansion or a Florida bungalow would be an extravagance to delight in, not an objective to pursue.

In the meantime, while she daydreamed, Tino cleaned the chicken, dipping the carcass into the boiling water to loosen the feathers so that he could pull them off easily. He gutted the chicken, setting aside the heart, liver, gizzard, and the ovary and eggs. Then he cut the chicken into pieces and browned them in a pot with a little of the chicken's fat. Later, he added water and seasonings—only salt and pepper—and returned it to a boil before adding the giblets and eggs. While Tino cooked some rice, Vivian finished the soup with onions that they had brought with them, some of the long beans and bell pepper that she had picked, and the thick coconut milk she had made.

It was midafternoon by then, and the three were hungry.

Tino kept all his kitchen utensils stored in an old army footlocker. He also stored two small Mason jars, one each for salt and pepper, and a bottle of soy sauce. The black pepper and soy sauce were store bought, but the sea salt was homemade by a boyhood friend of Tino's who lived in Inarajan, at the southern end of the island. Tino pulled out three old metal bowls and three tablespoons that didn't match and sloshed them around in the water drum. Philip looked askance; there were mosquito larvae in the drum, but it didn't seem to bother Tino or Vivian. He hid his misgivings and figured if mosquito larvae didn't kill them, they wouldn't kill him either. He was also too hungry to skip the meal. Philip wondered how such a ramshackle hovel became so well stocked with cooking and eating utensils, chipped, battered, and dented as they were.

"Where do all these things come from, Mr. Camacho?" he asked, hoping to take his mind off the mosquito larvae.

"I brought them," Tino said. "Not all at once, of course, but little by little, whenever I find something useful. People can be so wasteful. They throw away things that still have plenty of good use." By "people," Tino meant the Americans, but intentionally didn't specify for fear of offending Philip. Unlike the Chamorros, who saved and reused almost everything, including used butcher paper, paper bags, and even gift wrap, strings, wire, and ribbons; many of the American families threw away highly desirable and reusable things like glass bottles, jars, and metal cans.

As Tino explained how and where he collected things, Vivian scooped a large spoonful of rice into each bowl, sprinkled it with a little soy sauce, and ladled the soup on top. With a light breeze wafting through the lancho, the three sat down to eat. After having a second helping, Philip said it was the best chicken soup he had ever tasted. Tino chuckled.

"That's only because you were hungry, my boy," he said, unconscious of his use of an endearment. But Philip caught it immediately; he wasn't sure whether to take it as an indication of Tino's affection or as impertinence—as an underling taking liberty with a superior. He decided on the former; at the lancho, Tino outranked him. Philip was the American lieutenant, but at the lancho, Tino was the Chamorro commander.

"Do you do this all the time?" Philip asked. He had enjoyed the whole day and wanted to do it again. "May I accompany you again sometime?"

"Of course, Lieutenant. Anytime," Tino said.

By the time Philip marked his first year in Guam, he knew the way to Tino's lancho and sometimes went there by himself. He loved to hike the area around the lancho, tracking the stream to its source and exploring the hills and valleys beyond. He spent almost more time in and around the lancho, both with and without Tino and Vivian, than he did with his navy buddies. He even met the neighboring lancho owners, the Cruz family, who were concerned at first. The sight of a lone American wandering in the area was not common, but after learning that he wasn't lost and after seeing him hiking several times, they grew accustomed to his occasional presence. They considered him "Tino's boy" because he was always coming from Tino's lancho and lived in Tino's house and may as well have been Tino's adopted son. They often invited him to eat with them or have a drink of *tuba*, the sap of the coconut spathe, the sheath that encloses immature coconut blossoms. Freshly drawn, tuba is sweet and refreshing. Allowed to ferment, it becomes a beerlike alcoholic drink; fermented even further, it becomes a distinctly flavored vinegar. Philip liked helping Tun Kiko's sons score the spathes to draw the liquid but couldn't shimmy up the coconut tree trunks with their skill and agility. He was too tall and lanky. Tun Kiko urged him to stop trying for fear of falling and breaking his neck.

Once, on his way home from the office, Philip passed a trash can in the government compound. A banged-up stainless steel washbasin was leaning against it. Although dented and misshapen, the washbasin had no cracks or leaks. Philip figured that with some gentle tapping, he could pound out most of the dents and the basin would be almost as good as new, or at least quite useable. He picked up the washbasin and brought it home. With Vivian sometimes watching, Philip spent several evenings after supper in the outside kitchen carefully smoothing out the dents. Vivian pretended to be interested in his progress, but she really just wanted to watch the muscles of his arms and chest, aroused by the sheen of sweat he worked up. When he was satisfied, he took the basin to the lancho. It came in handy, and he was proud to claim it as his first contribution to lancho life.

Chapter 23

As he did every year on Sylvia's birthday, Tino offered a Mass of thanksgiving and birthday blessings in remembrance. After he and Vivian attended the Mass, Tino would go alone to the cemetery to spend Sylvia's birthday at her grave. He would spend an hour or two talking to her, telling her about their daughter, his work, the house, and the latest goings-on in town. April 2, 1940, would have been Sylvia's fortieth birthday. "Ai, *asagua-hu,*[15]" Tino whispered. "I hope I'll be with you for your fiftieth birthday."

On a gray morning several days later, Tino woke up earlier than usual. Something about that morning was different; he felt it in his bones. The dry season was coming to an end, and the rainy season would be bringing storms as well as rain. As the morning progressed, the weather began to reveal itself. There was no breeze. Everything outside was calm and still. The sun, when it came up, shone brightly, but not with its usual heat. Within hours, the sky filled with thick clouds. A storm, a typhoon, was brewing somewhere to the east. The stillness in the air was worrisome. Tino read it as a signal that the storm would be a big one. He roused his daughter and alerted her. If the signs continued, they would have to start making preparations. Vivian got up and made breakfast. Philip was already dressed when he came downstairs; Parker followed a few minutes later.

"I think a typhoon is coming," Tino announced. "It's not a good sign this early in the year." Philip and Parker knew such storms as hurricanes, which generally were seasonal storms on the East Coast. In Guam, they could occur any time of year. The men, both of whom had experienced hurricanes in their lifetimes, sensed Tino's concern.

"If we get one, Reed and I will be required to report to Government House to ride out the storm there," Philip said. "When the 'all clear' is given, we'll have to start damage assessment right away. If it is severe, you may be called to assist, Mr. Camacho. You may even be called before it hits."

"I understand, Lieutenant. I'll be ready," Tino said. "You may want to secure your belongings in case this storm is a bad one. If it is, we may lose

[15] "My spouse."

the roof." Although the house was made of thick mamposteria walls, the tiled roof would be susceptible to severe damage.

"If your father is called in, will you be all right here alone?" Parker asked. Philip watched Vivian's face for her reaction. Tino was especially concerned about Vivian's response. He knew how terrified Vivian was of typhoons. He had always been with her through all of them since she was a child. If indeed he was needed at the compound, Tino was generally called in after a typhoon, not before. Lieutenant Avery's indication that he could be called in beforehand was a change in that protocol. If Philip was correct, Tino would have to comply, and for the first time ever, he would have to leave Vivian to face a typhoon by herself.

"Yes, of course I will." Although she answered bravely, Vivian was frightened. She couldn't stand the horrible screaming of the wind, the driving rain that seemed to penetrate any man-made barrier, and the loud crashing sounds that seemed to threaten certain doom. She also hated the backbreaking task of cleaning up and the stench of rotting vegetation in the days that followed. Tino didn't believe her; he knew she was only putting on a brave face. Philip, too, sensed the insecurity in her voice. He looked at her questioningly, hoping she could read in his eyes what he could not ask outright for fear of revealing to Tino and Parker how deeply he cared for Vivian. He wished he could stay and pass the storm with her, to hold her and protect her when she grew scared. He felt protective of her, not like a big brother, but like a lover.

"Tonight when we get home, we should start preparing ourselves," Tino said. "Gentlemen, I suggest you pack your belongings and bring them down here. I don't trust that old roof to last much longer. We will need to close the shutters and secure whatever we can."

The following morning dawned steely gray and ominous. Light breezes and drizzling rain occurred intermittently throughout the day. At school, Vivian and her students started standard typhoon precautions, storing their textbooks and personal belongings, their classroom decorations and posters, and all their other equipment in the supply closet. Then they pushed Vivian's heavy desk in front of the closet door and pushed their own desks to the center of the room. If nothing else, they had to guard against water damage. If the typhoon was a strong one, none of their precautions would prevent the inevitable destruction. Students and teachers in the other classrooms and in schools all over the island were doing the same.

As Vivian helped the boys push her desk to the closet door, she thought about what she would do if she had to brave the typhoon at home alone. Pray, of course, but beyond that? School let out early so that the children could go home and help their parents. The families living in thatched-roof houses would have to move to safer shelters. Vivian wanted to offer their home as a shelter, hoping to pass the time with some of her students and their families, playing cards and games, at least while they were able, but Tino advised against it. He worried about the roof and the danger it posed. He was certain it would sustain some damage, if not lost entirely. His worry heightened Vivian's fear of facing the typhoon by herself and doubled his about leaving her alone.

After her students were gone, Vivian rushed home to start her own preparations. She cooked a pot roast for supper and made a hearty vegetable soup, double the usual amounts of food she usually prepared. The excess would keep in the refrigerator for at least a day without electricity. Depending on when and if the electricity went out, the refrigerator would stay cold for a few hours. She then readied the kerosene lanterns, filling them from a five-gallon can that Tino always kept full and ready. They owned two flashlights, but the batteries were dead. She had to run to the store to buy new ones, irritated that she didn't think to buy them after leaving her classroom. The stores were crowded with people like her, buying last-minute necessities. Vivian managed to buy the batteries as well as some sweet rolls and flour titiyas made with coconut milk before the store shelves were emptied. She reached home as her father and the navy men arrived at the back door; they also had been released early. Without a word, they picked up where Vivian left off. While Tino gathered his pots, pans, tools, and several armfuls of firewood from the outside kitchen, Parker and Philip went upstairs to pack their belongings. Parker was the first to bring down his luggage and his favorite books, which he wrapped and tied in some oilcloth.

"I hope you won't mind keeping my books with you, Miss Vivvy. I'd hate to lose these," Parker said as he set down his suitcase and put the books down on top of it. "We'll need to keep our dress uniforms in your closet, if that's all right."

"Of course, it's all right, Mr. Reed. There's plenty of space," she replied. "Bring them in."

Parker had never been in Vivian's bedroom, which was located directly below his. He was surprised and humbled at how small and spartan it was. Her room was half the size of his and contained only a dresser, a narrow bed, and a beautifully carved chest at its foot. There was a crucifix on one wall and a magazine photo of a mansion on another. Nothing in the room suggested that it was occupied by a young woman. Even his bedroom looked more comfortable and inviting. Hers was like the cell of a cloistered monk. Parker ran his hand over the carved lid of the chest.

"That belonged to my grandmother," Vivian explained. "She gave it to my mother. Now it belongs to me."

"It's beautiful," he said, trying to mask how badly he felt for her.

"And heavy too. It's carved from ifil wood," Vivian added with a giggle. "No typhoon can blow it away, I don't think."

Vivian's closet wasn't large; there were only four or five dresses and items of clothing hanging inside. She pushed aside her clothing so that Parker could put his suitcase and books inside. There was space indeed for both his things and Philip's.

"I'll leave some space for Avery and get my uniforms," he said as he exited the room. Parker returned a few minutes later with several uniforms in protective suit bags. Philip followed with his own and hung them alongside Parker's. The pole in the closet bowed under the weight; it had never borne so much clothing.

Parker hurried back upstairs to start moving furniture. Tino followed behind him. They met Philip coming down the stairs with his valise and suitcase. He put the suitcase down beside Parker's in the closet and his valise on Vivian's bed. There was no more space in her small closet. He then glanced around to make sure Tino and Parker were still upstairs. He could hear them moving furniture to the center of the room, away from the parlor windows. Turning back to Vivian, he cupped both his hands around her face and looked deep into her eyes. "If I could, I would stay here with you," he said and kissed her forehead.

Philip had never said or done anything affectionate to her before. Had she not been so anxious about his eyes, she would have seen the warmth growing for her there. Before she could say anything, Philip dashed back upstairs. He stopped at the top, surprised by what he had said. He was concerned about her being alone in a storm, but he realized that what he felt was more than concern.

With rain squalls hampering their efforts, Tino, Philip, and Parker secured the shutters on all the windows, closed and bolted the storm doors upstairs, and tied down or stored anything that was loose in the yard. They did not stop to eat supper until the house and yard were as secure as they could make them. By then, it was dark and they were exhausted and soaking wet. Philip asked about the lancho. Tino said there was no time left to try to secure anything there. He expected the damage to be extensive. He felt badly about leaving the chickens imprisoned in their coop, but there was no time left to get to the lancho and set them free.

"What can I do with these?" Parker asked as he came downstairs holding his wadded-up wet uniform and underclothing.

"Leave them on that chair," Vivian said. "I'll get them with Papa's and Mr. Avery's."

She would have enough wet clothing to fill the washing machine. If left unwashed, the wet, soiled clothing would start to stink, get mildewed, and be ruined in no time. Vivian loaded the wet clothes into the washing machine, filled the tub with water and some laundry soap, and let the machine agitate for several minutes. She then put the clothes through the wringer, emptied the tub, and filled it again to rinse. She refilled the tub, put the clothing back in, and lashed the machine's cover to its leg on two sides. Filled as it was with water and clothing, the machine would be heavy enough to stay put in strong winds. Since the clothes were already clean, they would only need to be wrung out again and hung to dry as soon as that was possible.

Throughout supper, Vivian stole glances at Philip and wondered about his sudden show of affection. She welcomed it happily but suspiciously. *Why did he say that? Does he care about me, or does he just feel sorry for me?* she wondered. Philip was wondering too. He had no business taking such liberty, no right to assume he could overstep his bounds with Vivian. But it felt so right, and the rightness of it outweighed the inappropriateness.

By nightfall, the winds picked up, and a steady rain started to fall. Throughout the night, they listened to the wind grow stronger. The rain also fell in torrents. They could hear loose debris flying around, hitting the walls and shutters. In the morning, the ground was carpeted with leaves and broken branches, and the wind was starting to whistle and howl. The sky was dark gray, and the rain fell heavily. After a light breakfast, the navy men donned foul-weather gear and galoshes that had been issued to them the day before. Tino only had an old raincoat and rubber boots, which he put on before following Philip and Parker out the door.

"Listen for the telephone, Vivvy, I'll try to call you as soon as we know what's going on," Tino said and kissed her forehead. He didn't want to leave her alone.

Vivian watched them scurry against the wind whipping at them as they crossed the street, skipping through deep puddles filling the road.

"Wait! I forgot something," Philip yelled against the howling wind. He whirled around and ran back to the house. Vivian saw him coming and stepped back as he rushed through the door. He quickly closed it behind him. Rainwater dripped from his hat and foul-weather coat and left puddles on the floor. Without a word, Philip took her in his arms and kissed her passionately. Then with rainwater dripping from his face onto hers, he said, "I care about you, Vivian."

Before Vivian could react, he darted out the door and dashed back across the street. Tino and Parker were still waiting for him.

"Is everything all right?" Tino shouted.

"Yes, everything's good," Philip answered. His heart was racing, more from the kiss than the sprint. He was filled with delicious wonder; Vivian's lips were the softest he had ever kissed.

Her head reeling, Vivian touched her wet lips and smiled. She was alone but still blushed. It was her first kiss. Her lips still tingled from the pressure of his. Philip had forced his tongue into her mouth, probing it briefly before he pulled himself away. The sensation was strange and wonderful. She could still taste him. Her face and the front of her dress were wet, and there were puddles and muddy footprints on the floor from Philip's galoshes. Her heart was racing too. Philip liked her, maybe even more than liked. From that moment, Vivian was in love. She spent the rest of the day in a lovesick daze, humming happily and giggling as she mopped the floor. She touched her mouth now and then, reveling in Philip's kiss and wanting more of them. Shortly after four o'clock, the sudden ringing of the telephone upstairs broke her reverie. She ran upstairs to answer it. Philip was on the other end.

"Vivian," he said crisply. "We have to stay here, your father too. You'll be by yourself tonight. We'll get home as soon as we can."

Vivian's heart instantly dropped. She was petrified and wanted to cry. She wanted to beg Philip to let her father come home, but she knew it was beyond his authority. She knew also that her request was childish and it would embarrass her father. "All right," she said uneasily.

She could hear nervous voices chattering in the background as she held the receiver to her ear. Philip had not hung up yet, but he wasn't speaking.

"Mr. Avery, are you still there?" she asked, unable to steady her quivering voice. The voices faded somewhat, and she could tell that Philip had either moved or turned away from them. He then whispered into the receiver, "Be brave, Vivvy. Stay safe for me." Then he abruptly hung up. His kiss and his whispered words steeled her somewhat for the night ahead, but fear soon returned and overwhelmed her.

Chapter 24

By eight o'clock, the wind was howling wildly, driving the heavy rain horizontally. She could hear it clattering continuously against the walls outside. Then the thunder and lightning began. The house shuddered with each deafening thunderclap and every powerful wind gust. She huddled in her bedroom with one of the lanterns and a flashlight. She tried to be brave, but the high-pitched screeching winds, the thunder, and the crashing of objects hitting the house petrified her. Water soon started seeping into the kitchen from under the back door. She could hear it trickling in, but there was nothing she could do to stop it. She waited for it to seep into her bedroom, but it didn't.

Vivian lit the kerosene lantern, even though she kept all the electric lights on downstairs. She knew the lights wouldn't stay on much longer, and she didn't want to fumble for matches in the dark. She kept her shoes on her feet, afraid she wouldn't be able to find them in the dark if she had to flee. She leaned over onto Philip's valise and started praying. She fell into a light, fitful sleep, flinching with every loud crash. Shortly after midnight, a tremendous ripping sound pierced the storm din and jerked her awake in a panic. She thought the roof was ripping off. The electricity was out, and the lights were dead, leaving only the dim light from her lantern. She screamed in terror as another deafening crash sounded above her head. Sobbing hard, she was certain the floor above would fall in on her. When rainwater started dripping onto her from between the floorboards above, Vivian knew that the roof had been breached and she was in real danger. She could only try to protect herself as best she could and await rescue or for destruction and death to take her.

She pushed her bed into a corner and curled up on it, with one wall behind and the other beside her. She held Philip's valise against her exposed side and hugged her pillow. The howling wind and loud banging continued for hours longer. Exhausted, Vivian finally fell asleep. She woke with a start to all three men shouting her name. It was early morning; the sky was just starting to lighten. Except for the dim glow from the lantern, its fuel almost gone, her room was dark. Her small window was still shuttered. She was still clinging to Philip's valise. Her clothes and her bed were wet. She was stiff and sore and started shivering uncontrollably. Tino threw open her bedroom door and lifted her off the bed, hugging and kissing his precious daughter. She hugged him tightly and cried.

"It's over, Vivvy. You're all right. I'm here now," he said soothingly. He took off his old raincoat, still warmed by his body, and wrapped it around her. He hugged her tightly and let her sob into his chest for a few moments. Behind him, Philip and Parker awaited proof that she was unhurt. Philip offered his arms, hoping Tino would let him embrace her, but he refused to let her go. Vivian's brave assurance that she would be all right by herself didn't fool her father, but he had no choice. He had to leave her alone, and he felt deeply guilty.

"Come, let's make some coffee and eat breakfast. I'll start a fire," he said. He knew that getting her back on a normal track would help restore her sense of security. "Get your soup, and we'll heat it up."

He let go of Vivian and nudged her toward the refrigerator. She immediately went back into her room to change into dry clothes then went into the bathroom. She emerged a few minutes later, her face washed, teeth brushed, and hair combed. She didn't want Philip to see her looking so terrible, even though she had already been seen at her worst.

"Reed and I have to get back to the compound as soon as we get some breakfast and change into work clothes," Philip said to Vivian as Tino and Parker headed outside. Alone for a few moments, he stroked Vivian's cheek and said, "I wish I could have stayed with you." She looked up into his face and steadily into his eyes, hoping he would kiss her again. Instead, he hurried outside to help Tino and Parker. The men surveyed the yard and slowly walked around, gathering large broken branches and tossing them into a pile to burn once dry. The morning was gray with light, drizzly rain carried by blustery wind. As soon as the wind died down, the work of cleaning up commenced around the island. Those whose homes were not damaged or were only slightly damaged helped their neighbors, especially those who had lost everything. Everyone, including children, helped with clearing the streets and yards of debris. The work would continue for days until the island was back to normal.

While Philip and Parker opened the storm shutters on the windows, Vivian swept the puddles out of the kitchen and mopped up what remained. Tino's outside kitchen survived with minor damage; its sheet metal roof was gone. He threw a piece of canvas over the rafters above the fire pit and scraped out the wet sand and debris from it. He carried out some of the dry firewood he had stored inside the house and started a fire. Vivian brought out the pot of soup she had prepared the day before and set it on the fire to reheat. Tino filled a kettle with water to boil for coffee. While they waited for breakfast, the officers went upstairs. Parker checked every room for leaks and water damage. Philip pried open part of the ceiling and looked into the darkness under the roof with one of Tino's flashlights.

Vivian set out three bowls, soup spoons, and the coffee mugs. She also set out the rolls, titiyas, some hard biscuits, and some butter and jam. When the coffee was done and the soup was hot, Vivian helped her father bring the pots into the house and called the officers to eat. She finally felt safe again and ready to face the tedious task of cleaning up.

As they ate, Philip delivered his preliminary assessment of the roof damage. The three men had already seen—as they approached the house—that Sylvia's bougainvillea bushes were leafless and several limbs were broken and the veranda had blown away, as had the screens of the parlor windows. The veranda's destruction caused the terrible crashing sound that scared Vivian out of her wits. The roof also sustained damage, particularly where the veranda ripped away. Many of the fired clay tiles were gone, Philip said, adding that the underlayment looked all right but needed better inspection. Through a narrow gap between the outer wall and the roof where the veranda had been, he was able to view the trusses. He marveled at the quality of the massive, hand-hewn, old-growth hardwood timber used for the ceiling joists and rafters. Even the wall plates were in good condition, wet, but not in need of replacement.

"You'll need to bring in a contractor to do a more thorough assessment, but I'd say you're in pretty good shape," Philip said. "This will be a good time to put in some metal collar ties and straps. The wood is great, but those old iron nails are not. Of course, a good part of the ceiling will have to come down and be replaced."

"How bad is the roof above Mr. Reed's room? The rain poured into my room from upstairs last night," Vivian said, trying not to reveal how badly the leaking had frightened her.

"Yes, we lost most of the tiles on the roof above Reed's room," Philip said. "The underlayment couldn't hold back the rain. When the wood dries out or is replaced and the roof is retiled, there shouldn't be any more leaks."

Tino said nothing; he was already calculating the cost in his mind: the time the repairs would take and the loss of rental revenue if the officers had to move out, even if only temporarily.

"Reed might have to move out for a while, but the repairs shouldn't take more than a couple of weeks. My room is fine. I can stay put," Philip said, guessing at Tino's thoughts.

"Not me!" Parker said. "I'm not moving. I'll buy buckets for the leaks if I have to."

"It'll be noisy and uncomfortable while repairs are going on, but luckily, none of us will be here to be bothered by it," Philip said as he stood up. "Well, man, we have to go. Mr. Camacho, Vivian, I'm not sure when we'll get back. Looks like I'll be working late for a while."

The officers rose from the table and headed to Vivian's room to retrieve clean uniforms and underwear. They headed back upstairs to their respective bathrooms to take cold showers, shave, and get dressed to report back to the government compound. Tino stayed up to wait for them that night. Without electricity, the streets and houses were dark. Tino went upstairs before dark and lit some candles in the parlor and a lantern in each of the men's bedrooms. Only Parker came home that night, and it wasn't until late. Parker's clothes were wet and dirty, and he looked exhausted.

"Have you had anything to eat, Mr. Reed? Shall I have Vivian prepare something for you?" Tino asked. Parker shook his head.

"No thanks. I ate at the mess. I'm going to take a shower and hit the sack," he said.

"How bad is it out there?"

"Not too bad. There's been lots of damage, but no deaths have been reported, thank God. Lots of cleaning up though," Parker said and yawned.

"Good night, Mr. Reed."

"G'night."

Parker headed to his bathroom with a towel around his waist and a lighted candle. He turned on the tap and suddenly remembered that without electricity, there would be no hot water. Trying desperately not to awaken the entire town with his yelps, he took the quickest, coldest shower he had ever taken.

When the electricity returned four days later, so did the sun, hot and bright all day long. Vivian spent days washing clothes and bedding. Tino strung extra clotheslines throughout the backyard, to catch up with the extra loads.

To keep the rain out of Parker's room, Tino and Parker tacked a tarpaulin over the exposed tile underlayment. The temporary solution would suffice until permanent repairs could be made. After doing what he could to secure the house, Tino hitched a ride to Sumay to check on his mother's house. If it was damaged, and the four marine officers renting it had to move out, he would lose the income needed to make the repairs to both houses. As he neared the house, Tino's heart sank. His parents' house, his boyhood home, was destroyed. Luckily, the marine tenants were not in the house at the time. Like Philip and Parker in Agaña, the marines were at their headquarters above the village. Sumay and the southern part of the island suffered the brunt of the typhoon's fury. Rehabilitation and reconstruction island-wide would take months.

Tino debated whether to rebuild the veranda or simply seal up the roof and replaster the gouges in the wall where the veranda had been. When he received the cost estimate, he decided not to replace the veranda. Without it, sunlight streamed into the parlor, and the upstairs seemed more cheerful with the added light. Philip's time estimate for the repairs would have been accurate, but Tino had to wait over a month for a contractor to become available. Although damage throughout the island was light, several homes and some military facilities, especially in the south, were badly damaged or destroyed. Rebuilding homes and making repairs were the priorities. Tino decided to wait to build a new house in Sumay; the need was not urgent.

In the two months following the typhoon, Vivian rarely saw Philip, and she missed him. Although her father's work hours remained relatively the same, Philip would be gone for days at a time, working on-site at reconstruction or major repair projects somewhere in the northern or southern end of the island. Even when his work brought him back to Agaña, he spent long hours in his office, sometimes staying overnight in the BOQ so as not to awaken anyone at home. If he came home at all, it was usually to get clean uniforms and work clothes. Vivian felt badly for him, for the demands being made upon him and the pressure he was under.

"Don't worry about your laundry, Mr. Avery, I'll take care of it," Vivian said.

"Thank you, Vivian. I wasn't sure I would have the time," Philip said, relieved weariness showing in his face and voice. Tino's house had become home to him by then, and Vivian, Tino, and Parker had become like family. He told himself that he missed Vivian's cooking, but it was actually Vivian he missed most. He wanted to kiss her again. Once was not enough. He promised himself he would kiss her—really kiss her—as soon as the opportunity presented itself.

Philip wondered about the lancho and what damage it sustained. He also wondered about the fate of the chickens and the shack. He knew Tino would have already gone there and checked, but they found little time to talk about it.

CHAPTER 25

Tino did not go to the lancho until nearly a week after the typhoon. He was worried about the chickens. They would have been trapped in their cages, unable to find safe shelter had they been freed to look. As he anticipated, many of the chickens were dead. The coop had fallen over, collapsing on top of the birds. He let loose the few that were still alive and buried the many dead ones. The garden was ravaged. The bean trellis had blown away, pulling the bean vines with them. Most of the furrows were puddles of mud, his crops broken or buried underneath.

The shack lost its sheet metal roof, but the upright posts survived, as did the water-filled drum. It was too heavy for the wind to topple. The army footlocker was blown almost to the edge of the plateau but became wedged between a coral boulder and the base of one of the mango trees. The Mason jars inside were broken, but the rest of the contents remained intact, though more battered and dented than before. Tino found Philip's stainless steel basin at the bottom of the ravine. He chuckled, knowing Philip would be pleased.

Well, he thought to himself, *we'll just have to start over.* He was glad Philip enjoyed the lancho. The work of rebuilding it would be easier with an enthusiastic partner. Philip was indeed enthusiastic and eager to labor with his hands—to do actual construction and not just push a pencil. In the months that followed, Philip helped Tino rebuild the shack with scrap lumber and discarded materials they collected from project sites. They built a sturdier, fenced-in chicken coop and purchased two roosters and half a dozen young hens. They also built a new and larger open-air shed with a small store room for the footlocker and the cooking pots and pans.

Philip salvaged a discarded solid wood exterior door from one of his public works sites and persuaded a truck driver to haul it up San Ramon Hill to the parking lot of the officers' club. From there, he dragged the door along the jungle path to the lancho. He removed the doorknob and hinges, added stumps of scrap four-by-four lumber for legs, and turned it into a "nap" bench in the shack. He didn't show it outwardly, but he was exceptionally proud of his work; it was the first thing he ever built by himself. Although the bench was hard and uncomfortable, it was long enough to accommodate Philip's full length. Vivian purchased a couple of thick palm fiber mats to cushion the surface and covered the mats with an old quilt to make sitting or lounging on it more comfortable.

Parker never expressed interest in going to Tino's lancho, but as often as Philip chose the lancho over pursuits with him and other officers, he started to feel left out. When Philip and the Camachos prepared for their next outing to the lancho, Parker meekly asked to come along. Once there, Vivian gave him a tour of the newly constructed shed and chicken coop and of the fruit trees, pointing out which was which. Later, he watched incredulously as Tino and Philip, both wearing well-worn broad-brimmed straw hats, worked in the garden. Parker was amazed at Philip's skill with Tino's *fosiños*, a long pole tipped with a sharpened iron blade that looked like the straightened head of a hoe. Philip skimmed the *fosiños* blade just beneath the surface of the soil, slicing through the roots of weeds around a row of pepper plants. After a while, Philip laid down the unwieldy implement and sauntered over to the water-filled drum at the corner of the shack. Parker blanched when Philip sloshed his hands in the water before cupping some in his palms and drinking it. Dozens of mosquito larvae were wriggling in the water, but Philip didn't seem bothered by them.

"You drink that?" The look on Parker's face was one of shocked revulsion.

"Sure. You wriggle your hands in the water to drive them away then you drink. They won't hurt you," Philip said.

Philip had also mastered the art of selecting, husking, cracking, and grating coconuts, although he was never as skilled or as fast as his tutors. He proudly showed off his skills to Parker, who was as impressed as Philip had been when he watched Vivian do it. By then, Philip was thoroughly at home at the lancho and knew every inch of it. During the mango season that summer, he climbed one of the mango trees, nestled himself on a branch, and ate his fill of ripe and almost ripe mangoes. He thought it was so wonderful an experience that he wrote home about it. Philip especially enjoyed breadfruit season. He had read the Bounty trilogy in high school and had watched the 1935 blockbuster motion picture, *Mutiny on the Bounty*, starring Charles Laughton and Clark Gable. At the time, Philip knew nothing about breadfruit except that collecting breadfruit saplings was Captain Bligh's mission in the South Pacific. Philip felt privileged to see, firsthand, full-grown breadfruit trees and to know how breadfruit looked and tasted. He also learned that there was a seeded breadfruit unique to the Marianas, whose fruit contained nuts called *hutu*, which, when boiled, were almost like roasted chestnuts but not sweet.

Parker was not as romantic about breadfruit, although he liked it also. Both liked it roasted black on an open fire. Tino would roast at least two good-sized ones then break them open, and the four of them would eat it, piping hot, with butter or pork fat. Philip's favorite way to eat it was boiled in thick coconut milk. Parker liked it when it was ripe and oven-baked like a sweet warm dessert. Parker liked going to the lancho, but only went occasionally. Philip eventually spent almost all his free time there and often went on his own. He loved the lancho.

I could live here, he said to himself before dozing off on his nap bench one afternoon. There was a sense of freedom at the lancho that Philip had never experienced before. He was a city boy, the proverbial rich kid who spent his summers at a camp that lacked nothing. The lancho was crude, primitive, devoid of luxuries—there was not a toilet for at least a mile around.

The first time Philip had to "go," after his second or third visit to the lancho before the typhoon, he excused himself to find a private spot. He only needed to urinate, but Tino and Vivian shot each other concerned looks when he stood up.

"What?" Philip was puzzled.

"You have to ask permission first," Vivian said.

"Mr. Camacho, may I go find a place to pee?"

"Not Papa, Mr. Avery. You have to ask the *taotaomo'na.*"

There was a curious smile on Tino's face, but he said nothing, leaving Vivian to explain.

"They're the spirits of our ancestors, the people who came before us," Vivian said. "The jungle is their domain. Before you enter it or take anything from it or defile it in any way, you must respect them and ask their permission first. If you don't, they'll pinch you and leave you with strange bruises on your body, or else they'll make you sick. So sick you could die."

"But I've gone into the jungle many times before," Philip said, wondering why they were just then telling him this strange story.

"That's because we always asked for you, but now you have to start asking for yourself because we noticed you had bruises."

"So how are you supposed to ask?"

"You say, 'grandfathers and grandmothers, allow me to'—you tell them what you want to do. If you need to use the bathroom, you ask to go— 'here on your land because I cannot reach mine in time.' Then you do what you need to do," Vivian said. She was quite serious about the custom.

At first Philip thought it was a cruel way to take advantage of an ignorant American, to make him the brunt of jokes. But it was not like Vivian or Tino to make fun of anyone or to treat them like fools. He didn't think they would ever humiliate him in such a manner. Later, after discreetly asking around, he learned that asking permission was a universal Chamorro practice and that the Chamorros were in earnest about observing it. From then on, Philip always asked. He didn't believe in the jungle spirits, but asking their permission seemed a simple, respectful way to enjoy the jungle. He didn't get any more strange bruises either.

Philip promised to help Tino dig a pit and build an outhouse in a discreet spot safely within the lancho property before leaving the island for his next duty station.

If and when the water drum needed to be filled, Philip no longer hesitated to splash Vivian and knock her down. He would sit beside her in the water and talk, sharing stories of their childhood and school years. Having never gone to college, Vivian was intensely interested in Philip's accounts of campus life. Then with their backsides dripping wet, they would race up the slope, seeing who would spill the least amount of water from their water can. Philip would win as many times as Vivian.

Vivian was an inseparable part of the lancho experience. She was a jungle orchid, one made of steel—confident, capable, and completely at home in the jungle. Philip thought about the girls he grew up with and the women he dated back home. Unlike Vivian, none of them would have been as comfortable in the jungle. They would have balked at the notion of squatting in the wild to relieve themselves, at least until the urge was too great. They wouldn't have considered eating from discarded dishes rinsed in mosquito larvae-laden water. They were a different breed of female. Vivian, on the other hand, was as much at home in their world as in the jungle. She could be as unbridled and carefree as Tarzan's Jane or as proper and refined as any other ladies in polite company. With a better wardrobe, she would have been indistinguishable from them, except more tan.

Vivian was constantly on Philip's mind. He was beginning to realize that his admiration for her had turned into something deeper. He still didn't believe he could truly fall in love—not in the same undying way Tino loved Sylvia, but he was at a loss to define what he was feeling. He decided it was only infatuation, a different kind of spark for a different kind of girl, one that would eventually fizzle out like all the other sparks in his life. He waited for the fizzle, but it never came.

CHAPTER 26

On a beautiful Wednesday morning in July 1940 at ten o'clock, the earth shook. Somewhere deep in the ground, something shifted and sent powerful shockwaves to the surface. The low, distant rumble could be sensed, both as a sound and a shudder. At first there was a strong, sudden jolt followed by a steady vibration that quickly escalated to violent shaking. Panicked people ran screaming from their houses and into the streets. Sitting as they do on the lip of the Marianas Trench, the deepest part of the Pacific Ocean, Guam and its sister islands, one of which is home to an active volcano, experienced earthquakes almost daily. Most are quick shudders, lasting only seconds, and many are not felt at all. The July temblor was exceptional. It was the most powerful one in ten years. Some thatched houses collapsed. Mamposteria walls cracked, some beyond repair. Even the navy government compound wasn't spared. The first quake was followed by several aftershocks throughout the rest of the day.

At school, Vivian and her fellow teachers fled into the courtyard. The school year was over, and they were closing up the classrooms for the summer. Shoppers in the stores and navy personnel and employees at the Governor's Palace also fled outdoors. In the immediate aftermath, people frantically searched for loved ones. Tino ran as fast as he could toward Leary School to look for Vivian. Philip wanted to follow him, but his duty was to stay put, to attend to his responsibilities in and around the compound. As soon as Tino found Vivian, father and daughter raced home to see if and what damage their house might have sustained.

The house that Tino and Sylvia bought withstood many earthquakes and typhoons over the years, but it was not indestructible. Since damage repairs from the recent typhoon had been completed only a month earlier, Tino hoped for the best. As he and Vivian approached the house, they saw that outwardly, it appeared undamaged. To their relief, there were a few cracks in the plaster walls, but nothing serious. Inside, they found broken dishes and overturned furniture on both levels. As Tino started righting the furniture upstairs, Vivian began sweeping up the broken dishes and glassware downstairs. Sylvia's statue of the Virgin Mary, which Vivian kept in her bedroom, fell from its place on her dresser and onto her bed. It did not break. Vivian picked it up, kissed Mary's head, and then nestled the statue in one of her dresser drawers until the danger of strong aftershocks had passed.

Again, Philip and Parker did not come home until late that night. Vivian heard them come in and go straight to their rooms. *They must be exhausted,* she thought as she drifted into uneasy sleep.

The earthquake claimed the lives of forty-six people throughout the island. Over the following days, Tino and Vivian attended the rosaries and funerals of at least a dozen distant relatives and friends, including three children in one family. The children, twelve-year-old Pedro, his eleven-year-old brother Antonio, and their eight-year-old sister Emily were crushed to death when their home collapsed before they could get out. Their mother was outside, hanging her wash when the earthquake occurred. Screaming, she dug desperately through the rubble to get to her children. Her husband, a worker at the navy yard, ran home to find his wife lifting Emily's body into the yard. With the tortured cries that only an inconsolable father could make, he carried out the bodies of his sons and laid them on the ground beside his daughter. Emily was one of Vivian's students. With a heavy heart, Parker accompanied Vivian and Tino to the children's funeral and stayed for their burial at the cemetery. He knew all three children.

The children were always together, roaming the streets around the plaza and government compound and selling homemade coconut candy, pumpkin *buchi-buchi* (deep-fried turnovers) and banana or *lemai* (breadfruit) *buñelos* (doughnuts). They, or at least their mother, knew that *merienda* time, around three or four in the afternoon, was a profitable time to peddle her fresh, warm sweets among the government workers and navy personnel. Parker was a loyal customer, especially of the *buchi-buchi.* It tickled the children to tears to hear him pronounce the word. They made him say it at least thrice and giggled and laughed hysterically before they gave him the three turnovers his nickel purchased. And Parker laughed with them; it was the high point of his day, a real stress reliever.

The children's marketing strategy—trying to charm him into buying more sweets than he wanted—always amused him. He enjoyed countering their sales pitches with good-natured teasing and conversing with them about school and their plans for the future. Emily was a little chatterbox who asked endless questions and freely offered her ideas and opinions on nearly any topic. Antonio was the skeptical one who couldn't reconcile why Parker's parents gave him three last names: Parker Winston Reed. Pedro, the eldest, was bright and ambitious. He bombarded Parker with questions about joining the navy and becoming a seagoing officer. The enlisted ranks were not for him; Pedro wanted to command a gunboat up the Yangtze

River or a battleship in the Atlantic. A week before the earthquake, Pedro proudly told Parker that he was going to pursue his dream and become a navy officer when he grew up. Parker had no doubt the boy would make it, even if he had to work his way out of the galleys, where most Chamorro navy men were relegated.

After having experienced a dreadful typhoon four months prior and done more hard labor than he had ever done before, Parker was truly shaken. The earthquake had frightened him badly. It was so powerful and so damaging that he genuinely thought he was going to die. He saw buildings actually vibrate and shudder before collapsing. He and everyone around him were thrown to the ground. Parker had never experienced earthquakes before coming to Guam. His first experience with one, although not a strong one, shattered his sense of reality. Solid ground was not supposed to convulse. The earth beneath his feet was not supposed to move on its own. The sensation was so shocking, so unnerving, so frightening that he thought the world was coming to an end. In the year since his arrival, he had felt others, but none frightened him as badly as the big one that killed his three little friends.

By then, Parker was physically and emotionally exhausted, and grief caught up with him. A few days after the children's funeral, he was at his desk in the compound when the cathedral bells sounded the three o'clock hour. He looked up, expecting to see the children standing at his door with their basket of goodies, smiling and ready to talk him into spending more than a penny apiece for three doughnuts if they were sold out of *buchi-buchi*. Parker's heart sank. There was no one in his open doorway.

"Doesn't this island ever get a break? Don't you people ever give up?" he said out loud, not expecting the workers around him to respond. He knew he would lose his composure if anyone said a word. He rose from his desk and left the building. He walked around the plaza and read from his Bible before he could return to his desk.

Having experienced a devastating typhoon and a killer earthquake and several lesser ones of each in between, Parker realized that facing natural disasters was a fact of life for the people who live on Guam. Yet no matter what struck them, they immediately picked themselves up and kept on going. He had witnessed the cleanup efforts and even participated in them. He had watched how everyone, even the children, helped one another without argument or complaint. He realized that the strong Chamorro instinct for survival had developed not only out of their will to live, but also on their recognition of nature's foibles, their stoic acceptance of the consequences, and on their dependence on one another. Though casual and short-lived, Parker's acquaintance with the children connected him to the people and the island in a way he never expected. Guam was not his home; it was not the land of his birth, but it was no longer a strange, foreign place. Its people were not Spanish-speaking brown-skinned natives, as old news reports described, but were English-speaking American loyalists with brown skin. Parker would be forever linked to the island, the people, and to the memory of a little pixie, her owlish brother, and a young man who would never grow up to be a navy officer.

Chapter 27

Philip's work schedule after the earthquake did not return to normal until the middle of October. The quake occurred shortly before the anniversary of his arrival on Guam, and he missed its commemoration. Vivian bought a small chocolate cake and made a special dinner for him, but he couldn't come home to enjoy it.

Philip would have preferred staying home for Thanksgiving or spending the day at the lancho. Somehow, another Thanksgiving—without a New England autumn when the leaves change color and the weather starts growing cold and people put pumpkins on their doorsteps and he could take the train home to his family—just didn't feel right. But orders were orders. Like the year before, he and Parker were required to attend the governor's family dinner for all officers, including the unmarried ones. They had attended the dinner and had enjoyed it very much. This year was different; they had grown close to Vivian and Tino and felt badly that they couldn't bring them as their guests. The governor specifically ordered Philip to attend. Philip had been on Guam for fifteen months by then and was reputed to have "gone native." The governor wanted to see for himself how his renegade lieutenant would do in a social situation among his own kind. Philip, of course, was the perfect Yankee gentleman, suave and sophisticated, and masterfully charming all the wives, especially the governor's.

Thanksgiving had yet to become the American holiday Chamorros would adopt with a passion. They were not American citizens, although they tried several times to ask for citizenship, starting as early as 1901, and even sending envoys in 1936 to lobby directly with President Franklin Roosevelt and Congress but to no avail. The navy testified vigorously against the grant of citizenship, saying the Chamorros were not ready to fulfill the duties and obligations of citizenship. Since the holiday was focused on a specific dinner menu, it had limited appeal among Chamorros. They could not relate to pilgrims with blunderbusses and Indians with baskets of multicolored ears of corn, nor did they have any connection to the Civil War. Giving thanks with family and for family is supposed to be done daily, not just once a year.

And marinated grilled chicken was as good as roasted turkey, perhaps even better.

For the most part, the Americans could secure many of their Thanksgiving menu items locally, others had to be imported. The navy went to extraordinary lengths annually to provide its dependents and personnel with a traditional Thanksgiving dinner—from cranberry sauce to pumpkin pie. Although he had been reluctant to go to the governor's Thanksgiving dinner, Philip was delighted to find oyster stuffing—his favorite—and cranberry sauce, not jellied but whole, on the menu. Parker enjoyed everything that was served. For him, the only dish missing was pecan pie. The governor's Thanksgiving dinner for enlisted personnel and their families, which took place the day before, was much larger but equally as grand as the dinner for the officers.

Christmas made Philip and Parker homesick and yearn for home. The holiday was not celebrated in the Camacho home in any way to which the navy men were accustomed. The previous Christmas, the men's first on Guam, passed quietly. There was a Christmas Eve party at the compound. Philip and Parker wanted to bring Vivian and Tino as their guests, but it was open only to navy personnel and their families. Both men attended the party, but stayed only long enough for their presence to be noted. They spent Christmas day at the officers' club, which was all but deserted.

For Christmas in 1940, Parker was determined not to go through another disheartening holiday. By then, he, Philip, and the Camachos were much better acquainted, and Parker was not uncomfortable about celebrating as he knew how. He tried his best to create a taste of his and Philip's home for Tino and Vivian to experience and for the four of them to enjoy together. He purchased a potted Norfolk pine and placed it in the parlor. It was a scrubby little thing with long skinny branches and tiny needles. It looked nothing like a spruce or a fir and didn't give off any scent, but it was a pine and it was the closest he could come to a real Christmas tree.

Seeing the little tree reminded Philip of home. He missed reveling in the wonderful fragrances emanating from the kitchen beginning a few days before Thanksgiving and continuing past New Year's to his birthday on January sixth. From the time he was five years old and until he left for college, he would sneak into the kitchen when mother wasn't watching and cajole Mrs. Mueller, the cook, into giving him a warm, freshly baked cookie or a piece of whatever pie she had baked or some other wonderful treat she made only at that joyous time of year.

Though Parker's tree was small and scrawny, it also made him think about the cold and the snow and all the traditional activities that came with the season: going on sleigh rides and skiing, sledding and skating all afternoon then warming up in front of a crackling fire, roasting chestnuts and sipping rum toddies or eggnog spiked with fine old Irish whiskey. He wondered how Vivian would react to all the New England traditions he loved so much. He wished he could introduce her to them to watch her reactions. She, of course, would be colder than she had ever been in her life, but he would bundle her up in furs and hats, in earmuffs and gloves, in snow boots and scarves, and keep her warm in his arms. *Someday*, he thought.

Parker invited Vivian and Tino to join them upstairs to decorate his tree, imbibe in some spiked eggnog, and sing some Christmas carols. Father and daughter were familiar with many American Christmas traditions, but not with bringing a live potted tree into the house. While Vivian eagerly joined in, Tino savored his mug of eggnog and simply watched the tree-decorating process. Philip attached hooks to the glass figures and balls Parker had purchased and handed them, one at a time, to the decorators. Laughing, Vivian chided Parker for his terrible decorating skills; he had too many decorations on one branch and not enough on others.

"I do declare, Mr. Reed," she said, feigning the accent of a Southern belle. She had read an excerpt of *Gone with the Wind* in *Reader's Digest* and was eager to see the movie when it finally came to Guam. "You know absolutely nothin' 'bout decoratin', suh!"

"Well, ma'am, that's why we need you here to guide us clumsy oxen," he shot back.

Philip watched Vivian intently, charmed by her laughter and her playful nature, something she only displayed at the lancho. After a little bit of whiskey in the eggnog, her playful side was on full display. She was different from all the other girls he knew, but different in a most entertaining and captivating way. He liked watching her, listening to her, being with her, even if it was always in the company of others, either Tino or Parker, and usually both.

On Christmas morning, Vivian and Tino woke up late; they had attended midnight Mass the night before. After the Mass, they greeted their neighbors and friends and enjoyed some traditional refreshments, especially some *buñelos dagu* (yam doughnuts available only at Christmastime.) They didn't get home until after two in the morning. They awoke at ten and found four gaily wrapped gifts on the kitchen table. The gifts were from Parker and Philip. Father and daughter were surprised. They were not accustomed to exchanging gifts at Christmas. Like most Chamorros, exchanging gifts—usually special food items or sweet treats—occurred on the Feast of the Three Kings on January sixth, which, unbeknownst to them, was also Philip's birthday.

In anticipation of Christmas morning, Tino and Vivian prepared a hearty breakfast of bacon, ham, fried and boiled eggs, Tino's cinnamon rolls and fresh bread, butter, cheese, sliced fruit, freshly squeezed tangerine juice, and coffee. Since it was Christmas, the menu throughout the day would be more generous than usual. The fragrance of the foods brought Parker and Philip clattering down the stairs; they were accustomed to breakfast at seven and by eleven-thirty, when the table was set, they were ravenous. Vivian laughed out loud when Parker referred to the meal as "brunch." She had never heard the term before, but both men assured her that it was an actual term for a midmorning meal that was both breakfast and lunch.

After eating, and with boyish anticipation and smiles, Parker and Philip watched Tino and Vivian open their gifts. From Philip, Tino received a bottle of Johnnie Walker Black Label scotch whiskey. Tino was speechless; he allowed himself only the cheapest brand of scotch. Only the wealthiest civilians could afford Black Label. Tino looked at Philip who was smiling broadly. From Parker, Tino received a handsome, multitool pocketknife with his initials, *CFC*, engraved on the side. The pocketknife became a treasured possession that Tino would carry for the rest of his life and leave to his eldest grandson, Christopher. Deeply touched, all Tino could say was "thank you." His gratitude was genuine and sincere.

Parker gave Vivian an unabridged, hardcover copy of *Gone with The Wind*. It made her squeal with delight. The *Reader's Digest* excerpt left her wanting to read more, to know the whole story. Now the book—every delicious chapter—was hers. She threw her arms around Parker and kissed his cheek several times in quick succession. Philip's gifts were a tortoiseshell barrette and a beautiful lace veil to wear at church. Vivian wondered why he gave her two gifts; he wouldn't have known that her birthday was on December 20. She and her father had never mentioned their birthdates. Since childhood, she received only one present and had to choose whether to receive it on her birthday or on Three Kings. Philip had purchased the barrette the month before and intended it as his Christmas gift, but when he saw the veil, he couldn't resist. It was prettier than Vivian's old one. At five dollars, the veil was pricy, but Vivian was worth it, and he could afford both gifts.

"Damn it, Avery, you outdid me again," Parker complained in jest.

"Yes, but you got a hug and a bunch of kisses. I didn't." Philip felt slighted. He wondered why Vivian didn't also give him a hug and at least one kiss . . . for each gift. He didn't think Tino would have taken offense or suspected anything untoward about it under the circumstances. It was Christmas after all.

Vivian let the comment pass unnoted; she caught Philip's meaning. She wanted to hug and kiss him also, but not in the same way. She wanted a real hug, an embrace, and a real kiss on the lips, the way Philip had kissed her before the typhoon. None of that could take place in front of her father, and none of it would have meant anything if Philip wasn't sincere. Since he had made no attempt to kiss her since April, she wondered whether he thought of her only as a flirtatious distraction to take his mind off having to be in Guam, even if only temporarily. Her heart sank at the thought. She had foolishly allowed herself to fall in love with him and would have to suffer the heartbreak when it was time for him to leave. It hurt her to think that his words about caring for her were empty ones.

"These gifts are far too much for us, but we are very grateful," Vivian said.

"Some of us are not so bad," Philip said, hoping to ingratiate himself to her. He had come to the realization that Vivian meant more to him than he could understand. She was not a fleeting spark. He had tried to suppress and control the spark, primarily out of respect for Tino, but it didn't fizzle as he had expected. Instead, it grew larger, steadier, and warmer. Was it love? He didn't know; he had never been in love before.

Vivian was now all Philip could think about. He ached to hold her in his arms. He made up his mind to reveal his feelings to her and hoped she felt the same way about him. He sensed that she did but had no real proof. He wanted Vivian in his life somehow, but she was not the kind of girl who would consider a tawdry love affair. A short-term mistress wasn't what he wanted either, and he wouldn't have insulted her to ask for such. For the first time in his life, Philip thought about marriage. "Tying the knot" always seemed to him to be a strange and cautionary way of referring to marriage, but now it made sense. He wanted to be tied to Vivian and her to him. Although the prohibition against marriage to native women had been lifted some twenty years earlier, such marriages were still frowned upon, especially for servicemen, and securing approval to marry, which was required, was a bureaucratic nightmare, an effective way to discourage it. Philip would have gladly waded through the required process, but marriage to Vivian, even if she would have him, was not a smart career move.

Three days after Christmas, among the Christmas and early birthday cards from old girlfriends and college buddies, and a gift box from his mother and Jennifer, Philip received a startling letter from his father.

"I have good news for you, son," his father's letter started.

> I have learned that the navy department is considering organizing a special unit of fighting men whose primary

> mission will be to undertake construction projects. It is to be unique in the annals of U.S. military history.
>
> This is still hearsay, but likely to come to fruition, given the war in Europe and growing tensions in Asia. Should that be the case, I have let it be known that I would like you to be considered for a slot. I received certain assurances this morning that, despite your lack of experience, you will be among the civil engineers considered for selection. It will be your responsibility to qualify. If this appeals to you, I shall press my advantage.

It did appeal to Philip, very much. He wrote back immediately and thanked his father for the news. It was better than a transfer or a shortened assignment. He was elated by the news and excited by the prospect. A unit free of the limitations and constraints of the army's corps of engineers and the navy's civil engineering corps, of which he was a part, would be unique and historic when established. It would be trained to fight as well as to fix, to do battle as well as to build, and to defend as well as to destroy. To be in on the ground floor of such a unit presented untold career opportunities and advantages.

As he dropped his response letter in the outgoing mail slot, Philip thought about his chances. He was already hampered by a lack of experience on large-scale commercial engineering projects, which was what was being sought. His actual time in the service also was limited; he had been in the navy less than three years. His education and personal life would be factors also. His education was not a worry; he earned his degree from one of the finest engineering schools in the nation, but having a wife who wasn't of equal station or color would not have boded well for his advancement.

Philip kept his father's news and his decision to pursue the opportunity to himself. He grappled with his emotions and decided to give up any future with Vivian. Until he met her, his only objective in life was to succeed in his career. Since his commitment to a naval career had come well before wanting a wife, his career would remain at the forefront of his purpose. There would be other women in his life, someone better suited, more acceptable in the world of high-ranking military men and their ladies. Libby Morton immediately came to mind. She was that sort of woman, groomed and polished for that world. Philip thought of her as a plaything, someone to have fun with when the mood struck. He recoiled at the prospect of spending the rest of his life tied to her simply because she fit the role.

Philip chose his career over Vivian, but the decision didn't make him happy. He cared too much to ask her to compromise her morals and values, her dignity, and self-respect for anything less than lawful marriage. He had kissed her passionately only once in a moment of weakness. He could leave it at that, and Vivian would never know that there was any more to his feelings. If Vivian felt anything deeper for him, she hid it well. She was naturally affectionate but never gave him any indication that her affection for him was any greater than for Parker. Yet there was something between them, a connection. He felt it the moment their hands first touched.

His rotation date would be coming up in August, seven months away, but an eternity to continue longing for Vivian. If his father was successful, he could leave Guam even earlier. Philip wished for the sooner departure.

Chapter 28

On Saturday, January fourth, two days before Philip's twenty-fifth birthday, a stateside dance band was slated to perform at the officers' club. The band was touring the Pacific and was stopping briefly on Guam after the New Year. Everyone in town was excited about the upcoming dance. It was the most exciting event to come about in months, especially after the typhoon and the horrible earthquake, and it was the talk of the town. Parker was looking forward to hearing live music, dancing, and letting off steam, but Philip was not eager to celebrate. He was reaching the quarter-century mark in his life and was facing a momentous career opportunity, but his heart was heavy.

"Come with us, Miss Vivvy," Parker said. By then, both men were using Tino's pet name to address her. It didn't bother Vivian, but it annoyed Tino. "Vivvy" was his pet name, not theirs. He thought it was rude of them to take such liberty. Of course, he said nothing to them about it. He figured their Christmas presents more than "paid" for the privilege.

"I don't think so, Mr. Reed," said Vivian. "I don't know how to dance, and I'd be uncomfortable."

"But you have to! Don't you want to celebrate Avery's birthday?" Parker countered. "I promise you won't be a wallflower."

To Vivian's surprise, Tino encouraged her to take up Parker's invitation. It was uncharacteristic of him. She had turned twenty the month before, and Tino knew that he had to start letting her get exposed to an adult world. She was still so naive about life, or so he believed. He even persuaded her to buy a new dress and shoes for the event and gave her the money, a sizeable amount, as her Three King's gift.

On the evening of the dance, Vivian wore her new dress—a pretty, floral-patterned satin dress with a daring, scooped neckline, crinoline skirt, three-quarter length sleeves, and a black patent leather belt. On her feet she wore new, black patent leather pumps with two-inch heels. Vivian thought her mother's jewelry—the heavy Spanish rose-designed gold bracelet and matching earrings, chain, and pendant—were too flashy for her taste, but she dared not say anything about them since they were her father's wedding gifts to her mother. He had entrusted them to her, along with the Japanese lacquer box, when she turned sixteen. She wore them only on special occasions; otherwise she wore her grandmother's simple gold ear studs. Vivian donned the Spanish pieces and brushed out her dark auburn hair, allowing the waves to frame her face. She even bought some face powder, rouge, and lipstick and tried her hand at a little primping. The results were worth every penny she spent. Polished up, Vivian was very pretty. Satisfied, she smiled at herself in the mirror and prepared to make her entrance.

"No, Miz Scarlet, you're not going to be a wallflower tonight," Parker said when she opened her bedroom door. He, Philip, and Tino were sitting at the dining table waiting for her. They instinctively stood up as she emerged from her room. Tino gasped audibly and looked as if he would shed tears. He could see Sylvia in Vivian's face. Philip's heart skipped, but he said nothing. He suppressed a reaction that would have mirrored Tino's. Vivian was lovelier than the men had ever seen her. Philip smiled weakly, acknowledging her triumph, and saddened by it even more.

The expression on Philip's face was difficult to interpret. Vivian looked specifically for his reaction. He was smiling, but it seemed like only a polite gesture; there was no sparkle behind it. Vivian hoped to impress him but couldn't tell whether she had or not. She turned her face away and blushed, embarrassed that she had failed to elicit a more enthusiastic reaction from him. She didn't know that at that moment, Philip was trying to keep his mind in charge, his heart in check, and his emotions under control. He thought about backing out of the evening and staying home, alone in his misery, but he couldn't, not without revealing himself. Vivian had slowly filled a void in his life with wonder and joy and love. He became aware of that void only after choosing his career over her. He now felt hollow and empty and realized that he needed her. But he had made a decision and had to stick with it. He said nothing during the cab ride to the officers' club on San Ramon Hill.

The club, still trimmed with Christmas and New Year's decorations, was more crowded than at the New Year's Eve party the previous Wednesday. The mood was even more lively and festive. The lights were dim, the music was blaring, and couples mobbed the dance floor. Parker immediately went to the bar. Philip spotted an empty table for two and rushed to claim it. Vivian followed behind him, wondering why he was more uncommunicative and remote than usual. Lost in their respective thoughts, neither noticed the attention their entrance had drawn, several young officers to Vivian and a bevy of local girls and navy nurses to Philip.

Philip pulled out a chair for Vivian and asked, "Would you care for something to drink?" After she politely said no, he excused himself and headed for the bar. He returned with a drink several minutes later. He sat beside her and stared at his glass, swishing around the ice and liquid inside, and drinking in large gulps. Minutes later, he held up his empty glass and motioned to a waiter for another one. The busy waiter ignored his signal and hurried by with a tray of drinks to deliver. Philip excused himself again and went back to the bar. Vivian watched as he spoke with a woman standing next to him. A minute later, they were on the dance floor. A couple of dances later, the two returned to the bar.

Vivian watched Philip flirt blatantly with every woman who looked his way. He was on the dance floor with different partners for several songs in a row. Between dances, he returned to the bar and ordered drinks, one after another. Already uncomfortable, Vivian grew alarmed by his strange behavior. Although she had never witnessed his conduct in a public setting, his behavior was far out of character. Philip finally returned to Vivian's side, sat down beside her, and scowled at every man who neared their table. He ignored her, trying desperately to prove to himself that he didn't want or need Vivian's company and attention.

As they sat there, Bernice Cruz Frasier, who had been Vivian's classmate, and Norma Kirkwood, who was a year ahead of them, smiled and said hello as they passed by. Vivian acknowledged them with a nod and a feigned smile, certain that they, the daughters of Guam's elite, were being condescending toward her. She couldn't accept that they were being genuinely friendly and probably a little envious. She was sitting with a tall, strikingly good-looking man. They giggled as they walked away and Vivian heard Bernice say, "Gosh, he's gorgeous!"

They captured Philip's attention immediately. He turned in his seat and watched where they went. Bernice and Norma joined three other local girls—their equals, the beautiful daughters of American fathers and Chamorro mothers. All of them had the flair and worldly finesse of social experience. Some, like Rosemary Perkins, who was twenty-two, had attended high school and college in California, and had only recently returned home to Guam. Rosemary had traveled widely and could speak on many topics like politics and economics. She was also very beautiful, well-schooled in California on how to wear makeup and look like a movie star. Philip headed straight for Rosemary and asked her to dance.

Vivian overheard Rosemary's companions giggling and talking loudly at their table, over the blaring music, behind her.

"Who is that guy?" Norma asked.

"That's Phil Avery. He's a lieutenant. He's one of the officers who rent Vivian Camacho's upstairs apartment. It's that house near the back gate. Isn't he handsome?" Bernice said. "The other officer isn't bad looking either. That's him over there on the dance floor."

Rather than point him out impolitely, Bernice described Parker to her companions and told them his name and rank. Vivian wondered how Bernice knew such details.

"Is the lieutenant dating anyone?" Norma asked.

"Not that I know of. Maybe Rosemary after tonight," Bernice said.

"Who's she, and why's he with her?" Norma didn't know Vivian.

"That's Vivian," said the all-knowing Bernice. "Her father works with him in the same office. Maybe he's doing Mr. Camacho a favor by bringing her here."

Bernice's statement shocked Vivian. Maybe Philip and Parker were just doing her father a favor. Maybe bringing her to the dance wasn't really what they wanted. Maybe her father put them up to it. Had he paid them off too? She didn't know how to dance, didn't drink liquor, and didn't know how to behave in a nightclub. And given her companions' behavior, she wasn't needed there. Vivian felt the last shred of her confidence drain from her body and sink into the floor.

As Philip led Rosemary onto the dance floor, Vivian could hear her companions giggling triumphantly. She was crushed. Not only was Philip ignoring her, his attention was now focused on girls with whom she couldn't compete. She was not as pretty as they were. Their clothes were finer, more expensive than hers. They were of the upper class; she was a working girl. Their fathers were big, important men in the community, and their mothers commanded groveling attention. Her father was just a government worker and she grew up without a mother. Her father's words about reaching for the moon—about trying to grasp for what is always beyond reach—rang in her troubled mind.

When he returned after walking Rosemary back to her party, Philip sat down and drummed his fingers on the table, lost in thought and still not saying much to Vivian. He then ordered another drink, his fifth or sixth since they arrived. Philip was obviously trying to numb himself. Vivian assumed it was to her presence beside him. Hurt, she decided to solve his problem and remove herself as soon as an opportunity arose.

"Sure you wouldn't like something to drink? A Coca-Cola or a ginger ale?" he asked after a while. "No, thank you," she answered, trying not to sound sarcastic, or as annoyed as she really felt. His suggestion of something nonalcoholic made her feel less than adult. Although she didn't drink, she felt like she was being treated like a child.

Vivian tried to act relaxed and nonchalant, but she couldn't pull it off. She was certain everyone could see her discomfort and irritation. Despite his promise, Parker never sought them out to rescue her from the loneliness and awkwardness she was feeling. Vivian caught a glimpse of him gyrating on the dance floor, beer bottle firmly in hand. *At least he was having a good time,* she thought.

From across the room, near the bar and among a small group of navy nurses, Vivian noticed that one of them, a tall, attractive woman with flaming red hair and pouty red lips, was eyeing Philip. The woman was swaying to the beat of the music with a cigarette in one hand and a drink in the other. Philip caught her staring and smiled at her. A few moments later, he rose, sauntered over, and asked her to dance. Vivian watched as he followed the woman onto the dance floor. When a romantic ballad began, he took her in his arms and began a slow waltz, their bodies pressed together. The woman was speaking to him, but Vivian couldn't make out any words. As they swayed to the music, the redhead slid her arms up around Philip's neck and rested her head on his shoulder. Her face fit perfectly in the space between his jaw and his chest. He wrapped his arms around her and locked his fingers together at the small of her back. The sight of them at that moment made Vivian nauseous.

Jealousy, something that Vivian had never felt before, welled up from deep in her belly and scorched her neck and face. The realization startled her. Who was she to be jealous of a woman who was Philip's equal in age, education, affiliation, and more importantly, in ethnicity? She was only his landlord's daughter with no entitlement to his attention or affection.

As Vivian watched, her spirits sinking by the second, Philip waltzed the red-haired nurse over to the table and said, "This is Vivian, my landlord's daughter." The nurse had apparently asked about the companion he had abandoned at his table, and they made their way over so that Philip could tell her. His words were not an introduction but an explanation. The look on the redhead's face was dismissive, as if saying, "Go home, little girl, you're out of your league."

Vivian did feel out of her league; she *was* out of her league. She had no league. She felt miserable, and anger began to gnaw at her. She was alone and self-conscious. She felt belittled and forsaken by the escorts who had coaxed her into being there and abandoned by the friends she thought they were. With both men's attention on their dance partners, Vivian calmly rose from her seat and casually walked out, smiling at the people she passed.

Outside the club, she broke down and cried—hot, angry, humiliated, hurt, jealous tears. She started the long walk home down the paved road from the officers' club to the rear of the government compound and through its entire length to reach home. Her walk downhill would have been shorter on the jungle path to her backyard, but she couldn't manage it in high heels in the dark.

"Back already?" Tino asked as Vivian came in the back door. The threesome had left the house at seven-thirty, only two hours earlier.

"Yes, Papa, it was too loud and boring. That kind of place is not for me," she said, trying to sound indifferent. But her eyes were bloodshot and the powder on her face was smeared. She sailed into her room and closed the door. Her feet were blistered and bleeding. She kicked off the new shoes and threw them in her closet, never to be worn again. She carefully removed her mother's jewelry and replaced them in the lacquer box. She emerged in her cotton nightgown a few minutes later and headed to the bathroom to wash her tear-streaked face and get the lipstick off her mouth.

"Where are those two?"

"Still up there, drinking and dancing."

"Oh. Well, good night, Vivvy," Tino said as he kissed her forehead. He was relieved not to smell liquor on her breath.

"Good night, Papa."

Vivian cried into her pillow for a long, long time. Her emotions were in turmoil. She was angry and jealous and offended and hurt and unhappy and in pain all at the same time. She was angry with herself for having agreed to go to the dance. What a stupid place! She was angry at being such a coward; she was as good as Rosemary and Bernice and their companions. She was offended at being treated like a child out of place. She was jealous of the red-haired nurse and hurt that Philip preferred her company. Vivian was in love with a man she could never have, a man so close, yet further away than the moon. A man who had just reminded her, so painfully, that she did not belong in his world.

Chapter 29

From his perch at the bar, Philip watched a young ensign approach Vivian, sitting alone, smiling prettily, and attracting male attention. He intercepted the ensign and scared him off with a scowl. Philip knew that Vivian could have had a pleasant evening, meeting new people, making new friends, and learning to dance with partners eager to teach her. But that was exactly what he feared; he glared jealously at every man who came near her. He knew she would be uncomfortable in the unfamiliar setting, but he did nothing to comfort or assure her. He had never behaved so ungentlemanly or treated anyone so rudely, and he hated himself for it. He wanted to drive Vivian out of his heart and head. He assumed she would react as other women would—slapping him soundly and snuffing out his affection. But Vivian was unlike any other woman he knew.

After another dance with the redhead, Philip glanced over at the table. Vivian was gone. He scanned the dance floor and the rest of the room, but she was nowhere in sight. He asked the ladies emerging from the ladies' room if they had seen her inside. None had. Philip looked but couldn't find her. A chill washed over him. Had he driven too far? He never meant to drive her away. He never expected her to disappear surreptitiously into the night. He started drinking more heavily after Vivian disappeared. The redheaded nurse tried to discourage him, coaxing him onto the dance floor again, but he was no longer interested. By midnight, he was plastered. Racked with guilt, he staggered outside the club and began calling for Vivian, crying out apologies down the darkened road. The redheaded nurse led him gently back inside. She sought out Parker, who was flirting with some of her companions, and urged him to take Philip home.

"Your buddy's going to have one hell of a hangover," she told him. "Give him some Alka-Seltzer tomorrow, and you better take some yourself."

"Sure, sure," he said, not really paying attention as he led one of the nurses onto the dance floor. When they returned, the redhead motioned to Philip's table, where he sat glum-faced and alone. Parker looked around, searching the room in alarm. He hurried over to Philip.

"Avery, where's Vivian?" he demanded. By then, Philip was morose.

"Gone. She left me. I don't know how she feels."

Philip started babbling about being all mixed up and confused and wanting her and wanting home, wanting to stay, wanting to go, to go home to New York, where everything was right and proper, and constant and reliable, like her, and cold and dry, and not so goddamned hot and humid but so soft and sweet and warm. Philip's thoughts and words were jumbled and difficult to follow; he wasn't making sense.

"Reed," Philip said, slurring. "Ice cold logic is telling me to get my f—king head out of my ass."

"I agree. Where's Vivian, Lieutenant?" Parker demanded again, his concern mounting.

"Sound judgment and reason should guide life decisions, shouldn't they? Prudence and practicality should prevail?"

"Yes, yes. Where's Vivian? Did she leave? Did she leave *alone*?" Parker continued to press for an answer.

"Everyone should be who God says they are and what they are, right?"

"Avery, what the hell are you talking about?" Parker said, growing tired of Philip's nonsense.

"I love her, Parker," Philip said sadly, finally admitting to himself, as well as to Parker, what he had been trying desperately to hold back and deny.

"Who? That redhead?" Parker said, suddenly taken aback.

"No, dummy, I love Vivian!" Philip's ramblings finally made sense. *Damn,* the thought raced through Parker's mind, *you do this, buddy boy, and your career is in the toilet.*

"But I treated her so badly, I treated her like shit."

Philip's disjointed description of his actions and discourtesy toward Vivian angered Parker. He had promised not to let Vivian become a wallflower and had purposely stayed away from the table so that she and Philip could enjoy a nice, casual evening together, like a date, without his being a third wheel. But as Philip described it, Vivian must have been terribly hurt and humiliated.

"Why, Philip, why would you do that?"

"Because I need to stop loving her. I *tried* to stop loving her, Parker, but I can't. What am I going to do?"

The thought of Vivian trying to make her way home alone on foot, in the dark, sent a chill through Parker. He could not dictate Philip's behavior or do anything to undo the damage he had done, but Parker felt responsible. Having broken his promise to Vivian, how could he face her again? How could he face Tino after not having better protected his daughter?

"What am I going to do?" Philip repeated.

Angered, Parker snapped, "We're gonna go home, we're gonna apologize. You're gonna pull your shit together and we're gonna fix this."

Philip and Parker staggered home after two in the morning. Tino heard them come up the front steps and into the house—stumbling drunk and shushing each other to be quiet. He realized that something disturbing had occurred at the dance. First Vivian came home alone hours earlier, her face streaked with tears. Then Philip and Parker came home drunk; it was not like them. The behavior of all three was uncharacteristic, so much so that Tino was afraid to ask what had happened. So long as his daughter was safe in her bed, and she was, he felt no need to pry.

Vivian and Tino were up at dawn on Sunday and had gone to Mass, returned, and had both breakfast and lunch before their tenants awoke. Vivian had to wear slippers to church and couldn't hide the sores on her feet or her puffy eyes that morning. Tino noticed them right away. He heard her crying in the night but didn't ask her for an explanation. She didn't offer one either. He pointed upward and said, "Remember the moon."

Tino knew that Vivian was in love with Philip; he could now see it in her eyes, in the way she spoke to him, the way she smiled at him, and he feared for her. Tino had done his best by her and trusted her completely. She never gave him cause to doubt her. Vivian was older and wiser than her adolescent grandmother Amanda had been when she was betrayed. He was certain that Vivian would never have yielded to any man as easily or outside of marriage. Tino didn't worry about that, but he knew that she was not numb to temptation. She was not blind to attraction or immune to love and affection. He was fond of Philip also, but Philip could not be the husband for her. Once his time was up, Philip would be gone, and another navy officer would take his place—at the Governor's Palace and probably at their house as well. And his daughter would be left with a broken heart. It was inevitable.

Neither Philip nor Parker woke until late afternoon. Vivian and her father heard no movement upstairs until around four o'clock. From the direction of the footsteps, they could tell that Parker was up first. He trudged into his bathroom, relieved himself then turned on the shower. About an hour later, Philip staggered into his bathroom, gagged, and threw up in the toilet before climbing into his bathtub. Whether they were too hung over or were embarrassed by their behavior the previous night, neither man came downstairs for supper. Father and daughter ate alone. The men also didn't come downstairs for breakfast the following morning, which was Philip's birthday, nor did they come home for supper. Vivian and her father ate supper by themselves again, but they hardly spoke. She didn't want to hear from him what might have been discussed at work. On Tuesday evening, the three men came home together, walking silently. Vivian prepared supper, but left the men's portions on the stove upstairs. Later that night, Parker mustered the courage to venture downstairs to make his apologies, hoping his request for a snack would lighten the atmosphere.

"Miss Vivian," he started, "May I make a sandwich, please?"

Without looking at him, Vivian pulled out a loaf of bread and a jar of peanut butter from a cupboard and some strawberry jam from the refrigerator. She placed these on the table in front of him and walked away to her room. He followed after her and spoke through her closed door.

"I'm sorry, Miss Vivvy. I'm an asshole for breaking my promise," he said. "It was never my intention to leave you alone with a jerk. I hope you'll forgive me. I promise I'll never do that again."

"Your promises don't mean much, Mr. Reed," she said through the door. Parker had nothing to do with her feelings of inferiority and he did nothing to magnify them, as Philip had. She was upset with him because she became a wallflower despite his promise. Worse, he never came to her table to see if she was all right.

"I truly am sorry," Parker said. He wanted to say more, but the sound of footsteps coming down the stairs silenced him. He scowled at Philip and jogged back up the stairs, abandoning the peanut butter and jam. Tino, who was in the laundry, also heard the footsteps. He stepped back into the shadows, expecting angry words and tears to ensue. His daughter was clearly displeased with both men, but Philip was the focus of her upset. Tino would, if necessary, protect his daughter . . . or Philip. He was taken aback when Philip boldly entered Vivian's room without knocking.

Philip closed the door behind him. Vivian was sitting on her bed, head bowed, looking down at her hands in her lap.

"I hope you don't think me forward," he said softly. He wanted to kneel at her feet and beg her forgiveness, but he remained standing at her door. "I owe you an apology."

"You don't owe me anything, Mr. Avery," she said. There was no anger in her voice.

"Please stop calling me Mr. Avery, Vivian. Call me anything you want, anything but Mr. Avery," Philip said. Vivian didn't answer but in her head thought, *How? I'm just your landlord's daughter.*

Philip spotted her new dress crumpled on the floor. He picked it up and laid it on the bed beside her. "You looked so pretty that night," he said.

He wanted to confess that he loved her, to ask her about their relationship, and if they even had one. He wanted to know if she loved him and if there was hope for him. He wanted to tell her about his father's letter and the unprecedented opportunity that lay before him. He wanted to discuss it with her and to ask her to make the final decision with him as partners.

"You don't need to flatter me, Lieutenant," she said without looking up. Philip flinched. Addressing him by his military rank cut him deeper than her usual "Mr. Avery." He had chosen his career over her, and she unknowingly reminded him that he had done so. "I don't think you really mean it. Please leave."

"I do mean it," he said, "more than you know."

Philip turned and left, closing the door behind him. He was heartsick; he couldn't confess or even apologize. Courage had failed him.

Vivian crumpled up the dress again and threw it at the door. She wanted to scream at him, but why? What right did she have? Who was she to think she could win the affections of such an accomplished man? She allowed herself to reach for the moon, knowing from the start that Philip was beyond her grasp. She thought she could enjoy the ride and jump off unscathed before it ended. But the ride hadn't ended yet, and she was already injured. She loved him but could never have him. Philip was the first man to take her breath away, the first to make her heart beat faster. He was the first man to kiss her and awaken her desires. He filled her life with beautiful fantasies, but she could have him only in fantasies. No matter how high she climbed or how far she stretched, she would never reach his level. Papa was right: the moon is unattainable.

Vivian kept recalling the sight of Philip and the redheaded nurse in each other's arms. At least with Rosemary Perkins, Philip ignored her after the one dance and moved on to other dance partners. His reaction to the redheaded nurse was different. Vivian interpreted Philip's eagerness to dance with her as the delight of someone who finally met his match, a woman of his own kind, and a beautiful one at that. Vivian couldn't compare, couldn't compete. Not with Rosemary and especially not with the redheaded nurse. Vivian would love Philip until he was gone from her life. Maybe after he left Guam, and enough time had passed, her heart would stop aching for him. In the meantime, the only thing she knew to do was avoid him as much as possible.

Vivian started preparing supper early, setting the men's portions on the stove upstairs and setting her father's plate downstairs. She dined alone in her room. Philip and Parker thought she was still angry with them, but Tino assured them that was not the case. Vivian was not the type to stay angry or hold a grudge. Something was troubling her deeply, and he intended to find out. Philip knew that he was the cause of her remoteness and feared that he had destroyed any affection she may have had for him. In a way, he was relieved. If she felt nothing for him, he could leave Guam, knowing only one of them would have a broken heart. His would heal eventually.

"Vivvy, what's wrong?" Tino asked, finally insisting on an explanation. He entered her bedroom and sat beside her on her bed. He suspected her reasons and felt badly for her. With tears welling up in her eyes, she pointed toward the sky.

"My heart is reaching for the moon, Papa, and I'm trying to make it stop," she said, giving in to her sadness and letting the tears fall. "But it's so hard, Papa, it's so hard."

Tino embraced Vivian and let her sob into his shoulder. He didn't need his daughter to name her love; he knew it was Philip. The lieutenant would complete his second year on Guam in seven months. Then he would leave for a new duty station. Tino had to help his daughter hold on until then. He hoped she would not pine as other women had—falling in love with a serviceman who left them so brokenhearted that they never married, never had children, and died as lonely old spinsters. There were several in the community already.

"Vivvy, I know what it is to love someone deeply then lose them," Tino said. "It is hard, it's very hard. In time, the pain eases, but it never goes away. It is a hard thing to accept, but once you do, you can live with the pain much easier."

"Like you, Papa? When you lost Mama? Do you still grieve for her?" Vivian asked.

"Yes, I do. I will never stop loving her," Tino said.

"Are you saying I will live the rest of my life grieving for the one man I love?"

"Vivvy, he is only your first love," her father said. "There will be others in your life. Someday you will meet the right man, and all of this will be a sad memory, only a memory."

"Mama was the first woman you ever loved, Papa. She was the only one. Maybe love comes only once for you and me."

Tino had no comeback. On that point, Vivian was right. Perhaps they were the sort destined only for one love in a lifetime. Although he thought about remarrying someday, Tino did nothing to pursue it. He never met anyone who could replace Sylvia in his heart and mind. Vivian attracted the attention of many boys while she was in school, but none ever turned her head. Philip Avery was the first and only man in whom she showed interest. Her mention of his height and looks following their initial meeting hinted to her father that something about Philip appealed to his daughter. In the months since then, Tino watched Vivian's interest develop into affection, especially after the typhoon. He had also seen changes in Philip and recognized his struggle to suppress his feelings. Tino was caught between lovers who were not supposed to love each other but did. Philip would leave

Guam in less than a year, and the problem for all of them would be solved, Tino hoped.

Vivian could not escape Philip no matter how hard she tried. He seemed to go to extraordinary lengths to get her attention, seeking her out for the simplest of tasks, asking the silliest of questions, inventing excuses to speak with her or be near her. He even curtailed his outdoor activities and excursions and stayed at home, unknowingly thwarting Vivian's efforts to stay away from him. It worried him that she no longer giggled at the funny faces he made at her or blushed if he complimented her. Then one day, she smiled, and for him, all was right with the world again. If all he could hope for was her smile, he would bask in it and try to regain her affection.

Chapter 30

In the days following the New Year's dance, Parker and Philip held lengthy discussions about the letter from Philip's father, about Philip's career goals, and about his feelings for Vivian. Parker initiated their exchange with some terse but carefully couched words about the way Philip had treated Vivian at the dance. Although they had become friends, Parker didn't think their friendship was secure enough for him to be disrespectful to a superior officer, even in private. Philip still outranked him.

"Had I known you were ignoring her, I would have come to her rescue right away," Parker said, trying to remain civil. "She didn't deserve what you did to her."

Philip could see the displeasure behind Parker's eyes. Philip freely admitted that Parker's gallantry would have been welcome relief for Vivian and for himself as well.

"The girl loves you, Avery, don't you know that? You're the only one who doesn't see it."

"You don't know how badly I want to believe that, but I can't let myself," Philip said. "I want her so badly it hurts, but I can't let it happen. I can't be in love with her.

"Why, for God's sake? Because she's not white?" Anger flashed in Parker's eyes. Equally angered, Philip glared at Parker. "How dare you!" he spat. "It has nothing to do with her color."

Philip rose, disappeared into his room, and returned a minute later. "Here's why," he said and handed Parker the letter from his father. Parker's eyes widened as he read it.

"Wow! Congratulations! That's a big deal," Parker's reaction was what Philip expected. No navy man could take such news without awe.

"It's not a done deal, but if it happens, I want in," Philip said. "And that's why I can't be with Vivian."

Parker needed no further explanation. It took his family four generations to "heal" from his great-grandfather's marriage to his great-grandmother, an Indian. Shunned, the couple lived in seclusion in the backwoods of Virginia. Their children, eight in all, were bullied mercilessly. Only Parker's grandmother, Miriam, survived to adulthood; her brothers and sisters succumbing either to injury, disease, or gunshot wounds. Miriam, who was light-skinned, took up with a man from whom she hid her mixed-race heritage. She was pregnant when he found out, and he nearly beat her to death. A kindly Baptist minister named Joshua Parker and his wife took Miriam in and sheltered her until she gave birth. She named her baby Parker, as a way to honor both the minister and his wife. Miriam later married an English farmer named Winston Reed, who didn't care about her race and loved her deeply. He raised her child as his own and fathered seven more children. At his grandmother's insistence, Parker was named after his father and grandfather.

"If she loved me the way I think she loves you, I'd marry her in a heartbeat," Parker said.

"No, I'll marry her and you be my best man," Philip said flippantly, but deep down, he meant it.

Near the end of January, Parker received the news he had been hoping for—he had won promotion to lieutenant, junior grade. He also received Permanent Change of Station orders to Bremerton, Washington. His assignment on Guam was at an end; he had one month to prepare himself to leave. On one hand, his little Chamorro family was proud and happy for him. On the other, they were sad about having to say good-bye. Philip was happy about Parker's promotion, but not about his impending departure. He had come to enjoy his conversations with Parker. Although they talked about many things—the war in Europe, the growing tensions between the U.S. and Japan, the possibility of all-out war and what it meant for them as servicemen, and about returning stateside and what it would be like to be at home again—Philip especially liked hearing from Parker about how Vivian felt about him. Like a grade-school boy, he pressed Parker for every detail, every indication, and every shred of evidence that Vivian cared.

To celebrate Parker's promotion, Philip bought an expensive bottle of champagne, the best he could find on the island. There had been a toast for Parker at the Governor's Palace that afternoon and another at the officer's club early that evening. Philip's toast was to be private, intimate and reserved only for the four of them. He asked Tino and Vivian to join them in the parlor upstairs.

"Here's to one of our nation's newest and finest young officers and my good friend, Lieutenant, Junior Grade, Parker Winston Reed, United States Navy," Philip said as he held up his glass and as Parker blushed. He, Tino, and Vivian held up theirs too. "Hear, hear," Tino said.

Vivian tasted the dry champagne and wrinkled her nose. She didn't like the bitter taste but emptied her glass, forcing it down and chiding herself for having felt slighted by Philip's offering her only soft drinks at the New Year's dance. Tino welcomed a second glass. After father and daughter retired downstairs, Philip and Parker lounged in the parlor to finish off the bottle.

Lieutenant, Junior Grade, Parker Reed left Guam on February 24, 1941. Tino and Vivian were dockside in Piti, insisting on seeing him off. A launch would carry him and several other navy passengers out to the *Henderson* anchored in the harbor.

Vivian kissed Parker's cheek and handed him a coconut that had been carved and painted to look like two parrots perched on either side of a feed bowl. On the back was painted the message "Souvenir of Guam." The coconut shell, which was cut in half, cleaned of the meat, polished, and left intact, served as the feed bowl.

"We got you this souvenir to keep on your desk at your new duty station," Vivian said, her voice breaking and tears rolling from her eyes as she pointed out the coconut shell bowl. "See here, you can keep your paper clips in here."

Tino held out his hand to shake Parker's, but Parker instead gave him a bear hug. "Thank you, Mr. Camacho. Thank you for treating me like family. It meant a lot to me. I will never forget you and Vivvy," Parker said with a lump in his throat. "Someday, God willing, I'll come back to visit you. You can count on that."

Parker wrote several letters and sent pictures from North Carolina, where he spent thirty days leave with his parents, grandparents, three sisters, and an army of uncles, aunts, and cousins. Parker also wrote to Vivian and Tino from his new duty station in Washington. Vivian answered every letter faithfully, sharing all the news that was happening in Agaña, in the compound, and at home. Tino wrote too, but not as regularly. In June, Parker received a disturbing letter from Vivian. Worried, he wrote back for more details, but his letter and all the others he sent thereafter were returned, marked "Undeliverable."

PART THREE

Chapter 31

Life in the upstairs apartment was lonely and quiet after Parker left. He was a good sounding board and good company, and Philip missed him. Parker Reed was not easily replaced. Philip had no intention of sharing the apartment and was glad to pay the entire monthly rent by himself. He asked Tino not to look for another tenant. He liked the privacy and didn't relish the idea of another young ensign or lieutenant making Vivian's acquaintance. Without Parker's company, however, he felt uncomfortable being with Tino and Vivian at supper. The unsaid words and unacknowledged sentiments among them made for an awkward atmosphere. He began to make up excuses for having to eat out. He also volunteered for work assignments outside the government compound, in Sumay, or at the northern or southern end of the island. Those assignments could keep him away for a day or two at a time.

He reluctantly returned to the house in time to see Lieutenant Commander Pitt off to a new duty station and to welcome his replacement, Lieutenant Commander Joseph Flynn. The following week, on April 20, the island's new commanding officer was to be installed and inaugurated as the next navy governor. Philip had no feeling one way or the other about Pitt's departure. Rotating to somewhere else was part of navy life. Pitt was a good man. Flynn was older and appeared to be more experienced, both in his profession and in the navy.

No one knew yet what the incoming governor would be like. Those who preceded him varied from harsh and unpleasant to compassionate and sympathetic toward the Chamorro people. Whatever their character, no governor ever ranked higher than captain and none stayed in office for more than two years. Several held office in an acting capacity for only a few months; others were removed from office for reasons never explained but not difficult to conclude. The new one had only recently arrived with his family, and the outgoing one would leave with his on the next ship. Pitt and his wife would be on the same ship out.

While the change over from Pitt to Flynn would take place without fanfare, the governor's change of command would be a formal ceremony, complete with flags, gun salutes, sailors and marines in formation in dress uniforms, and marches rendered by the navy band. It would take place in the plaza with the island's elected officials, village commissioners, and business leaders as invited guests. Navy and Marine Corps personnel not on duty were required to attend. The ceremony was a major social and official military event, with a reception and luncheon to follow. It was a holiday for schoolchildren, and after the ceremony, nearly all the government workers and some military personnel, except for the governor's immediate staff, got the rest of the day off.

Vivian followed her father upstairs to meet Philip. The two men were going to walk to the plaza together. Vivian would follow behind soon after; she had housework to do that day and wanted to get her laundry sorted first.

Tino was dressed in his beige linen suit and blue bowtie, the only suit and tie he owned. "Are you ready, Lieutenant?" Tino asked.

"Yes, sir," Philip answered as he emerged from his room, resplendent in his full dress whites. Vivian had to catch her breath. How handsome he was! With his visor cap tucked under one arm, he glowed with regal confidence, like a storybook prince. He stood stately and proud, and teased Vivian with a wink, which made her blush immediately. She watched Philip and her father make their way toward the plaza. Philip's uniform was dazzlingly white under the morning sun.

It was mid-April, the middle of the dry season, and already so hot that Vivian longed for a cool shower, but by the time she would be ready for one, even the water in the cold tap would be uncomfortably warm. She felt sorry for Philip and her father and everyone who had to attend the ceremony in the unrelenting heat. As a spectator, she didn't have to attend the entire ceremony and could leave when she wanted. She stayed only long enough to watch her father take his place among the other navy government employees and Philip take his among the naval officers.

The ceremony in the plaza lasted more than two hours. The outgoing governor spoke longer than anyone expected. By eleven thirty, the sun was blazing, threatening a humid and even hotter afternoon. Philip hurried back to the house to change his clothes. Although he was expected to attend the governor's reception and luncheon, he opted instead to steal away to the lancho. He also wanted to steal a few minutes with Vivian, his first opportunity since the typhoon. If nothing else, he could enjoy being with her. Tino and the boys would be at the reception, and he could be alone with Vivian, at least until Tino noticed his absence. He was sure that Tino recognized his interest in Vivian.

Sweating profusely and eager to get out of his stifling uniform, with its choking stand-up collar, Philip tossed his cap on the dresser and kicked off his white dress shoes and socks. In a frenzy, he peeled off his heavy tunic and wet undershirt. He had readied his "lancho clothes"—hiking boots, thick socks, denim pants, and cotton shirt—intending to change quickly, but he was sticky with sweat. He marched out of his damp trousers and skivvies and stood with his eyes closed and his arms outstretched in front of his electric fan running at its highest setting. The stiff cool breeze it generated felt wonderful against his clammy skin. As he turned to cool his back side, Vivian suddenly came through his door.

Vivian entered to collect his sheets and had assumed he was at the governor's reception, where he was supposed to be. She didn't expect him to be at home or naked in his room. Vivian caught a quick glimpse of him and gasped in shock. She had never seen a fully naked man and was horrified. She whirled around to flee and cringed with shame at having invaded his privacy accidently. Philip was startled too, but only for a second. Whether it was the heat or because he was naked before Vivian, his inhibitions evaporated. He felt no need to hide and was glad to be exposed to her. Nothing else mattered. Not race. Not color. Not clothing, uniform or rank. Before she could escape, Philip came up behind her, reached over her shoulder, and closed the door.

"Wait," he said gently.

"I, I'm . . . I didn't know you were here," she said nervously, keeping her back to him.

"I know," he whispered again. Vivian felt his lips brush against her ear, and it sent shivers through her.

She froze and nearly fainted when he nuzzled the side of her neck below her ear. She could smell him—a blend of shaving cream, bath soap, and sweat. He reached his arms around her waist and pulled her body against his. Vivian wanted to turn around and melt into his arms. She wanted to study him from head to toe, to run her hands over his skin and feel his body, and to kiss his face and taste his lips again. But she couldn't yield to such wants; chastity and propriety had to prevail. Until then, she would allow just this one sweet moment. Vivian closed her eyes and leaned back against his bare body. Philip continued to kiss her neck and shoulder, tasting her skin with his mouth and tongue. He moved his hands slowly and gently, one toward her chest, the other down her belly to the front of her skirt, his desire mounting. Vivian felt something firm press against the back of her dress. Her eyes shot open; she knew instantly what it was, and it frightened her. At that same moment, from downstairs, Tino called out, "Vivvy, are you there?"

In a panic, Vivian pulled away from Philip and dashed out the door, breathless and trembling. "Up here, Papa," she said unsteadily, her heart banging wildly in her chest. "I'm just getting the linens."

Philip quickly closed the door, tore the sheets from his bed, and tossed them out to Vivian. He shut the door again and put his ear to it, listening as she nervously gathered the sheets and as Tino came up the stairs.

"*Hafa*[16]? Need help?" her father asked suspiciously. Vivian's face was flushed.

Behind his closed door, Philip grinned. Vivian had accepted his caresses. Philip was accustomed to winning women into his bed easily, but no conquest was as sweet as seducing Vivian. Philip waited until his body had calmed before getting dressed and heading downstairs.

In the days that followed, Philip realized he was in love, truly in love. He felt different; everything felt different. His every waking moment was filled with bouts of either heart-soaring happiness or tearful depression. He found himself smiling for no reason, even when he was alone. He even had moments of giddiness and laughed at his own silliness. Although he had no solid proof, he felt that Vivian loved him too. The way she looked at him aroused him. Her very nearness sent him into ecstasies about what delights awaited him in her bed. But Vivian was a virgin, pure and undefiled. Until the time was right, until she invited his passion and yielded to him, he would be patient. He would caress her tenderly and tell her that he belonged to her, body and soul.

Vivian and Philip tried to avoid each other since that fateful afternoon. If they did encounter each other, both would blush. Vivian was ashamed at having nearly succumbed to temptation, and Philip was ecstatic that she had allowed him to touch her, although he wouldn't have forced himself on her if she had balked. Trying to behave normally in front of Tino was exceptionally difficult. To Vivian's relief, Philip continued to work long hours and kept to himself upstairs.

In his solitude, Philip began to rethink his decisions. He had launched himself on a naval career and was well on his way. But he was now also inescapably in love. After several sleepless nights, he decided to try to keep his career and marry Vivian. He needed only to figure out how to manage both. He decided he would marry her before his pending reassignment, no matter how many hoops he had to jump through to secure approval, and take her with him to his next duty station. If that was not possible, he would request an extension of his assignment on Guam. If the proposed new navy unit was created and he was called up for consideration, he would accept the challenge only with Vivian at his side. If his requests were denied, if he was forced to choose one or the other, he would leave the navy. His mind

[16] Literally, "what." *Hafa* is both a question and a greeting.

was set; his plan was workable. He latched on to Parker's belief that Vivian loved him and he felt his world settling comfortably into place.

Philip was ready to declare his intentions and wouldn't let his courage flag this time. He was certain about his decision, and nothing would sway him from it. He would tell Vivian he loved her, straight out, and ask if she loved him in return. He wanted to give her something he hoped would convey how he felt. He designed a locket and gave the drawing to a goldsmith in town. The locket would be small and oval shaped. Vivian wouldn't have worn anything too large or gaudy. It would have a filigree border and eight tiny garnets, his birthstone, around a blank center. The letter *A*, without the crossbar, would be engraved in the blank. Inside, sealed behind tiny glass panes, would be his photo and a lock of his hair, to represent giving himself to Vivian. She would interpret the incomplete *A* as her initial and ask why it was upside down. He would explain that it wasn't her initial, that he would complete it with a tiny diamond chip after they were married. It would then be a proper *A*, for Avery, her new surname.

Philip purchased a gold chain that had tiny links shaped like a ship's anchor chain. He liked the symbolism of anchoring Vivian to him. He planned to give her the locket and chain as soon as the locket was finished. He imagined her opening the little jewel box and being thoroughly impressed. He hoped she would throw her arms around him and smother him with kisses, real ones, not just quick pecks on the cheek. The goldsmith said it would take about a month to produce the locket. A week after placing the order, however, Philip was forced to address a fatal blow to his plans.

Philip didn't swear Parker to secrecy about his father's letter. There wasn't much information for him to divulge, but in the two months since Parker's departure, whispers with outlandish exaggerations began to circulate throughout the government compound. Philip was eventually cornered to confirm or deny them. The rumors, he said, were partially true. He did hear from his father that the navy was considering the creation of a new unit. No, the unit had not been created yet. If and when it was created, yes, he did express interest in joining it, but he would have to compete and qualify first. Philip was slated to rotate in late August or early September, at the end of his assignment, but if he was selected for consideration, he could be called to leave Guam sooner.

Chapter 32

Tino would certainly have told Vivian the news. Philip felt frustrated at having to respond to the rumors before he had the chance to lay out his plans to Vivian. He worried about how she took the news. She would have known he would eventually move on, but had no notion of his intentions. Philip was desperate for an opportunity to be alone with her, to explain. He had so much he wanted to tell her, so much he wanted to say. He took leave on the day Vivian usually collected the sheets and waited for her. Tino left for the lancho early that morning and wouldn't immediately find out that Philip stayed home.

Vivian knew that Philip was still upstairs and was nervous about facing him. Tino had indeed told her about Philip's decision to try out for a new navy outfit. The news cemented the inevitability of his leaving the island and why she would never see him again. Philip belonged to the United States Navy; his stay on Guam was only temporary. Vivian was aware of that from the start and couldn't hold it against him. She had allowed herself to fall in love with a man who wasn't free to grant her any more than a moment of his time. She knew she meant something to him, but maybe only as a convenient plaything. How else could she interpret his one kiss and one erogenous embrace, spaced months apart? She knew she should never have allowed it. Now she would have to pay the penalty of unending heartache.

Knowing that he was still upstairs, Vivian tried to steel herself against any attempt he might make to touch her or kiss her. She climbed the stairs quietly and looked around. Philip was not in the kitchen or the parlor, as she had hoped. His bedroom door was closed, and she grew uneasy. *I am not your plaything, Mr. Avery,* she said to herself, trying to muster the resolve to make facing him easier, but she loved him. She loved him with her heart and with her mind and, if he wanted it, with her body too. Her heart racing, she knocked on his door and prayed that he wouldn't be naked again. She didn't know if she could resist him.

"Come in, Vivian," he said in a tone that reminded her of a school disciplinarian. Like a student facing admonishment, she entered cautiously. Philip was sitting by the window. He was fully clothed, and Vivian sighed with relief. He stood up and came toward her.

Before he could say a word, Vivian demanded, "Why did you kiss me and let me see you undressed?"

"Because I love you, Vivian," he said without hesitation.

His blunt response took her aback. She was expecting him to take advantage of the moment to seduce her again, the plaything conveniently delivered for his carnal pleasure. She needed to resist him, but was ashamed that she didn't want to resist. She wasn't expecting a declaration of love, and her feelings of inadequacy and unworthiness flooded back.

"Mr. Avery, you shouldn't love me," she said softly, trying to remind him that loving her was against the rules in his world.

"Why?" Philip was instantly crushed. He had allowed himself to believe the things Parker told him. Had Parker been wrong? After struggling to reconcile his conflicting feelings and to decide a course of action, Philip didn't expect Vivian to reject him. He felt foolish for revealing his feelings and more exposed and vulnerable than when she caught him naked.

"I know about that new navy group you want to join and that you'll be leaving soon," she said. "I think you are a fine naval officer and the navy is fortunate to have you."

"That's not how I wanted you to find out." Philip couldn't fault Tino for sharing the news with Vivian; it was a hot topic in the compound and no longer a private affair. Philip felt defenseless and started pacing, trying to find the words to explain. "I wanted to tell you myself. I wanted to discuss it with you," he said.

"There's nothing to discuss," Vivian said, wondering why her opinion would matter to him. Was she more than a plaything? She tried to remain distant and aloof, but her resolve was beginning to crumble. She could see his struggle and wanted to reach out to him.

"You've made a good decision, good for your career," she said, hoping to assure him that she supported his aspirations, and herself that she was strong enough to see him go.

"Your future beckons, Mr. Avery. It's a wonderful one and I sincerely wish you well."

But her words had the opposite effect. At that moment, addressing him as "Mr. Avery" magnified the distance she had always placed between them. He had similarly tried to keep her at a distance, but he never succeeded as masterfully as she did with those two words. The shock of rejection destroyed his confidence. The strange sensation of helplessness and defeat flashed into anger. Philip's face turned red and his eyes flashed.

"Goddammit, stop calling me Mr. Avery!" he roared as he whirled on his heel and slammed his fist into the wall. It made a strange sound—a muffled thud—and left a dent in the plaster. "Shit!" he yelped.

Curses and obscenities spewed from his mouth as he shook his hand and glared at the dent in the wall. Vivian shrank back in horror, her eyes widening in fear. She had never seen him angry or heard him use foul language. "Add the damage to the f—king rent," he spat the words at her.

His chest heaving, he snapped, "Is that all I am to you, Vivian—a f—king tenant?"

The question burned into Vivian's heart. Philip was never just a tenant; he was everything. "No, sir. You are so much more," she said softly.

"How much more, Vivian? Tell me; how much more must I be?"

"Papa once told me that falling in love with a serviceman is like reaching for the moon. It is not possible to have or to hold. You are the moon to me, Mr. Avery, and —"

Vivian sat down on the edge of Philip's bed and hung her head. How could she make him understand the futility of anything between them? He was a fleeting dream from which she would awaken when he left. He was foreign to her island and her home, an alien to her history and language and culture—and she even more so to his. He was the moon she could never reach, never keep. He was her beautiful mansion there, her icon of wealth and privilege, her symbol of race, rank, and status. He was appointed with advanced schooling and professional credentials. He possessed attributes and circumstances she could never achieve. Now a great opportunity lay before him.

"You are worthy of someone better than me."

"What do you mean 'better'?" Philip couldn't stomach her words. He had grappled with the same words, the same ideas, and they were as repulsive in his mind as they were from Vivian's lips.

"You should be with someone who's like you," she said. "Someone from your own world, your own kind; an American, like you. Someone who's pretty and well-educated; someone who will be helpful in your career."

Philip's heart leaped into his throat. Vivian's words echoed the same notions that had prevented him from admitting to himself and to Vivian that he loved her. They were the same words—the same inescapable reality—that would affect his advancement up the ranks. It broke his heart to hear the woman he loved conceding that she would be a detriment to his career. In that moment, his career ambition disintegrated; he was willing to give it up, now he didn't want it anymore. He could feel tears filling his eyes, but he fought them back. He knelt down in front of her and looked into her face.

"Vivian," he started, swallowing hard, "you are all I want, all I need. I want to go to sleep at night for the rest of my life with you in my arms. I want to wake up every morning with you beside me. I want to make love to you for as long as I can. I want only you."

Philip wrapped his arms around her waist and tried to rest his head against her chest, but she pushed him away.

"But your career, your future—" Vivian started, but Philip interrupted her.

"Vivian, without you, I have no future," he said. "I am not the moon. I'm right here—with you. It's where I want to be. I love you, Vivian. I want you in my life and I want to be in yours."

Vivian held his face in her hands and looked deep into his eyes. She was no longer afraid to stare into them. A single tear trickled from his right eye and onto her hand. She leaned forward and kissed his forehead. Philip closed his eyes and sighed with relief.

"Do you love me, Vivian? I need to know," he whispered.

"With all my heart," she said. She tilted his head back and pressed her lips to his.

Philip rose to his feet and pulled her up to hers. He wrapped his arms around her; she seemed so small in his long arms. They kissed long and deep, again and again.

The joy in Philip's heart overwhelmed the pain in his right hand, but it soon started to throb. He winced in pain when he tried to cup Vivian's cheek. Something in his hand was broken, and it was starting to swell. Although breaking from his embrace was difficult, Vivian hurried to the kitchen and took some ice cubes from the refrigerator's freezer compartment. Philip went to his bathroom and started running cold water over his hand. As Vivian wrapped his hand in a damp towel with the ice cubes, Philip kissed whatever part of her he could reach: her cheek, her nose, her eyebrows, her forehead, the back of her neck, the top of her head, the top of her shoulder, and his favorite, her lips. His kisses made her giggle. The more she giggled, the more he reached for places to kiss. Vivian also was giddy and dizzy with joy, returning his kisses with equal enthusiasm.

Vivian had to push Philip away and out the door, to get to the hospital. He came home three hours later with his arm in a sling and a plaster cast from the middle of his fingers to halfway to his elbow. He told everyone, including Tino, that he had tripped on the front stairs and broke his hand trying to catch himself. Tino didn't believe him. Despite what should have been a painful injury, Philip was in high spirits. The tension in the air at home was lifted; the atmosphere was light and bright. Vivian hummed as she prepared dinner. When it was ready, Philip clattered down the stairs, cheerful and smiling. Whatever had occurred between them, Tino knew it had ended well. He prayed it wasn't what he feared.

A few nights later, as Tino sat in the outside kitchen, Philip quietly came outside to join him. Vivian had already gone to bed; she knew nothing of

Philip's intentions. Tino looked up at Philip as he sat down beside him. He knew the man had come to a decision or had come to confess.

"Some scotch?"

"No, thank you."

Both men sat quietly for a few minutes—Tino waiting for Philip to start talking, Philip striving to find the words and the courage.

"Mr. Camacho," he said, feeling nervous and awkward. His mouth was dry. He regretted turning down the scotch; it would have given him the jolt he needed to get the words out. "I must tell you something and I hope you won't think ill of me."

"What is it, Lieutenant?" Fear stabbed into Tino's heart. *Please don't tell me you've defiled my daughter,* he implored inwardly as he steeled himself for such a confession.

"I'm in love with Vivian. Sir, I respectfully request your permission to marry her," Philip blurted out the words before he lost courage. He was certain that Tino could hear his heart pounding. Asking Tino to marry Vivian was more difficult than telling his father about joining the navy. Philip didn't expect his father to approve, but he also knew that his father wouldn't have tried to stop him. On the other hand, a negative answer from Tino would send Philip's hopes into a tailspin. Vivian would never defy her father.

"You didn't—"

"No, sir," Philip wouldn't let him finish. He felt insulted that Tino would think him so crude. *I'm not that kind of sailor, sir. Not anymore,* the thought raced through his mind.

"How did you hurt your hand? I want the truth," Tino said, pressing for the details. He was now not afraid to demand the truth from a man who was his superior at work but not under his roof, especially the one seeking his only daughter's hand. Philip carefully explained, keeping to himself the more intimate details.

"Then I lost my temper and punched the wall."

"And what made you do that?" Tino asked.

"Vivian wouldn't believe me."

"She does now?"

"Yes, sir," Philip answered with a smile so bright that Tino could see it in the dimness. He could even sense Philip's happiness.

Tino gazed at him then turned, sighed heavily, and slowly shook his head. Philip's heart sank, believing Tino was about to turn him down. If he did, Philip hoped Vivian loved him enough to marry him anyway.

"Lieutenant Avery," Tino began slowly. "Vivian was four years old when her mother passed away. She has had only me to raise her. I did my best and I am very proud of the woman she has become. There is no one in this world I care more about. I love her and I would defend her with my life.

"I see that she has impressed you, and now you love her too," he continued. "Thank you, sir, for seeking my permission. If you are the man she chooses, I will stand by her choice."

Philip wasn't sure whether or not Tino actually granted his permission. Except for the "if," Tino's tone and words seemed positive.

Tino stood up. "It's nearly midnight, Lieutenant, we should head inside."

His heart soaring, Philip said, "Mr. Camacho, please call me Philip, at least here at home."

"I'll try, but it'll take some getting used to."

There was a touch of sadness in Tino's heart. He believed Philip truly loved his daughter and he knew that Vivian loved him. He had witnessed them struggle to deny what their hearts demanded. Tino had no reason to doubt them, but Philip was a serviceman. He was not in full control of his destiny, at least not while he was in the navy. He knew Philip to be a man of honor and integrity, someone any father would be proud to have as a son-in-law, but the navy still held sway over him.

Chapter 33

Knowing for certain that Vivian loved him, Philip would persist until she agreed to marry him. Tino said he would abide by her decision, and Philip knew in his heart what her decision would be. Whatever obstacles appeared in their path, he and Vivian would conquer them together; he was sure of it.

Philip began checking into the process of securing approval to marry a local girl and decided it was nothing he couldn't handle. He picked up the paperwork from the judge advocate general's office, filled it out, and handed it to the registrar clerk, a skinny, bespectacled sailor who apprehensively asked, "Do you really want to do this, sir?" Philip grinned at him and said, "Just do your job, yeoman, and process my application."

Vivian's locket would be finished and ready to be picked up in a day or two. Philip planned to give it to her right away. He also sent a telegram to a noted jeweler in New York City, a longtime friend of his father, and ordered a half-carat solitaire engagement ring and matching diamond-studded wedding band, and a plain gold wedding band for himself. After the set arrived, he planned to propose in the traditional and expected manner—to get down on one knee, present Vivian with the engagement ring, and with all the sincerity and formality he could muster, again declare his love and ask her to marry him. He would make Vivian a June bride and explain the tradition to her on their wedding night. He smiled at the thought and quivered with anticipation.

The goldsmith apologized when Philip came to pick up the locket. He was out of necklace cases and wouldn't have any for another month, if Philip could wait. Philip didn't want to wait. He was giving Vivian the locket that night. He was not displeased when the goldsmith stuffed the locket and chain into a small, red velvet ring box.

"Don't worry about it," Philip said with a smile as he paid the man, "they won't be in the box for long."

Philip tucked the ring box in his desk drawer and sat down with a fresh cup of coffee when the mail boy handed him a letter. It was from his father. Still grinning in anticipation of Vivian's happy reaction, Philip opened the letter and read it. His heart stopped and the smile left his face. He was among several officers selected for consideration to the new navy unit. He was to report to Davisville, Rhode Island, by 1 July 1941 for testing and trials. His transfer orders were in the pipeline.

> By the time you receive this, your captain will have been informed. Your orders should follow soon after. Your mother and I hope you will be able to spend some time with us before you report to Davisville, Preston wrote.

Ignoring the protocol of informing his superiors first, Philip handed the letter to Tino whose brow furrowed as he read it. Tino had misgivings about the strength of Vivian and Philip's relationship. He was uncertain about their ability to withstand the many difficulties and obstacles that lay before them. He wondered whether they could make the sacrifices, each to the other, to secure a successful marriage. Their first major difficulty was at hand.

"Congratulations, Lieutenant," Tino said, not sure how to react. His first thought was of his daughter and what devastating news this would be to her. The look on Philip's face was troubled and gloomy as well.

"Please, let me tell Vivian," Philip said. His world was turned upside down again. He pulled out his desk drawer and stared down sadly at the little red jewel box that contained Vivian's new locket and chain. Tino watched him worriedly as he readied himself to accompany Lieutenant Kaplan on an outdoor assignment.

"You ready, Tino? Let's go," Kaplan said as he made for the door.

"If you don't mind, Kap, I'd like to take Mr. Camacho's place," Philip said as he jumped up from his desk. "I need some air and I can't do much around here anyway."

With his writing hand in a cast, Philip was of little use in the office. His time would be better spent on assignment with Kaplan, who was going to examine a little-used roadway at the southern end of the island. The two-hour drive to get there would give Philip time to sort out his thoughts.

"Then let's get a move on," Kaplan said. "Time's awastin'."

Tino was glad not to have to go. He wanted to get to the lancho after work, mainly to avoid facing Vivian. He wouldn't have been able to mask the disheartening news Philip had in store for her. Philip's eagerness to take his place was an indication that he too wanted to forestall having to face Vivian. He and Kaplan wouldn't get back to Agaña until after dark.

Although fewer in number, reports of infrastructure damage, especially in isolated rural areas, were still coming into the engineering division a year after the earthquake. Kaplan was following up on a report of some cracks that had recently appeared in a road near a bridge. He was going to make an on-site inspection to determine whether they were caused by the earthquake or were simply due to normal wear and tear. The road in question was situated along a narrow rocky ledge and used mainly by heavy utility vehicles. It led down to an old wooden bridge straddling the mouth of a small stream that opened out to the sea. The contractor and some of his men would be there, awaiting Kaplan's arrival and his preliminary determination of the repairs needed. For Philip, the assignment was far more interesting and distracting than sitting at his desk, doing little to pass the time.

With Lieutenant Kaplan at the wheel of their government vehicle, an old Ford sedan, the trip south would take them through thick jungle and over steep hills and deep ravines. Philip usually relished every opportunity to get out of the office, to rumble over the narrow coral roads and enjoy the beauty of the jungles and the seashore along the way, but his mind was too unsettled that afternoon to appreciate the ride. He had to think, to decide what to do next, how to proceed, and more importantly, how to tell Vivian. He had to be in Rhode Island, half the world away, by the first of July. It was already the middle of May. Six weeks, that was all the time he had left. Even if Vivian loved him enough to marry him the next day—if that was even possible—she would never leave her father on such short notice. She would never agree to leave behind her home, her world, to follow him into the unknown. He couldn't and wouldn't disrupt her life so drastically. As he wrestled with the options, which were few and unacceptable, Philip realized what Vivian meant about reaching for the moon; it was exactly what he was trying to do.

Before he realized it, he and Kaplan had arrived at the site. Kaplan drove the sedan up the narrow paved road along the cliff above the bridge. He parked in the middle of the road and left the motor running. Since the road was rarely traveled, there was no need to worry about blocking traffic. The two men climbed out of the sedan and walked down to the bridge a few yards away. They examined several fissures that were parallel with the roadway in front of the bridge. Most were superficial, but at least three were questionable. They were narrow but ran deep down into the roadbed, suggesting serious instability. The engineers decided the roadway was hazardous, not only in front of the bridge, but also for several yards behind it, where they were standing. It was too dangerous to take the sedan across.

They walked uphill and climbed back into their vehicle. As soon as they closed the doors, a loud gravelly rumble shook the ground beneath them.

The construction workers on the other side of the bridge began shouting at them in alarm.

"Back up! Back up!"

"Get out of the car! Get out! Get out!"

Philip and Kaplan tried desperately to get out of the car quickly, but it was too late. Several large boulders broke free from the cliff face and rolled downward into the stream. Kaplan threw the sedan in reverse and jammed on the gas pedal, trying frantically to shoot backward to solid ground, but time ran out. The undermined roadway buckled and collapsed, and the sedan lurched over the embankment. Philip grabbed for the door handle but the cast on his hand blocked his grip. As the vehicle tipped, Philip slid across the seat toward Kaplan, who had gotten his door open and immediately fell out. Philip tried to grab for him but managed only to clutch Kaplan's sleeve, which ripped away in his hand. Philip slid rapidly, following Kaplan out the open door. He grabbed the steering wheel with his left hand and dangled in space for a split second. His fingers slipped and he plunged helplessly downward. The sedan followed behind the men. It glanced against some boulders and landed on its roof, its tires still spinning. Kaplan was killed instantly, the lower half of his body was crushed beneath the sedan. Philip landed face down in a crumpled heap in the water, his right leg and torso pinned under a pile of large rocks.

Still shouting, the construction workers scrambled across the stream toward the upturned vehicle. Several men lifted it while others pulled Kaplan's body out from underneath. Two men tossed aside the rocks on top of Philip while two others turned him over before he drowned. Philip was barely breathing, but was still alive. The men could tell that Philip was broken inside and out; he was bleeding from his mouth, nose, and ears. A deep gash across his forehead was bleeding profusely. With a woefully inadequate first aid kit, one of the men wound a roll of gauze around Philip's head while others splinted his mangled leg with some rags and a piece of two-by-four lumber. They carried him to one of their pickup trucks not far away. They loaded him into the bed and nestled his head and neck between two cement bags. They then signaled the driver who drove the truck across the shallow stream on the inland side of the bridge and gunned the engine to climb up the rough, shattered terrain. At the top, they started the drive back to Agaña at breakneck speed. A second pickup truck transported the deceased lieutenant; there was no need for speed.

The truck carrying Philip arrived in Agaña at five o'clock, well over an hour and a half after the accident. By then, his body was swollen and covered with huge bloody scrapes and angry bruises. His uniform was in shreds. Philip was rushed to the hospital and immediately into surgery.

So much vital time had been lost in transit that the doctors didn't think he would survive. Philip's liver and spleen had been lacerated and he was bleeding internally. Calls went out immediately for blood donors. The bones of his right leg were broken. His femur was fractured and both his tibia and fibula needed to be pinned back together. His right foot was also fractured in several places. The doctors also suspected damage to his spine and spinal cord. If his back was broken, his manhandling at the accident scene and the wild ride back to Agaña would have left him paralyzed, at least from the waist down. They worked frantically to save him.

Word about the accident was immediately reported to the governor by radio and spread rapidly throughout the compound. Commander Flynn was chatting leisurely with Tino, Kiko, and Chu'. They were about to close the office and head home when they heard the news. Lieutenant Kaplan was dead? Lieutenant Avery was barely alive? They stared at one another in numbed shock. Flynn rushed out, heading toward the hospital. Kiko and Chu' followed behind him. Tino was badly shaken; he was supposed to have been with Kaplan, not Philip. His heart racing, Tino ran in the opposite direction, toward Leary School, to get Vivian.

The school year had ended and Vivian had to inventory the sets of textbooks assigned to her. She had finally completed the task and stored the books and materials in the storage closet. She was cleaning up the little ice-cream-and-cake celebration she had had for her students when her father rushed into her classroom, his face flustered and pale.

"Come," he said hoarsely. He grabbed her hand, pulled her roughly to her feet, and dragged her to the door. Startled, Vivian balked.

"Papa, what's wrong?" she said, growing frightened by the alarm in his face.

"There's been an accident," he said, still clutching her hand tightly and dragging her, half stumbling, across the plaza and toward the hospital. "It's Philip. He might not make it."

If someone can freeze and still be moving, it was Vivian. Everything came to a standstill inside her, her heart, her mind, the breath in her lungs, though her feet and legs were still driving her forward. A heavy, invisible blanket of cold seemed to drape over her.

This is not real; it can't be real, she said to herself. She was running as fast as she could but seemed to be moving in slow motion. She was choking on her own breath and fighting back tears. *Stay safe for me, Philip,* again and again she repeated in her mind the words Philip had whispered to her over the telephone before the typhoon.

There were at least forty people crowding the hospital waiting room—officers, sailors, and employees from the governor's office, people who were already in the waiting room and others who were attracted by the commotion. Vehicle accidents of any kind were uncommon. That this one might result in the deaths of two naval officers was highly unusual and unprecedented. Everyone was murmuring, wondering and asking one another for any details they may have heard. Kiko spotted Tino and Vivian as they rushed into the waiting room. He hurried over and embraced them both.

"Don't know very much right now," he said, and looked sadly at Vivian, "but it doesn't look good. One of the contractor's men said the roadway collapsed under their car. They couldn't get out in time."

Kiko looked at Tino and quietly added, "The car landed on top of Lieutenant Kaplan. He died right away."

As Kiko completed his report, the murmur in the waiting room instantly stopped. Kaplan's body, wrapped in a blood-stained sheet, was wheeled in on a gurney and taken to the morgue.

As the hours passed and as more details of the accident came to light, people began trickling away, shaking their heads. At Tino's insistence, Kiko and Chu' left the hospital for home at eight o'clock. Commander Flynn was ensconced with the governor and his chief of staff in the medical director's office, discussing the accident and their next course of action. Philip was still on the operating table. At midnight, a doctor finally appeared. He grimly described the extent of Philip's injuries to the governor and Flynn, whispering loud enough for Tino and Vivian, standing discreetly behind them, to hear. The doctor was not optimistic.

"He's stable now, sirs, but barely. He has a fractured skull and is in a coma," the doctor said. "Right now, we have to worry about brain swelling. His condition is grave and he may not survive the night. If he does, he might have a chance, but only a slim one. The next few days will be critical. The only good news is that his back is not broken."

After rendering his report, the doctor watched as the governor and Commander Flynn walked away and exited the hospital. He remained in the hallway then turned to Tino and Vivian. He didn't know who they were but concluded that his critically ill patient had to be someone important to them. With a kindly expression on his face, the doctor said to them, "You might want to get some rest. There's nothing more you can do here."

Chapter 34

Tino and his daughter walked home silently in the dark. Their house was dark also; they hadn't been home since early that morning. Tino never made it to the lancho that afternoon. The chickens would have to go without fresh water and scratch for a day, but they would be all right. Tino and Vivian had had no supper, either, but they weren't hungry.

"Get some sleep, Vivvy. We'll go back tomorrow," Tino said to her as he closed his bedroom door. Exhausted and emotionally drained, Tino sat on the edge of his bed and struggled with the guilt that one man was dead and another might follow, and with relief that he was the one still alive. He did not ask to be relieved of the assignment, but he was anguished that it was Philip, his daughter's beloved, who displaced him. If not for Philip, he would have been the one fighting to survive or lying dead with Lieutenant Kaplan.

Vivian couldn't sleep, although she tried. At three in the morning, she rose and went upstairs to Philip's room. She switched on the light and looked around, examining how he had arranged his belongings. *He is such a meticulous man,* she thought, trying desperately to cling to hope. *He's so neat and orderly.*

Indeed, Philip's clothes, his uniforms, and his shoes were precisely arranged in his closet. Even his toilet bag on his dresser was well ordered. His soiled laundry was in a large mesh bag hanging from a peg inside the closet. There wasn't enough in it yet for a wash load. Vivian recalled all the times he asked for her help with the washing machine, always pretending he had forgotten how to operate it. She remembered the boyish look and impish smile on his face as he hovered around her. She smiled at the realization that he had invented hundreds of other such excuses to be near her, to be with her. He did truly love her.

Vivian opened the wardrobe and smiled again. All his civilian clothes, including the old denim pants and the much-mended cotton shirt he always wore to the lancho, were kept separate from his uniforms and were folded neatly and stacked inside. She opened his dresser drawer and saw his clean underwear, also neatly folded. She wondered again about his upbringing and how someone who grew up wealthy and privileged, with servants and maids, could be so neat and orderly on his own. She realized she was wrong to think that all rich people were spoiled and snobbish. Philip was not a spoiled snob.

She lay down on Philip's bed. It smelled of him, clean and pleasing. She buried her face in his pillow and inhaled deeply, drawing his scent, his essence, into herself. Tears trickled from her eyes and onto his pillow.

"Please, God, don't let him die," she whispered then fell asleep.

***

In a whirlpool of searing, crushing pain, Philip found himself spinning in inky blackness. His head throbbed. His whole body was in excruciating pain. Loud, crashing noises filled his ears. The clamor seemed to last for hours, then suddenly all was quiet. Deathly quiet; he could hear no sound at all, not even his own breathing. Only the throbbing pain and the darkness remained. Philip was floating in it, and he was cold, icy cold. The sensation puzzled him. He hadn't felt cold in a long time. *Is it winter?* he wondered, *am I home?* He didn't know where he was. He knew only that he was cold; he was shivering uncontrollably, and he was in terrible pain. He couldn't remember anything before waking up in this terrible place. Every part of his body ached with layers of pain—crushing, slicing, wrenching, pounding, stinging, and burning sensations, inside and out. Philip wanted to close his eyes and let the darkness swallow him, hoping that drowning in it would end his pain.

Before he could drift into oblivion, Philip became aware of a pinpoint of light far ahead of him. Although his head was spinning and he couldn't see clearly, he watched the tiny light twinkle as he drifted toward it. Philip was drawn to it, but as he reached out to try to touch it, the light glided away. It slowly widened into a circle that grew larger and larger, and brighter and brighter. Wonderful warmth spilled from the circle, which grew large enough for Philip to climb through. The circle of warm light offered an escape from the cold blackness. He hurtled himself into the now blinding white light and emerged in the quiet warmth of his bedroom in the house at the base of San Ramon Hill.

The colors of the walls, the floor, the woodwork, and even the ceiling, which he never noticed before, were rich and vibrant. Vivian was asleep in his bed. The waves of her dark auburn hair were fanned out on his pillow. Her features were peaceful and serene in slumber; her breathing slow and deep. Philip knelt down beside her and gazed upon her face. She was beautiful, the most beautiful woman he had ever known. He closed his eyes and kissed her temple. The sweet smell of her hair filled him with comfort.

He rested his cheek against hers. The warmth of her skin felt wonderful. He wanted to climb into the bed to lie beside her and warm his shivering body against hers. He stood up to try, but the darkness suddenly yanked him back, sucking him back into the black whirlpool.

He tried to reach for her, but his arms would not respond. He tried to call out to her, but no sound came from his mouth. The circle of light drifted away, shrinking rapidly until he was enveloped in darkness again. But Vivian's warmth stayed with him. It spread from his lips into the rest of his face and head. Like a warm bath, it washed over his body. It soaked into his chest and settled in his heart, not like a flame or an ember, but like golden sunshine. All the pain melted away. Strengthened, Philip glared defiantly into the darkness. "You will not take me!" he shouted.

In that strange, dark, nether place, Philip held on tightly to Vivian's warmth and felt safe enough to let sleep overtake him. "Good night, Vivvy, my love," he whispered and drifted off.

***

Vivian only slept for two or three hours. Before eight, she called the school to say she would not be in that day, the first absence she had ever made. Her principal and all the other teachers had heard the shocking news about the accident which claimed the life of one navy officer and threatened the life of another, Vivian's tenant. Her principal assured her that her classroom would be secured. Vivian prepared breakfast, but neither she nor her father was hungry.

Tino dressed for work as usual, unsure what was to happen there. He thought about Lieutenant Kaplan's family and the grief that would be theirs, not only over the loss of their loved one, but also in the difficulty of observing their traditions under the circumstances. Kaplan was Jewish. Tino knew that Jewish people had certain death and funeral tenets that had to be observed, although he didn't know exactly what those were. He knew that Kaplan was not supposed to be chemically embalmed and that meant that his remains would have to be kept on ice until he could be shipped home. Lieutenant Kaplan was a good man who treated them fairly and considerately; he deserved to be treated with dignity and respect. Keeping him refrigerated like a side of beef was necessary, but seemed terribly disrespectful. Tino didn't envy the naval governor's burden of having to inform Kaplan's family and carry out their wishes.

Tino kissed Vivian's cheek and told her that if she wanted to go to the hospital, he would understand. He didn't want to tell her that Philip had already asked for her hand or about the letter from his father; Philip had asked him not to and he agreed to let him handle it himself. It was the least he could do for the man who had taken his place, the man who was in love with his daughter. Now all was moot. Tino had fully expected Philip to leave Guam healthy and whole, to go on with his life—perhaps with Vivian—at a new duty station somewhere else, but he was haunted by his own words about the futility of reaching for the moon. In Philip, Vivian had captured her moon. Tino never imagined that death could rob her of the victory and leave her in a dark place, a place he knew well.

Chapter 35

Vivian crept slowly into Philip's hospital room, afraid of what she was about to see. An oxygen tent surrounded his head and the top half of his body. Except for his dog tag and chain, he was stripped of clothing beneath the sheet covering him. His head and right eye were swathed in bandages. The remainder of his face was so swollen he didn't look like himself. His cheek and jaw were badly scraped, as were his arms and shoulders. She wanted to kiss him but was afraid to lift the oxygen tent to touch him.

Philip's leg was wrapped, from groin to ankle, in a wicked-looking metal brace with at least a dozen leather straps and buckles. The brace was suspended at an angle by thin cables to a rack above his bed. His right foot was splinted and wrapped in gauze bandages. Since the hospital bed was not long enough for his body, his uninjured left foot protruded between the bars at the foot of his bed. His head and pillow rested up against the bars at the head.

Philip's hands and fingers were swollen; the fingers of his right hand looked blue and were bulging from the cast still on his hand and forearm. Vivian looked questioningly at a corpsman who came through the door.

"We'll be taking off that cast today. He won't need it right now," the corpsman said.

"But his hand is still broken," she said, more like a plea than a statement, worried that the hospital staff thought so little of his chances that mending his broken hand wasn't important.

"We have to take it off," the corpsman said. "Because of the swelling, it's doing more harm than good. We'll immobilize his hand again when the swelling goes down. Same goes for his leg. Anyway, he's not moving or using it, so it'll be all right. Don't worry." The corpsman tried to sound confident, but he knew that Philip's condition could deteriorate rapidly and there would be little they could do to save him.

The corpsman's calm assurance relieved Vivian somewhat. She took Philip's left hand in hers; it was cold and puffed up. The skin was stretched and taut. She sat by his bed, holding his hand to her cheek, and watching his chest rise and fall, and sometimes shudder as he took shallow, erratic breaths. That evening Tino came to see him. Father and daughter sat together watching a navy lieutenant fighting for life. With every labored breath Philip fought to take, by force of will and hope, Tino breathed with him. Vivian silently prayed a rosary, counting the Hail Marys on her fingers. They sat together quietly until a nurse said they could only stay a few minutes more and they would have to leave.

As Vivian and her father headed down the corridor to the hospital's main entrance, the redheaded nurse approached them. Vivian recognized her from the officers' club at that horrible New Year's dance. The nurse smiled warmly at her; she recognized Vivian as well. She handed Vivian a brown paper bag.

"I know he would want you to hold on to these for him," she said. "You're a lucky girl; he's quite a catch. Good luck to you both." There was no sarcasm or contempt in her voice, and the sympathy in her eyes seemed genuine and sincere.

The bag contained Philip's belongings. His clothes—his uniform—and underwear and socks had to be cut away from his body and were discarded. Vivian looked into the sack but waited until she was at home before examining its contents more carefully.

Philip's visor cap, which had been retrieved from the accident scene, was crushed, wet, and ruined. It lay in the bag on top of his white uniform shoes. Vivian lifted it out of the bag; there was no way to straighten or repair it, and she wondered whether she was supposed to throw it away. His shoes, scuffed and smeared with mud, were at the bottom of the bag. She peeked inside one shoe and giggled. His shoes were size 12, four sizes larger than her father's. Philip's valuables—his wristwatch and billfold—were in the other shoe. Vivian opened the wallet. Inside were twenty-three dollars, several receipts and calling cards, Philip's military identification card, his New York driver's license, and a small formal photograph of his family.

The photograph was taken in a studio but was not recent; Philip looked younger than the man she knew. She studied every person—there were five in all. Everyone was nicely dressed in expensive looking suits and dresses. Philip's mother was a beautiful woman, elegant and stately. Vivian could see where Philip inherited his good looks; he looked like his mother. Like Philip, she didn't look like anyone who could or would howl with laughter at a funny joke. Mrs. Avery and her daughter were sitting side by side on a chaise lounge. Philip, his father, and brother were poised behind them. His father looked dignified and important, and was tall and slender, like Philip. Vivian didn't know the names of Philip's brother and sister. His brother looked like a younger version of their father, but not as tall. His sister looked to be about fifteen years old and was already as beautiful as her mother.

Behind Philip's family photo, Vivian found a picture of herself, clipped from a page of a school yearbook. It was a reproduction of an unflattering photo which Vivian never liked. Seeing it made her giggle; of all the photos he could have chosen, Philip picked that one. That he had made the effort to secure one proved to her once and for all that Philip truly cared, that she was someone special to him. Before releasing Philip's wallet to the navy, Vivian exchanged the printed picture with a more flattering original photo. If he survived, he would find it and would know also that he was someone special to her.

For weeks, Philip lay oblivious to the world. Vivian came to see him every day. After her school was secured for the summer, she stayed almost all day. At first, the nurses wouldn't let her help with his care, but they eventually relented. She helped to change Philip's bedding every day. She bathed his face and cleaned his mouth and teeth with a washcloth, and smeared petroleum jelly on his dry, cracked lips. She washed his hair and ears but left the rest of his bath to the nurses. She left his room whenever it was time for his sponge baths. The task seemed to require the hands of a half a dozen nurses and aides. She wondered if they were being morbidly curious or whether it actually required that many people to attend to him. Vivian knew he would have been humiliated if he had been aware of everything happening to him.

When the bandage was removed from Philip's abdomen, Vivian shrank at the sight. There was a long raw incision across his torso. More than a dozen ugly black stitches were holding his flesh together. A small rubber tube was sticking out at the lower end of the incision. A corpsman explained that it was for drainage. The wound and drain tube were covered with a sponge—a smaller, thicker bandage that was changed twice daily. The sutures, and eventually the drain, were removed a few days later.

In the days and weeks following the accident, Vivian saw every part of Philip's naked body and had touched and handled almost every part of it, but not in the loving, intimate way she had hoped to experience it. She helped the nurses and aides keep him clean and comfortable as if he could sense anything. She helped to manipulate his body—bending, massaging, and stretching his arms and unfettered left leg to stimulate his muscles, and rolling him on his sides to relieve the pressure on his shoulders, back, and hips, to prevent bedsores. She massaged his left leg and foot to keep the blood flowing, but his foot was always cold to the touch. She eventually brought his thick hiking socks to the hospital and put it on his foot, alternating the pair daily. She knew the manhandling was necessary, but the loss of his dignity and privacy dismayed her immensely.

As careful as Vivian and the hospital staff tried to be, with a patient so fragile, Philip developed pneumonia. His doctor said it was not unusual in traumatic coma cases. They would fight it as best they could with antibiotics and hope he survived. The pneumonia scare prompted Philip's father to bring his son home. If Philip was to die, he would do so at home, or at least on U.S. soil. Near the end of June, the naval governor received Preston Avery's telegram, requesting that Philip be transported to California and admitted to the naval hospital in San Diego as soon as feasible. He would pay the airfare for Philip and a nurse escort aboard the first available Pan American flight from Guam. He, his wife, and their eldest son William, a doctor, would meet Philip upon his arrival. Since military wives, dependents, and some personnel were already being removed from Guam, Preston's request was granted. Philip was breathing better but was still in a coma.

After the proper clearances were secured and the arrangements were made, Philip was readied for the trip. Vivian bought a silver St. Christopher medal, and after Mass on the Sunday before Philip's departure, she asked the bishop to bless it. Then she said a novena and asked St. Christopher to keep Philip safe on the long journey back to the States. At the hospital, she helped the nurses prepare him for the drive to Sumay, where Pan American World Airways was based.

Philip had more than a month's growth of facial hair, but none of the hospital staff seemed concerned about his unkempt hair and face. Vivian wanted to shave his beard, and though she didn't know how, she was willing to try, but Tino advised against it. The beard was the least of Philip's problems. He was being fed through a tube up his nose. A needle in his arm was attached by a tube to a glass bottle of clear liquid. Another tube drained his urine into a bag hanging beside his bed. Vivian knew how every tube was attached and had even helped clean and replace each one. Philip's right hand was again in a plaster cast, though a shorter one, but the dreadful metal brace, with all its straps and buckles, remained on his leg. As soon as Philip and all his tubes and bags were settled on a gurney, which was even shorter than his hospital bed, he was ready to be wheeled onto an ambulance along with a packing case of the medical supplies he would need on the trip.

The hospital staff gave Vivian a few minutes alone with Philip to say good-bye. She added the St. Christopher medal to his dog tag chain and tenderly kissed his lips, but they were chapped and unresponsive. She kissed his cheek and bandaged forehead and whispered into his ear. "I love you, Philip. Come back to me. I'll be waiting," she said softly, hoping he could hear and remember her words. With tears streaming down her face, she watched as Philip's ambulance drove away. His plane left Guam on July 2,

1941. On the east coast of the United States, the date was July 1, the day he was supposed to be in Rhode Island.

Three days after Philip's departure, a lieutenant and three sailors came to the Camacho house to collect Philip's belongings for shipment back to the States. Vivian showed them to Philip's room and pointed out where he kept all his clothing and shoes. She opened his closet and retrieved the brown paper sack containing Philip's cap and valuables. She had cleaned his shoes before putting them in his closet with the others.

"This was given to me at the hospital, to hold for him. There's some money in his wallet," she said as she handed the sack to the lieutenant. "I think his hat is beyond repair, but I've left it in the bag." She wanted to keep the cap, even though it was ruined. It belonged to Philip, and that's all that mattered to her. But since it wasn't hers to keep, she let it go.

"Thank you, ma'am," he said. "I'll take care of disposing it, and I'll add his things to the items from his desk. They'll be safe." The lieutenant removed the items from the sack and placed them in a large manila envelope.

Vivian watched sadly as the navy men removed Philip's clothing from the drawers in the wardrobe and from the closet. She then led them to the third bedroom, where Philip and Parker had kept their dry-cleaned service dress whites. Only Philip's uniforms remained in the closet. The sailors removed the uniforms to Philip's bedroom and started quickly and methodically packing. Philip's valise and suitcase—her companions during the typhoon—could not contain all his belongings; he had acquired more civilian clothing than what he had arrived with. One of the sailors was sent back to the compound to get a large cardboard shipping box. When he returned, the sailors filled it with the rest of Philip's clothes. After they left, Vivian looked around the stark and empty bedroom. Except for the electric fan, which the lieutenant said they were not authorized to pack, all of Philip's belongings were gone.

Vivian stripped the bed and buried her face in the wadded up sheets, but his scent was no longer there. She had laundered his sheets days after the accident, hoping he would eventually recover and come home, but Philip never returned to the Camacho house. Vivian pressed her fingers into the shallow impression Philip's fist made in the wall and recalled how their encounter that day began so dreadfully and ended so wonderfully. Reluctantly, she shuttered the window and closed his bedroom door. She went into the parlor, to the spot near the front door where he stood with Parker that afternoon nearly two years ago. She remembered how her heart jumped when she saw him for the first time. He was so tall and handsome.

"I think I fell in love with you the moment I saw you, Philip Avery," she said out loud as she looked up at where his face would have been.

She remembered the startling color of his eyes, so distracting then but so longed-for now. Vivian wanted to remember Philip as the handsome lieutenant who conquered her heart; the man who kissed her lips for the first time, who made secret funny faces at her, and knelt at her feet to declare his love. She prayed Philip would make it back to the States alive. Even if he never returned to Guam, or ever wrote to her, even if she never saw him again, Vivian hoped he would survive to live a long and happy life.

"Good-bye, Mr. Avery, I love you," she whispered. She heaved a sad, heavy sigh and closed the wooden doors. The apartment in the Camacho house was vacant again. No one lived upstairs anymore.

PART FOUR

Chapter 36

Pan American Airways' "flying boat," the *California Clipper*, departed Guam once a week, on the return of its transpacific flight from San Francisco to Hong Kong. It made the four-thousand-mile leap from Guam to Honolulu, Hawaii, with refueling stops on Wake and Midway islands. The huge Boeing seaplane could seat seventy-four passengers, had sleeping berths for thirty-six, and featured a full-service dining room, separate bathrooms for men and women, a lounge, and a deluxe private compartment. Philip required only a sleeping berth and a nearby seat for his nurse escort. At each stop, he was removed to a hospital or dispensary for his condition to be assessed before he was cleared to continue. Because of the stops, and having to wait for the next flight, the trip took almost three weeks. By then, Philip was starting to awaken from the coma. His left eye fluttered occasionally, and he turned his head from side to side but was not conscious.

From Honolulu, the flight terminated in Alameda, California, specifically at Treasure Island in San Francisco Bay, where his parents and brother William met the seaplane. From there, they boarded a train to San Diego and admitted Philip to the naval hospital there. Preston and William remained in San Diego until they were assured that Philip would survive and was on the road to recovery then they returned to New York. Lydia stayed behind, refusing to leave her son. She was shocked by Philip's appearance; his beard and hair were long and unkempt. At her insistence, a barber was brought in to groom him, cutting his hair and shaving his face. Lydia was at his bedside when he opened his left eye and his limbs started to twitch more often and more consistently.

Philip remained semicomatose for another two weeks. He awoke slowly, confused, disoriented, and agitated by his surroundings. He didn't know where he was or what had happened to him. He remembered nothing about the accident and could only recall being with Vivian, but he didn't know where or when that was. Through a blur, Philip eventually recognized his mother. When he was more awake, a few days later, he became less distressed and started to calm down, especially at the sound of his mother's voice. Although Philip was not yet himself, doctors marveled at his recovery; he was regaining his faculties more quickly than normal.

When his appetite returned, and he was in relatively good spirits, his mother asked, "What is a 'vivvy,' Philip? You mumbled it several times."

"It's a pet name, Mother, short for Vivian," he said, matter-of-factly. "She's the girl I'm going to marry."

In the days that followed, Philip told his mother about Vivian. Although he had regularly written letters home, he never mentioned anything about Vivian and how he felt about her. Initially, as he struggled with his feelings, he had nothing to report. Later, he wrote nothing because he feared his parents' reaction to his marrying outside his race and social standing. He had only come to grips with his decision himself shortly before his accident. Bolstered by the possibility of losing Vivian, Philip swallowed his doubts and fears and boldly confessed his love and his decision to marry a brown-skinned Chamorro girl from Guam. He watched his mother's face as he spoke and realized that she would have respected his choice and supported his decisions though not without trepidation.

"Would you like me to break this to your father?" his mother asked, revealing her misgiving. Philip flinched at her use of the term "break." Did she expect his father to react negatively to his news? It didn't matter. He loved Vivian enough to oppose his father on the issue.

"No, thank you, Mother. I'll handle this myself," Philip said. He sincerely believed that if and when they met Vivian, they would see past her ethnicity and would come to know and love her as he did. How could they not? But he also feared that they would reject her. If they did, he decided, he would make it clear to them that they would be rejecting him as well. And if that was their decision, he would dismiss himself and his wife from their presence and return to Guam. He hoped it wouldn't come to that. Although he knew Vivian would have great difficulty leaving behind her father and her island, Philip hoped she would agree to frequent and regular visits, not only to New York, but to any other place she wanted to see.

His mother also asked about the religious medal attached to his dog tag chain. Until then, Philip hadn't noticed it. He couldn't see out of his bandaged right eye, and the vision in his left was still blurred. He couldn't read the lettering on the medal. He didn't know who the saint was or what the medal was supposed to do for him—for luck? He guessed that Vivian put it there, so he kissed it every night and said, "Saint Whoever-you-are, please watch over my Vivian."

Though he was no longer in a coma and most of his wounds had healed, Philip still suffered pain and frustration as he recuperated. His mangled leg and foot had yet to heal, and he faced several weeks of physical therapy to regain normal, pain-free use of it. Sometimes, in the wee hours of morning, he would awaken to stabbing pain in his leg, or somewhere else on his body. Unable to get back to sleep, he would stare up at the ceiling or out the window and into the night. He would recall his days on Guam and find himself missing his nighttime scotch-and-water conversations with Tino, the wonderful times they spent at the lancho, his excursions with Parker and the other fellows, and Vivian.

Mostly he found himself missing Vivian. He missed her so much, it hurt more than all the physical pains that plagued him. Sometimes, from deep sleep, he would be jolted awake by Vivian's voice cheerfully calling, "Mr. Avery?" He would sit bolt upright and search the darkness for her, only to realize sadly that it was a dream, a vivid memory. He yearned for Vivian. He longed to see her, to be near her, even if he couldn't touch her. He wanted to see her face and get lost in the warmth of her dark eyes. He longed to listen to her laugh and to hear her say, "Mr. Avery." Knowing that she loved him, Philip now welcomed her "Mr. Avery" as endearment. He was determined to marry her and to cherish the privilege of addressing her as "Mrs. Avery" as often as he wanted. He had to get word back to Vivian somehow that he was alive and to wait for him.

At his parents' insistence, Philip returned to New York to complete his convalescence at home, under the care of his brother and a hired physical therapist. The vision in his left eye returned to normal, but his right eye remained blurred. He could not yet walk and had to rely on first a wheelchair and later a cane. His surgery scars were completely healed, but he continued to experience terrible headaches. He had lost a considerable amount of weight and was gaunt and pale.

He took the train with his mother and along the way, spoke more about Vivian and his life in Guam. Between their conversations, Lydia watched him stare silently out the windows for hours with a faraway look in his eyes, not really seeing the landscape speeding by. She could see that her son was lonely, and deeply in love. His face brightened and his eyes sparkled whenever he spoke about Vivian. Lydia realized that her son's love for this strange native girl from some faraway island was what kept him alive and fueled his determination to live. The doctors, including William, were astounded by his survival. They said his injuries were so severe and life-threatening that he should have died. *What a debt of gratitude I owe that girl. Thanks to her, my son lives,* Lydia thought to herself.

Philip and his mother arrived home to find the foyer and great room filled with floral arrangements from friends and old girlfriends. There were also stacks of cards and letters wishing him well and asking to pay him visits. Mrs. Mueller, the cook, and the rest of the household staff were in the great room as well, ready to welcome him home. The physical therapist

Preston hired—a burly man named Jan—was on hand also. Mrs. Mueller paled when she saw Philip.

"We shall have to put some meat back on those bones," she declared in her gruff German accent. Until he heard it again, Philip didn't realize how much he missed her.

"And it'll all be muscle," Jan added. Philip turned to his parents and in jest shot them a feigned look of panic.

After greeting everyone, Philip went into his father's den to try to make a long-distance telephone call to Guam, not taking into account the time difference, but it didn't matter. His calls, both to the Governor's Palace and to the old telephone upstairs in the Camacho house, didn't connect. He tried almost daily without success. He also tried several times to send a telegram, again without success, something about technical difficulties crossing the Pacific. He finally resorted to writing letters. He wrote several, to Vivian directly and in care of Tino at the Governor's Palace. He waited anxiously for a reply, but none came.

Wearied by the homecoming, Philip retired to his bedroom. There were floral arrangements there too. Although the room and its furnishings, including his custom-made extra-long bed, and all his boyhood trophies and treasures were just as he left them, Philip felt alien to his surroundings. He last slept in his room when he was home on leave before he reported to Guam. It seemed so long ago, and everything in his bedroom now seemed to belong to someone else.

After a long, hot bath, he caught a glimpse of his naked body in the mirror and balked; he was scarred and skinny. He held up his arms, sucked in a deep breath, and watched in horror as his ribs appeared under his skin. The surgery scar was an angry red line that ran diagonally across his abdomen. Another diagonal scar ran across his forehead, brow, and eyelid. He looked awful. Philip worried that Vivian would cringe at his disfigurement and shrink from him. *If she truly loves me, she wouldn't,* he told himself. He knew he would have to regain his health, his strength, and at least his weight if he had any chance of getting back to her. That goal would be a strenuous and painful one, especially with as unyielding a trainer as Jan looked to be.

Among the cards and letters on his dresser, Philip found four letters from Parker, who wrote at least once a month since leaving Guam. The first two letters were received at the Governor's Palace then forwarded to Philip's New York address. Parker's first letter chronicled his new assignment in Washington and the cold, wet weather there. He also wrote about his new superiors and civilian coworkers. The second letter, dated in May, only days before Philip's accident, went into detail about his new job, finding a small apartment near the base, and about missing Tino and Vivian—and him also. Philip chuckled. Parker ended his letter with a question about whether Philip had proposed yet.

Parker's third letter, a long one, was addressed to Philip's parents and dated in June. The envelope had been opened and the letter was left for him to read. Parker wrote that he had received terrible news from Miss Vivian Camacho, the daughter of his and Philip's landlord in Guam and a dear friend, about Philip's accident and the gravity of his injuries. Parker told the Averys that he had written back to Vivian for more information but received no response. He asked if they would share with him any information they might have had.

> I know nothing of Philip's condition and I fear for him. He is my friend. If he has passed on, I apologize sincerely for this intrusion, but please know that I send my deepest condolences and mourn with you.
>
> Sincerely,
> Lt.j.g. Parker W. Reed, USNR

Philip was touched. *That ole' chowhound,* he thought, *I have to give him a phone call.* Parker's last letter was addressed to Philip. His parents had responded and filled him in. The letter started with, "Glad you made it. Did you pop the question? Don't forget, I'm your best man!" The rest was about the great fishing in Washington and the even greater seafood. He urged Philip to make a trip out there if and when he could.

Philip telephoned Parker and the two spoke for nearly two hours, talking mainly about Philip's accident and catching up on news about the people they worked with at the Governor's Palace, and they especially shared their concerns about Tino and Vivian and why neither of them could make contact. Philip had little in common with Parker when they first met, but in less than two years of being housemates, Parker turned out to be a first-rate friend. Philip had many high school and college friends, but he never let anyone get close to him, not even the women he dated. He never saw the need, not until he met Parker and the Camachos. Each changed his life in ways he never expected, and he counted Parker as his closest, dearest friend. Philip's telephone call cost a fortune, but Preston did not complain.

The package from his father's jeweler friend was also on Philip's dresser. It contained the diamond engagement-and-wedding ring set he had ordered for Vivian. It too had been received at the Governor's Palace and forwarded to his parents' address. The Averys recognized the sender's name and address and suspected the package's contents. They speculated for months as to who might have been the intended recipient. Philip left the box unopened. If he couldn't propose and eventually slip the wedding ring on Vivian's finger, there was no need to open it, no need to explain what he had purchased or why. He had already revealed his intentions to his mother and she would have explained to his father.

In a corner of his bedroom, near a window, were his now-battered suitcase, valise, and a large, equally banged-up cardboard box. They had been sitting in his room for weeks while he was in the hospital. Knowing what they contained, he didn't bother to open them. He assumed the box held whatever didn't fit in the suitcase. When he finally opened the box, he found the uniform shoes he was wearing during the accident, his hiking boots, and his extra civilian clothes. The new set of lancho clothes that Vivian had ordered for him was a bittersweet surprise.

Nestled among several sets of relatively new skivvies was a large manila envelope. It was rubber-stamped to indicate that the seal had not been broken. Philip could tell by the feel that the envelope contained several small, bulky items. He ripped it open and out fell his wallet, broken wristwatch, and the red velvet ring box from his desk drawer. There was also a legal size envelope addressed to him at the engineering division. He sat down on the edge of his bed and opened the letter. It was from the judge advocate general's office and listed at least half a dozen signatures, including those of the judge advocate and the governor. Philip's application to marry Vivian had been approved. He stared at it in disbelief. He picked up the little ring box, opened it, and, for the first time since he was six years old, he wept.

CHAPTER 37

Two days after Philip arrived home, someone banged loudly on his bedroom door. Jennifer rushed home from college to see him. When she was informed of his accident and the uncertainty of his survival, she realized that the threat to his life was the source of the strange foreboding she had felt before Philip went to Guam. Fearing Philip would die, she had begged and pleaded to accompany her parents and William to California, but her father wouldn't allow it, telling her to wait until they brought Philip home. She hoped it wouldn't be in a casket. Not waiting for permission to enter, Jennifer came bounding into his room, laughing and squealing happily, ready to jump into his arms. She stopped short suddenly.

"Will I hurt you if I hugged you?" she asked, shocked by his appearance.

Philip had lost almost forty pounds and looked frail. His hair was cropped short and scars were visible on his scalp. There was another one across his forehead and through his right eyebrow. His cheeks and temples were sunken and his clothes hung on him. He looked like he was wearing someone else's clothes, someone two sizes larger. When Philip answered negatively, Jennifer threw her arms around him and kissed his cheeks; she could feel his ribs. She said nothing about the ugly scar on his forehead, but inwardly, she wanted to cry at the sight. Her brother's face was now marred. The scars and the weight loss were not the only changes she noted. Philip was different; there was a sense of purposeful resolve about him.

"And what's this about a gir-r-r-r-l, and wanting to get ma-a-a-a-rried? You? The playboy of this family?" she asked, eager to hear all the details. Philip obliged her, knowing she would be the most enthusiastic listener of all he had to tell.

"Oh Philip, I can't wait to meet her. I hope we'll be good friends. I'll have another sister . . . in-law," Jennifer's eyes sparkled at the idea.

"Hold your horses, Jenny, I haven't asked her yet," Philip said with a laugh. "But I fully intend to as soon as I can."

"Is she a nurse? Is she in the navy too? How did you meet her? Where's she from?"

Philip realized that his sister was assuming he had fallen in love with an American, someone who was white.

"She's Chamorro, Jenny, a native of Guam. She's a grade school teacher," he said, waiting for her reaction. The smile on Jennifer's face held fast, but Philip could actually see the muscles behind it sag a little. Her reaction was barely noticeable and was as he expected. Jennifer was the Avery least affected by racial prejudice and unconcerned about social status, but she also knew that they were inescapable realities.

"Would you like to see a picture of her? It's not a very good one; I clipped it from one of her yearbooks."

Until that moment, Philip didn't bother to look into his billfold. In it, Vivian's picture and the family photo were the only items he valued. He didn't remember, nor was he concerned, about the twenty-three dollars, which were still inside. He reached into a slot, expecting to retrieve the yearbook clipping along with the family photo, but instead found the original photograph that Vivian had switched. On the back, Vivian had written: "I love you, Mr. Avery. Please come back to me." Vivian's handwriting and her declaration of love—committed to paper—made his heart soar and sent his spirits flying. Jennifer watched as a huge, beautiful smile lit up his face. "She gave me a better photo," he said as he handed it to his sister.

Jennifer read the back first and asked, "Why does she call you Mr. Avery?"

Philip's smile grew even wider and happier. "It's a joke between us," he said.

The woman in the picture was not at all the type that usually captured her brother's attention. She had dark wavy hair and large dark eyes; her skin was not dark, but it wasn't pale either. Vivian was not unattractive. In fact, Jennifer sincerely thought she was pretty but vastly different from the girls Philip usually chased. And he chased, and caught, a lot of them. Vivian wasn't a blue-eyed blonde or a freckled redhead, and she didn't look anything like a bubbly brunette. Jennifer tried to imagine what it was about Vivian that captivated her brother so dramatically. Maybe it was because she was different, she figured. Until Vivian came into his life, Philip never talked about any particular girlfriend, and none had ever lit up his face the way Vivian's photo did. Even more surprising, Philip had never ever said anything to anyone about marriage. Jennifer was sure he would remain a happy-go-lucky bachelor for a long, long time.

"She's pretty," she said with a little hesitation, due mainly to studying Vivian's features and wondering about what kind of power this woman had to convert an avowed playboy into a lovesick puppy. Warmth and gentleness shone in the woman's dark eyes. She wasn't smiling widely or showing any teeth. Instead, her lips were held together with only a slight, demure smile.

Philip watched Jennifer's reaction and assumed she wasn't impressed. He grew defensive.

"Yes, she *is* pretty!" he said defiantly. "She's the most beautiful, wonderful, amazing girl I've ever met. And I'm the lucky bastard she fell in love with."

Jennifer threw her arms around her brother's neck and kissed him again.

"If you love her, Philip, I know I will too!"

"I do love her, Jenny, more than I can say."

Jennifer could only stay the weekend before she had to return to school. The fall semester was already well underway. She made Philip promise to write her as often as he could, to let her know when and how he proposed—did he get down on one knee—what Vivian's response was, and when the wedding would take place. She was determined to attend it, no matter where in the world it was to occur. Philip's smile faded as Jennifer spoke of marriage proposals and weddings. He couldn't bring himself to tell her that the little box on his dresser contained the wedding ring set he had ordered, or to show her the locket he designed and had made for Vivian and which he kept hidden in a drawer.

"Jenny, she doesn't know I'm alive, that I survived the accident," he said, recalling the last time he was with her, how he kept kissing her as she wrapped his throbbing hand in a towel. He suddenly remembered his broken hand and realized the cast was gone. He studied both sides of his right hand. There was a small scar on his middle knuckle. He rubbed his knuckles and added, "I broke my hand and she made me go to the hospital."

Another memory flashed, one so frightening that the color drained from his face. "I couldn't get the car door open because of the cast," he said, "and I fell out."

For several days after he came out of the coma, his mother and several of the hospital staff had to repeat to him several times the details of the accident. He remembered nothing and struggled to recollect something—anything—about it. He couldn't accept that Lieutenant Kaplan was killed, or that he almost died also, and that nearly three months of his life had passed without his knowing. He knew only that his father had him flown to California and that no word as to his fate was ever relayed back to the Governor's Palace or to Vivian and Tino.

"When I woke up, I was in San Diego," he said.

He showed Jennifer the religious medal on his dog tag chain. "Vivian must have put this on me. I don't know what it's supposed to do, but it must be important."

Jennifer recognized it instantly. "I know what that is; it's a St. Christopher medal," she said. "My roommate's Catholic and her mother gave her one when she left for college. She never takes it off. He's supposed to be the patron saint of travelers and he protects you on your journey."

"Well, thanks to Vivian, he protected me, I guess," Philip said, and added sadly, "Jenny, I'm trying every way I can to contact her, to let her know I made it, but I can't reach her."

His anguish alarmed her. It wasn't like him to sound sad and defeated. Of her brothers, Philip had always been the boldest, bravest, the most daring and adventurous, and the most determined. Whenever she was frightened or anxious about attempting something new, he was the one who boosted her courage. Now she hoped to do the same for him, repeating the words he often told her.

"Remember, Avery Bravery! You already have most of what you need. Find the rest, Philip, find a way," Jennifer said and patted his cheek.

"By the way," she added, "scarecrows don't look good in tuxedoes."

The comment lifted his spirits and made him laugh.

Jennifer said good-bye to Philip and their parents two days later and sailed out the door to the cab waiting to drive her to the train station. "Don't forget, I'm coming to the wedding," she called out.

Philip and his mother watched the cab pull away. As they turned to go back inside, Lydia reminded him that several of his friends were awaiting his call. Several wanted to come for a visit.

"At least four of your old girlfriends would like to call on you," she said. "Libby Morton has telephoned every day since we arrived. What shall I tell them, Philip? What shall I say to Libby?"

"Mother, please hold them off a while longer," Philip said. "I really don't want to see anyone right now. Especially Libby."

"Well. I'm afraid you're going to have to face them sooner or later."

"I know. But I'd rather it be later than sooner. I have to contact Vivian first."

Despite his mother's and the staff's efforts to keep well-wishers at bay, at least until Philip felt up to entertaining visitors, Libby Morton showed up on their doorstep, insisting on seeing Philip. Although he still didn't want to face anyone, especially old girlfriends, Philip realized he needed to face his past, to see if someone like Libby could take his mind off Vivian.

Libby was a high-class beauty. She was the kind of girl who turned men's heads everywhere she went. She was the kind most guys could only dream of escorting. Family friends often said that he and Libby looked like they could have been the models for the bride and groom figures on the tops of wedding cakes, hinting at their hopes for the couple. But Philip was never sure of her. He liked her; she was easy to take to bed and she satisfied his urges, but she never filled his thoughts and fantasies the way Vivian did. Philip had been a girl watcher almost all his life but realized he hadn't paid attention to any since coming home. He wondered whether seeing Libby again would rekindle his attraction to her, realizing how superficial it had always been. Philip donned his robe and slippers and headed downstairs to the sunroom where Libby had been led to wait.

Libby rose gracefully to her feet when he entered, but the bright smile on her face disappeared immediately. She was stunned. She was expecting to see the handsome, debonair Philip; the man she hoped would marry her. Instead, he was thin and frail, and she was repelled. She realized what a horrible mistake she had made in showing up uninvited and sought to make a quick exit.

"I'm glad to see you, Libby," Philip lied.

Libby Morton was as beautiful as ever, her peaches-and-cream complexion still flawless, her azure eyes clear and sparkling. Her blonde hair was silky and shiny and brushed smoothly into a pageboy. She wore a handsome blue suit with a fox stole around her shoulders. Behind Libby's finery, however, Philip knew how ambitious, self-centered, and manipulative she could be. Marriage to her would have been hellish in a very short time—picture perfect on the outside, poisonous and bitter on the inside.

Libby couldn't hide her disenchantment either. She wanted to marry a handsome, wealthy man who would provide for all her wants, make her the envy of her friends, eventually seek his pleasures elsewhere, and never ruin her figure by making her pregnant. She didn't want any children or a scrawny husband who had such an obvious and distractingly scarred face. Philip was no longer the perfect specimen she expected of a mate.

"You look wonderful, Philip," she said, lying also. After some awkward small talk, she added, "I really can't stay. I just wanted to pop by to welcome you home."

"Thank you for coming, Libby. I hope to see you again," Philip said as he walked her to the foyer and opened the front door. He lied again and knew she was lying too.

Life with her would have been one lie after another, he thought as he watched her saunter down the walkway to her car. He recalled the look of shock and revulsion on her face at seeing him and wondered whether Vivian would react the same way. No, he decided, Vivian would not. Philip smiled and waved at Libby from the doorstep as she drove away.

"No more visitors, Mother," he said as he closed the front door and headed back upstairs. "If anyone else calls, tell them I died and went to heaven. Tell them anything."

Chapter 38

Over breakfast in the sunroom that October, Preston summoned Philip to join him. Philip had taken breakfast in his bedroom and was hobbling around in pajamas. Before going downstairs, he changed into gym shorts and a sweatshirt to start the exercise program Jan had outlined for him. The program included flexibility, endurance, strength training, and a carefully planned muscle-building weight-gain diet.

"I understand we have important matters to discuss," Preston said to him as he took a seat opposite his father. The trees along the rolling lawn outside the glass walls of the sunroom were glorious in their fall colors. Philip could only glance at them quickly. He wondered if he could ever bring Vivian into that very room to marvel at the colors. *Someday,* he assured himself.

On the table before him was a small bowl of plain yogurt with wheat germ, raisins, honey, and slivered almonds, and a large glass of orange juice. Philip frowned at the second breakfast but started eating it. He was determined to return to good health and would do everything Jan demanded. Preston was paying for the man's services. More important, Vivian would expect him to return to her healthy and whole. He hoped she would still love him, scars and all, if he at least didn't look like a scarecrow.

"Yes, Father, we do," Philip said, surprised by his lack of anxiety. He had never been afraid to speak with his father about anything, even when he decided to enlist, but he was nervous about telling him about Vivian. Preston was not pleased with Philip's decision to join the navy and he expressed his disapproval clearly, but he didn't thwart it. Knowing his father's prejudices, however, Philip dreaded having the conversation that had to occur. But when that moment arrived, Philip's qualms disappeared.

"Father, I have met the girl I want to marry," Philip said confidently. "Her name is Vivian de Leon Camacho. She is a native of Guam and will be twenty-one years old this December. I have been trying—"

His father cut him short. "So have you managed to make contact?"

"No, sir, I have not," Philip said, "but I shall return to active duty as soon as I'm cleared medically and will endeavor to return to Guam at my earliest."

Preston had tried through his own political channels to get word to his son's mysterious sweetheart, but his efforts were equally unsuccessful. He heard about Vivian from his wife, despite Philip's request to disclose the news himself.

"Our son should have perished immediately in that accident. But he didn't. If loving that girl kept Philip alive, then I will not stand between them," Lydia told her husband. The look in her eyes warned Preston to follow her lead.

Preston had no confirmation that his messages were received and no reply ever came back. He said nothing to Philip about his efforts. There was no point to it; telling him simply would have added to his son's worry.

For the next half hour, Preston pressed his son on what Guam was like, and what he remembered of his accident. Philip knew his father was simply being polite and was not really interested in Guam, but he gave him a greatly abbreviated description and said he didn't remember much about the accident, although he had vivid nightmares reliving it.

"Davisville was informed through official channels of your accident in Guam and why you were unable to report as ordered. The admiral who's putting the unit together assures me that you will not lose your spot, although you would still need to prove yourself able and qualified," Preston said.

"Thank you, Father," Philip responded. "I will report and I will qualify. And I will return to Guam and marry Vivian if she'll have me." He left the sunroom with a joyful feeling. His father did not react negatively to his wanting to marry Vivian.

In the weeks that followed, Philip worked doubly hard to regain his health. Jan often had to slow him down. By the end of September, Philip had regained fifteen pounds; by October, he was back up to a hundred and seventy. By Thanksgiving, he weighed two hundred and ten pounds and was well muscled. He looked almost as brawny as Jan. When he looked at himself in his bathroom mirror and flexed his biceps, he hoped Vivian would be impressed.

At the end of November, Philip received a letter from Davisville. His new report date, 29 December 1941, would allow him to spend Christmas with his family. But it was not to be.

On December 7, 1941, the United States entered World War II. The following day, Philip and his parents listened intently to the radio as President Roosevelt addressed a joint session of Congress. "The attack yesterday on the Hawaiian Islands has caused severe damage to American naval and military forces," the president said.

> I regret to tell you that very many American lives have been lost. In addition, American ships have been reported torpedoed on the high seas between San Francisco and Honolulu.
>
> Yesterday the Japanese Government also launched an attack against Malaya.
>
> Last night Japanese forces attacked Hong Kong.
>
> Last night Japanese forces attacked Guam—

Philip froze. His heart seemed to drop into his stomach and bounce back up. The sensation made him gasp for breath. The color drained from his face. His parents watched his reaction and saw fear grow in his eyes. The president's voice faded to a whisper as Philip's mind turned immediately to Vivian and Tino. He now understood why communicating with them had been impossible. *Were they hurt,* he wondered, *were they alive? Were they safe?*

The president continued,

> As Commander in Chief of the Army and Navy, I have directed that all measures be taken for our defense, that always will our whole nation remember the character of the onslaught against us. Victory Will Be Absolute. No matter how long it may take us to overcome this premeditated invasion, the American people, in their righteous might, will win through to absolute victory.

In the days that followed the attack on Pearl Harbor, which dominated the news, Philip scoured the newspapers for more details about the attack on Guam, but the *New York Times* simply mentioned the island by name. To his horror, Philip later learned that Japanese warplanes had strafed the government compound in Agaña, that there had been widespread panic and that several people had been killed. Philip wouldn't let himself think about what might have happened to Vivian and Tino. Their house was only steps away from the government compound. If it had been strafed, might they have been harmed? The probabilities were too unbearable to contemplate.

As more details came to light, Philip learned that the Japanese had aimed for strategic targets in Sumay and the navy docks in Piti. The air strikes lasted two days and were followed by a landing force of several thousand, which split up and marched on Sumay, Piti, and Agaña. Against overwhelming odds, the naval governor surrendered the island. He, the few remaining navy personnel, and all other Americans were taken prisoner.

Philip knew the places that had been bombed; he had been to all of them. He knew the governor and his staff, as well as some of the civilians and insular guardsmen. They were not nameless strangers. In their letter exchanges, Philip and Parker shared their worries about the navy men they worked with, about the Chamorro people they had come to know, and about Vivian and Tino, in particular. Guam to them was not a strange foreign place worth only a mention in a newspaper article; it was not just a tiny outcropping in the Pacific Ocean.

"Wish me luck, Parker," Philip said in a final telephone call to his friend. "I'm going back there. I'm going to find a way somehow."

"Good luck, Philip. I hope you find them," Parker said.

Preston Avery was well acquainted with the look of unassailable determination on his son's face. He knew from whom he had inherited it, but he also feared it. His son was going off to war; there was no stopping him. Philip would not wait until after Christmas to report to Davisville; he would take the first train to Rhode Island and beg, if necessary, to be accepted into the new navy unit.

At the train station, Philip hugged his mother tightly and kissed her cheek. He also kissed Mrs. Mueller, who had insisted on seeing him off. She was crying inconsolably, afraid that he would not come home alive again this time. He cupped her cheeks and said, "Don't worry, Mama Mueller, I'm going to bring back a wife and you can spoil both of us." Mrs. Mueller blew her nose noisily and smiled at him through her tears. "I just want you to come home."

"I promise I will!" Philip said.

"Watch your back, son," Preston whispered in his ear as they embraced each other.

"I will, Father," Philip whispered back.

Philip was among dozens of navy civil engineers eagerly volunteering to join the new Naval Construction Battalions, which were organized a month after the United States entered the war. Although the recruitment priority was for men for the enlisted ranks, officers were selected also. The navy wanted experienced construction tradesmen—masons, carpenters, steelworkers, heavy equipment operators, electricians, plumbers, and whoever had already proven their worth in every aspect of the building industry—to enlist and be ready to build and fight.

"You were stationed in Guam?" asked a captain who was poring over Philip's file.

"Yes, sir," he answered.

"Are you the guy who was in an accident?"

"Yes, sir, but I'm fine now."

"We'll see. It's not going to be easy."

"I'm fine, sir. I assure you."

"Says here you haven't had much experience."

Philip's heart sank. "No, sir, but I'm a quick study and I'll learn. Please give me a chance."

The captain handed Philip's file to a yeoman sitting behind a desk piled high with other file folders then walked away without a word. The yeoman behind the desk yelled, "Next!"

Philip remained standing before him, waiting to learn his fate. The yeoman looked up at him and said, "Lieutenant, please step aside."

"In which direction?"

"Officers' quarters are behind you, to the left, sir."

Philip wanted to jump for joy. He made the first cut.

Training for everyone began immediately. Officers of the navy's civil engineer corps, who, like Philip, were selected to lead the new construction battalions, underwent additional training and indoctrination to authorize them to exercise military authority and command over other officers and enlisted men. In addition to hours in the classroom, Philip and his companions spent hours in the field and in exercises. The officers, like the enlisted construction experts, were expected to fight as part of their mission and underwent rigorous combat training as well. Although they were masters of the construction trades, the enlisted recruits had to learn to become navy men. They underwent military indoctrination, discipline, and weapons and combat training, in order to defend themselves and their projects.

Together, all the men of the construction battalions would eventually become known by their initials *CB*, which evolved into "Seabees." A heavily armed bumblebee became their emblem. The first group of builders left the advanced base depot at Davisville for Guadalcanal before the end of January 1942. The following month, another group of nearly three hundred went to Bora Bora in the Society Islands.

Within weeks of the war's start, a second advanced base depot was established in Port Hueneme, California. In time, the Seabees trained in Rhode Island were deployed to Europe; those in California fanned out into the Pacific—north to Alaska and the Aleutian Islands; south to the Society Islands, Tonga, the New Hebrides, the Solomons, and New Guinea; and straight ahead from Hawaii to Midway, Wake, the Marianas, the Carolines and the Palauan Islands; all three prongs eventually converging and aiming toward the Philippines and Japan itself.

Having undergone several weeks of fitness training to regain his health and strength, Philip was well ahead of his colleagues physically.

He completed the training as a full lieutenant and was slated to leave for Port Hueneme, where his battalion underwent staging and outfitting. From California, the battalion would be shipped to Hawaii and then out to island-hopping campaigns in the Central Pacific. In his pocket, Philip carried Vivian's locket. He vowed to keep it on him until he could place it around her neck.

While at Davisville, Philip wandered around town one morning and passed a Catholic church. The sign outside told him Mass would begin in a few minutes. Curious, he went into the church. Vivian and Tino were devout Catholics who went to church every Sunday, and even on some special weekdays, without fail. He wondered about their piety and what it was that spurred their devotion. He himself hadn't been in any house of worship since he was a teenager and then only on special occasions. The Averys didn't belong to any particular church, but they did believe in God and went sporadically to churches of different Protestant denominations.

Inside the church, Philip was surprised to see several of his fellow Seabees, both officers and enlisted men. He stood at the back of the church, not sure what to do. He noticed as people entered, they dipped their hand into some water in marble fonts on either side of the front doors. With moistened fingertips, they crossed themselves before proceeding down the aisle, genuflecting to the floor on one knee then taking a seat in a pew.

The church, St. Michael the Archangel, was an old one, filled with statues, ornate accoutrements, and tall candles in elaborate candelabras, and filled with the faint scent of fragrant smoky incense, candle wax, and polished wood. The tabernacle atop the altar was a spectacular masterpiece of gold, brass, pewter, and silver. Off to the left of the altar was a large, beautifully detailed statue of a fierce looking knight with huge wings, thrusting a spear into the chest of a bat-winged gargoyle pinned beneath his sandaled foot. The winged knight represented St. Michael, the defender of Christians against the Devil, represented by the gargoyle. It was a dramatic statue, and Philip liked studying all its details.

A tiny bell sounded, and the priest, dressed in scarlet vestments, and several altar boys entered the sanctuary. The choir started a hymn, and the Mass began. Except for the priest's sermon, the service was conducted entirely in Latin, some of which Philip recognized from his college Latin classes, but much was incomprehensible to him, as was the puzzling standing, sitting, and kneeling, repeated several times. Throughout the service, Philip could think only of Vivian and how this ceremony, this Church, meant so much to her. He wondered if she and her father were in their church now, attending Mass as they always did on Sunday mornings.

He still heard no word about the plight of the Chamorro people now under enemy occupation.

Although the Catholic Mass made little sense to him, Philip went to the church again the following Sunday. He found comfort in knowing that Vivian would be at a similar service halfway around the world. After his third visit, he waited to speak to the priest, a Father Manella, a venerable old Italian who still spoke with a lilting accent. Philip asked about converting to Catholicism.

"And why do you seek to convert?" the priest asked.

Philip freely admitted that he hoped someday to marry a particular girl, a Catholic girl.

"That is not a good enough reason, my son," the priest said. "A conversion occurs between you and God. He called you and you answered. If your only intention is to marry a Catholic, then yours is not a true conversion, a transformation of your life as you now live it, to a life that you alone wholeheartedly devote to God.

"I would gladly welcome you into the Roman Catholic faith and all the ways in which we worship God, but you must also welcome all that this faith believes in and requires of you. Think about what I have told you. In the meantime—"

The old priest rose from his chair and studied a shelf of books before pulling one out.

"I suggest you read this and study on it, then decide what it is you want to do," he said as he handed Philip a catechism for adults. He placed both hands on Philip's head, mumbled something in Latin, and then waved his right hand in the pattern of a cross in the air in front of Philip. "Go with God, my son," he said.

Chapter 39

December 8 is the Feast of the Immaculate Conception. It is the holiday Catholics commemorate as the day God brought the Blessed Virgin Mary into being without original sin to become the mother of his son, Jesus. The feast day is celebrated also as Agaña's fiesta, the home of the Dulce Nombre de Maria, or Sweet Name of Mary, Cathedral. A large procession gathering people from all over the island would take place through the streets of Agaña. In 1941, the holiday fell on a Monday, a regular workday. Tino and all other government employees were allowed the morning off to attend the festal Mass.

Tino and Vivian, along with most of Agaña's residents, were at Mass that morning when the strange drone of aircraft engines sounded overhead. The bishop froze, as did the altar boys and everyone in their pews, listening intently. The rumble of engines was followed by loud, high-pitched whistling sounds, which grew louder as they drew closer. Then several horrific explosions, one after another, rocked the ground around the cathedral. His face white with alarm, the bishop turned to the congregation.

"Leave here, my brothers and sisters," he said calmly, hoping not to cause a panic. "Seek shelter for yourselves and your families. God have mercy on us all!"

But panic did ensue. People fled the cathedral in terror, first into the streets then later into the jungles and into the hills to hide. They had lived in relative peace for nearly two hundred years, had never been exposed to armed conflict, and didn't know what to expect. They would find out in the days and months ahead. Their nightmare began that morning.

His heart pounding, Tino grabbed Vivian's hand and dashed out the nearest door, dragging his daughter roughly behind.

"Papa, what is it? What's happening?" Vivian asked, feeling panic rising.

"I think this is war," he answered.

Some in the community, especially among the government workers like Tino, knew that tensions between the U.S. and Japan were growing. When the navy began sending away its families, a few at a time, starting in 1940, it was clear that danger was stirring. The evacuation of dependents and nonessential personnel was completed by October 1941. Some American civilians who were married to Chamorros and who sensed danger also moved their families to the States months earlier. Others refused the offer to be evacuated, opting instead to remain with their wives and children who were not included in the evacuation offer.

Tino and Vivian ran home and hurriedly packed some food, clothing, and tools. Though he had never experienced war, Tino believed that as with typhoons, effective preparation offered the best chance for survival. He had a good machete and his gardening tools at the lancho but not much else. He had another machete in the outside kitchen and a well-stocked toolbox. Although the load was heavy, he and Vivian struggled to haul everything they could carry uphill to the lancho.

Less than four hours after the attack on Pearl Harbor, at eight-thirty in the morning of December 8 in Guam, Japanese aircraft from Saipan launched bombing attacks on the navy government compound and the naval hospital in Agaña, hitting several nearby homes. The Marine Barracks, the Standard Oil Company, the Pan American Hotel, and the Pacific Cable Station in Sumay; the navy yard in Piti, and the navy radio antenna at Libugon were primary targets.

With fear and uncertainty canceling out hunger, thirst, and all other feelings, Tino and Vivian sat at his makeshift picnic table. Without walls, the lancho shack offered no protection, especially from the swarms of mosquitoes that descended upon them at dusk. All they could do was watch great plumes of black smoke rising from behind the hills in the direction of Piti and Sumay and pray for the people who lived there.

The air attacks in Sumay and Piti continued until sundown and resumed the following morning. On December 10, the Japanese landed a two-pronged invasion force of several thousand. One prong landed in Apotguan, north of Agaña, and headed toward the capital. Along the way, they gunned down and killed all in a large family fleeing northward. The second prong marched to Sumay. In Agaña, men of the Chamorro insular guard put up a valiant defense in the Plaza de España, but they were quickly subdued. The navy governor was forced to surrender. He, the few remaining navy personnel, including a half dozen navy nurses, were taken prisoner and held in the cathedral. The insular guardsmen were held in the jail but were later released.

Tino and Vivian spent two miserable nights at the lancho. They had only the picnic table and Philip's nap bench. With a fiber mat and an old quilt each, Vivian slept on the nap bench, Tino on the picnic table. They had no mosquito netting or mosquito coils and were plagued by swarms of the annoying, biting, yammering insects. They both disliked the pungent smell of smoldering mosquito coils, so they never bought or used them.

Tino set fire to some empty coconut shells and let them smolder, but with no walls to enclose and concentrate the oily smoke, it did little to drive away the mosquitoes. Tino made note of the items they would need to retrieve from their house or purchase as soon as the opportunity arose. His list included buying a good supply of mosquito coils and some netting.

He was glad he had convinced Vivian to buy some sturdy work pants and boots to wear at the lancho. Dresses were impractical. She had torn or stained several of her cotton dresses, ruining them beyond further wear to church or school. Likewise, dainty shoes were not made for slogging through mud or climbing slippery inclines. In the rush to flee, Vivian changed into denim pants, a shirt, and her new work boots. She packed the remainder of her lancho clothes and some of her undergarments into a pillowcase. She had ordered three pairs of pants, four shirts, and the boots from the boys' section of the Sears Roebuck catalogue for herself. She also ordered a pair of denim pants and a shirt each for her father and Philip, who had worn out his old pants. His favorite cotton 'lancho shirt' also was beyond further mending. Vivian knew her father's sizes but could only guess at Philip's. She ordered the largest size available and hoped they would fit. She placed the order a month before Philip's accident, and it arrived the day he was flown away. The new clothes were packed and shipped with the rest of his belongings.

Three days after the invasion, Tino heard from his lancho neighbors that the Japanese had ordered all people to report to Agaña to be identified. Anyone who could not produce the proper identification would be shot on the spot. Not knowing what to expect from the Japanese, Tino felt complying with the order would be safer than continuing to hide out. Returning to town also provided the means to gather other necessities in case they had to flee again. They made their way to the yard in front of the officers' club and joined several other people on the road back down to town. They rounded the government compound and found thousands of others, their neighbors and people from outlying villages, in the plaza, waiting to be processed. Dozens of heavily armed soldiers roamed the plaza, glaring at people. Several Japanese-speaking Chamorros from Saipan swaggered alongside them, barking at people in Chamorro.

The Japanese required the people to provide their names and addresses and to itemize all their valuables and useable possessions, especially livestock. These were recorded and people were given identification badges made of cloth to pin on their clothing and wear at all times. They also pulled all the American civilians from the ranks and herded them into the cathedral with the captured navy personnel, the American Capuchin priests, and the bishop, who was a Spaniard. No one could understand why the civilians and priests were taken. They were not military men. They posed no threat, committed no crime. A few days later, the Chamorro-American families and their relatives and neighbors watched tearfully as their American husbands and fathers, the priests, and the navy personnel, stripped to their underwear, were marched to Piti, to be shipped off to wintery-cold prison camps in Kobe, Japan, and Manchuria, China.

The Americans had already been removed to the cathedral when Tino, Vivian, and the people they were with arrived in the plaza, which was still crowded. The processing took hours. Those who were the last to arrive at the plaza were also the last to be processed. Tino and Vivian were not processed until well after midnight and tried fearfully to make their way home through the tangle of military tents filling the plaza. There was not enough space in the Governor's Palace compound to accommodate the great number of soldiers so they commandeered other government buildings or abandoned residences nearby. Most pitched their tents in and around the plaza, filling it to capacity. Although the plaza was filled with soldiers and tents, the whole of Agaña was dark and quiet. The Japanese-imposed curfew and blackout worsened an already frightening situation. Rather than try to make their way back to the lancho in the dark, Tino decided it would be safer for them to go home. He and Vivian picked their way around the dozens of tents to leave the plaza and cross the street to their house.

The house was dark—all the windows had been shuttered, but it was not quiet. A ruckus was taking place upstairs. At least two dozen soldiers seemed to be squabbling over the vacant rooms. Quietly and carefully, Tino and Vivian entered their apartment to find a handful of soldiers exploring their bedrooms.

"This is my house!" Tino barked at them in Chamorro, scowling at the soldiers and trying to mask his fear of them. He dared not speak English and hoped his voice and demeanor would convey his meaning. To his surprise, the soldiers didn't attack him. Instead they began bowing toward him as they backed out the side door. Tino concluded they were likely fresh conscripts who had not yet perfected a seasoned arrogant swagger.

The goings-on upstairs were not as easily settled. Tino and Vivian could hear men ransacking Parker's empty bedroom, pulling out empty drawers, and apparently fighting over who was going to get the bed. More were in the bedroom that Parker and Philip used for storage, again arguing over the bed. Philip's room caused the biggest quarrel of all. The shouting became so loud and angry that Tino and Vivian feared fistfights would follow. In the end, however, several officers entered the house, and the bickering stopped suddenly. Four junior officers ran the soldiers out of Parker's room.

Another four took the spare room. The four highest ranking officers—Tino assumed they were the highest-ranking ones—prevailed in Philip's room. The rest, the enlisted men, slept on the floor in the parlor and dining room and even in the kitchen.

The Imperial Japanese Army remained on the island for three months to impose order and establish the new rules to live by. Within days of the invasion, the Japanese arranged a public execution to demonstrate their brand of justice. Two men were caught in an American contractor's warehouse in Sumay and were accused of stealing from the stores of construction materials and food supplies, all of which the Japanese now claimed. The men were sentenced to death by firing squad. The remaining residents of Agaña, those who did not immediately return to hiding in the jungles, were rounded up and forced to witness the execution, not knowing beforehand what they were about to see. Tino and Vivian were among them, as was Vivian's godfather, Kiko Taisipic. Tino had not seen Kiko since the Friday before the invasion.

"How are things with you?" Tino whispered to him.

"We're hiding out at my lancho in Maite[17]. There are three other families with us and at least twenty children. We need food," Kiko said, adding that he had crept into town for supplies and was caught in the roundup.

"Do you know what's happening?"

Tino looked sadly at Kiko and shook his head as they were herded along. The purpose of their gathering became frighteningly clear when they arrived at the cemetery at the western edge of town. The condemned men were blindfolded and standing before two freshly dug graves. A couple of Saipanese Chamorros armed with rifles strutted among the crowd.

"Pay attention!" one of them yelled. "You will not close your eyes. You will not make a sound. You will watch this demonstration in silence, or else." With that, he hit the man standing near him in the stomach with the butt of his rifle. The man crumpled to the ground, coughing and gagging. Two others near him helped him back up to his feet.

Vivian grabbed her father's arm, ready to bury her face in his shoulder, but he whispered to her to be brave. He put his arm around her shoulder and pulled her tight against himself.

"Don't look directly at them," he whispered, "Look above their heads."

Vivian could feel him trembling also. Her legs started to quake, and she started to sink, but Tino held her up. Around them, the other people were equally terrified.

---

[17] Pronounced "my tee."

The condemned men had been beaten and could barely stand. Some in the crowd knew the men and their families. Upon seeing them, a woman in the crowd stifled a cry and started whispering prayers. Others immediately joined in, keeping their voices low. But as the number of people praying grew, so did the sound of their murmuring until a Saipanese interpreter shouted angrily for silence.

The Saipan Chamorros, long influenced by their Japanese colonizers, were among the many brought to Guam to serve as interpreters. The Guam Chamorros, fiercely loyal to the Americans, looked upon their Saipanese brethren as enemy collaborators. The Saipan Chamorros considered the Guam Chamorros as arrogant and bigheaded as the Americans. Culturally and linguistically, the Chamorros were one people divided politically by their colonizing nations, which were now pitted against each other in war. The sense of betrayal and the animosity among the estranged Chamorros lingered long after the war. Some of the Saipanese interpreters were as cruel as their bosses and savored the sway they now had over the high and mighty Guam Chamorros.

A truck pulled up, and several armed soldiers jumped out. They took positions and readied their rifles. The people collectively held their breath. Vivian kept her eyes open and her face aimed in the direction of the condemned men, but her focus, blurred by her tears, was locked on the hillside above the firing squad. At a signal, the rifles were fired. Smoke from the rifles and the smell of burnt gunpowder filled the air. Her tears now streaming down her cheeks, Vivian kept her eyes on the hillside, but she could not escape flinching at the loud reports and glimpsing the bodies fall into the graves. She and almost all the other women and children wailed in shock and revulsion. Some women fainted; others vomited. Vivian also felt light-headed and began to lose consciousness, but Tino hugged her tightly and kept her from falling. Once the crowd was released, Tino, Kiko, and many other men half dragged, half carried their women and children home. Not one among them had ever seen another human being die in such a manner. None of them had ever seen anything so gruesome and horrifying, and none of them would ever forget it.

Kiko helped Tino get Vivian home. She had passed out as they left the cemetery. After getting her settled, the two men said good-bye. They did not see each other again for several months.

Vivian cried for hours. The execution haunted her for many nights. Even years later, especially if she was stressed or ill, the horrifying sights, sounds, and smells of the execution would return in a nightmare as vividly as the day it happened. She would awaken in a panic, her heart pounding. The terrified scream that she had to keep locked inside would escape her lips. Only the loving arms of her husband could calm her back to sleep.

Chapter 40

Over the days that followed, many residents moved away from Agaña, leaving the town all but deserted. Many chose the discomfort of staying at their lanchos rather than risk having to witness another execution or angering any of the soldiers wandering the streets with their bayoneted rifles always at the ready. It was safer to stay in isolation away from town and return only as needed. To stay was to tempt fate. Those who remained were watched, their whereabouts and activities monitored carefully.

With so many soldiers occupying the upstairs apartment, Tino was worried. Several of the men had already cast lecherous smirks at Vivian and suspicious looks at him. Like so many other townspeople, Tino also wanted to flee to the lancho, but he and Vivian were stuck. They had already been identified as the residents of the house and were expected to continue in residence, as part of the new order. He and Vivian could disappear for the length of a typical workday—tending their garden, harvesting fruits and vegetables, and collecting eggs for themselves and their nonpaying tenants, or shopping for supplies in town, but if they were absent longer or without prior explanation and approval, they would have been reported missing. A search might have followed, and they certainly would have been questioned and punished when found, as had already happened to several other runaway residents.

The soldier-tenants also knew that the door in the kitchen led downstairs into Tino and Vivian's apartment. Tino thought about dismantling the stairs but could not do so until all the soldiers were out of the house, and that rarely occurred. Still, he quietly pried up and removed the treads from the first six bottom steps, leaving a large gap at the bottom of the staircase. Anyone who came uninvited downstairs in the dark would find a nasty surprise halfway down. If questioned, Tino would claim that termites had destroyed the stairs and that he had yet to repair the damage. He hid the treads in the closets and planned to take them to the lancho if and when the opportunity arose.

For added safety, to protect Vivian, Tino again moved her bed into his room. Though crowded, uncomfortable, and highly improper, he felt it was the best way to safeguard her at night. Tino also worried about his bottle of Johnnie Walker, the scotch that Philip had given him for Christmas the year before. It was valuable, highly desirable, and distinctly American. If it had been found in his possession, the soldiers would immediately take it from him and beat him for not divulging that he had it. And, of course, they would have guzzled every last drop immediately, without savoring or appreciating it at all. Late one night, as the soldiers slept, Tino tightly wrapped the bottle, along with about two hundred and fifty dollars in cash, in several layers of butcher paper then tied the bundle up in his old raincoat. He dug a hole under the bougainvillea and buried it.

Upon its departure in March 1942, three months after invading, the Japanese army relinquished control of Guam to the navy. Under navy rule, a relative calm settled over the island for the remainder of 1942 and throughout 1943. Except for being forced to perform labor several times a month, people were otherwise left to themselves. However, the punishment for violating any of the numerous rules and regulations, like failing to show proper respect by bowing low to all Japanese persons encountered, was swift and merciless. Constantly having to bow to the numerous roaming patrols and off-duty sailors was another reason to stay away from town. Even in their own home, Tino and Vivian were expected to bow whenever their lodgers, now navy men, sought them out.

Although the Japanese imported dozens of women from occupied Korea to serve as "comfort women" or sex slaves, many local young women, especially pretty ones, were forced as well. Fearing Vivian might be "drafted," Tino urged her to disguise herself as a male as best she could.

"Why, Papa?" she protested, shocked by his suggestion.

"I've heard that some young girls have already been taken from their families and put with those poor Korean girls at Adelup to service the troops with sex," he said.

Without further question, Vivian complied. In the brief span between the departure of the Japanese soldiers and the arrival of the sailors to their house, she cut off her hair, leaving the "sideburns" long enough to cover her pierced earlobes. She bound her chest with bandages and dressed only in her boys' clothing and boots. As far as the new upstairs occupants were concerned, Vivian was a quiet, scruffy thirteen-year-old boy named Victor. Tino called her "Bik-tot", the Chamorro pronunciation of the name. He moved her bed back to her bedroom and felt better about the arrangement. They entertained themselves in the evenings by making up elaborate and funny stories about how a twenty-one-year-old daughter turned into a thirteen-year-old son.

The aim of the Japanese navy's rule was to turn Chamorro loyalty away from American influences and toward the Japanese emperor instead, as well as to inform them of their new place in the new order, the Greater East Asia Co-Prosperity Sphere. Like the American navy, the Japanese navy used socialization to indoctrinate the people. Schools to teach the Japanese language and culture were established, and Japanese entertainment in the form of propaganda films, parades through the streets, live performances in the cathedral-turned-auditorium, and cultural demonstrations and displays in the plaza was introduced. Anything and everything American was strictly forbidden, even music and songs. But Chamorro loyalty to Uncle Sam never wavered. They could not believe or accept that a tiny nation like Japan could prevail over the great United States; it was impossible. And Uncle Sam would return to Guam and prove it! In the meantime, the Chamorros would wait patiently and try to stay alive.

Under navy rule, men, women, and children were put to work at various tasks and were expected to complete work assignments and deliver food measures according to monthly quotas. Like the Americans, the Japanese decided that the Chamorros (and other island peoples) were suited only for agricultural and manual labor. Unlike the Americans, however, who thought Chamorros should farm for themselves for self-sufficiency, the Japanese wanted the people to grow rice, fruits, and vegetables, and to raise livestock to feed the fighting troops. Little was left for family consumption. Except for a rooster and a hen, the chickens at Tino's lancho were confiscated with other people's livestock to support the war effort.

By a certain deadline, everyone had to exchange their U.S. dollars for Japanese yen at an insultingly low rate. After the deadline, American money was prohibited and anyone caught with it was punished severely. Tino and Vivian's joint savings account in the U.S. Navy's Bank of Guam contained their navy government pay and the rental income from the upstairs apartment and the house in Sumay. At the time of the invasion, they had more than six thousand U.S. dollars in savings. After the money conversion, they had three thousand yen. Tino had withdrawn some money and had cashed his and Vivian's paychecks in anticipation of the December 8th fiesta and to pay their monthly bills. The cash was what he buried with his bottle of scotch. He regretted not having withdrawn more, but at the time there had been no need.

Tino never left home without Vivian, even though she remained disguised as a boy. He didn't know how long they could keep up the charade and feared leaving her at the mercy of the swarm of men upstairs. He watched and waited for the opportunity to steal away from them for good. Father and daughter were together always, shopping for needed supplies, which were getting harder to come by. They purchased nonperishable foods, mostly canned meats and vegetables, and necessities like mosquito nets and coils, kerosene, and laundry and bath soap, which wouldn't arouse suspicion, but which they could slowly stockpile in Vivian's closet and later take to the lancho. On some shopping outings, Tino would slip away while Vivian paid or bartered for what they needed. There were men who risked their lives—and those of their family—to hide and operate radio sets and to listen clandestinely to American news broadcasts out of California. They would then share the latest news with a small trusted group who passed it on by word of mouth. Tino was among the recipients who helped pass on news.

When labor and production quotas were established, certain numbers of men and women from each village were expected to turn out for work details, usually clearing the jungles and building airfields and bunkers by hand. They also were forced to cut down, paint, and make coconut tree trunks look like large gun emplacements protruding from the jungles and along the cliffs and shorelines. When Tino's turn came up, he and Vivian reported for work as father and son. He urged her to wear a floppy hat to further hide her earlobes and to keep her face as dirty as she could tolerate; it was the only part of the deception she detested. Vivian worked as hard alongside the men for many weeks. They were assigned to clear the land and build an airstrip at Jalaguak, a farming area about three miles northwest of Agaña.

Many of the men, especially Tino's friends, knew that he had a daughter, not a son, and they tried to ease the work on Vivian. As hard as it was, Tino begged them not to expose her by easing her workload. If the overseers noticed that she was receiving preferential treatment, the ruse would be up. For Vivian, having to drink sparingly (to minimize needing to pee) and finding a well-hidden place to attend to monthly female issues was uncomfortable, horribly embarrassing, and potentially disastrous. On these issues, Tino relented and accepted any offer of help to divert attention away from Vivian and allow her the needed secrecy and privacy.

As the tide of war turned against the Japanese, the forced labor and food production demands intensified, and the people on work details were brutalized. When the laborers and the women forced into sexual slavery were no longer needed, they were simply shot to death and left to rot in the jungles.

By January 1944, it was clear that the Americans were winning their way across the Pacific and pushing the Japanese back toward their homeland. In anticipation of the battle to come, the Japanese navy returned control of the island to the ruthless army. As the Americans had done in 1941, the navy evacuated its dependents, a clear indication of a do-or-die fight to come. Hell-bent on revenge, the U.S. Marines were determined to take back their barracks in Sumay. The Japanese were equally determined to fight to the death to hold on to their strongholds in Saipan to the north of Guam and Palau to the south. The battles for the tiny Palauan island of Peleliu and for Saipan and Guam in the Marianas were among the bloodiest of the Pacific war, not only for the Japanese and the Americans but for the Chamorros as well.

American fighter planes began to appear in the skies over Guam in February 1944. They bombed and strafed the Japanese airstrip on the Orote Peninsula and the one that Tino and Vivian helped to build at Jalaguak. The air attacks were the first indications to the Chamorros that the Americans were returning. In response, the Japanese forced work crews to continue building fortifications and repairing damaged airstrips even while the Americans attacked. Many Chamorros were wounded and killed in the process. The Chamorros of Saipan, Tinian, and Guam didn't know it at the time, but the Americans were determined to capture the Marianas to use them as the stepping stones to Japan. The Japanese were determined not to give them up. The air battles that preceded the Americans' intense naval "softening up" bombardments and troop landings were called the Great Marianas Turkey Shoot.

That January, when the Japanese navy moved on, Tino took the opportunity to move too. He and Vivian made several trips to and from the lancho, transporting whatever they could carry in gunnysacks. They created two staging areas well-hidden in the jungle. The first was halfway up San Ramon; the second, halfway to the lancho. Although it was clear that the Americans were returning, Tino didn't know how long they would have to stay in hiding. As with fiesta planning, he knew that being well prepared was better than desperately needing something left behind.

Tino wanted only necessities to be packed—food, clothing, and tools—but he couldn't refuse Vivian's tearful request not to abandon her few prized possessions. He yielded to her insistence on taking her mother's jewelry and lacquer box, her lace wedding veil and the christening gown, and her statue of the Virgin Mary. The ifil wood chest, handed down from Tino's mother to Sylvia then to Vivian, was too big and too heavy to carry. The antique wedding gown inside was too bulky to pack. Both had to remain behind.

Since she no longer had to disguise herself as a boy, Vivian put her grandmother's gold earrings back on her earlobes. She carefully packed the tortoiseshell barrette and lace veil that Philip had given her for Christmas three years before. She had worn the veil to church exclusively and the barrette both to work and to church since that Christmas. They were her only connection to Philip. Since her hair was cut like a boy's, she could no longer wear the barrette. And since the Japanese had turned the cathedral into a theater and auditorium, there was no church to attend, although

Mass was celebrated sporadically at secret locations. News of one was spread by word of mouth. Vivian was not going to leave her treasures behind. She wrapped them all in the layers of a bedsheet and packed the bundle carefully in a pillowcase.

From the lancho, Tino led the way further inland. After descending into the ravine, they followed the shallow stream to its source, a small spring deep in the jungle. They walked in the stream to hide their tracks as they traveled back and forth between the lancho and their new hiding place. The old oil drum and the heavy footlocker were exceptionally difficult to move, although the drum was empty. Rolling and dragging them across the ground and getting them down the slope to the stream left obvious gouges and drag marks of their movement. Tino and Vivian had to work quickly to smooth over the telltale marks on the ground before any Japanese patrols discovered them.

Father and daughter also dismantled parts of the lancho shack and painstakingly dragged the lumber, including Philip's nap bench, and some of the metal roofing sheets, to their new hideout. With these, and the treads he removed from the back stairs, Tino built a shelter that was well hidden in the jungle. There they remained safe for nearly five months, rarely venturing above the ravine, eating sparingly from their store-bought supplies, and catching freshwater shrimp and eels from the stream. Once in a while, they would get an egg or two from the hen.

For the most part, all the other people in hiding stayed in hiding—at least from the Japanese. Among themselves, they knew where to find one another.

Philip's washbasin came in handy, as did the pocketknife Parker gave Tino. Both items were cherished, well used, and much sought after. Tino turned down several offers of trade for them. He even turned down a .22 rifle and a box of bullets.

"I have no need of a firearm," he told the man who wanted to trade the rifle and bullets for the basin, the pocketknife, and one of Tino's machetes. Having lost his machete, the man desperately needed one. Rifles are useless for cutting down trees or opening coconuts. Tino had never fired a weapon and was not comfortable having one around. If caught with it, he would have been killed on the spot. He wouldn't give up the basin and pocketknife but gave the man one of his machetes. The man was grateful beyond words.

"God will repay you for this, my friend," he said.

Chapter 41

The intense American bombardment to recapture Guam began in early July 1944 and continued for several hours around the clock until the Americans landed on July 21. Despite their distance from the target areas, Tino and Vivian could not escape the terrible explosions and the rocking ground beneath their feet. Thick clouds of acrid black and gray smoke filled the air in the distance and blotted out the sun. They didn't have to see to know that Agaña and the whole western coast were in flames.

One night, Tino wanted to see firsthand what was happening to the city. Although Vivian begged him not to go, he made his way in the dark, guided only by the red-orange glow of the raging fires. Tino inched his way to the edge of San Ramon Hill and looked down into the town. The tremendous roaring of the flames was deafening. Jets of sparks were shooting high into the night sky as combustible fuel sources ignited. He could feel the heat. He staggered each time the ground shook beneath his feet. American warships were continuing their relentless bombardments. Despite the danger, Tino made his way down the slope through the now splintered jungle, hoping to reach his backyard, if not the house itself, but the intense heat held him back. The choking smoke and acrid odors of burning rubber and other noxious materials were too intense. In the firelight, he could see that his house was engulfed in flames. The sight brought him to tears.

Tino sobbed all the way back up the hill. Sylvia's beloved house was gone. He was glad Vivian stayed at their hiding place and was spared the sight and the heartbreak. Her mother's beautiful carved ifil wood chest—his mother's chest—and the wedding dress that both wore and that Vivian also hoped someday to wear were gone. Tino washed his face in the little stream at the bottom of the ravine and made his way back to the hideout. Vivian saw the grief in his bloodshot eyes and knew that all was lost. The house, the only home she had ever known, was no more. Life, as they had always known it and lived it, was gone forever. Nothing would ever be the same again.

As their food supplies ran out, Tino and Vivian were forced to go back to the lancho to search for mangoes and maybe some bananas or tangerines or sweet potatoes still in the ground. It was summer and mangoes would be in season. They waited until sundown so as not to be caught in daylight. That afternoon, Vivian ate the last of their previous night's supper—a half cupful of rice and canned Vienna sausage cooked in tomato sauce. There wasn't enough for both of them, so Tino insisted on Vivian having what was left. She ate it but said nothing to her father about the strange metallic taste it left in her mouth. By the time they reached the lancho, Vivian was feeling queasy.

They wandered along the edge of the now barren garden and were disappointed to see that the lancho shack, stripped as it had been, was gone. It had been blown to bits by a bomb that left a huge crater in the ground. The trees were gone also; they were only splintered stumps. The American bombardments had destroyed everything. The whole plateau was a muddy wasteland. By then the rainy season was in full swing, and hard rain fell almost daily, sometimes not stopping at all for as long as three or four days straight. As they headed back to the edge of the plateau, an angry shout came from behind them. They turned around to see a Japanese roving patrol at the end of the trail from town. They had been spotted and were trapped. There was no escape.

"Vivvy, don't be scared," Tino said, feeling his own fear rising. "And don't try to run, or they'll shoot us both. I love you, Vivvy."

They slowly raised their arms and proceeded toward the squad. As they approached, rain again began to fall heavily but stopped after a few minutes.

Five grim-faced soldiers surrounded them, their bayonets fixed and pointing menacingly at them. Another man, a sergeant, seemed to be in charge. Ignoring the rain, he approached Vivian and flashed a toothy grin in her face. Though her hair was cut short and she was wearing boy's clothing, she was undeniably female. Her chest was not flat and her brassiere was clearly visible through her wet shirt. When the sergeant barked a command, two men grabbed Vivian's arms. Tino lunged at them, but another soldier hit him in the head with the butt of his rifle. Tino fell to the muddy ground, dazed but still conscious. Blood gushed from a gash in his scalp and washed down his face and neck. He staggered to his feet. The soldiers laughed as he stumbled about, trying desperately to help Vivian.

They laughed even harder and snickered when the sergeant unbuckled his gun belt, handed it to another man, and started unbuttoning his fly. He was going to be the first to rape her. Vivian started screaming and struggling as hard as she could. Tino shouted at the sergeant to stop, but the same soldier hit him in the head again. This time, Tino slumped unconscious into the mud, unable to prevent what was going to happen to his daughter.

The soldiers near him took turns kicking him. Vivian screamed and wailed, certain that her father was dead.

With his eyes drilling into hers, the sergeant didn't look away as he drew a knife from another soldier's belt and waved it in Vivian's face. She stared wide-eyed at the blade, certain he was about to slit her throat. Instead, he ripped open her shirt. Vivian froze as the man slid the blade under her bra between her breasts. She winced in pain; the pointed tip sliced her skin and drew blood. The sergeant pulled the knife away quickly, severing her bra and exposing her breasts. He then dug his fingers into the waistband of her pants and flicked off the button with the knife. He handed the knife back to another man and then began fondling Vivian's chest. His hands were calloused, rough, and dirty. He drew a finger across the cut between Vivian's breasts, collected some of the blood, and sucked it off, smiling diabolically at Vivian as he did so.

Vivian started to cry, not the tears of pain, but of fear and helplessness. She was about to lose her virginity—not lovingly to a husband, not to Philip—but forcibly to an ugly stranger, an animal. The thought made her angrier than she had ever felt before, and with it came a sense of growing strength and an overwhelming urge to fight. At that moment, she hated that sergeant and every man with him and decided she would rather die than allow any of them to defile her. She stomped on the foot of the soldier on her right and started growling and kicking at whatever parts of the soldiers she could reach.

"Kill me too! Kill me!" she shrieked, hoping to enrage them enough to end her life. She nearly broke free, but the sergeant cuffed her with a fist to her ear. When the sergeant drew close enough to her face, her ear ringing loudly and painfully, Vivian defiantly spat in his face. He wiped the spittle away with the back of his hand then slapped her hard with an open palm.

As the other soldiers snickered in anticipation, the two men holding Vivian tried to force her to the ground. Aroused and ready, the sergeant stepped toward her again. Vivian fought hard to stay on her feet, snaking her legs around the boots of the men trying to force her down. When she spat at the sergeant again, he punched her hard in the belly. Before he even pulled his fist away, Vivian vomited into his face and chest. Her stomach heaved again and more vomitus—the spoiled and partially digested rice, sausage, and tomato sauce—shot from her mouth. She let the remaining stuff dribble from her mouth and down her chin onto her bleeding chest, hoping he would be too revolted to continue. He was. Shouting angrily, the sergeant balled his fist and began to pummel her face and head. Blood poured from her mouth and nose. Her knees buckled, but the men holding her kept her upright and the sergeant punched her in the belly again. Then they let her fall to the muddy ground. Screaming and shouting angrily in Japanese, the sergeant kicked at various parts of her body several times before he was satisfied.

Vivian was unconscious and bleeding when Tino came to. He crawled to his daughter, cradled her, and cried out in anguish. Sobbing profusely, he pulled the open sides of her shirt together and tried to cover her chest, but the buttons had been ripped away. He wiped the mud, blood, and vomitus away from her face and chin, wiped his hand on his pants, and sat there in the mud, crying and rocking her body. When Tino ignored the sergeant's command to get up, he was struck unconscious again.

Night had closed in by the time Vivian and Tino awoke. The soldiers were sitting on the trunk of one of the splintered mango trees and were drinking from their canteens. Father and daughter had been dragged to a spot several yards from where they were beaten. Their mouths and throats were parched and they needed water badly, but the soldiers had no mercy and drank tantalizingly from their canteens. Desperate, they sipped carefully from a nearby mud puddle.

Vivian tied the tails of her shirt in front of her, but it did little to cover her chest. The knife cut was superficial and bled only a little. Tino tried to give her his shirt, but the soldiers laughed and swiped his hands away as he tried to unbutton it. Tino and Vivian were forced to their feet and were prodded at gunpoint to walk. They didn't know where they were being led and they stumbled in the dark several times along the way. Exhausted and in great pain, they held on to each other and pulled each other up each time one tripped. With one hand free, Vivian clutched together the two halves of her shirt front. Within hours, the swelling and bruises from their injuries hampered their vision and their pain was excruciating. They had difficulty breathing; every breath, every step, brought on new waves of pain. Both had broken ribs and blackened, swollen eyes and faces.

Tino and Vivian were made to walk a couple of miles before a truckload of soldiers drove up behind them. The truck stopped and an officer disembarked. He started yelling angrily at the sergeant who cowered under the onslaught. The men in his squad jumped at the officer's shouted command and meekly lifted Vivian and Tino onto the back of the truck with the other soldiers. The truck drove away, leaving the would-be rapist and his men in the mud on the dark road. The truck drove Tino and Vivian ten miles to an area in the Ylig Valley called Mañenggon. There, they were pushed off the truck before it drove away.

Chapter 42

Mañenggon was the largest of three or four other internment areas around the island. The people were gathered from their homes and villages and marched into the jungle to fend for themselves for food and shelter. There were no facilities of any kind at any of the "camps," not even fences, only raw jungle and a machine-gun nest manned by a crew of two with orders to shoot anyone attempting to escape. The sight of the machine gun was enough to keep people compliant, even though they vastly outnumbered their guards. It was said that the Japanese planned to slaughter all the Chamorro people and herding them together would make the job easier. Several thousand people were already at Mañenggon when Tino and Vivian were dumped there. Most of the people were their neighbors from Agaña and Anigua and gathered from the smaller surrounding villages and those in the north.

Tino and Vivian hit the ground hard and were too debilitated to drag themselves off the trail. Several people came to their aid immediately, including the man who wanted to trade his .22 rifle. Another man, Benny Cruz, one of Tino's high school classmates, took charge of caring for Tino and his daughter. Benny and Tino were not particularly close friends, but in school, Tino often helped Benny with their arithmetic homework and Benny felt more than obligated to help Tino, a friend and neighbor, a brother. Benny and his teenaged son Tony carried Tino and Vivian into their family's shelter and tended to their wounds. Tino wove in and out of consciousness for two days; Vivian, for three.

When Tino was better, Benny helped him scrounge for materials and helped him fashion a makeshift shelter next to his family's hovel. Unlike the other people in the camp who had been given a short time to pack and prepare for the move, Tino and Vivian were dumped at the entrance with nothing but the clothes they were wearing and the pocketknife in Tino's pocket. Tino always carried it and if the soldiers had searched him, they would have found it. With a heavy heart because the pocketknife was a cherished gift, Tino offered it to Benny in return for his kindness, but Benny refused it.

"No, you keep it, my friend," Benny said. "If it was a good machete, I'd take it, but that little thing is only good for looks."

Having heard about Tino's offer and Benny's refusal, the man to whom Tino gave his second machete offered to give it back so that Tino could give it to Benny instead. Benny again refused. "That's all right, my friend," he told the man. "You need it more than we do."

When Vivian came to, she was wearing a man's shirt and Bernice Frasier was dabbing her face with a wet rag. Benny was Bernice's uncle, her mother's brother.

"There you are," Bernice said with a sweetness and gentleness that surprised Vivian.

"Where am I?" she asked, her voice hoarse and her throat sore.

Bernice held a cup of water to Vivian's lips and explained that they were in a camp somewhere far from Agaña but that she and her father were safe. The look on Bernice's face was troubling.

"What's wrong, Bernice?"

"Oh, I'm just a big ole softy," she said, not wanting to alarm Vivian. Bernice had never seen anyone, especially a girl, so badly beaten, not even among the boxers who lost to stronger opponents. Bernice's father owned the boxing arena in Anigua, and she knew almost all the boxers who trained and fought there. Vivian's injuries were horrendous, and they looked even worse when Vivian opened—or tried to open—her eyes. The whites of her eyes were dark red and frightening. Vivian guessed that Bernice was reacting to her horribly swollen and discolored face.

"How bad do I look? Be honest," Vivian said.

"Pretty bad, Vivian. Really bad," Bernice said, feeling terrible for being honest.

"Like a scary monster?" Vivian said, trying to muster a laugh with her swollen face.

Bernice smiled sadly and nodded, her eyes watering with tears.

"The ladies who know about these kinds of injuries say you won't have any scars, and you'll be good as new in no time," she said.

Vivian swirled her tongue slowly around the inside of her mouth feeling for her teeth. Although she tasted blood and some teeth were loose, none were missing.

"At least I still have my teeth," she said and smiled, trying again to lift Bernice's spirits.

Bernice stayed with Vivian nearly every day in a hovel next to theirs. Vivian wondered why Bernice was suddenly so interested in befriending her.

"I've always wanted to be your friend, but you were so stuck-up," Bernice said. "Well, maybe not stuck-up, but you didn't seem to want to be friends with anyone."

Vivian was taken aback. While she had been intimidated and envious of the half American girls like Bernice, Vivian realized that it was she who would not allow them into her friendship. She recalled the many times in school when Bernice would smile and say hello, how she tried to engage her in conversation, and how Vivian acknowledged her coolly and turned away, believing Bernice was patronizing her. And she felt guilty, five years after the fact.

Bernice helped Tino look after Vivian until she was completely recovered. She spent most of the day with Vivian and shared her clothing and underwear with her. They laughed about the impropriety of the necessity, but Vivian was grateful and glad to have women's clothing to wear again. Bernice's things were of fine quality, exactly what Vivian expected someone like Bernice would own. One of Bernice's dresses, a very pretty pink-and-yellow striped one, seemed too beautiful and so inappropriate to wear in their horrible jungle-camp setting.

"We didn't have much time to pack, so I just grabbed whatever I could," Bernice explained. "I grabbed a bunch of under things out of my drawers and things hanging in my closet. They turned out to be mostly church clothes."

"Oh, Bernice, I can't wear that. It's too pretty," Vivian protested when Bernice handed her the pink-and-yellow dress.

"Sure you can," Bernice insisted. "Just because we're in this awful place doesn't mean we can't look nice. Who knows? We might land dates for tonight."

After Vivian put on the dress, Bernice burst into hysterical laughter. The only footwear Vivian had was her muddy work boots. Still laughing uproariously, Bernice said, "Well, Cinderella you are not. Those are definitely not glass slippers."

Without a mirror, Vivian could only imagine what she must have looked like, and it wasn't a pretty picture. Both girls laughed until they cried.

Over the next few days, friendship soon began to develop between them. There were times, however, when Bernice stayed away. Vivian thought it was because Bernice needed the privacy. When she could move around without pain, Vivian went in search of her new friend and found Bernice crying by herself in a relatively secluded part of the camp. She approached her and laid a hand on Bernice's shoulder.

"What's wrong, Bernice?" Vivian asked.

"Oh, I'm being a crybaby," Bernice said through her tears.

"Come on, Bernice, I know something's wrong."

"I miss my daddy, Vivian, and I'm so scared I'll never see him again!"

Bernice hid her sorrows from the rest of her family—her mother and three younger brothers. Her mother was grief-stricken, and worrying was taking its toll on her. Bernice told Vivian how she and her family had gathered in the plaza with all the other residents of Agaña to be identified and processed. To everyone's horror, Bernice's father and all the other American civilians were pulled from the crowd and herded into the cathedral. The American priests were soon made to join them.

"Mama tried to hold on to him, but the soldiers pulled him away. We didn't know why they were separating us," Bernice said. "Mama started crying, but he told her not to worry, that he'd be back. Then they took him away. That's the last I saw of my father, Vivian. I don't know where he is or what's happening to him or if I'll ever see him again."

Vivian was humbled. She had her father and had never been separated from him. She never stopped to think about Bernice's feelings and the terrible turmoil she, her family, and all the other Chamorro-American families were going through. Their fathers, their husbands, were taken from them as prisoners of war. They were civilians, not military men. They were businessmen, working to fill community needs and provide for their families. No one knew where they were taken or why. No one knew anything about their fate. Vivian didn't know anything about Philip's fate either, but she knew that if he was still alive, he was safely back in the United States. Vivian hugged Bernice and let her cry as hard as she wished. She rocked her back and forth, trying to soothe both their aching hearts.

As the days passed, Vivian's friendship with Bernice deepened. Vivian related how she and her father lived for weeks in their jungle hideaway and how they were eventually caught. They laughed triumphantly when Vivian told about spitting then vomiting in her would-be rapist's face, making surviving the beating that followed part of the victory. They also shared stories about growing up and going to school and laughing and giggling about the same teachers or gossiping about the people they both knew. Then one day Bernice brought up that awful New Year's dance and Philip's accident.

"I heard about what happened to your boyfriend," she said gently. "Is he all right?"

"What makes you think he's my boyfriend?" Vivian asked beaming, although she never thought the word *boyfriend* applied to Philip in their situation. A boyfriend was a schoolboy who followed around the girl he liked. He was an awkward juvenile who bought his girlfriend an ice cream if he had enough pennies. Nothing about Philip was awkward or juvenile.

He was a man, confident, self-assured, and mature. But as she thought about him, she remembered the funny faces he made at her, the boyish looks on his face, and his secret playful smiles. Oh, how she loved his face. The recollection warmed her heart. It felt good to realize that Philip was indeed her boyfriend and more. He was the love of her life, and would always be, even if he was no longer alive.

"I don't know, Bernice. He was in a coma when he left, and I don't know what's happened since," Vivian said, not wanting to cry. She told Bernice what she knew of the accident—as her godfather and father related the details. "Lieutenant Kaplan was killed right away, and Philip was badly injured. The doctors didn't think he would survive. He was not conscious when he left here. I don't know if he made it home or if he's alive or not."

"Well, I know he loved you," she said.

Bernice's statement made her feel good and she chuckled. She remembered wondering how Bernice knew so much and where she seemed to collect all her information, accurate as it always seemed.

"How do you know that? Where did you get such an idea?" Vivian demanded.

"You silly nincompoop! Remember that New Year's party when he asked Rosemary Perkins to dance?"

Vivian nodded. She didn't like recollecting that night and all the terrible emotions she felt, especially all the times Philip left her to dance with other women.

"By the way, why'd he do that?"

"He wanted to make me jealous, I guess. And I was!" Vivian left it at that; she didn't want to share how dismal and heartbroken she felt. She was ashamed to admit that she had walked home alone in the dark, crying bitterly the whole way.

"Well, you were all he talked about, and Rosemary got the message loud and clear: that gorgeous man was yours! Of course, Rosemary can recognize a lost cause when she sees one, so she wasn't about to waste her time," Bernice said, sounding like a radio gossip reporter.

Vivian recalled how kindly the red-haired nurse had been at the hospital when she gave her Philip's belongings. She told Vivian that Philip was quite a catch and that she was a lucky girl. *Perhaps Philip talked about me to her too,* she thought.

"Well, not long after that," Bernice continued, stirring Vivian from her reverie about seeing the red-haired nurse in Philip's arms, "your lieutenant commissioned the goldsmith to make a special locket for you. He designed it himself. Did he ever give it to you?"

"No," Vivian said. "Maybe the locket wasn't for me."

"Oh, yes it was. It was for you," Bernice countered. "The goldsmith was working on it when I went there to pick up my gold necklace. I broke it, and he fixed it for me. Anyway, he showed me the locket and said the lieutenant was having it made for Vivian Camacho. You're the only Vivian Camacho I know. It wasn't finished yet, but it was really pretty. After that, a rumor went around that Lieutenant Avery was going to get married. Did he ever propose to you?"

"No. If he was going to, he never got the chance," Vivian shook her head sadly. "How do you know all this, Bernice?"

Bernice smiled coyly and said, "I keep my ear to the ground."

As a war not of their making raged around them, the two brokenhearted girls became best friends in what was meant to become a death camp.

CHAPTER 43

For the aid he received from Benny, Tino felt obliged to help him in any way. Benny was trying to take care of his wife and six children, including his eldest daughter, her husband, and their child, and his sister, Julia Frasier, and her four children; Bernice was the eldest. His brother-in-law, Herbert Frasier, was among the American civilians taken prisoner. For at least two weeks, Benny also looked after Tino and, with Bernice's help, Vivian. Seventeen people in all, including himself. Tino could see that Benny was struggling under the pressure and strain of carrying the responsibility alone. To the extent that he could, Tino would help him bear the burden.

With so many mouths to feed, finding enough food was Benny's most difficult task. He and his son Tony needed Tino's help to forage for food in the jungle, especially as many other people foraged too. The Japanese were not familiar with tropical jungles and didn't know what was edible and what wasn't. The Chamorros did know, and that knowledge helped keep them alive. But as edibles in and around the Mañenggon valley were consumed, foragers had to risk venturing deeper and further into the surrounding jungle and being absent from the camp throughout the day or night. Since people were still being gathered every morning to work on bomb-damaged airfields, being absent when names were called was dangerous.

Benny's son-in-law, Billy, was taken on a work detail with twenty other young men the day after they arrived in Mañenggon. A week later, none of the men had been returned. Benny's daughter, Margaret, who was seven months pregnant and uncomfortable, was distraught and worried about her husband, as were the wives and mothers of the other missing men. To ease the burden on Margaret, Bernice and Vivian took charge of her two-year-old toddler, Dolores, whose nickname was Loling. The nickname suited the little girl's pretty brown eyes and curly hair. Playing little girl games with Loling and hosting pretend tea parties with leaves, sticks, and empty coconut shells were welcome distractions in the midst of the nightmare they were living.

No one in camp had a safe, sturdy shelter or real protection from the elements. They were in the middle of the rainy season, nearly always wet, and wary of typhoons. As fuel and candles were used up and batteries died and a ban on fires continued, they had no reliable source of light in the darkness. They had no clean water, except from the muddy stream that everyone used. Although there were a couple of local doctors and some nurses and midwives, they could do little without medical supplies and equipment. The only saving grace was that Mañenggon's location in the Ylig Valley, behind the rim of an ancient volcano and not too far from the island's eastern coast, shielded the people from most of the teeth-jarring noise and stomach-turning quaking of the American bombardments.

The bombing continued around the clock along the western coast, even on July 21, the day the marines and army soldiers landed to retake Guam. The landing forces came ashore in Agat and Asan and fought uphill from the beaches while the entrenched Japanese fired down upon them from the hills and cliffs above. Although their losses were heavy, the Americans prevailed and drove the Japanese northward.

Among the rank and file, the Japanese knew the end was near. Before the end of July, guards at the Mañenggon camp abandoned their machine-gun nest and ran away. Many of the thousands in the camp didn't know they were no longer under guard, but word spread quickly. Cautiously, some of the bravest people ventured away. They were among the first people to be "liberated," having liberated themselves. Slowly, more small groups started to leave, moving westward over the hills and toward the coast where the Americans were. Those who made it to the top were greeted by the most awesome sight they had ever seen. Hundreds of American warships speckled the ocean all the way to the horizon. The ships were still pounding the central and northern parts of the island with their mighty guns. With his arm around Vivian, Tino and his daughter watched in awe as the big guns were fired.

Around them, hundreds of others from the Mañenggon camp streamed downhill toward the Americans on the beaches. Thousands of military men and their equipment darkened the coast for miles in both directions. Tino, Vivian, Benny, and his family were caught up in the surge and ran too. Calling out in English and laughing and crying with joy and relief, they ran toward rescue and freedom. Some people waved crudely made American flags fashioned in secret from bits of clothing and hidden away for the moment everyone knew would come: when Uncle Sam returned. No one doubted that. Many among the American fighting men on the beaches were moved to tears at the sight. The Americans were still engaged in battle and were unprepared to attend to the needs of bedraggled refugees. But it didn't matter. The Chamorros were just grateful beyond words to be among Americans again. Although they didn't have much in the way of food, medicine, and supplies, especially needs like baby diapers, the soldiers and marines shared whatever they could spare.

The island was declared back in American hands on August 10, although sporadic fighting continued for weeks afterward. The Seabees followed the landing forces and immediately began hauling ashore the equipment and materiel to begin the task of repairing the Japanese airfields, building new ones, and turning the island into the largest supply depot in the entire Pacific. In short order, Guam became the staging area for more than a hundred thousand service personnel, hundreds of ships, thousands of planes, with five gigantic airfields, and the unrivaled production capacity and largess of the United States of America.

As soon as they were safe, Tino asked for a lift from the Asan beachhead and into Agaña. A Seabee chief told him the trip would be futile since there was little left of the town. Still, Tino persisted, eager to see what was left of his home. He and Vivian were among the first couple of dozens who hitched a ride from Asan then walked the rest of the way to Agaña. With so many people to care for, Benny opted to stay put until he and his family learned one way or another what became of Billy and the other members of his work detail.

Relief efforts began immediately after Guam was declared militarily secured. Within days, the returning navy provided the people with tents and tarpaulins and turned the cemetery in Anigua into a refugee camp among the tombstones. Nearly all the residents of Agaña and the surrounding villages were homeless. Tino pitched his tent next to Sylvia's headstone, which was among the many that were damaged or destroyed.

Tino and Vivian were only about a mile and a half from home, but their house was in ruins. He had watched the town burn a few weeks before and knew that his house burned down too. Vivian knew from her father that the house was gone and didn't want to see what remained. She wanted to go back to their jungle hideout to collect their few belongings there. Tino assured her they would return as soon as they were better settled. From the refugee camp, Tino walked to the base of San Ramon Hill and what was left of his home. He went there by himself; Vivian opted to stay in the camp. Tino wanted to dig up his bottle of scotch, if it survived, and the American money buried with it. He also wanted to salvage Sylvia's bougainvillea if possible. By some miracle, the bottle of scotch was unscathed, even its label was intact. Tino's cash, nearly three hundred dollars, was wet but undamaged. Tino dug up two bougainvillea bushes that still looked viable. If they survived, they would produce red flowers. The bushes that produced white ones were burnt black, but Tino took some cuttings anyway, hoping they would bounce back. He planted them in empty tin cans with cemetery soil.

"You're in sacred ground, so you should pull through," Tino said to them.

Tino and Vivian, along with all the other homeless people, were made to move from one temporary relief camp to another. From the cemetery, they were moved back to the staging area in Asan then from Asan up to Sinajana, about a mile or so north of the lancho in Tutujan. Knowing what the barrette meant to Vivian, Tino promised her they would return to the hideout to retrieve it, along with her statue of the Virgin Mary and whatever else was salvageable and useful to their condition. After moving to Sinajana, Tino and Vivian hitched a ride to Tutujan from a couple of marines in a jeep. A new gravel road coursed through what had been Tino's shack and chicken coop. Father and daughter made their way down the ravine and back to the hiding place deep in the jungle. Vivian was determined to retrieve her treasures and Tino wanted his tools.

Their hiding place, which had been abandoned for less than a month, was as they had left it, although the rain had soaked almost everything. Water had seeped into Tino's toolbox, and most of the tools were rusted but were salvageable. Vivian burst into tears at finding her mother's wedding veil, the veil that Philip had given her, and the christening gown—wet, moldy, and ruined beyond repair. Her statue of the Virgin Mary was broken in pieces and her mother's lacquer jewelry box was warped and had split apart. Her mother's gold jewelry and her barrette, which were inside, were undamaged but dirtied by the mud and debris that had washed into the box. Vivian found an old tin can to hold her jewelry and barrette then helped her father carry his rusted tools back to the coral road. There they waited to hitch a ride back to Sinajana. With all the servicemen on the island and the massive construction activity taking place in numerous areas, it was easy to get a ride.

Though moving from camp to camp was taxing, Vivian and Tino were grateful to have a roof, a floor, and a clean, dry place and, eventually, army cots with blankets and pillows to sleep on. Although they and all the other homeless refugees had to take turns drawing water from spigots, the water was clean and several spigots were scattered throughout the camps. The Seabees who built the camp also put in separate latrines and shower facilities for males and females and devised an ingenious way to warm the water for the showers with fifty-gallon gasoline drums, cleaned, painted black, and laid on their sides on elevated platforms in the sunshine.

Even before 1944 came to an end, the Seabees were busy mowing down the jungles and building new roads where none had been before, repairing the airstrips built by slave labor, and constructing resettlement camps for the homeless Chamorros. At least two battalions landed with the invasion force and started unloading tons of machinery, equipment, and supplies, even as the battles raged. The taking of Saipan and Tinian and the recapture of Guam were crucial to the American plan to attack Japan. Guam became the home base for the B29s that bombed Japan and home to more than a quarter of a million military men and women, as well as the largest supply depot in the Pacific. Unbeknownst to Tino and Vivian, Philip was among the battalions that landed on Guam in the days after its recapture. He desperately wanted to find them, but he could find no one who knew anything about what happened to the local people or where they might be found. He was in Guam only a week before shipping out to Tinian where the battle to capture that island was raging.

Tino, along with other homeowners and landowners from Agaña and the surrounding areas, were eager to find out from the reestablished navy government when they could expect to get their lands back so that they could start rebuilding their homes and lives. But the answers they received were troubling. Bulldozers were already pushing the rubble of Agaña into the sea near the coal barge channel. Worse, surveyors were also marking off the whole of Agaña into large blocks, with new wide straight streets surrounding them. The new blocks and the planned streets were plotted without regard to private property lines. The navy government was not forthcoming as to why property lines were ignored or what was to become of the property owners.

Tino and his neighbors soon found out that properties throughout the island were being taken and occupied for military use. At first, the need for Chamorro land was obvious. The Americans were still fighting and the war still needed to be won. Grateful to be liberated from enemy occupation and eager to do their part to win the war, the Chamorros gladly stepped aside, believing their lands would be returned after the war. But Tino was among those property owners who realized they would never get their lands back. A new road was already coursing through his lancho, leaving only a sliver too narrow for any building. In Agaña, another new road was under construction along the base of San Ramon Hill, at the rear of what had been the old government compound and where his house had once stood.

A rumor soon started to spread that the navy intended to relegate the Chamorros to the southern end of the island in what was tantamount to a reservation, like the Indians. As military encampments took more permanent shape, the rumor seemed to be true.

In Sumay, the village was erased completely and the entire Orote Peninsula, including Apra Harbor, was taking shape as the gigantic new

Naval Station Guam. Libugon, which was renamed Nimitz Hill after Admiral Chester Nimitz, became the headquarters of the Commander of Naval Forces, Marianas. The northern quarter of the island was taken to house Andersen Air Force Base. Further south, the navy's new communications center and vast antennae fields were also taking shape. In all, Naval Communications Station Guam, Naval Air Station Agana, Naval Hospital Guam in Tamuning, Naval Supply Depot, and Naval Magazine Guam, along with dozens of various unit headquarters and smaller encampments, would occupy three-quarters of Guam's two-hundred-and-ten square miles of land area. The highly restricted Naval Magazine included Fena Lake, Guam's only freshwater body. Landowners were assured that monetary compensation would follow. When it did, decades after the war, few were satisfied.

In the immediate afterglow of liberation, the Chamorros could not believe that Uncle Sam, to whom they had been unwaveringly loyal, would treat them unjustly.

Chapter 44

Philip made his first confession, received first communion, and was confirmed as a Roman Catholic before being deployed with the construction battalion detachment that landed on Midway in June 1942. His St. Christopher medal, as well as a St. Michael the Archangel medal, a gift from Father Manella, remained on his dog tags throughout the war.

Philip did think long and hard about Father Manella's counsel and decided that God was calling him through Vivian. He confessed to the old priest that wanting to marry Vivian remained his motivation for wanting to become a Catholic.

"Only God grants love, my son," Father Manella said. "If your love for this woman brings you here, then perhaps it is how God has called you."

Philip took his catechism lessons with Father Manella. They had many discussions on theological issues and church doctrine. Philip came away from the lessons and discussions sometimes with profound understanding, sometimes with confusion and uncertainty, but always with deepening affection for Father Manella. Before Philip left for Port Hueneme, Father Manella gave him the medal, a rosary, and a pocket prayer book. Philip hadn't been a Catholic long enough to have memorized the prayers that most Catholics learn in childhood. With a knowing twinkle in his eyes, Father told Philip that the prayer book was made small explicitly for converts who might be too self-conscious to be seen studying it.

"Next time we meet, I'll expect you to know these prayers by heart. Recite them often, my dear Philip," Father Manella said, knowing that Philip was heading off to war. He gave him his blessing and said he would pray for him and all others who would be facing the dangers and horrors of combat.

Philip's new dog tags, now that two were required for all service personnel, included the letter *C*, indicating that he was a Catholic. He went to Mass and communion as regularly as he could, sometimes in the chapels of warships, in bombed-out fields or jungle clearings, on sandy beaches, and in coconut groves, wherever and whenever the chaplains could set up makeshift altars. He was never embarrassed to be seen reading his prayer book, especially because it was not uncommon to be with others poring over their pocket bibles or fingering their rosary beads as they waited to hit the beach and wade into battle.

Philip was assigned to the Central Pacific at his request. He hoped the Seabees' intended island-hopping route would eventually get him back to Guam. He also bounced from one battalion to another, from small detachments to even smaller special assignment units, and back again. He and the Seabees often landed and fought alongside the marines then immediately started to repair the damage left in the wake of the battles. They rebuilt infrastructure and built anew whatever was needed, from airfields to latrines. He spent six months hopping from Midway, backtracking to Johnston Island, then back to Midway.

The Seabees who had served at least eighteen months overseas were required to return to Camp Parks in Shoemaker, California, for thirty days of rest and recuperation. At Camp Parks, battalions were reorganized or disbanded, and men were reassigned to other battalions or discharged. Philip had been away from the United States for seventeen months and intended to duck having to return. He had come halfway across the Pacific and didn't want to start over from square one. He remained on duty until he was wounded in the terrible battle for Tarawa Atoll in the Gilbert Islands in November 1943.

The marines who had preceded them ashore were pinned down behind a seawall on the beaches until the third wave, which included the Seabees and their heavy equipment, hit the beach. The Seabees used their bulldozers like tanks and plowed ahead to the Japanese stronghold, filling in bomb craters in the airfield—which was their objective to capture—as they progressed. Philip, along with other men—marines and Seabees—fought from behind the cover of the 'dozers. An enemy bullet ricocheted off the blade of one of the bulldozers and hit him in the upper chest, earning him a Purple Heart. He fought to remain conscious, afraid he would again slip into a long-lasting coma and awaken weeks or months later somewhere back in the States. A medic was at his side immediately doing what he could to staunch the bleeding. Philip and dozens of other wounded were taken back to their ship and eventually removed to a hospital ship. Philip was slated to be flown back to Camp Parks. He reluctantly agreed to take leave but to go only as far as Honolulu.

While in Honolulu, Philip sought out a jeweler in Waikiki and showed him Vivian's locket and chain. It needed to be cleaned and polished. Inside, sealed behind their miniature glass frames, his portrait and lock of hair remained intact and undamaged. Philip also asked the jeweler to complete the unfinished engraved *A* with a tiny diamond chip.

"You say this was done in Guam?" the jeweler asked. "It's very well made."

Philip proudly told him that he had designed the locket himself and that it was for the girl he was going to marry. He also admitted that the girl was from Guam and that he didn't know if she was all right.

"I don't wanna be mean, but what if she—" the jeweler paused, not sure how to say, 'what if she's dead?' He knew that Guam was still being held by the Japanese, and no one knew the fate of the islanders. All the islands surrounding Guam had been under Japanese rule since the turn of the century. Just as the people of Guam were loyal to Uncle Sam, it was a given that their island neighbors would be just as loyal to Emperor Hirohito. As such, the Chamorros of Guam, especially the more stubborn ones, were likely to be subjected more vigorously to reindoctrination efforts. Philip knew what the jeweler meant, but wouldn't let him finish the question.

"She's a smart cookie," he said. "She'll be fine. I'm not worried."

But he *was* worried. Philip had no way of knowing whether Vivian and Tino were dead or alive. He wondered whether his snap decision to complete the *A* was a subconscious acceptance of losing her. With a heavy heart, he decided that if Vivian was lost to him, he would bury the locket on her grave. If she married someone else, he would throw it into the sea. He got drunk that night and wandered into a tattoo parlor. He had the letters *VA* in a fancy wedding-invitation script about half an inch high tattooed below the bend on the inside of his right wrist. The tattoo artist wanted to add brightly colored hearts and flowers and other scroll work around the initials, but Philip refused; he wanted only the letters. After he sobered up, he didn't regret the decision. One way or another, he would have to give up the locket, but the tattoo would be his forever.

Philip returned to the jeweler a couple of days later and examined the completed *A*. His idea of completing the letter with a diamond chip worked out nicely. The jeweler placed the locket and chain in a new necklace display case. Philip had rubbed the old ring box so often that the velvet fuzz was worn away. He paid the jeweler and thanked him for the fancy case but returned it in favor of another ring box. "It fits better in my pocket, and I've grown attached to it," he explained. "I'd like another red one if you don't mind."

With an accelerated promotion to lieutenant commander, Philip returned to duty in January 1944 in time to join another Seabee battalion in Majuro in the Marshall Islands. From Majuro, he sailed on in February to Kwajalein and Eniwetok atolls.

Although he had earned his degree from a fine engineering school, his best teachers were the master magicians of construction, the seasoned workmen first called to become Seabees. He learned with awe what "Can Do!" really meant and became an even quicker innovative thinker and problem solver and a better leader. Once unaccustomed to manual labor or to a workman's tools, he now knew them all. He could handle any hand or power tool, operate any piece of heavy equipment, and work alongside any man his senior. His hands, once the pretty hands of a rich playboy, were now calloused and scarred.

Philip's first kill made him sick, but he was numb to the others that followed. He was a good shot and could kill the enemy easily from a distance, but killing up close with a bayonet remained difficult. In the heat of battle, however, with all its unrelenting deafening noise, with bullets and shrapnel and chunks of coral rock, sand, and human flesh and blood whizzing overhead, with the screams and shouts of angry men, frightened men, and the moans of the wounded and dying, killing up close was a way to stay alive. He had seen so much death and so many mangled bodies that he could no longer think of corpses as human beings; otherwise, he would go mad.

The death of one marine, a PFC no older than twenty, would haunt him for the rest of his life. They had overrun the enemy airfield on Eniwetok, and Philip's men were busy repairing craters in a landing strip. He took a break in the shade where the young marine was dozing, his helmet over his face. Upon hearing someone approach, the boy lifted his helmet to peek at who had drawn near. Seeing Philip, he jumped up, eager to bum a cigarette, but as he raised his helmet to his head, a shot rang out. A sniper hidden somewhere to Philip's left fired on them. Philip watched in horror as the shot tore through the boy's hand, sending two of his fingers and his helmet flying. The bullet then ripped into his cheek, below his right eye, which bulged out and popped like an egg. The rest of the boy's face exploded in blood, his left ear and part of his hair and skull spinning away. The marine died instantly. Philip dropped to the ground immediately, on top of the marine, his head on the boy's chest, which was covered with blood and bits of bone. The boy's body was still warm and twitching. Philip's face was covered in the boy's blood and he could see a spattered trail of blood, bone, and brain matter leading to the boy's ear lying in the sand a few yards away.

Having heard the shot and seen their commander and the marine fall, Philip's men spun their rifles from their backs and opened fire, killing the sniper who had lashed himself near the top of a coconut tree, its draping fronds providing cover.

The young marine was not a friend; Philip didn't even know the kid, but watching him die made him feel a profound kinship. And he mourned him like kin, like a brother. Philip waded numbly into the surf to wash the blood from his face and chest. He knelt down, scooped handfuls of water to his face, and cried despondently into his cupped hands. In the months that followed, he watched life fade from the eyes of other wounded men and had mourned them as well, but never again with the same intensity. Philip became even more wary of making friends for fear of losing them. He had seen what losing a friend did to men. In grief and anger, many reacted irrationally and often endangered or got themselves and others killed. There were so many times that his heart, his whole being, seemed to be filled only with sorrow and pain and anger and hate.

Getting back to Vivian was the only thing that kept him fighting for his life. It was the goal that made everything else tolerable. By then, he was no longer the naïve young junior lieutenant who suffered in dress whites to attend outdoor ceremonies and the naval governor's social functions. He worked and fought alongside his men, not content to stand idly by. He spent days in the same filthy fatigues, some parts of which rotted or tore away. Like so many other men, his feet suffered from being imprisoned in wet, muddy leather boots and rotting socks. He was battled-hardened and cynical of interests he once thought important.

But on rare quiet nights, when it was comforting to lay on a beach and gaze up at the stars in the night sky, he would ponder the future and wonder if his love for Vivian was real or only a romantic fairy tale he had created for himself. He would recall the last time he was with her; he remembered the pain of their confrontation, but not of breaking his wrist, both of which were real. He also remembered the joy that filled his heart when Vivian welcomed him into hers. The memory of her smile, her giggles, and her kisses warmed his heart. No, he concluded, his love for her was not a delusion, not a fleeting spark. It was real. He needed to find her to recover his humanity, to know that he was not beyond hope.

The red velvet ring box was with him all the way. It was his talisman. He rubbed it for luck and drew from it the comfort and courage he needed to keep going, to fight on. No matter how many times he opened the box, the locket never lost its beauty. Even on the darkest, loneliest nights or the ugliest, bloodiest battlefield, the glittering gold locket reminded him that there was another reality beyond war, that it was meant for Vivian, and holding on to the belief that if she was still alive, she would be waiting for him. And he would be whole again.

In June 1944, the horrific battles for the Marianas began. By then, Philip had rubbed away much of the velvet on the new ring box. He was drawing closer to his personal objective and was growing nervous about surviving to the end. So many others, so many "short-timers" got killed just days, sometimes only hours, before departing for home. He prayed every night for his saints Christopher and Michael to bless his journey and shield him from harm.

The battle for Saipan was tougher and took longer than military planners expected. By the time his battalion of Seabees could go ashore, the fleet had moved on to take Guam. Philip was heartsick about missing the recapture of Guam. He landed on the island a few days after the American landing but was called back to Tinian after only a week. Agaña had been destroyed in the bombardment, and nothing was known about the residents, how many had survived or where they were located. Disappointed, Philip returned to Tinian but he knew the military plans for Guam were enormous. The Seabees would be on the island for a long, long time, and he would eventually return there to stay for good, even if he had to quit the navy.

From Guam, the Americans captured Tinian, the largest of three tiny islands between Guam and Saipan. The battle for Tinian was brief and uncomplicated. Philip was confident he could then get to Guam quickly, but he received orders to move on. The next assignment for his battalion was to follow behind the marines after the capture of Iwo Jima. The battle, one of the costliest of the war, began in February 1945. Philip's Seabees moved in three weeks later. They remained there until May 1945. Philip was promoted to full commander and assigned to lead a special detachment back to Tinian. There he and his men were tasked to construct a special building to exacting specifications. They were told nothing else about the project. It wasn't until after the *Enola Gay* took off in August 1945 that Philip and his men realized they had built the storage shed for the atomic bombs dropped on Hiroshima and Nagasaki.

Chapter 45

After missing the chance to search for Vivian and Tino in early August 1944, Philip finally returned at the end of July 1945, a year after the island was recaptured and four years after his comatose departure. His plane landed at the navy airfield in Maite. The airfield had been carved out of the jungle and built by force for the Japanese by Chamorro labor, including that of Vivian and Tino. It was captured by the marines, repaired by the Seabees, given over to the navy, and eventually became U.S. Naval Air Station, Agaña. It was less than three miles from town. After getting settled in a barrack, Philip hitched a ride into Agaña.

The damage in Guam was massive. Agaña was unrecognizable. Over the next few days, Philip watched as hundreds of Seabees with heavy equipment everywhere busily piled up the wreckage and debris. Hundreds of others were building the road that would become Marine Drive in honor of the marines, running the length of the western coast, from the new Army Air Force base in the north to the new Naval Station in Sumay. The name of the highway was later expanded to be specific: Marine Corps Drive.

The Seabees had their work cut out for them. They would be on the island for a long time. And that suited Philip just fine. It guaranteed him an assigned stay of two years at least—time enough to obtain the navy department's required security clearances[18] for Parker and Jennifer to enter Guam for the wedding, complete the church's required marriage preparation course with Vivian, and prepare her for eventually leaving Guam with him to his next duty station. He was certain it would be somewhere stateside. As he thought about it, Philip realized that fate had arranged for the fulfillment of his aspirations: to keep his career, rise through the ranks, and marry Vivian, if she was alive and he could find her. Although it took a world war and four years, he would have his heart's desires.

---

[18] President Franklin D. Roosevelt imposed a security curtain around Guam by executive order in 1941. After Guam's recapture, the navy restricted entry to anyone who could not obtain a navy department security clearance. President John F. Kennedy rescinded the navy's restriction and security clearance requirement in 1962.

Philip made his way to the Plaza de España and gazed sadly at what was left of the naval government compound. It had been all but obliterated, so had the Dulce Nombre de Maria Cathedral yards away. Only a few partially damaged buildings, a small portion of the pillared wall surrounding the compound, and the kiosk in the center of the plaza remained. The memories of ceremonies and parades in the plaza, of navy band concerts at the kiosk, of watching Vivian cheer for her students, of days spent working with Tino, Kaplan, Pitt, and the boys in the Governor's Palace flooded back. They seemed to come from a distant time, another place, completely unconnected to the ugly ruins before him.

On his first day off, Philip returned to Agaña and from the plaza, headed toward Tino's house at the base of the hill. The path he had walked daily from home to work for nearly two years was unrecognizable. He couldn't even distinguish where it had been. It was buried somewhere beneath a thick layer of compressed crushed coral gravel. The flattened coral was the slate upon which would lay the grid of city blocks and paved streets of the new Agaña. Here and there, however, still lay great piles of fire-blackened debris—jumbled chunks of mamposteria rubble, bricks, and clay tiles, tangled electrical wires, and burnt tree stumps and roots. There were shards of broken glass, bits of charred clothing, and the shattered pieces of people's lives. The Seabees would eventually bulldoze all the wreckage into the sea, to create the Paseo de Susana, which the federal government would give back to the Chamorros strictly for recreational use.

Philip climbed over a mound of debris searching until he found the area where Tino's house had been. Like almost everything else in Agaña, the house did not survive the bombing. Nor could it ever be rebuilt or replaced. Crushed coral gravel, the foundation bed for a new street, covered the ground where the house had stood. In the narrow strip remaining of the backyard, piled on the remains of the low retaining wall, was the wreckage of Tino's house—the rubble of its mamposteria walls, charred pieces of lumber and furniture, broken dishes and pottery, and shredded cloth, some of it familiar to Philip. The parts that could burn—the roof, the doors, and all the woodwork—were gone. Whatever didn't burn was bulldozed away. Philip picked his way through the area and wondered whether Tino and Vivian were anywhere near the house when the bombing began. He prayed they weren't.

His heart heavy, Philip surveyed the area one last time. As he turned to leave, a Seabee who was operating a steamroller stopped his machine and turned off its engine.

"You lookin' fer sumpin, sir?" he called out.

"I used to live here," Philip replied.

"Oh, sorry, sir. Yer house didn't make it. Nuthin' made it," the man said, lifting his hard hat and wiping the sweat from his forehead with his sleeve. "Funny, you don't look like a local. Whadder they called, 'Guamians'?"

"Chamorros. They're called Chamorros. I was stationed here. I'm from New York," Philip said.

"You just get here, sir?"

"About a week ago. Came in from Tinian."

"You with the guys what built the bomb?" News of the bombing of Hiroshima had just broken out.

"No. I built the shed for the guys who assembled it."

"Well, sir, my hat's off to you and those guys," he said and stuck out his hand. "This goddamn war is gonna end real soon, and we can all go home."

Philip shook the man's hand. *I am home,* he said to himself.

It was another week before Philip could look for Vivian and Tino. After days of checking, he learned that Agaña's residents were scattered among resettlement camps in Anigua, Sinajana, and Maite. The American bombardment had left nearly all of Agaña's families homeless. Those who owned property elsewhere left the camps to start building new homes. Others, like Tino, had nowhere to go, no place to rebuild. The Sinajana camp, which was located uphill and about a mile inland from Agaña, was one of several temporary housing sites for the people not slated by the navy to get their lands back. Philip narrowed his search to the Sinajana camp.

As soon as he got some time off and could get away, Philip made himself as presentable as he could. If he found her, he wanted Vivian to be impressed. He bought a new set of khakis and had them washed and pressed, his silver commander's insignia gleaming on his collar and cap. He also got a haircut and shave. He signed out a jeep from the motor pool and headed to Sinajana.

The camp was a sea of small plywood-and-canvas structures, some of them empty of occupants. Philip stopped at the camp's entrance and wondered how he was going to find Vivian and Tino among the dozens of identical, unpainted huts. Several children were running around happily chasing one another around the grounds. Seeing them reminded him of how ruthlessly the war had spared no one, not even the most innocent. He had seen refugee children in other camps on other islands, but he had no connection to them. These children were different. They could have been Vivian's pupils or the children who roamed the neighborhoods around the Governor's Palace, selling fresh vegetables or homemade treats, the children who played in the plaza and saluted smartly as he and Parker walked to the compound every morning. It was good to see them playing and just being children.

Philip stopped a boy of about ten years and asked if he knew where the Camachos were staying. Breathless from running, the boy saluted Philip and said, "Which ones, sir?"

The salute made Philip smile; it reminded him that he owed Parker a letter. He hoped he could write him some wonderful news.

"Ah . . . Mr. Constantino Camacho and his daughter Vivian?"

"Oh, them. They're in thirty-four, over there," the boy said, waving his arm to the left but at no specific hut before running off.

Philip wandered to the left, searching the numbers on the unpainted huts until he found Number Thirty-Four. Near the door were four coffee cans with bougainvillea plants; some were struggling to survive, others were doing nicely. He knew he was at the right hut. It would be like Tino to make such an effort to save Sylvia's flowers. Philip could now relate to the kind of deep-seated love Tino had for his wife, love that would even survive death. Philip took a deep breath and knocked on the door, his heart in his throat. He didn't know what he was going to say; he hadn't planned that far ahead. Finding Vivian and her father was his first priority, his only priority. No sound came from inside the hut. He knocked again but got no answer.

A few yards away, he heard the voices of women and children laughing in a dusty play area dotted with wooden benches. The children were playing on tire swings, a little wooden merry-go-round, and a couple of teeter-totters. He had no doubt the play equipment and the playground itself were the products of Seabee ingenuity, construction, and compassion. He was proud to be a Seabee but never more than at that moment.

Three women were sitting on one of the benches, talking and laughing. One of them was Vivian. Her back was to him, but Philip recognized her voice and her frame immediately. As he watched them, Vivian stood up, glanced around, and sat down again. She looked right at him but didn't recognize him. Philip was wearing dark sunglasses, a garrison cap, and the khaki uniform with the insignia of a commander. Several rows of colorful little ribbons and a couple of medals were affixed to his chest. He was not in the white service dress uniform of a junior lieutenant, the only one Vivian ever saw him wearing. His once pale skin was now golden-brown from endless days working shirtless under the tropical sun. And he was more muscular than the last time she saw him, although he had lost some weight. He was also older, and so was she.

Philip marveled at how beautiful Vivian had become. At twenty-four, she had lost her pubescent roundness. She was thinner too and seemed taller than he remembered. She was wearing trousers and a short-sleeved white shirt. Her hair was much shorter, barely clearing her shoulders, and was quite stylish. She was also wearing the tortoiseshell barrette he had given her for Christmas. Her face was now that of a woman and her eyes were still wide and beautiful but had lost their innocence. They were like his—the eyes of someone who had witnessed terrible sights. Philip wondered if she was still the same person, the rare little orchid he fell in love with. He was a different person as well. Would she still love him? Vivian once told him that he was her moon, her mansion on the moon. He knew what she meant; for four years she was his moon: distant and bright but out of his reach. She was his mansion there—the beautiful home where his heart resided. Now only a few yards separated them.

As Philip started to approach the women on the bench, a little girl of about three years ran up to Vivian. She reached down and scooped up the child, laughing as she kissed and nuzzled her neck. The child squirmed and giggled happily in Vivian's arms. Philip froze. Was Vivian a mother? Had she gotten married? He watched them for several moments. They were the picture of a loving mother and a contented child. But the child wasn't his, not the product of his love. Philip was not the man who had made Vivian a mother. Shaken, he turned and walked away, feeling empty and cold. Vivian's locket, still in the little box in his pocket, would have to be thrown into the sea.

Philip had tried hard to contact her after his accident, to tell her to wait for him, that he would return to her or die trying. The last time she saw him, he was clinging to life. She would not have known whether he lived or died. Then, during the occupation of the island, he had no way to reach her, no way of knowing or finding out if she was still alive. *She must have thought I died, and moved on,* he reasoned sadly. He would have to be satisfied knowing that she was alive and well and that she once loved him. His long quest to find her was over, and he wanted to cry.

Philip intended to leave and not look back. There was no point in reconnecting with Vivian if she belonged to someone else. He knew that if he stayed on Guam, he would run into her, probably with her husband and daughter, at some point. He didn't want that. With a heavy heart, he decided to seek an immediate transfer. He returned to his jeep and started to climb in, but before he could start the engine, he heard a familiar voice behind him, frantically calling his name.

Chapter 46

Tino was sitting under a breadfruit tree on a hill overlooking the camp. He could have hitched a ride from Tutujan but decided to walk back instead. The distance to Sinajana wasn't great, and the walk would give him time to mull over his dilemma. As he rested in the shade, a military jeep sped past on the dusty coral road. Tino watched the jeep pull up at the entrance of the camp. At first, he thought the serviceman driving it was just another occupancy inspector, checking to see who had moved out and who still remained. But the driver of the jeep was not one of the scruffy sailors who usually conducted the weekly survey. The driver was a commander in neatly pressed khakis. Tino grew apprehensive.

Why would such a ranking officer come to the camp? he wondered. Did he come to deliver more bad news? Evict them from the camp and take more land? Tino still had nowhere to go. He had yet to finalize any plans. He had just come from meeting with Tun Kiko, his lancho neighbor in Tutujan. Tino had asked Tun Kiko to buy a small portion of his large property, which adjoined his lancho. Tino needed only a small piece—at least enough to add to what remained of his own property so that he could build a house for Vivian and himself. Tino's neighbor was willing to sell, but Tino didn't have enough for the five-hundred-dollar asking price. He gave the man a good-faith deposit of a hundred dollars from the stash he had buried with his scotch. He promised to pay the rest in full as soon as he and other landowners were compensated for the taking of their lands. But there was no indication from anyone as to when compensation would be made. Frustrated by his inability to secure a place to live, Tino's apprehension quickly turned into resentment.

You bring your war here. You bomb my city and burn it down. You destroy my house, take my lands, and leave me with nothing, Tino fumed as he continued to keep an eye on the officer whose face was hidden behind dark sunglasses. *Now you send your henchman to chase us out?*

Tino watched as the commander stopped and spoke to a small boy. The boy gestured a direction then ran off. The officer strode in the direction the boy had indicated and, to Tino's alarm, stopped at the hut he and Vivian shared. The man knocked twice on Tino's door, but getting no answer, he walked toward the playground and disappeared behind some huts.

Oh hell, Tino thought, *he'll confront Vivian and scare her to death.*

Tino hurried to try to intercept the officer, but before he could reach the camp entrance, the officer had returned to his jeep and was starting to climb in. As Tino drew closer, something about the man struck him as familiar. He couldn't see the man's face behind the dark glasses, but he suddenly recognized him, and his heart leaped.

"Lieutenant Avery! Philip! Philip, wait! It's me, Tino!" Tino ran toward Philip with a huge smile on his face. Tears filled Tino's eyes as the two men embraced each other.

"You're alive! You're here," he stammered in disbelief.

"How are you, Mr. Camacho?" Philip asked, trying to mask the sadness he felt.

"Come, let's talk," Tino said as he led Philip to a bench in the shade. "Take off your sunglasses, I want to see your face."

As Philip did so, Tino's face softened. The accident left a diagonal scar from left to right across Philip's forehead. The scar, a thin, crooked line, ran from his hairline down through his right eyebrow to his eyelid. Philip had no trouble seeing out of his right eye, but the scar on his eyelid was jarringly evident against his tanned skin. Despite the scar and the bronzed skin, Philip was the same man but with a ruggedness that hardened his features. He turned twenty-nine that January, and age, the sun, and the war took a toll on his good looks.

"It is you," Tino said, ignoring the changes. "We never knew what happened to you. The Japanese came five months after you were taken away."

For nearly twenty minutes, the two men exchanged basic accounts of their lives in the years since their last meeting. Philip was eager to ask about Vivian—was she married? Who took his place in her heart? But he resisted the urge to ask. Tino might not have appreciated his prying into Vivian's married life.

***

Vivian was overjoyed when Bernice and her mother and brothers moved into the camp. They had not seen each other for several weeks after leaving Mañenggon. They were separated while Bernice's Uncle Benny searched for information about Billy, Margaret's husband. Margaret gave birth to a son in September 1944, a day after Billy and the rest of the men in his work group were found dead in the jungle. Uncle Benny and the rest of his family moved to Sinajana a month later. Although still in mourning, Margaret's spirits brightened once she was surrounded with neighbors and friends again. She named her baby William, after Billy who had hoped for a boy. Margaret was nursing William and keeping an eye on Loling who was frolicking with other children when Vivian and Bernice joined her on a bench beside the playground. The three women gossiped and laughed all morning. As lunchtime approached, Vivian started to worry. Her father still hadn't returned.

She hoped his mission to try to purchase some land alongside their lancho met with success. He was under tremendous stress at not having secured a permanent place for them to live. They also needed to find jobs and start earning a living. While Vivian could return to teaching, Tino feared the new navy government would have no place for him. He was forty-nine years old and knew that finding work might be as tricky as finding a place to live. Vivian feared he was making himself sick with worry.

Vivian stood up and looked around, searching the road for her father. As she scanned the camp, she noticed a navy officer a few yards away. There were so many military men—soldiers, sailors, and marines—on the island that seeing them anywhere was commonplace. As she sat back down, Loling came running up to her. Vivian scooped up the child and nuzzled her neck, distracted from any second thought she might have had about the officer. No longer were the servicemen around them enemies to fear but liberators to thank. They were guardians and protectors, and it felt good to be protected. It felt good to feel safe, to laugh and be free again.

"Let's go get some apple juice," Vivian said as she led Loling to Hut Thirty-Four. She hoped her father would be there, back from his mission to Tutujan.

***

Tino was not ready yet to tell Philip about how he and Vivian had gone into hiding far beyond the lancho, how they were eventually captured, how Vivian escaped being raped, and the price she paid for her defiance. The horrors were behind them and there would be time later to tell of them and, in the telling, relive them. Tino was sure Philip had his own horrors to bear, his own nightmares. He could see it in Philip's eyes. He could also see his desperation to find peace. Tino knew what Philip wanted, what he needed, and he knew where Philip could find it.

"Have you seen Vivian yet?" Tino knew his daughter would be beside herself with joy.

"I saw her over at the playground, but she was with some ladies," Philip said, trying to sound detached. Tino was taken aback. Philip's reply puzzled him. Philip should have been ecstatic at seeing her again, but he seemed indifferent. Was he no longer in love with Vivian? Tino knew that Vivian would be devastated if Philip's feelings had changed. He couldn't understand why Philip didn't approach her.

"You didn't talk to her?"

"I didn't want to disturb them," Philip could no longer hide his sadness. "How is she? Is she married now? Is she happy?"

Tino looked at him quizzically then realized why he was downhearted. "Vivian's not married," he said.

"But I saw her with a little girl."

"That's not her child," Tino said and laughed. *No, my boy,* he thought, *she saved herself for you and almost got herself killed.*

"That little girl is the granddaughter of my old classmate," Tino explained. "If not for him, Vivian and I would be dead." Tino related how Benny and his family came to their rescue in Mañenggon and how Vivian and Bernice, Benny's niece, helped to care for the child.

"Philip, Vivian never gave up hope that you would survive. She never stopped believing."

Tino knew that if not for the outbreak of war, without the invasion and occupation which interrupted their lives, Vivian would have been one of the women likely to wait in vain for the return of their loved one. He thought back to the words he had said to his daughter so many years prior—that if a man, a serviceman, truly loved an island girl and found a way back to her, they would both be fortunate. He didn't believe it could actually happen, yet here it was; Philip had returned. He couldn't deny the incredible series of events that had brought it about. The war had changed everything—the island, the people, everything.

Philip was part of that ruthless military entity that had rescued them from enemy enslavement and taken their lands in payment. But he was also the man who nearly died in his place, the man his daughter loved, the man who could well become his son in marriage—a man in whom any father would be proud. Tino studied Philip's face again and saw the longing in it. *If this good man fought his way through hell to marry my daughter,* he reasoned, *and she risked getting killed to save herself for him, how could I deny them?* Tino smiled inwardly. Indeed the future ahead was more uncertain than ever before. Nothing in Guam or for any of its people was ever going to be the same again. Yet the people of Guam would triumph over it all, as they always had. And so also would Vivian and Philip.

Philip couldn't hide his joy. His face, his whole bearing, brightened. Vivian wasn't married and could still become his wife. His head swam with all sorts of wonderful thoughts and emotions. Whatever Vivian wanted, whatever she and Tino needed, whatever it would take to make her his wife and make her happy, he would provide, he would do. His strong little orchid never gave him up for dead; she never stopped believing that he would return. She never stopped loving him. From the moment their hands first touched, their fate as lifelong lovers was sealed. Philip knew it now. He tried to pull himself together, to be the confident, self-assured man she fell in love with. But what he really wanted was to be scooped into her arms, and cuddled and nuzzled and kissed and held safe, the same way she did that little girl. He knew that when he was held in her arms, all his fears, all his pain and sorrow, and all the horrors he had witnessed would melt away—at least for a while.

"Come on, Philip," Tino said. "Let's go find her."

Philip hesitated. He still didn't know what he was going to say to Vivian or what his reaction would be to seeing her face-to-face. Or what her reaction would be to seeing him. For the first time since emerging from the coma, he began to doubt Vivian's reaction, and he grew frightened. He didn't think Vivian knew how disfigured his face had become. He didn't know that she had already seen all his wounds and more. Instinctively, he reached into his pocket and grabbed the red velvet ring box, rubbing it as he always did when uncertainty and fear swept over him. Looking down at his feet as he followed Tino up the path toward Hut Thirty-Four, Philip tried to find the right words to say to her. As they came to the hut, Philip lifted his head to see Vivian standing motionless in front of it, staring disbelievingly at him. Loling was holding her hand and staring wide-eyed also. Vivian didn't say a word as Philip approached.

"Come, Loling, let me take you back to your mama," Tino said as he gently took the little girl's hand. "Who's that scary man, Uncle Tino?" Loling asked as the two walked away.

Philip smiled inwardly—he might have looked scary to the little girl, but Vivian wasn't running away in fear. He was right; Vivian still loved him, scars and all. He didn't hear Tino's answer.

Neither Philip nor Vivian spoke. Their eyes locked; no words were necessary. Vivian stepped toward him and stared up into Philip's beautiful, incredible eyes and saw only love. She raised her hand to his forehead and gently traced the scar down to his eyelid. *It healed nicely,* she mused. In her eyes, the scar did not mar his handsome face. She let her fingers slide gently to his mouth. The last time she felt his lips, they were chapped and dry and unresponsive. Now his lips were soft and warm, and they were kissing her fingers. Vivian rested her cheek against his chest and closed her eyes. She could hear Philip's heart and could feel it beating strongly against her cheek. "You're alive," she said sweetly.

Vivian wrapped her arms around Philip's chest and hugged him tightly. She started to cry, letting more than four years of worry and sadness and grief, of horror and revulsion and pain, of relief and jubilation and triumph, and happiness pour out at last. Philip in turn reached his arms around her and rested his cheek against her head. He closed his eyes, sighed deeply, and allowed the magic of the moment to wash over him. The four years that had separated them melted away and he felt as amazed and wonderful as when they last kissed. "I will never leave you," he whispered.

Vivian and Philip held on to each other for a long time, standing silently in the sunshine outside Hut Thirty-Four. The warmth that Philip had felt in a dream after his accident, that had sustained him through many nights of pain and loneliness; the warmth that carried him through countless days of fear and desperation, through months of longing; the warmth that had kept him alive now glowed. Philip's reason for living was now safe in his arms, and he was safe in hers.

Philip pulled a handkerchief from his pocket. Vivian took it from him, sniffling and smiling embarrassedly up at him as she mopped her face and nose.

"I have something for you," he said. He reached into his pocket again and pulled out the ring box. "I meant to give this to you a long time ago."

She took the battered little box from his hand and studied it for a moment. The velvet fuzz was worn away, and it had obviously spent a long time in his pocket. Vivian wondered about the awful moments of fear and desperation Philip must have endured to rub the box down to dark bare metal. She opened the box and looked at the locket. The all-knowing Bernice was right; the locket was beautiful. The tiny diamond chip in the engraved letter *A* glittered in the sunlight. Vivian loved it immediately. She opened the locket and giggled at Philip's little portrait and lock of hair.

"When I'm old and gray, you can open your locket and remember that I wasn't always old," he said.

"May I?" he asked, taking the locket from her hands to open the clasp and fasten the chain around her neck. As he did so, Vivian noticed the tattoo inside his right wrist, the one he broke when he punched the wall. Although she saw it upside down, she could see that it was the letters *VA*. The tattoo made her heart soar. *VA*—Vivian Avery. The initials stood for what she longed to become but didn't think would happen. That Philip made it an indelible part of his body proved that he wanted it too. She raised his hand to her lips and kissed the tattoo.

"I did that for you too," Philip said. "Do I still owe you for the damage to the wall?"

"Well, since there's no wall anymore, you don't owe anything," she said and laughed.

Philip had longed to hear her laughter. Upon hearing it again, he decided not to wait any longer. "This is not exactly how I wanted to do this," he said. "Your ring is in New York. I bought it before my accident. If it's all right with you, I'll do this properly when it gets here."

Philip looked around, pleased that he would have a small, intimate audience. Tino, Bernice, and Margaret had gathered near the hut and were watching them. Holding both of Vivian's hands in his, Philip said, "Vivian Camacho, please say you'll marry me."

"Mister—" she started, but Philip pressed a finger to her lips. He tilted his head and smiled coyly. "Say it, Vivian. Please let me hear you say it."

Vivian smiled her special smile, the one exclusively for Philip. The one he prayed for years to see again.

"Philip," she said. "I will marry you, Philip Avery."